THE

C000182105

Also in Legend by Robert Asprin

Another Fine Myth
Myth Conceptions
Hit or Myth
Myth-ing Persons
Little Myth Marker
Mythnomers and Impervections
Myth Inc. Link
Phules Company
Phules Paradise

THE SECOND MYTHING OMNIBUS

Robert Asprin

This Legend Paperback Edition published by
Arrow Books Limited in 1992

3 5 7 9 10 8 6 4 2

© Robert Asprin 1983, 1984, 1985

The right of Robert Asprin to be identified as the
author of this work has been asserted by him in accordance
with the Copyright, Designs and Patents Act, 1988

This book is sold subject to the condition that it shall not,
by way of trade or otherwise, be lent, resold, hired out, or
otherwise circulated without the publisher's prior consent in
any form of binding or cover other than that in which it is
published and without a similar condition including this
condition being imposed on the subsequent purchaser

Random House, 20 Vauxhall Bridge Road, London SW1V 2SA

Random House Australia (Pty) Limited
20 Alfred Street, Milsons Point, Sydney,
New South Wales 2061, Australia

Random House New Zealand Limited
18 Poland Road, Glenfield
Auckland 10, New Zealand

Random House South Africa (Pty) Limited
PO Box 337, Bergvlei, South Africa

Random House UK Limited Reg. No. 954009

A CIP catalogue record for this book
is available from the British Library

ISBN 0 09 921471 1

Printed and bound in Great Britain by
Cox & Wyman Ltd, Reading, Berkshire

HIT OR MYTH

Chapter One:

*"There's something to be said for relatives
. . . it has to be said because it's unprint-
able!"*

—A. EINSTEIN

PERHAPS if I hadn't been so preoccupied with my own
thoughts when I walked into my quarters that day, I
wouldn't have been caught unawares. Still, who expects
to get caught in a magikal attack just walking into their
own room?

Okay, okay! So I *am* the Court Magician of Possiltum, and maybe I *have* been getting a bit of a reputation
lately. I still should be able to walk into my own room
without getting jumped! I mean, if a magician isn't safe
in his own quarters, can he be safe anywhere?

Scratch that question!

It's the kind of thing my teacher says to convince me
that choosing magic for a career path is not the best way
to insure living out one's normal life span. Of course, it
doesn't take much convincing. Actions speak louder
than words, and the action since I signed on as his apprentice has been loud enough to convince me that a
magician's life is not particularly quiet. I mean, when
you realize that within days of meeting him, we both got
lynched by an angry mob . . . as in hung by the neck . . .

1

But I digress.

We started out with me simply walking into my room. Yeah, simple! There was a demon waiting for me, a Pervect to be exact. This in itself wasn't unusual. Aahz, the teacher I mentioned earlier, is a Pervect. In fact, he shares my quarters with me. What *was* unusual was that the demon waiting for me wasn't Aahz!

Now I haven't met many Pervects . . . heck, the only one I know is Aahz . . . but I know Aahz very well, and this Pervect wasn't him!

This demon was shorter than my mentor, his scales were a lighter shade of green, and his gold eyes were set closer together. What's more, he wasn't smiling . . . and Aahz always smiles, even when he's mad . . . *especially* when he's mad. To the average eye Aahz and this stranger might look alike, but to me they were as different as a Deveel and an Imp. Of course, there was a time when I couldn't tell the difference between a Deveel and an Imp. It says something about the company I've been keeping lately.

"Who are you?" I demanded.

"You Skeeve?"

"Yeah. Me Skeeve. Who you?"

For an answer, I suddenly felt myself snatched into the air by an invisible hand and spun end over end until I finally stopped dangling head down four feet off the floor.

"Don't get smart with me, punk. I understand you're holding a relative of mine in some kind of bondage. I want him back. Understand?"

He emphasized his point by lowering me to within a few inches of the floor, then using that surface to rap my head sharply.

I may not be the greatest magician ever, but I knew what he was doing. He was using his mind to levitate me about the room. I've done it myself to small objects from time to time. Of course, it occurred to me that I wasn't a small object and that I was dealing with someone a bit better versed in the magikal arts than myself. As such, I deemed it wiser to keep my temper and my manners.

"You know Aahz?"

"Sure do. And I want him back."

The latter was accompanied by another head rap. So much for holding my temper.

"Then you should know him well enough to know that nobody holds him against his will!"

My head started for the floor again, but stopped short of its target. From my inverted position I could get a partial view of the demon tapping himself thoughtfully on the chin.

"That's true," he murmured. "All right. . . ."

I was turned into an upright position once more.

". . . Let's take it from the top. Where's Aahz, and what's keeping him in this backwater dimension?"

"I think *and* talk better with my feet on the ground."

"Hmm? Oh! Sorry."

I was lowered into a normal standing position. Now that I was self-supporting again, I realized the interrogation had left me with a splitting headache.

"He's back in General Badaxe's quarters arguing military tactics," I managed. "It was so boring I came back here. He should be along soon. They were almost out of wine when I left."

"Tactics and wine, eh?" my visitor grimaced. "That sounds like Aahz. What's the rest of it? Why is he staying around a nowhere dimension like Klah and how did he get mixed up with the Great Skeeve?"

"You've heard of me?"

"Here and there around the dimensions," the demon

acknowledged. "In some circles they think you're pretty hot stuff. That's why I started wondering if you'd managed to cage Aahz somehow. I was braced for a real battle royale when you walked in."

"Well, actually I'm not all that good," I admitted. "I've only really started making headway in the last couple years since I started studying under Aahz. I'd still be a total nothing if he hadn't lost his powers and taken me on as an apprentice."

"Bingo!" my visitor declared, holding up his hand. "I think you just explained everything. Aahz lost his powers and took on a new apprentice! No wonder he hasn't been home in a while. And all this talk about the Great Skeeve is just a standard Aahz-managed hype job for a new talent. Right?"

"We *have* taken on a few rough assignments," I said defensively.

"In which Aahz choreographed, then set you up to take the credit. Right?"

"What's 'choreographed'?" I asked. Obviously the family similarity was more than scale deep.

"Well, I hope you're up to operating on your own, Skeeve, 'cause I'm taking your mentor back to Perv with me."

"But you don't have to rescue him from me!" I protested. "He's free to come and go as he wants."

"I'm not saving him from you, I'm saving him from Aahz. Our colleague has an overblown sense of responsibility that isn't always in his own best interest. Do you know how lucrative a practice he's letting fall apart on Perv while he clowns around with you?"

"No," I admitted.

"Well, he's losing money every day he's gone . . . and that means the family is losing money."

Right there I gave up the argument. Early on in my

association with Aahz I learned the futility of trying to talk a Pervect out of money. The fact that Aahz was willing to sacrifice a steady income to work with me was an incredible tribute to our friendship . . . or his sense of duty. Of course, there's more than one way to win an argument.

"Well, as I said before, I can't keep him here," I said innocently. "If you can convince him he's not needed any more. . . ."

"No way, punk," the demon sneered. "We both know that won't get him to desert an apprentice. I'm going to lure him back to Perv with a blatant lie. And *you're* going to keep your mouth shut."

"But . . ."

". . . Because if you don't, I'll make sure there's nothing left to keep him in Klah . . . meaning you! Now before you even think about trying to match magik with me, remember something. *You've* been studying under Aahz for a couple years now. *I* graduated after over three hundred years of apprenticeship. So far, I'm willing to live and let live. You should be able to earn a living on what you've learned so far, maybe even pick up a few new tricks as you go along. *However*, if you cross me now, there won't be enough of you to pick up with a sponge. Do we understand each other?"

I was suddenly aware why nobody we met in our dimension-crawling ever wanted to tangle with a Pervect. I was also aware that someone had just walked into the room behind me.

"Rupert!"

"Uncle Aahz!"

The two pounded each other on the back. I gave them lots of room.

"Hey kid, this is my nephew Rupert . . . but I see you've already met."

"Unfortunately," I grumbled.

That earned me a black look from Rupert, but Aahz
missed it completely.

"So what brings you to Klah, nephew? A bit off your
normal prowl pattern, isn't it?"

"It's Dad. He wants you."

"Sorry," Aahz was suddenly his normal self again.
"I've got too many irons in the fire here to get drawn
into some family squabble."

"But he's dying."

That stopped Aahz for a moment.

"My brother? Nonsense. He's too tough to kill. He
could even beat me in an unfair fight."

"He got into a fight with Mom."

A look of concern crossed Aahz's face. I could see he
was wavering.

"That serious, huh? I don't know, though. If he's
really dying, I don't see what I can do to help."

"It shouldn't take long," Rupert urged. "He said
something about his will."

I groaned inwardly. Trust a Pervect to know a
Pervect's weaknesses.

"Well, I guess my business here can keep for a few
days," Aahz declared with false reluctance. "Stay out
of trouble, kid. I'll be back as soon as I can."

"Let's get going," Rupert suggested, hiding his
triumphant grin. "The sooner we get to Perv, the
sooner you can be back."

"But Aahz. . . ."

"Yeah, kid?"

I saw Rupert's brow darken.

"I . . . I just wanted to say 'goodbye.' "

"Hey, don't make a big thing of this, kid. It's not like
I was going forever."

Before I could respond, Rupert clapped an arm

around Aahz's shoulder and they both faded from view.

Gone.

Somehow I couldn't make myself believe it had happened. My mentor had been spirited away . . . permanently. Whatever I had learned from Aahz would have to do, because now I was totally on my own.

Then I heard a knock at my door.

Chapter Two:

*"When things are blackest, I just tell myself
'cheer up, things could be worse!' And
sure enough, they get worse!"*

—SKEEVE

I DECIDED that as Court Magician of Possiltum, my response should be gracious.

"Go away!"

That *was* gracious. If you knew what my actual thoughts were, you'd realize that. Very few people ever visited me in my chambers, and I didn't want to see any of them just then.

"Do you know who you're talking to?" came a muffled voice from the other side of the door.

"No! And I don't care! Go away!"

"This is Rodrick the Fifth. Your King!"

That stopped me. Upset or not, that title belonged to the man who set and paid my wages. As I said earlier, I *have* learned a few things from Aahz.

"Do you know who *you're* talking to?" I called back, and hoped.

There was a moment's pause.

"I assume I'm talking to Skeeve the Magnificent, Court Magician of Possiltum. At best, he'll be the one to bear the brunt of my wrath if I'm kept waiting out-

9

side his chambers much longer."

So much for hoping. These things never work in real life the way they do in jokes.

Moving with undignified haste, I pounced on the door handle and wrenched it open.

"Good afternoon, Lord Magician. May I come in?"

"Certainly, Your Majesty," I said, standing aside. "I never refuse a fifth."

The King frowned.

"Is that a joke? If so, I don't get the point."

"Neither do I," I admitted calmly. "It's something Aahz my apprentice says."

"Ah, yes. Your apprentice. Is he about?"

Rodrick swept majestically into the room, peering curiously into the corners as if he expected Aahz to spring forth from the walls.

"No. He's . . . out."

"Good. I had hoped to speak with you alone. Hmmm . . . these are really quite spacious quarters. I don't recall having been here before."

That was an understatement. Not only had the King never visited my room in his palace, I couldn't recall having seen him when he wasn't either on the throne or in its near vicinity.

"Your Majesty has never graced me with his presence since I accepted position in his court," I said.

"Oh. Then, that's probably why I don't recall being here," Rodrick responded lamely.

That in itself was strange. Usually the King was quite glib and never at a loss for words. In fact, the more I thought about it, the stranger this royal visit to my private chambers became. Despite my distress at Aahz's unplanned and apparently permanent departure, I felt my curiosity beginning to grow.

"May I ask the reason for this pleasant, though unexpected audience?"

"Well . . ." the King began, then shot one more look about the room. "Are you sure your apprentice isn't about?"

"Positive. He's . . . I sent him on a vacation."

"A vacation?"

"Yes. He's been studying awfully hard lately."

The King frowned slightly.

"I don't remember approving a vacation."

For a moment, I thought I was going to get caught in my own deception. Then I remembered that in addition to the various interdimensional languages, Aahz had also been teaching me to speak "bureaucrat."

"I didn't really feel your authorization was necessary," I said loftily. "Technically, my apprentice is not on your Majesty's payroll. I am paying him out of *my* wages, which makes him my employee, subject to my rules including vacations . . . or dismissal. While he is subject to your laws, as is any subject of Possiltum, I don't feel he actually is governed by Subparagraph G concerning palace staff!"

My brief oration had the desired effect: it both confused and bored my audience. Aahz would have been proud of me. I was particularly pleased that I had managed to sneak in that part about dismissals. It meant that when Aahz didn't return, I could claim that I had dismissed him without changing the wage paid me by the crown.

Of course, this got me brooding again about Aahz not coming back.

"Well, whatever. I'm glad to see your philosophy regarding vacations mirrors my own, Lord Magician. Everyone should have a vacation. In fact, that's why I came to see you this afternoon."

That threw me.

"A vacation? But your Majesty, I don't need a vacation."

That threw the King.

"You? Of course not. You and that apprentice of yours spend most of your time gallivanting around other worlds. You've got a lot of nerve asking for a vacation."

That did it. All the anger I had been storing up since Rupert's arrival exploded.

"I didn't *ask* for a vacation!"

"Oh! Yes. Of course."

"And furthermore, that 'gallivanting around other worlds' you mentioned is stock in trade for magicians, court or otherwise. It enables us to work our wonders . . . like saving your kingdom from Big Julie's army. Remember?"

"How could I forget. I . . ."

"If, however, your Majesty feels I have been lax in fulfilling my duties as his court magician, he need only ask for my resignation and it's his. If he recalls, *he* approached *me* for this position. I didn't ask for *that* either!"

"Please, Lord Magician," Rodrick interrupted desperately, "I meant no offense. Your services have been more than satisfactory. In fact, any reluctance I expressed regarding your vacation was based on a fear of having to run the kingdom for a period without your powers available. If you really feel you want a vacation, I'm sure we could work out something to . . ."

"I don't *want* a vacation. All right? Let's drop the subject."

"Certainly. I just thought . . . very well."

Shaking his head slightly, he headed for the door.

Winning the argument put me in a much better mood. After the beating my ego had taken from Rupert, it was nice to hear *someone* say they thought my powers were worth something.

It occurred to me, however, that winning the argument with the man who paid my wages might not have been the wisest way to bounce back.

"Your Majesty?"

The King stopped.

"Aren't you forgetting something?"

He frowned.

". . . Like the original reason for your visit? Since I wasn't asking for a vacation, and you weren't offering one, I assume you had something else on your mind?"

"Oh, yes. Quite right. But all things considered, this might not be the time to discuss it."

"What? Because of our misunderstanding? Think nothing of it, your Majesty. These things happen. Rest assured I am still your loyal retainer, ready to do anything in my power to assist you in the management of your kingdom."

As I said before, I was getting pretty good at shoveling when the situation called for it.

Rodrick beamed.

"I'm glad to hear that, Master Skeeve. That is precisely why I came to you today."

"And how may I be of service?"

"It's about a vacation."

I closed my eyes.

For a brief moment, I knew . . . *knew*, mind you . . . how Aahz felt. I knew what it felt to be sincerely trying to help someone, only to find that that someone seems bound and determined to drive you out of your mind.

The King saw my expression and continued hastily, "Not a vacation for you. A vacation for me!"

That opened my eyes. Figuratively and literally.

"You, your Majesty? But Kings don't take vacations."

"That's the whole point."

Rodrick began pacing the floor nervously as he spoke.

"The pressures of being a King mount up like they do on any other job. The difference is that as a King you never get a break. No time to rest and collect your thoughts, or even just sleep late. From the coronation when the crown hits your head until it's removed by voluntary or forcible retirement, you are the King."

"Gee, that's tough, Your Majesty. I wish there was something I could do to help."

The King stopped pacing and beamed at me again.

"But you can! That's why I'm here!"

"Me? I can't approve a vacation for you! Even if it were in my power, and it isn't, the kingdom needs a king on the throne all the time. It can't spare you, even for one day!"

"Exactly! That's why I can't leave the throne unattended. If I wanted a vacation, I'd need a stand-in."

An alarm bell went off in my mind.

Now, however much Aahz may have nagged me about being a slow student, I'm not stupid. Even before I met Aahz . . . heck, before I learned my letters . . . I knew how to add two and two to get four. In this case, one two was the king's need for a stand-in; the second two was his presence in my quarters, and the four was. . . .

"Surely your Majesty can't mean me!"

"Of course I mean you," Rodrick confirmed. "The fact is, Lord Magician, I had this in mind when I hired you to your current position."

"You did?"

I could feel the jaws of the trap closing. If this was indeed why the King had hired me, I would be ill-advised to refuse the assignment. Rodrick might decide my services were no longer needed, and the last thing I needed with Aahz gone was to get cut off from my source of income. I wasn't sure what the job market was like for ex-court magicians, but I was sure I didn't want to find out first hand.

"As you said earlier, the powers of the Court Magician are at my disposal, and one of the powers you demonstrated when we first met was the ability to change your own shape, or the shape of others, at will."

The disguise spell! It was one of the first spells Aahz had taught me and one of the ones most frequently used over our last several adventures. After all the times it's bailed me out of tight spots, who would have guessed it would be the spell to get me into trouble? Well, there *was* the time it had gotten me hung. . . .

"But, your Majesty, I couldn't possibly substitute for you. I don't know how to be a King!"

"Nothing to it," Rodrick smiled. "The nice thing about being a King is that even when you're wrong, no one dares to point it out."

"But. . . ."

"And besides, it will only be for one day. What could possibly go wrong in one day?"

Chapter Three:

"Once a knight, always a knight,
But once a King is once too often!"
—SIR BELLA OF EASTMARCH

NOW, I don't want you to think I'm a pushover. I drove
a hard bargain with the King before giving in. I not only
managed to get him to agree to a bonus, but to cough up
a hefty percentage in advance before accepting the
assignment. Not bad for a fledgling magician who was
over a barrel.

Of course, once I accepted, I was no longer over a
barrel, I was in over my head!

The more I thought about it, the worse the idea of
standing in for the King seemed. The trouble was, I
didn't have a choice . . . or did I? I thought about it
some more and a glimmer of hope appeared.

There was a way out! The only question was, how far
could I run in a day? While not particularly worldly (or
off-worldly for that matter) I was pretty sure that
double-crossing kings wasn't the healthiest of pastimes.

It was going to be a big decision, definitely the biggest
I ever had to make on my own. The King (or to be exact,
his stand-in) wasn't due to make an appearance until
noon tomorrow, so I had a little time to mull things

over. With that in mind, I decided to talk it out with my last friend left in the palace.

"What do you think, Gleep? Should I take it on the lam, or stick around and try to bluff it out for one day as king?"

The response was brief and to the point.

"Gleep!"

For those of you who've tuned in to this series late, Gleep is my pet. He lives in the Royal Stables. He's also a twenty-foot long blue dragon . . . half grown. (I shudder to think what he'll be like when he's fully grown! Groan!) As to his witty conversation, you'll have to forgive him. He only has a one-word vocabulary, but he makes up for it by using that word a lot. Wordy or not, I turned to him in this moment of crisis because with Aahz gone, he was the only one in this dimension who would be even vaguely sympathetic to my problem. That in itself says a lot about the social life of a magician.

"Come on, Gleep, get serious. I'm in real trouble. If I try to stand in for the King, I might make a terrible mistake . . . like starting a war or hanging an innocent man. On the other hand, if I double-cross the King and disappear, you and I would spend the rest of our lives as hunted fugitives."

The unicorn in the next stall snorted and stamped a foot angrily.

"Sorry, Buttercup. The *three* of us would be hunted fugitives."

War unicorns aren't all that common, even in Royal Stables. That particular war unicorn was mine. I acquired him as a gift shortly after I acquired Gleep. As I said before, this life-style is more than a little zooish.

"In a kingdom with a bad king, a lot of people would get hurt," I reasoned, "and I'd be a terrible king. Heck, I'm not all that good a magician."

"Gleep," my pet argued sternly.

"Thanks for the vote of confidence, but it's true. I don't want to hurt anybody, but I'm not wild about being a hunted fugitive, either."

Tired of verbalizing his affection, Gleep decided to demonstrate his feelings by licking my face. Now, aside from leaving a slimy residue, my dragon's kisses have one other side effect. His breath is a blast of stench exceeded only by the smell of Pervish cooking.

"G . . . Gleep, old boy," I managed at last, "I love you dearly, but if you do that twice a week, we may part company . . . permanently!"

"Gleep?"

That earned me a hurt expression, which I erased simply enough by scratching his head. It occurred to me that dragons had survived because each of them only became emotionally attached to one being in its lifetime. If their breath reached the entire population instead of a single individual, they would have been hunted into extinction long ago. No, it was better that only one person should suffer than . . .

Another part of my mind grabbed that thought and started turning it over.

"If I run, then I'll be the only one in trouble, but if I try to be king, the whole kingdom suffers! That's it! I have to leave. It's the only decent thing to do. Thanks, Gleep!"

"Gleep?"

My pet cocked his head in puzzlement.

"I'll explain later. All right. It's decided. You two stock up on food while I duck back to my room to get a few things. Then it's 'Goodbye, Possiltum!' "

I've had pause to wonder what would have happened if I'd followed my original plan: just headed for my room, gathered up my belongings, and left. The timing for the rest of the evening would have changed, and the rest of this story would have been totally different. As it was, I made a slight detour. Halfway to my room, Aahz's training cut in. That is, I started thinking about money.

Even as a hunted fugitive, money would come in handy . . . and the King's advance would only last so long. With a little extra cash, I could run a lot farther, hide a lot longer . . . or at the very least live a lot better. . . .

Buoyed by these thoughts, I went looking for J. R. Grimble.

The Chancellor of the Exchequer and I had never been what you would call close friends. Blood enemies would be a better description. Aahz always maintained that this was because of my growing influence in court. Not so. The truth was that my mentor's greed for additional funding was surpassed only by Grimble's reluctance to part with the same. Literally the same, since my wages came out of those coffers so closely guarded by the Chancellor.

I found him, as expected, in the tiny cubicle he used for an office. Scuttlebutt has it he repeatedly refused larger rooms, trying desperately to impress the rest of the staff by setting an example of frugality. It didn't work, but he kept trying and hoping.

His desk was elbow deep in paper covered by tiny little numbers which he alternately peered at and changed while moving various sheets from stack to stack. There were similar stacks on the floor and on the only other available chair, leading me to believe he had been at his current task for some time. Seeing no available space for sitting or standing, I elected to lean against the door frame.

"Working late, Lord Chancellor?"

That earned me a brief, dark glare before he returned to his work.

"If I were a magician, I'd be working late. As Chancellor of the Exchequer, these *are* my normal hours. For your information, things are going rather smoothly. So smoothly, in fact, I may be able to wrap up early tonight, say in another three or four hours."

"What are you working on?"

"Next year's Budget and Operating Plan, and it's almost done. That is, providing someone doesn't want to risk incurring my permanent disfavor by trying to change a number on me at the last minute."

The last was accompanied by what can only be described as a meaningful stare.

I ignored it.

I mean, what the heck! I was already on his bad side, so his threats didn't scare me at all.

"Then it's a good thing I caught you before you finished your task," I said nonchalantly. "I want to discuss something with you that will undoubtedly have an impact on your figures. Specifically, a change in my pay scale."

"Out of the question!" Grimble exploded. "You're already the highest paid employee on the staff, including myself. It's outrageous that you would even think of asking for a pay increase."

"Not a pay *increase*, Lord Chancellor, a pay cut."

That stopped him.

"A pay cut?"

"Say, down to nothing."

He leaned back in his chair and regarded me suspiciously.

"I find it hard to believe that you and your apprentice are willing to work for nothing. Forgive me, but I always distrust noble sacrifice as a motive. Though I dislike greed, at least it's a drive I can understand."

"Perhaps that's why we've always gotten along so well," I purred. "However, you're quite right. I have no intention of working for free. I was thinking of leaving the court of Possiltum to seek employment elsewhere."

The chancellor's eyebrows shot up.

"While I won't argue your plan, I must admit it surprises me. I was under the impression you were quite enamored of your position here in 'a soft job,' I believe is how your scaly apprentice describes it. What could possibly entice you to trade the comforts of court life for an uncertain future on the open road?"

"Why, a bribe, of course," I smiled. "A lump sum of a thousand gold pieces."

"I see," Grimble murmured softly. "And who's offering this bribe, if I might ask?"

I stared at the ceiling.

"Actually, I was rather hoping that *you* would."

There was a bit of haggling after that, but mostly on the terms of our agreement. Grimble *really* wanted Aahz and me out of his accounts, though I suspect he would have been less malleable if he had realized he was only dealing with me. There was a bit of name calling and breast beating, but the end result is what counts, and that end result was my heading for my quarters, a thousand gold pieces richer in exchange for a promise that it was the last money I would ever receive from Grimble. It was one more reason for my being on my way as soon as possible.

With light heart and heavy purse, I entered my quarters.

Remember the last time I entered my quarters? How there was a demon waiting for me? Well, it happened again.

Now don't get me wrong. This *isn't* a regular occurrence in my day-to-day existence. One demon showing up unannounced is a rarity. Two demons . . . well, no matter how you looked at it, this was going to be a red-letter day in my diary.

Does it seem to you I'm stalling? I am. You see, this demon I knew, and her name was Massha!

"Well hel-lo, high roller! I was just in the neighborhood and thought I'd stop by and say 'Hi!' "

She started forward to give me a hug, and I hastily moved to put something immobile between us. A 'hi!' and a hug might not sound like a threat to you. If not, you don't know Massha!

I have nothing against hello hugs. I have another demon friend named Tananda (yes, I have a *lot* of demon friends these days) whose hello hugs are high points in my existence. Tananda is cute, curvaceous, and cuddly. Okay, so she's also an assassin, but her hello hugs can get a rise out of a statue.

Massha, on the other hand, is *not* cute and cuddly. Massha is immense . . . and then some. I didn't doubt the sincere goodwill behind her greeting. I was just afraid that if she hugged me, it would take days to find my way out again . . . and I had a getaway to plan.

"Um . . . Hi, Massha. Good to see you . . . all of you."

The last time I had seen Massha, she was disguised as a gaudy circus tent, except it wasn't a disguise. It was actually the way she dressed. This time, though, she had apparently kicked out the jams . . . along with her entire wardrobe and any modicum of good taste. Okay, she wasn't completely naked. She was wearing a leopard-skin bikini, but she was showing enough flesh for four *normal* naked people. A bikini, her usual wheelbarrow full of jewelry, light green lipstick that clashed with her

orange hair, and a tattoo on her bicep. That was
Massha. Class all the way.

"What brings you to Klah? Aren't you still working
Jahk?" I asked, mentioning the dimension where we
met.

"The boys will just have to work things out without
me for a while. I'm on a little . . . vacation."

There was a lot of that going around.

"But what are you doing here?"

"Not much for small talk, are you? I like that in a
man."

My skin started to crawl a little on that last bit, but
she continued.

"Well . . . while I'm here, I thought I'd take another
little peek at your General Badaxe, but that's not the
real reason for my visit. I was hoping you and me could
talk a little . . . business."

My life flashed before my eyes. For a moment,
neither Aahz's departure nor the King's assignment was
my biggest problem . . . pun intended.

"Me?" I managed at last.

"That's right, hot stuff. I've been giving it a lot of
thought since you and your scaly green sidekick rolled
through my territory, and yesterday I made up my
mind. I've decided to sign on as your apprentice."

Chapter Four:

> *"Duty: A fee paid for transacting in good(s)."*
>
> —U.S. DEPT. OF COMMERCE

"BUT your Majesty, he promised me he'd pay the other half before spring, and . . ."

"I did not."

"Did too."

"Liar!"

"Thief!"

"Citizens," I said, "I can only listen to one side at a time. Now then, you! Tell me what you remember being said."

That's right. *I* said. There I was, sitting on the very throne I had decided to avoid at all cost.

Actually, this king business wasn't all that rough. Rodrick had briefed me on basic procedure and provided me with a wardrobe, and from there it was fairly simple. The problems paraded before me weren't all that hard to solve, but there were lots of them.

At first I was scared, then for a while it was fun. Now it was just boring. I had lost count of how many cases I had listened to, but I had developed a new sympathy for Rodrick's desire to get away for a while. I was ready for a vacation before lunch rolled around. It was beyond my comprehension how he had lasted for years of this nonsense.

You may wonder how I went from talking with Massha to sitting on the throne. Well, I wonder myself from time to time, but here's what happened as near as I can reconstruct it.

Needless to say, her request to work as my apprentice caught me unprepared.

"M . . . my . . . but Massha. You already *have* a job as a court magician. Why would you want to apprentice yourself to me?"

In response, Massha heaved a great sigh. It was a startling phenomenon to watch. Not just because there was so much of Massha moving in so many different directions, but because when she was done, she seemed to have deflated to nearly half her original size. She was no longer an imposing figure, just a rather tired looking fat woman.

"Look, Skeeve," she said in a low voice that bore no resemblance to her normal vampish tones. "If we're going to work together, we've got to be honest with each other. Court magician or not, we both know that I don't know any magik. I'm a mechanic . . . a gimmick freak. I've got enough magik baubles to hold down a job, but any bozo with a big enough bankroll could buy the same stuff at the Bazaar at Deva.

"Now, mind you, I'm not complaining. Old Massha's been kicked around by some of the best and nobody's ever heard her complain. I've been happy with what I have up to now. It's just when I saw you and your rat pack put one over on *both* city-states at the Big Game with some *real* magik, I knew there was something to learn besides how to operate gimmicks. So whattaya say? Will you help me learn a little of the stuff I really got into the magik biz for?"

Her honesty was making me more than a little un-

two of you can't decide the problem be-
ems to me there's only one solution. Cut
d each of you keep half.''

osed to inspire them to settle their dif-
uick compromise. Instead they thanked
dom, shook hands, and left smiling,
arve up their cat.

me, not for the first time today, that
zens of Possiltum don't have both oars
hat anyone could do with half a dead
ead cat fo: that matter, was beyond me.
s very tired. With an offhanded wave I
ald forward.

ore are waiting out there?'' I asked.
last. We deliberately kept the case load
ur Majesty could prepare for tomor-

lipped out reflexively. Actually, I
yhat happened tomorrow. My assign-
ad survived the day, and tomorrow
lem.

. . . when your bride arrives.''
o longer tired. Not a bit. I was wide
with every pore.
ed cautiously.
sty hasn't forgotten. She specific-
ival so that she would have a week
dding.''
d. Now I knew why dear Rodrick
so knew, with cold certainty, that
night to relieve me of my duties.
e not ever.

comfortable. I wanted to help her, but I sure didn't
want an apprentice right now. I decided to stall.

"Why did you choose magik for a profession,
anyway?"

That got me a sad smile.

"You're sweet, Skeeve, but we were going to be
honest with each other, remember? I mean, look at me.
What am I supposed to do for a living? Get married and
be a housewife? Who would have me? Even a blind man
could figure out in no time flat that I was more than he
had bargained for . . . a lot more. I resigned myself to
the way I look a long time ago. I accepted it and covered
up any embarrassment I felt with loud talk and flamboyant airs. It was only natural that a profession like
magik that thrives on loud talk and flamboyant airs
would attract me.''

"We aren't *all* loud talk," I said cautiously.

"I know," she smiled. "You don't have to act big
because you've got the clout to deliver what you promise. It impressed me on Jahk, and everyone I talked to at
the Bazaar on Deva said the same thing. 'Skeeve doesn't
strut much, but don't start a fight with him.' That's why
I want you for my teacher. I already know how to talk
loud.''

Honesty and flattery are a devastating one-two
punch. Whatever I thought about her before, right now
Massha had me eating out of the palm of her hand.
Before I committed myself to anything I might regret
later, I decided to try fighting her with her own
weapons.

"Massha . . . we're going to be honest with each
other, right? Well, I can't accept you as an apprentice
right now for two reasons. The first is simple. I don't
know that much magik myself. No matter what kind of
scam we pull on the paying customers, including the
ones on Deva, the truth is that I'm just a student. I'm

still learning the business myself."

"That's no problem, big bwana," Maasha laughed, regaining some of her customary composure. "Magik is like that: the more you learn, the more you find there is to know. That's why the really big guns in our business spend all their time closeted away studying and practicing. You know *some* magik, and that's some more than I know. I'll be grateful for anything you're willing to teach me."

"Oh." I said, a bit surprised that my big confession hadn't fazed her at all. "Well, there's still the second reason."

"And that is?"

". . . That I'm in a bit of trouble myself. In fact, I was just getting ready to sneak out of the kingdom when you showed up."

A small frown wrinkled Massha's forehead.

"Hmm . . ." she said, thoughtfully. "Maybe you'd better give me some of the details of this trouble you're in. Sometimes talking it out helps, and that's what apprentices are for."

"They are?" I countered skeptically. "I've been apprenticed twice, and I don't remember either of the magicians I studied under confiding in me with their problems."

"Well, that's what *Massha's* for. Listening happens to be one of the few things I'm *really* good at. Now give. What's happened to put a high-stepper like you on the run?"

Seeing no easy alternative, I told her about the King's assignment and my subsequent deal with Grimble. She was right. She was an excellent listener, making just enough sympathetic noise to keep me talking without actually interrupting my train of thought.

When I finally wound down, she sighed and shook her head.

"You're right.
I think there ai
reaching your fii

"Such as . . .

"Well, first, :
good king. The
no king at all. I
chair tomorrov
kingdom goes
peared."

"I hadn't th

"Then there
a little extra cash
comes out that Gri
King was counting
ping block f

I closed n

That did
masses, b
Grimble's
because

"You
for the

"Wi

"A
mean
he'll

"Well, if the
tween you, it se
the cat in two ai

This was sup
ference with a c
me for my wis
presumably to c

It occurred to
many of the citi
in the water. W
cat, or a whole d

Suddenly I wa
ckoned the her

w many m
That was the
ght today so y
ow."

"Tomorrow?"
The question
didn't really care
ment was done. I
was Rodrick's prob
"Yes, tomorrow
Suddenly I was n
awake and listening
"My bride?" I ask
"Surely your Maj
ally scheduled her ar
to prepare for your w
Case load be hange
wanted a vacation. I a
he wouldn't be back to
Not tonight, and mayb

Chapter Five:

"The only thing worse than a sorcerer is a sorcerer's apprentice."

—M. MOUSE

FOR once, I successfully suppressed the urge to panic. I had to! Without Aahz around to hold things together until I calmed down, I couldn't afford hysterics.

Instead, I thought . . . and thought.

I was in a jam, and no matter how I turned it over in my mind, it was going to take more than just me to get out of it.

I thought of Massha.

Then I thought about suicide.

Then I thought about Massha again.

With firm resolve and weak knees, I made my decision. The question was, how to locate Massha? The answer came on the heels of the question. Standing in for the king had been nothing but a pain so far. It was about time I started making it work *for* me for a change.

"Guard!"

A uniformed soldier materialized by the throne with impressive speed.

"Yes, your Majesty?"

31

"Pass the word for General Badaxe. I'd like to see him."

"Umm . . . begging your Majesty's pardon. He's with a lady just now."

"Good. I mean, bring them both."

"But . . ."

"Now."

"Yes, your Majesty!"

The guard was gone with the same speed with which he had appeared.

I tried not to grin. I had never gotten along particularly well with the military of Possiltum. Of course, the fact that my first exposure to them was when Aahz and I were hired to fight their war for them might have something to do with it. Anyway, the thought of some poor honor guard having to interrupt his general's *tête-à-tête* was enough to make me smile, the first in several days.

Still, sending a guard to fetch the person I wanted to see was certainly better than chasing them down myself. Perhaps being a king *did* have its advantages.

Two hours later, I was still waiting. In that time, I had more than ample opportunity to reconsider the benefit of issuing kingly summons. Having sent for Badaxe, I was obligated to wait for him in the throne room until he appeared.

At one point I considered the horrible possibility that he had taken Massha riding and that it might be *days* before they were located. After a little additional thought, I discarded the idea. There wasn't a steed in the Kingdom, including Gleep, who could carry Massha more than a few steps before collapsing.

I was still contemplating the image of Massha, sitting indignant on the ground with horse's legs protruding grotesquely from beneath her rump, when the herald sprang into action.

"Now comes General Badaxe . . . and a friend."

With that, the man stood aside. Actually, he took several sideways steps to stand aside.

I've already described Massha's bulk. Well, Hugh Badaxe wasn't far behind her. What he lacked in girth, he made up for in muscle. My initial impression of the General remained unchanged; that he had won his rank by taking on the rest of the army . . . and winning. Of course, he was wearing his formal bearskin, the clean one, which made him appear all the larger. While I had been there when they met, I had never actually seen Badaxe and Massha standing side by side before. The overall effect was awe-inspiring. Together, they might have been a pageant of a barbarian invasion gone decadent . . . if it weren't for the General's axe. His namesake, a huge, double-bitted hand axe, rode comfortably in its customary place on the General's right hip, and the glitter from it wasn't all decorative. Here, at least, was one barbarian who hadn't let decadence go to his sword arm.

"Your Majesty."

Badaxe rumbled his salutation as he dropped to one knee with an ease that denied his size. One could almost imagine the skull of a fallen enemy crackling sharply beneath that descending knee. I forced the thought from my mind.

"Greetings, General. Won't you introduce me to your . . . companion?"

"I . . . certainly, your Majesty. May I present Massha, Court Magician of Ta-hoe, and friend of both myself and Lord Skeeve, Magician to your own court here at Possiltum."

"Charmed, your Majesty."

I realized with a start that Massha was about to attempt to imitate Badaxe by dropping to one knee. Even if she were able to execute such a maneuver, it would require sufficient effort as to invite ridicule from the other court retainers present . . . and somehow I didn't want that.

"Ah . . . there is no need for that," I asserted hastily. "It was not our intention to hold formal court here, but rather an informal social occasion."

That caused a minor stir with the court, including the general who frowned in slight puzzlement. Still, I was already committed to a line of conversation, so I blundered on.

"In fact, that was the only reason for the summons. I wished to meet the lady dazzling enough to lure our general from his usual position by my side."

"Your Majesty gave his permission for my absence today," the general protested.

"Quite right. As I said, this is a social gathering only. In fact, there are too many people here for casual conversation. It is our wish that the court be adjourned for the day and the room cleared that I might speak freely with this visiting dignitary."

Again there was a general ripple of surprise, but a royal order was a royal order, and the various retainers bowed or curtsied to the throne and began making their way out.

"You too, General. I would speak with Massha alone."

Badaxe began to object, but Massha nudged him in the ribs with an elbow, a blow which would have been sufficient to flatten most men, but was barely enough to gain the general's attention. He frowned darkly, then gave a short bow and left with the others.

"So, you're a friend of our lord Magician," I asked after we were finally alone.

"I have that . . . honor, your Majesty," Massha replied cautiously. "I hope he's . . . well?"

"As a matter of fact, he's in considerable trouble right now."

Massha heaved a great sigh.

"I was afraid of that. Something to do with his last assignment?"

I ignored the question.

"General Badaxe seems quite taken with you. Are you sure you want to stay in the magik biz? Or are you going to try your hand at a new lifestyle?"

Massha scowled at me.

"Now how did you hear that? You haven't been torturing your own magician, have you?"

I caught the small motion of her adjusting her rings, and decided the time for games was over.

"Hold it, Massha! Before you do anything, there's something I have to show you."

"What's that?"

I had already closed my eyes to remove my disguise spell . . . faster than I ever had before.

"Me," I said, opening my eyes again.

"Well, I'll be . . . you really had me going there, hot stuff."

"It was just a disguise spell," I waved off-handedly.

"Nice. Of course, it almost got you fried. Why didn't you let me know it was you?"

"First of all, I wanted to see if my disguise spell was good enough to fool someone who was watching for it. This is my first time to try to disguise my voice as well as my appearance. Secondly . . . well, I was curious if you had changed your mind about being my apprentice."

"But why couldn't you have just asked me . . . I see.

You're really in trouble, aren't you? Bad enough that
you didn't want to drag me into an old promise. That's
nice of you, Skeeve. Like I said before, you run a class
act."

"Anybody would have done the same thing," I
argued, trying to hide my embarrassment at her praise.

She snorted loudly.

"If you believed that, you wouldn't have survived as
long as you have. Anyway, apprentice or not, a friend is
a friend. Now out with it. What's happened?"

Sitting on the steps to the throne, I filled her in about
the forthcoming wedding and my suspicions about the
king's conveniently scheduled vacation. I tried to sound
casual and matter-of-fact about it, but towards the end
my tone got rather flat.

When I was done, Massha gave a low whistle of sympathy.

"When you big leaguers get in trouble, you don't kid
around, do you? Now that you've filled me in, I'll admit
I'm a little surprised you're still here."

I grimaced.

"I'm a little slow from time to time, but you only
have to lecture me once. If one day without a king is bad
for a kingdom, a permanent disappearance could be
disastrous. Anyway, what I need right now is someone
to track down the real king and get him back here, while
I keep bluffing from the throne."

Massha scowled.

"Well, I've got a little trinket that could track him,
if you've got something around that he's worn, that
is. . . ."

"Are you kidding? You think court magicians dress
this way in Possiltum? Everything I'm wearing and two
more closetsful in his quarters belong to the king."

". . . But what I can't figure out is why you need me? Where's your usual partner . . . whatsisname . . . Aahz? It seems to me he'd be your first choice for a job like this. Wherever he is, can't you just pop over to that dimension and pull him back for a while?"

Lacking any other option, I decided to resort to the truth, both about Aahz's permanent departure and my own lack of ability to travel the dimensions without a D-Hopper. When I was done, Massha was shaking her head.

"So you're all alone and stranded here and you were *still* going to give me an out instead of pressuring me into helping? Well, you got my help, mister, and you don't have to bribe me with an apprenticeship, either. I'll get your king back for you . . . before that wedding. *Then* we'll talk about apprentices."

I shook my head.

"Right idea, but wrong order. I wasn't going to bribe you with an apprenticeship, Massha. I told you before I don't know much magik, but what I know I'll be glad to teach you . . . whether you find the King or not. I'm not sure that's an apprenticeship, but it's yours if you want it."

She smiled, a smile quite different from her usual vamp act.

"We'll argue about it later. Right now, I've got a king to find."

"Wait a minute! Before you go, you're pretty good with gadgets, right? Well, I've got a D-Hopper in my quarters. I want you to show me two settings: the one for Deva, and the one for Klah. You see, I'm not all *that* noble. If things get too rough or it takes you longer than a week to find the king, I want a little running room. If I'm not here when you get back, you can look for your 'noble' Skeeve at the Yellow Crescent Inn at the Bazaar at Deva.''

Massha snorted.

"You're putting yourself down again, Hot Stuff. You're going to try before you run, which is more than I can say for most in our profession. Besides, whatever you think your motives are, they're deeper than you think. You just asked me to show you two settings. You only need one to run."

Chapter Six:

"Good information is hard to get. Doing anything with it is even harder!"
—L. SKYWALKER

I HAD long since decided that the main requirement for Royalty or its impersonators was an immunity to boredom. Having already chronicled the true tedious nature of performing so-called "duties of state," I can only add that *waiting* to perform them is even worse.

There was certainly no rush on my part to meet the king's bride-to-be, much less marry her. After word had come that her arrival would be delayed by a full day, however, *and* as the day waxed into late afternoon waiting for her "early morning" reception, I found myself wishing that she would get here so we could meet and get it over with already.

All other royal activity had ground to a halt in an effort to emphasize the importance of Possiltum's greeting their queen-to-be. I hardly thought it was necessary, though, as the citizens decked the street with flowers and lined up three deep in hopes of catching a glimpse of this new celebrity. The wait didn't seem to dampen their spirits, though the flowers wilted only to be periodically replaced by eager hands. If nothing else, this reception was going to put a serious dent in Possiltum's flower crop for awhile. Of course, it might also put a dent in *all* our crops, for the streets remained packed with festive people who showed not the slightest inclination to return to their fields or guild shops when word was passed of each new delay.

"Haven't the citizens anything better to do with their time than stand around the streets throwing flowers at each other?" I snarled, turning from the window. "*Somebody* should be keeping the kingdom during all this foolishness."

As usual, J. R. Grimble took it on himself to soothe me.

"Your Majesty is simply nervous about the pending reception. I trust his wisdom will not allow his edginess to spill over onto his loyal subjects?"

"I was assured when she crossed the border that she would be here this morning. Morning! Ever see the sun set in the morning before?"

"Undoubtedly she was delayed by the condition of the roads," General Badaxe offered. "I have told your Majesty before that our roads are long overdue for repair. In their current state, they hinder the passage of travelers . . . *and* troops should our fair land come under attack."

Grimble bared his teeth.

"And his Majesty has always agreed with *me* that repairing the roads at this time would be far too costly . . . unless the General would be willing to significantly reduce the size of his army that we might use the savings from wages to pay for the road work?"

The General purpled.

"Reduce the size of the army and you'll soon lose that treasury that you guard so closely, Grimble."

"Enough, gentlemen," I said, waving them both to

silence. "As you've both said, we've discussed this subject many times before."

It had been decided that rather than having the King of Possiltum sit and fidget in front of the entire populace, that he should sweat it out in private with his advisors until his bride actually arrived. Royal image and all that. Unfortunately this meant that since morning I had been confined in a small room with J. R. Grimble and Hugh Badaxe for company. Their constant bickering and sniping was sufficient to turn my already dubious mood into something of record foulness.

"Well, while we're waiting, perhaps you can each brief me on your opinions of my future bride and her kingdom."

"But your Majesty, we've done that before. Many times."

"Well, we'll do it again. You're supposed to be my advisors, aren't you? So advise me. General Badaxe, why don't you start?"

Badaxe shrugged.

"The situation is essentially unchanged from our last briefing. Impasse is a small kingdom; tiny really—less than a thousand citizens altogether. They claim the entire Impasse mountain range, from which the kingdom gets its name, and which is the bulk of their military defense. Their claim stands mostly because the mountains are treacherous and there is little or no reason to venture there. At least ninety-five percent of their population is concentrated along the one valley through the mountains. They have no formal military, but rather a militia, which suffices as there are no less than five passes in the main valley where a child with a pile of rocks could hold off an army . . . and they have plenty of rocks. Their main vulnerability is food. The terrain is such that they are unable to support even their small population, and as they are still at odds with the kingdom at the other end of the valley who originally owned it, they are forced to buy all their food from us . . . at prices even a generous man would call exorbitant."

"Supply and demand," Grimble said with a toothy smile.

"Wait a minute, General," I interrupted. "If I understand this right, Impasse is not a threat to us militarily because of its size. If anything, it guards our flank against attack from the pass. Right?"

"Correct."

"Which it is already doing."

"Also correct."

Seeing an opening, I hurried on.

"We can't attack them, but from what you say they don't have anything we want. So why are we bothering with this marriage/alliance?"

The General looked pointedly at Grimble.

"Because even though Impasse is people-few and crop-light, they are sitting on the largest deposit of precious metal on the continent," The Chancellor of the Exchequer supplied.

"Precious met . . . oh! You mean gold."

"Precisely. With the alliance, Possiltum will become the richest kingdom ever."

"That hardly seems like sufficient reason to get married," I mumbled.

"Your Majesty's opinions on the subject are well known to us," Grimble nodded. "You have expressed them often and long every time the possibility of this marriage was broached. I am only glad that you finally gave your consent when the citizens of Possiltum threatened to revolt if you didn't accept the betrothal offer."

"That was only after you spread the word that such

an alliance would significantly lower taxes, Grimble,"
Badaxe scowled.

"I said it *might* lower taxes," the Chancellor corrected innocently. "Can I help it if the common folk
jumped to conclusions?"

Now that I had a clearer picture of the situation, I
might have mustered a bit of sympathy for the King's
predicament, if he hadn't stuck me in it in his stead.

"Enough about Impasse. Now give me your opinions
of my bride-to-be."

There was a brief moment of uncomfortable silence.

"Impasse doesn't have a monarchy," Grimble said
carefully. "That is, until recently. It was more a tribal
state, where the strongest ruled. When the last king
died, however, his daughter Hemlock somehow managed to take over and maintain the throne, thereby es-
tablishing a royal line of sorts. Exactly how she did it is
unclear."

"Some say that prior to the king's death she managed
to gain the . . . loyalty of all the able-bodied fighters in
the kingdom, thereby securing her claim from challenge," Badaxe supplied.

I held up a restraining hand.

"Gentlemen, what you're telling me are facts. I asked
for your *opinions*."

This time, there was a long uncomfortable silence.

"That good, eh?" I grimaced.

"Your Majesty must remember," Grimble protested,
"we are being asked to express our hidden feelings
about a woman who will soon be our Queen."

"Not until the marriage," I growled. "Right now, I
am your king. Get my drift?"

They got it, and swallowed hard.

"The words 'cold-blooded' and 'ruthless' come to

mind," the general said, "and that's the impression of a
man who's made a career of the carnage of war."

"I'm sure the rumors that she murdered her father to
gain control of the kingdom are exaggerated," Grimble
argued weakly.

". . . But your Majesty would be well advised to insist
on seperate sleeping quarters, and even then sleep lightly
. . . and armed," the general concluded firmly.

"No difficulty should be encountered with separate
quarters," Grimble leered. "It's said Queen Hemlock
has the morals of an alley cat."

"Terrific," I sighed.

The Chancellor favored me with a paternal smile.

"Oh, there's no doubt that the entire kingdom,
myself included, admires your Majesty for the sacrifices
he is willing to make for his people."

The trouble was, only *I* knew who the King was willing to sacrifice!

I studied Grimble's smile through hooded eyes, seeking desperately through my mind for something to disrupt his smug enjoyment of the situation. Suddenly, I
found it.

"I've been meaning to ask, does anyone know the
current whereabouts of our Court Magician?"

Grimble's smile disappeared like water on a hot
skillet.

"He's . . . gone, your Majesty."

"What? Out on another of his madcap adventures?"

The Chancellor averted his eyes.

"No, I mean, he's . . . gone. Tendered his resignation
and left."

"Tendered his resignation to whom?" I pressed. "On
whose authority has he quit his post during this, my
darkest hour?"

"Ahh . . . mine, your Majesty."

"What was that, Grimble? I couldn't quite hear you."

"Mine. I told him he could go."

Grimble was sweating visibly now, which was fine by me. In fact, an idea was beginning to form in my mind.

"Hmm . . . knowing you, Lord Chancellor, I would suspect money is behind the Great Skeeve's sudden departure."

"In a way," Grimble evaded, "you might say that."

"Well, it won't do," I said firmly. "I want him back . . . and before this accursed marriage. What's more, since you approved his departure, I'm holding you personally responsible for his return."

"B-ut your Majesty! I wouldn't know where to start looking. He could be anywhere by now."

"He can't have gone far," Badaxe volunteered casually. "His dragon and unicorn are still in the Royal Stables."

"They are?" the Chancellor blinked.

"Yes," the General smiled, "as you might know if you ever set foot outside your counting house."

"See, Grimble," I said. "The task I set before you should be easy for a man of your resources. Now off with you. The longer you tarry here, the longer it will be before you find our wayward magician."

The Chancellor started to say something, then shrugged and started for the door.

"Oh, Grimble," I called. "Something you might keep in mind. I heard a rumor that the Great Skeeve has recently been disguising himself as me for an occasional prank. Like as not the scamp is parading around somewhere with the royal features on his face. That tidbit alone should help you locate him."

"Thank you, your Majesty," the Chancellor responded glumly, reminded now of the shape-changing abilities of his supposed quarry.

I wasn't sure, but I thought General Badaxe was stifling a laugh somewhere in the depths of his beard as his rival trudged out.

"How about you, General? Do you think your men could assist in passing word of my royal summons to the Great Skeeve?"

"That won't be necessary, your Majesty."

With sudden seriousness he approached me, laid a hand on my shoulder, and stared into my eyes.

"Lord Magician," he said, "the King would like to see you."

Chapter Seven:

*"There is no counter for a spirited woman
except spirited drink."*

—R. Butler

"YOU'VE known for some time that I'm a fighting man. What you *don't* seem to realize is what that implies."

We were sitting over wine now, in a much more relaxed conversation than when I had been pretending to be King Rodrick.

"Fighting men recognize people as much by movement and mannerism as they do by facial feature. It's a professional habit. Now, you had the appearance and voice of the King, but your carriage and gestures were that of the Great Skeeve, not Rodrick the Fifth."

"But if you knew I was an imposter, why didn't you say something?"

The General drew himself up stiffly.

"The King had not taken me into his confidence in this matter, nor had you. I felt it would have been rude to intrude on your affairs uninvited."

"Weren't you afraid that I might be a part of some plot to murder the King and take his place?"

"Lord Magician, though we met as rivals, prolonged exposure to you has caused my respect for you to grow to no small matter. Both in your convincing Big Julie and his army to defect from the Mob and join Possiltum as honest citizens, and in fighting at your side in the Big Game when you risked life and limb to rescue a comrade in peril, you have shown ingenuity, courage, and honor. While I may still speak of you from time to time in less than glowing terms, my lowest opinion of you does not include the possibility of your having a hand in murdering your employer."

"Thank you, General."

". . . And besides, only a total idiot would want to assume Rodrick's place so soon before his marriage to Queen Hemlock."

I winced.

"So much for your growing respect."

"I said 'ingenuity, courage, and honor.' I made no mention of intelligence. Very well, then, a total idiot or someone under orders from his king."

"How about a bit of both?" I sighed.

"I suspected as much." Badaxe nodded. "Now that we're speaking candidly, may I ask as to the whereabouts of the King?"

"Good question."

In a few depressing sentences, I brought him up to date on my assignment and Rodrick's disappearance.

"I was afraid something like this would happen," the General said when I concluded. "The King has been looking desperately for some way out of this marriage, and it looks like he's found it. Well, needless to say, if there's anything I can do to help, just ask."

"Thanks, General. As a matter of fact, I. . . ."

". . . As long as it doesn't go against the good of the kingdom," Badaxe amended. "Like helping you to escape. Possiltum needs a king, and for the time being, you're it!"

"Oh. Well . . . how about using your men to help find the king?"

Badaxe shook his head.

"Can't do it. Massha has that assignment. If I sent my men to back her up, she'd think I didn't have any faith in her."

Terrific! I had an ally, if I could get around his loyalties and amorous entanglements.

The General must have noticed my expression.

"Anything else I'll be willing to do."

"Like what?"

"Well . . . like teaching you to defend yourself against your bride-to-be."

That actually sounded promising.

"Do you think we'll have enough time?"

With that, there was a heavy knocking at the door.

"Your Majesty! The carriage of Queen Hemlock is approaching the palace!"

"No," said the General, with disheartening honesty.

We barely made it to our appointed places ahead of the Queen's procession. The throne of Possiltum had been temporarily moved to a position just inside the doors to the palace, and only by sprinting through the corridors with undignified abandon were Badaxe and I able to reach our respective positions before the portals were thrown open.

"Remind me to have a word with you about the efficiency of your army's early warning system," I said to the General as I sank into my seat.

"I believe it was the Court Magician who complained about the excessive range of the military spy system," Badaxe retorted. "Perhaps your Majesty will see fit now to convince him of the necessity of timely information."

Before I could think of a sufficiently polite response,

the Queen's party drew to a halt at the foot of the stairs.

The kingdom of Impasse had apparently spared no expense on the Queen's carriage. If it was not actually fashioned of solid gold, there were sufficient quantities of the metal in the trim and decorations as to make the difference academic. I took secret pleasure that Grimble was not present to gloat at the scene. The curtains were drawn, allowing us to see the rich embroidery upon them, but not who or what was within. A team of eight matched horses completed the rig, though their shaggy coats and short stature suggested that normally the mountainfolk put them to far more practical use than dragging royalty around the countryside.

With the carriage, however, any semblance of decorum about the Queen's procession vanished.

Her escort consisted of at least twenty retainers, all mounted and leading extra horses, though whether these were relief mounts or the bride's dowry I couldn't tell. The escort was also all male, and of a uniform appearance; broad-shouldered, narrow-waisted, and musclebound. They reminded me of miniature versions of the opposing teams Aahz and I had faced during the Big Game, but unlike those players, these men were armed to the teeth. They fairly bristled with swords and knives, glittering from boot-tops, arm sheaths, and shoulder scabbards, such that I was sure the combined weight of their weapons offset that of the golden coach they were guarding. These weren't pretty court decorations, but well handled field weapons worn with the ease fighting men accord the tools of their trade.

The men themselves were dressed in drab tunics suited more for crawling through thickets with knives clenched in their teeth than serving as a royal escort. Still, they wrinkled their broad, flat features into wide smiles as they alternately gawked at the building and waved at the crowd which seemed determined to unload the earlier noted surplus of flowers by burying the coach with them. The escort may have seemed sloppy and undisciplined in the eyes of Badaxe or Big Julie, but I wouldn't want to be the one to try to take anything away from them; Queen, coach, kingdom, or even a flower they had taken a fancy to.

Two men in the procession were notable exceptions to the rule. Even on horseback they looked to be head and shoulder taller than the others and half again as broad. They had crammed their massive frames into tunics which were clean and formal, and appeared to be unarmed. I noted, however, that instead of laughing or waving, they sat ramrod stiff in their saddles and surveyed their surroundings with the bored, detached attention to detail I normally associated with predators . . . big predators.

I was about to call Badaxe's attention to the pair when the carriage door opened. The woman who appeared was obviously akin to most of the men in the escort. She had the same broad, solid build and facial features, only more so. My first impression was that she looked like the bottom two-thirds of an oak door, if the door were made of granite. Unsmiling, she swept the area with a withering stare, then nodded to herself and stepped down.

"Lady in waiting," Badaxe murmured.

I'm not sure if his comment was meant to reassure me, but it did. Only after did it occur to me that the General had volunteered the information to keep me from running, which I had been seriously considering.

The next figure in view was a radical departure from the other Impassers in the party. She was arrow thin and pale with black stringy black hair that hung straight past her shoulders. Instead of the now expected round, flat face, her features looked like she had been hung up by her nose to dry. She wasn't unpleasant to look at, in fact, I guessed that she was younger than I was, but the pointed nose combined with a pair of dark, shiny-alert eyes gave her a vaguely rodent appearance. Her dress was a long-sleeved white thing that would have probably looked more fetching on a clothes-hanger. Without more than a glance at the assembled citizens she gathered up what slack there was in the skirt, hopped down from the carriage, and started up the stairs toward me with the athletic, leggy grace of a confirmed tomboy.

"*That* is Queen Hemlock," the General supplied.

I had somehow suspected as much, but having received confirmation, I sprang into action. *This* part, at least, I knew how to handle, having had it drilled into me over and over again by my advisors.

I rose to my feet and stood regally until she reached the throne, then timed my bow to coincide with her curtsey . . . monarch greeting monarch and all that.

Next, I was supposed to welcome her to Possiltum, but before I could get my mouth open, she came up with her own greeting.

"Sorry I didn't curtsey any lower, but I'm not wearing a thing under this dress. Rod, it's beastly hot here in the lowlands," she said, giving me a wide but thin-lipped smile.

"Aahh. . . . ." I said carefully.

Ignoring my response, or lack thereof, she smiled and waved at the throng, which responded with a roar of approval.

"What idiot invited the rabble?" she asked, the smile never leaving her face.

"Aahh. . . ." I repeated.

General Badaxe came to my rescue.

"No formal announcement was made, your Majesty, but word of your arrival seems to have leaked out to the general populace. As might be expected, they are very eager to see their new Queen."

"Looking like this?" she said, baring her teeth and waving to those on the rooftops. "Six days on the road in this heat without a bath or a change of clothes and instead of a discreet welcome, half the kingdom gets to see me looking like I was dragged along behind the coach instead of riding in it. Well, it's done and we can't change it. But mind you, if it happens again . . . General Badaxe, is it? I thought so. Anyway, as I was saying, if it happens again, heads will roll . . . and I'm not speaking figuratively."

"Welcome to Possiltum," I managed at last.

It was a considerably abbreviated version of the speech I had planned to give, but it was as much as I could remember under the circumstances.

"Hello, Roddie," she said without looking at me, still waving at the crowd. "I'm going to scamper off for my quarters in a second. Be a love and try not to get underfoot during the next week . . . there's so much to do. Besides, it looks like you're going to have your hands full with other business."

"How's that?"

"You've got a wee bit of trouble coming your way, at least, according to the gentleman I met on the road. Here he comes now. Bye."

"But . . ."

Queen Hemlock had already disappeared, vanishing into the depths of the palace like a puff of smoke. Instead, I found myself focusing on the man who had stepped from the carriage and was currently trudging up the stairs toward my throne. I observed that he had the same weasel features and manners of J. R. Grimble.

Mostly, though, I noticed that the two broadshouldered predators previously assumed to be part of the Queen's escort, had suddenly materalized at his side, towering over him like a pair of bookends . . . mean looking bookends.

I sat down, in part because the approaching figure did not seem to be royalty, but mostly because I had a feeling I wanted to be sitting down for this next interview.

The man reached my throne at last, drew himself up, and gave a curt nod rather than a bow. This, at least, looked polite, since his flankers didn't acknowledge my presence at all.

"Forgive me for intruding on such a festive occasion, your Majesty," the man said, "but there are certain matters we need to discuss."

"Such as . . . ?"

"My name is Shai-ster, and I represent a . . . consortium of businessmen. I wish to confer with one of your retainers concerning certain employees of ours who failed to report in after pursuing our interests in this region."

As I mentioned earlier, I was getting pretty good at speaking "bureaucrat." This man's oration, however, lost me completely.

"You want to what about who?"

The man sighed and hung his head for a moment.

"Let me put it to you this way," he said at last. "I'm with the Mob, and I want to see your Magician, Skeeve. It's about our army, Big Julie's boys, that sort of disappeared after tangling with him. Now do you understand me?"

Chapter Eight:

"Choose your friends carefully. Your enemies will choose you!"

—Y. ARAFAT

WITHIN a few days of Queen Hemlock's arrival, the palace of Possiltum had the happy, relaxed air of a battlefield the night before the battle. The Queen's party and the mob representatives were housed in the palace as "royal guests," giving me a two-front war whether I wanted it or not.

Queen Hemlock was not an immediate problem; she was more like a time bomb. With specific orders to "stay out of her way," I didn't have to deal with her much, and even General Badaxe admitted that if she were going to try to kill me, it wouldn't be until after the wedding when she was officially Queen of Possiltum. Still, as the wedding day loomed closer, I was increasingly aware that she would have to be dealt with.

The Mob representatives, however, were an immediate problem. I had stalled them temporarily by telling them that the Court Magician was not currently in the palace, but had been sent for, and as a token of good faith had given them the hospitality of the palace. They didn't drink much, and never pestered me with

questions about "Skeeve's" return. There was no doubt
in my mind, however, that at some time their patience
would be exhausted and they would start looking for the
Court Magician themselves. I also had a felling that
"some time" would be real soon.

Needing all the help I could get, I had Badaxe send
one of his men for Big Julie. With minimal difficulty we
smuggled him into the palace, and the three of us held
a war council. On Badaxe's advice, I immediately
dropped my disguise and brought our guest up to date
on the situation.

"Ah'm sorry," Julie said to open the meeting, "but I
don't see where I can help you, know what I mean?"

Terrific. So much for Big Julie's expert military advice.

"I'd *like* to help," he clarified. "You've done pretty
good by me and the boys. But I used to work for the
Mob, you know? I know what they're like. Once they
get on your trail, they never quit. I tried to tell you that
before."

"I don't see what the problem is," General Badaxe
rumbled. "There are only three of them, and their main
spokesman's a non-combatant to boot. It wouldn't take
much to make sure they didn't report anything to anybody . . . ever again."

Big Julie shook his head.

"You're a good man, Hugh, but you don't know
what you're dealing with here. If the Mob's scouting
party disappears, the Big Boys will know they've hit
paydirt and set things in motion. Taking out their reps
won't stop the Mob . . . it won't even delay them. If
anything, it will speed the process up!"

Before Badaxe had a chance to reply, I interrupted
with a few questions of my own.

"Wait a minute, Big Julie. When we first met, you

were commanding the biggest army this world had ever seen. Right?''

"That's right," he nodded. "We was rolling along pretty good until we met you."

". . . And we didn't stop you militarily. We just gave you a chance to disappear as soldiers and retire as citizens of Possiltum. You and your boys were never beaten in a fight."

"We were the best," Big Julie confirmed proudly. "Anybody messed with us, they pulled back a bloody stump with no body attached, know what I mean?"

"Then why are you all so afraid of the Mob? If they try anything, why don't you and your boys just hook up with General Badaxe's army and teach 'em a lesson in maneuvers?"

The ex-commander heaved a deep sigh.

"It don't work that way," he said. "If they was to march in here like an army, sure, we could send 'em packing. But they won't. They move in a few muscle-men at a time, all acting just as polite as you please so there's nothing you can arrest 'em for. When enough of 'em get here, though, they start leaning on your citizens. Little stuff, but nasty. If somebody complains to you, that somebody turns up dead along with most of their family. Pretty soon, all your citizens are more afraid of the Mob than they are of you. Nobody complains, nobody testifies in court. When that happens, you got no more kingdom. The Mob runs everything while you starve. You can't fight an invasion like that with an army. You can't fight it at all!''

We all sat in uncomfortable silence for a while, each avoiding the other's gaze while we racked our brains for a solution.

"What I don't understand," Badaxe said at last, "is if the system you describe is so effective and so unstoppable, why did they bother having an army at all?''

"I really hate to admit this," Big Julie grimaced, "but we was an experiment. Some of the Mob's bean-counters got it into their heads that even though an army was more expensive, the time savings of a fast takeover would offset the additional cost. To tell you the truth, I think their experiment was a washout.''

That one threw me.

"You mean to say your army wasn't effective?''

"Up to a point we were. After that, we were too big. It costs a lot to keep an army in the field, and toward the end there, it was costing more to support my boys for a week than we were getting out of the kingdoms we were conquering. I think they were getting ready to phase us out . . . and that's why it's taken so long for them to come looking for their army."

I shook my head quickly.

"You lost me on that last loop, Big Julie. *Why* did they delay their search?''

"Money," he said firmly. "I'll tell you, nothing makes the Big Boys sit up and take notice like hard cash. I mean, they wrote the book when it came to money motivation.''

"Sounds like Grimble," Badaxe muttered. "Doesn't anybody do anything for plain old revenge anymore?''

"Stow it, General," I ordered, leaning forward. "Keep going, Big Julie. What part does money have in this?''

"Well, the way I see it, the Mob was already losing money on my army, you know? To me, that means they weren't about to throw good gold after bad. I mean, why spend more money looking for an army that, when you find it, is only going to cost you more money?''

"But they're here now.''

"Right. At the same time Possiltum's about to

become suddenly rich. It looks to me like the Big Boys have found a way to settle a few old scores and turn a profit at the same time.''

"The wedding!" I said. "I should have known. That means that by calling off the wedding, I can eliminate two problems at once; Queen Hemlock, *and* the Mob!"

Badaxe scowled at me.

"I thought we had already discarded that option. Remember Grimble and the citizenry of Possiltum?"

Without thinking, I slammed the flat of my hand down on the table with a loud slap.

"Will you forget about Grimble and the citizenry of Possiltum? I'm tired of being in a box, General, and one way or another I'm going to blast a way out!"

From the expressions of my advisors, I realized I might have spoken louder than I had intended. With a conscious effort, I modulated my tone and my mood.

"Look, General . . . Hugh," I said carefully. "You may be used to the pressures of command, but this is new to me. I'm a magician, remember? Forgive me if I get a little razzled trying to find a solution to the problem that your . . . I mean, *our* King has dropped in my lap. Okay?"

He nodded curtly, but still didn't relax.

"Now, your point has merit," I continued, "but it overlooks a few things. First, Grimble isn't here. When and *if* he does get back, he'll have the king in tow, and friend Rodrick can solve the problem for us . . . at least the problem with the Queen. As for the citizenry of Possiltum . . . between you and me I'm almost ready to face their protests rather than have to deal with Queen Hemlock. Now if you weigh the disappointment of our people over having to continue the status quo against having both the Queen *and* the Mob move in on a permanent basis, what result do you get? Thinking of the welfare of the kingdom, of course!''

The General thought it over, then heaved a great sigh.

"I was never that much in favor of the wedding, anyway," he admitted.

"Just a minute, boys," Big Julie said, holding up a weary hand. "It's not quite that easy. The money thing may have slowed up their search a bit, but now that the Mob is here, there are a couple other matters they're gonna want to settle."

"Such as?" I asked, dreading the answer.

"Well, first off, there's me and my boys. Nobody just walks away from the Mob, you know. Their pay scale is great, but their retirement plan stinks."

"I thought you said they didn't want their army anymore," Badaxe grumbled.

"Maybe not as an army, but they can always use manpower. They'll probably break us up and absorb us into various positions in the organization."

"Would you be willing to go back to work for them?"

Big Julie rubbed his chin with one hand as he considered the General's question.

"I'd have to talk to the boys," he said. "Like I said, this kingdom's been pretty good to us. I'd hate to see anything happen to it because we were here . . . especially if we'd end up working for them again anyway."

"No," I said flatly.

"But . . ."

"I said 'No!' You've got a deal with Possiltum, Big Julie. More important, you've got a deal with me. We don't turn you over to the Mob until we've tried everything we can do to defend you."

"And how do you propose to defend them from the Mob?" Badaxe asked, sarcastically.

"I don't know. I'm working on it. Maybe we can buy

them off. Offer them Queen Hemlock to hold for ransom or something.''

"Lord Magician!''

"Okay, okay. I said I was still working on it, didn't I? What's next, Big Julie? You said there were a couple things they wanted besides money.''

"You,'' he said bluntly. "The Mob isn't going to be happy until they get the Great Skeeve, Court Magician of Possiltum.''

"Me?'' I said in a small voice.

"The Mob didn't get to the top by ignoring the competition. You've made some pretty big ripples with your work, and the biggest as far as they're concerned is making their army disappear. They know you're big. Big enough to be a threat. They're gonna want you neutralized. My guess is that they'll try to hire you, and failing that, try for some sort of non-aggression deal.''

"And failing that . . . ?'' Badaxe asked, echoing my thoughts.

Big Julie shrugged.

"Failing that, they're gonna do their best to kill you.''

Chapter Nine:

"I don't know why anyone would be nervous about going to see royalty."

—P. IN BOOTS

"BUT why do *I* have to come along?" Badaxe protested, pacing along at my side as we strode towards the Queen's chambers.

"Call it moral support," I growled. "Besides, I want a witness that I went into the Queen's chambers . . . and came out again, if you get my drift."

"But if this will only solve one of our problems. . . ."

". . . Then it will be one less problem for us to deal with. Shh! Here we are."

I had switched back to my Rodrick disguise. That combined with the General's presence was enough to have the Honor Guards at the Queen's chambers snap to rigid attention at our approach. I ignored them and hammered on the door, though I did have a moment to reflect that not long ago, I thought the biggest problem facing a king was boredom!

"For cryin' out loud!" came a shrill voice from within. "Can't you guards get *anything* right? I told you I didn't want to be disturbed!"

One of the guards rolled his eyes in exasperation. I

favored him with a sympathetic smile, then raised an eyebrow at Badaxe.

"King Rodrick the Fifth of Possiltum seeks an audience with Queen Hemlock!" he bellowed.

"I suppose it's all right," came the reply. "How about first thing in the morning?"

"Now," I said.

I didn't say it very loud, but it must have carried. Within a few heartbeats the door flew open, exposing Queen Hemlock . . . literally. I can't describe her clothing because she wasn't wearing any. Not a stitch!

"Roddie!" she chirped, oblivious to the guards and Badaxe, all of whom gaped at her nakedness. "Come on in. What in the world are you doing here?"

"Wait for me," I instructed Badaxe in my most commanding tone.

"C-certainly, your Majesty!" he responded, tearing his eyes away from the Queen long enough to snap to attention.

With that, I stepped into the Queen's lair.

"So, what have you got for me?" She shut the door and leaned back against it. The action made her point at me, even though her hands were behind her back.

"I beg your pardon?"

"The audience," she clarified. "You wanted it, you got it. What's up?"

Somehow under the circumstances, I found that to be another embarrassing question.

"I . . . um . . . that is . . . could you please put something on? I'm finding your attire, or lack thereof, to be quite distracting."

"Oh, very well. It *is* beastly hot in here, though."

She flounced across the room and came up with a flimsy something which she shrugged into, but didn't close completely.

"Right after the wedding," she declared, "I want that window enlarged, or better yet, the whole wall torn out. Anything to get a little ventilation in this place."

She plopped down in a chair and curled her legs up under her. It eased my discomfort somewhat, but not much.

"Ahh . . . actually, that's what I'm here to talk to you about."

"The window?" she frowned.

"No. The wedding."

That made her frown even more.

"I thought it was agreed that I would handle all the wedding arrangements. Oh, well, if you've got any specific changes, it isn't too late to. . . ."

"It isn't that," I interrupted hastily. "It's . . . well, it's come to my attention that the high prices Possiltum is charging your kingdom for food is forcing you into this marriage. Not wishing to have you enter into such a bond under duress, I've decided to cut our prices in half, thereby negating the need for our wedding."

"Oh, Roddie, don't be silly. That's not the reason I'm marrying you!"

Rather than being upset, the Queen seemed quite amused at my suggestion.

"It isn't?"

"Of course not. Impasse is so rich that we could buy your yearly crop at double the prices if we wanted to and still not put a dent in our treasury."

My stomach began to sink.

"Then you *really* want this marriage? You aren't being forced into it for political reasons?"

The Queen flashed all her teeth at me in a quick smile.

"Of course there are political reasons. I mean, we are royalty, aren't we? I'm sure you're a pleasant enough fellow, but I can get all the pleasant fellows I want without *marrying* them. Royalty marries power blocks, not people.''

There was a glimmer of hope in what she was saying, and I pounced on it with all fours.

''. . . Which brings us to the other reason we should call off the wedding,'' I said grandly.

The Queen's smile disappeared.

''What's that?'' she said sharply.

For my reply, I let drop my disguise spell.

''Because I'm not Royalty. I'm people.''

''Oh, that,'' the Queen shrugged. ''No problem. I knew that all along.''

''You did?'' I gulped.

''Sure. You were embarrassed . . . twice. Once when I arrived at the palace, and again just now when I opened the door in my all-together. Royalty doesn't embarrass. It's in the blood. I knew all long you weren't Rodrick. It's my guess you're the Great Skeeve, Court Magician. Right? The one who can shape change?''

''Well, it's a disguise spell, not shape changing, but except for that, you're right.''

Between Badaxe and Queen Hemlock, I was starting to wonder if anyone was really fooled by my disguise spells.

The Queen uncoiled from her seat and began pacing back and forth as she spoke, oblivious to her nakedness which peeked out of her wrap at each turn.

''The fact that you aren't the king doesn't change my situation, if anything it improves it. As long as you can keep your disguise up enough to fool the rabble, I'll be marrying two power blocks instead of one.''

''Two power blocks,'' I echoed hollowly.

''Yes. As the 'king' of Possiltum, you control the first block I was after: land and people. Impasse by itself isn't large enough to wage an aggressive war, but uniting the respective powers of the two kingdoms, we're unstoppable. With your armies backed by my capital, I can sweep as far as I want, which is pretty far, let me tell you. There's nothing like growing up in a valley where the only view is the other side of the valley to whet one's appetite for new and unusual places."

"Most people content themselves with touring," I suggested. "You don't have to conquer a country to see it."

"Cute," Queen Hemlock sneered. "Naive, but cute. Let's just say I'm not most people and let it ride, okay? Now then, for the second power base, there's you and your magic. That's a bonus I hadn't expected, but I'm sure that, given a day or two, I can expand my plans to take advantage of it."

At one time, I thought I had been scared by Massha. In hindsight, Massha caused me only faint discomfort. Talking with Queen Hemlock, I learned what fear was all about! She wasn't just a murderess, as Badaxe suspected. She was utter mayhem waiting to be loosed on the world. The only thing between her and the resources necessary to act out her dreams was me. Me, and maybe. . . .

"What about King Rodrick?" I blurted out. "If he shows up, the original wedding plans go into effect."

"You mean he's still alive?" she exclaimed, arching a thin eyebrow at me. "I've overestimated you, Skeeve. Alive he could be a problem. No matter. I'll alert my escort to kill him on sight if he appears before the wedding. After we're married, it would be a simple matter to declare him an imposter and have him officially executed."

Terrific. Thanks to my big mouth, Massha would be walking into a trap if she tried to return the King to the castle. If Queen Hemlock's men saw him, then . . .

"Wait a minute!" I exclaimed. "If I'm walking around disguised as the King, what's to keep your men from offing me by mistake?"

"Hmm. Good thing you thought about that. Okay! Here's what we'll do."

She dove into her wardrobe and emerged with a length of purple ribbon.

"Wear this in full view whenever you're outside your chambers," she instructed, thrusting it into my hands. "It'll let my men know that you're the man I want to marry instead of their target."

I stood with the ribbon in my hand.

"Aren't you making a rather large assumption, your Majesty?"

"What's that?" she frowned.

"That I may not want to marry you?"

"Of course you do," she smiled. "You've already got the throne of Possiltum. If you marry me, you not only have access to my treasury, it also rids you of your other problem."

"My other problem?"

"The Mob, silly. Remember? I rode in with their representative. With my money, you can buy them off. They'll forget anything if the price is high enough. Now, isn't being my husband better than running from their vengeance *and* mine for the rest of your life?"

I had my answer to that, but in a flash of wisdom kept it to myself. Instead, I said my goodbyes and left.

"From your expression, I take it that your interview with the Queen was less than a roaring success," Badaxe said dryly.

"Spare me the 'I told you so's,' General," I snarled. "We've got work to do."

Shooting a quick glance up and down the corridor, I cut my purple ribbon in half on the edge of his axe.

"Keep a lookout for Massha and the King," I instructed. "If you see them, be sure Rodrick wears this. It'll make his trip through the palace a lot easier."

"But where are you going?"

I gave him a tight smile.

"To see the Mob representatives. Queen Hemlock has graciously told me how to deal with them!"

Chapter Ten:

"Superior firepower is an invaluable tool when entering into negotiations."
—G. PATTON

THE Mob representatives had been housed in one of the less frequented corners of the palace. In theory, this kept them far from the hub of activity while Badaxe and I figured out what to do with them. In fact, it meant that now that I was ready to face them, I had an awfully long walk to reach my destination.

By the time I reached the proper door, I was so winded I wasn't sure I'd have enough breath to announce my presence. Still, on my walk I had worked up a bit of a mad against the Mob. I mean, who did they think they were, popping up and disrupting my life this way? Besides, I was too unnerved by Queen Hemlock to try anything against her, which left the Mob as the only target for my frustration.

With that in mind, I drew a deep breath and knocked on the door.

I needn't have worried about announcing myself. Between the second and third knocks, the door opened a crack. My third knock hit the door before I could stop it, but the door remained unmoved by the impact.

"Hey, Shai-ster! It's the King!"

"Well, let him in, you idiot!"

The door opened wide, revealing one of Shai-ster's massive bodyguards, then a little wider to allow me entry space past him.

"Come in, come in, your Majesty," the Mob's spokesman said, hurrying forward to greet me. "Have a drink . . . Dummy! Get the King something to drink!"

This last was addressed to the second hulking muscleman who heaved himself off the bed he had been sprawled upon. With self-conscious dignity he picked up the end of the bed one-handed, set it down again, then picked up the mattress and extracted a small, flat bottle from under it.

I wondered briefly if this was what Big Julie meant when he referred to the Mob tradition of "going to the mattresses." Somehow the phrase had always brought another image to mind . . . something involving women.

Accepting the flask from his bodyguard, Shai-ster opened the top and offered it to me, smiling all the while.

"Am I correct in assuming that your Majesty's visit indicates news of the whereabouts of his court magician? Perhaps even an estimated time as to when he is expected back?"

I accepted the flask, covertly checking the locations of the bodyguards before I answered. One was leaning against the door, while the other stood by the bed.

"Actually, I can do better than that. The Great Skeeve . . ."

I closed my eyes and dropped my disguise spell.

". . . is here."

The bodyguards started visibly at my transformation, but Shai-ster remained unmoved except for a narrowing of the eyes and a tightening of his smile.

"I see. That simplifies things a bit. Boys, give the Great Skeeve here a chair. We have some business to discuss."

His tone was not pleasant, nor were the bodyguards smiling as they started for me.

Remember how Rupert jumped me so easily? Well, he took me by surprise, and had three hundred years plus of magical practice to boot. Somehow, I was not particularly surprised by the bodyguards' action . . . in fact, I had been expecting it and had been gathering my powers for just this moment.

With a theatric wave of my hand and a much more important focusing of my mental energies, I picked the two men up and spun them in midair. Heck, I wasn't adverse to stealing a new idea for how to use levitation . . . even from Rupert. I did like a little originality in my work, though, so instead of bouncing them on their heads, I slammed them against the ceiling and held them pinned there.

"No, thanks," I said as casually as I could, "I'd rather stand."

Shai-ster looked at his helpless protectors, then shot a hard stare at me.

"Perhaps this won't be as simple as I thought," he admitted. "Say, you've got a unicorn, don't you?"

"That's right," I confirmed, surprised by the sudden change in topic.

"I don't suppose you'd be particularly scared if you woke up in the morning and found him in your bed . . . not all of him, just his head?"

"Scared? No, not particularly. In fact, I'm pretty sure I'd be mad enough to quit playing games and get down to serious revenge."

The Mob spokesman sighed heavily.

"Well, that's that. If we can't make a deal, we'll just

have to do this the hard way. You can let the boys down now. We'll be heading back in the morning.''

This time, it was my turn to smile.

"Not so fast. Who said I didn't want to make a deal?"

For the first time since I met him, Shai-ster's poise was shaken.

"But . . . I thought . . . if you can . . ."

"Don't assume, Shai-ster. It's a bad habit for businessmen to get into. I just don't like to get pushed around, that's all. Now then, as you said earlier, I believe we have some business to discuss."

The spokesman shot a nervous glance at the ceiling.

"Um . . . could you let the boys down first? It's a bit distracting."

"Sure."

I closed my eyes and released the spell. Mind you, unlike the disguise spell, I don't have to close my eyes to remove a levitation spell. I just didn't want to see the results.

The room shook as two loud crashes echoed each other. I distinctly heard the bed assume a foolproof disguise as kindling.

I carefully opened an eye.

One bodyguard was unconscious. The other rolled about, groaning weakly.

"They're down," I said, needlessly.

Shai-ster ignored me.

"Big bad bodyguards! Wait'll the Big Boys hear how good dumb muscle is against magik!"

He paused to kick the groaner in the side.

"Groan quieter! *Mister* Skeeve and I have some talking to do."

Having already completed one adventure after antagonizing the military arm of a large organization, I was not overly eager to add another entire group of plug-uglies to my growing list of enemies.

"Nothing personal," I called to the bodyguard who was still conscious. "Here! Have a drink."

I levitated the flask over to him, and he caught it with a weak moan I chose to interpret as "thanks."

"You said something about a deal?" Shai-ster said, turning to me again.

"Right. Now, if my appraisal of the situation is correct, the Mob wants three things: Big Julie's army back, me dead or working for them, and a crack at the new money coming into Possiltum after the wedding."

The Mob spokesman cocked his head to one side.

"That's a bit more blunt than I would have put it, but you appear to have captured the essential spirit of my clients' wishes. My compliments on your concise summation."

"Here's another concise summation to go with it. Hands off Big Julie and his crew; he's under my protection. By the same token, Possiltum is my territory. Stay away from it or it will cost you more than you'll get. As to my services, I have no wish to become a Mob employee. I would consider an occasional assignment as an outside contractor for a specific fee, but full-time employment is out."

The Mob spokesman was back in his element, face stony and impassive.

"That doesn't sound like much of a deal."

"It doesn't?"

I reviewed the terms quickly in my mind.

"Oh! Excuse me. There is one other important part of my offer I neglected to mention. I don't expect your employers to give up their objectives without any return at all. What I have in mind is a swap: an army and maybe a kingdom for an opportunity to exploit an entire world.''

Shai-ster raised his eyebrows.

"You're going to give us the world? Just like that? Lord Magician, I suspect you're not bargaining with a full deck.''

"I didn't say I would give you the world, I said I would give you *access* to a world. Brand new territory full of businesses and people to exploit; one of the richest in the universe.''

The spokesman frowned.

"Another world? And I'm supposed to take your word as to how rich it is and that you can give us access?''

"It would be nice, but even in my most naive moments I wouldn't expect you to accept a blind bid like that. No, I'm ready to give you a brief tour of the proposed world so that you can judge for yourself.''

"Wait a minute,'' Shai-ster said, holding up his hands. "This is so far beyond my negotiating parameters that even if I liked what I saw, I couldn't approve the deal. I need to bring one of the Big Boys in on this decision.''

This was better than I had hoped. By the time he could bring one of the Mob's hierarchy to Possiltum, I could deal with some of my other problems.

"Fine. Go and fetch him. I'll hold the deal until your return.''

The spokesman gave one of his tight-lipped smiles.

"No need to wait,'' he said. "My immediate superior is on call specifically for emergencies such as this.''

Before I could frame a reply, he opened the front of his belt-buckle and began rubbing it, all the while mumbling under his breath.

There was a quick flash of light, and an old, hairy-jowled man appeared in the room. Looking round, he spied the two bodyguards sprawled on the floor and gripped the sides of his face with his open hands in an exaggerated expression of horror.

"Mercy!" he wheezed in a voice so hoarse I could barely understand him. "Shai-ster, you bad boy. If there was trouble, you should have called me sooner. Oh, those poor, poor boys."

The Mob spokesman's face was once again blank and impassive as he addressed me.

"Skeeve, Lord Magician of Possiltum, let me introduce Don Bruce, the Mob's fairy godfather."

Chapter Eleven:

"Tell you what. Let me sweeten the deal a bit for you. . . ."

—BEELZEBUB

"OH! This is simply *mar*-velous! Who would have ever thought . . . another dimension, you say?"

"That's right," I said off-handedly. "It's called Deva."

Of course, I was quite in agreement with Don Bruce. The Bazaar on Deva was really something, and every time I visited it, I was impressed anew. It was an incredible tangle of tents and displays stretching as far as the eye could see in every direction, crammed full of enough magikal devices and beings to defy anyone's imagination and sanity. It was the main crossroads of trade for the dimensions. Anything worth trading money or credits for was here.

This time, however, I was the senior member of the expedition. As much as I wanted to rubberneck and explore, it was more important to pretend to be bored and worldly . . . or other-worldly as the case might be.

Don Bruce led the parade, as wide-eyed as a farm-kid in his first big city, with Shai-ster, myself, and the two bodyguards trailing along behind. The bodyguards seemed more interested in crowding close to me than in protecting their superiors, but then again, they had just had some bad experiences with magik.

"The people here all look kinda strange," one of them muttered to me. "You know, like foreigners."

"They are foreigners . . . or rather *you* are," I said. "You're on their turf, and a long way from home. These are Deveels."

"Devils?" the man responded, looking a little wild-eyed. "You're tellin' me we're surrounded by devils?"

While it was reassuring to me to see the Mob's bully-boys terrified by something I had grown used to, it also occurred to me that if they were *too* scared, it might ruin the deal I was trying to set up.

"Look . . . say, what is your name, anyway?"

"Guido," the man confided, "and this here's my cousin Nunzio."

"Well look, Guido. Don't be thrown by these jokers. Look at them. They're storekeepers like storekeepers anywhere. Just because they look funny doesn't mean they don't scare like anybody else."

"I suppose you're right. Say, I meant to thank you for the drink back there at the castle."

"Don't mention it," I waved. "It was the least I could do after bouncing you off the ceiling. Incidentally, there was nothing personal in that. I wasn't trying to make you two look bad, I was trying to make myself look good . . . if you see the difference."

Guido's brow furrowed slightly.

"I . . . think so. Yeah! I get it. Well, it worked. You looked real good. I wouldn't want to cross you, and neither would Nunzio. In fact, if we can ever do you a favor . . . you know, bend someone a little for you . . . well, just let us know."

"Hey, what's that?"

I looked in the direction Don Bruce was pointing. A booth was filled with short painted sticks, all floating in midair.

"I think he's selling magic wands," I guessed.

"Oh! I want one. Now, don't go anywhere without me."

The bodyguards hesitated for a moment, then followed as Don Bruce plunged into negotiations with the booth's proprietor, who gaped a bit at his new customer.

"Does he always dress like that?" I asked Shai-ster. "You know, all in light purple?"

The Mob spokesman raised an eyebrow at me.

"Do you always dress in green when you travel to other dimensions?"

Just to be on the safe side, I had donned another disguise before accompanying this crew to Deva. It occurred to me that if I were successful in my negotiations, it wouldn't be wise to be known at the Bazaar as the one who introduced organized crime to the dimension.

Unfortunately, this had dawned on me just as we were preparing to make our departure, so I hadn't had much time to choose someone to disguise myself as. Any of my friends were out, as were Massha, Quigley, Garkin . . . in desperation I settled on Rupert . . . I mean, there was one being I owed a bad turn or two. Consequently, I was currently parading around the Bazaar as a scaly green Pervert . . . excuse me, Pervect.

"I have my reasons," I dodged loftily.

"Well, so has Don Bruce," Shai-ster scowled. "Now if you don't mind, I've got a few questions about this place. If we try to move in here, won't language be a problem? I can't understand anything these freaks are saying."

"Take a look," I instructed, pointing.

Don Bruce and the Deveel proprietor were haggling earnestly, obviously having no difficulty understanding each other, however much they disagreed.

"No Deveel worth his salt is going to let a little thing like language stand in the way of a sale."

"Hey, everybody! Look what I got!"

We turned to find Don Bruce bearing down on us, proudly waving a small rod the same color as his clothes.

"It's a magic wand!" he exclaimed. "I got it for a song."

"A song plus some gold, I'd wager," Shai-ster observed dryly. "What does it do?"

"What does it do?" Don Bruce grinned. "Watch this."

He swept the wand across the air with a grand gesture, and a cloud of shiny dust sparkled to the ground.

"That's it?" Shai-ster grimaced.

Don Bruce frowned at the wand.

"That's funny. When the guy back there did it, he got a rainbow."

He pointed the wand at the ground and shook it . . . and three blades materialized out of thin air, lancing into the dust at our feet.

"Careful!" Shai-ster warned, hopping back out of range. "You'd better read the instructions on that thing."

"I don't need instructions," Don Bruce insisted. "I'm a fairy godfather. I know what I'm doing."

As he spoke, he gestured emphatically with the wand, and a jet of flame narrowly missed one of the body-guards.

". . . But this can wait," Don Bruce concluded, tucking the wand into his waistband. "We've got business to discuss."

"Yes. We were just . . ." Shai-ster began.

"Shuddup! I'm talking to Skeeve here."

The force behind Don Bruce's sudden admonishment, combined with the Shai-ster's quick obedience, made me hastily revise my opinion of the Mob leader. Strange or not, he was a force to be recognized.

"Now then, Mister Skeeve, what's the police situation around here?"

"There aren't any."

Shaister's eyebrows shot up.

"Then how do they enforce the laws?" he asked, forgetting himself.

"As far as I can tell, there are no laws either."

"How 'bout that, Shai-ster?" Don Bruce laughed. "No police, no laws, no lawyers. You'd be in trouble if you were born here."

I started to ask what a lawyer was, but the godfather saved me from my own ignorance by plunging into the next question.

"How about politicians?"

"None."

"Unions?"

"None."

"Bookies?"

"Lots," I admitted. "This is the gambling capital of the dimensions. As near as I can tell, though, they all operate independently. There's no central organization."

Don Bruce rubbed his hands together gleefully.

"You listening to this, Shai-ster? This is some world Mister Skeeve is givin' us here."

"He's not giving it to us," Shai-ster corrected. "He's offering *access* to it."

"That's right," I said quickly. "Exploiting it is up to your organization. Now, if you don't think your boys can handle it. . . ."

"We can handle it. A layout like this? It's a piece of cake."

Guido and Nunzio exchanged nervous glances, but held their silence as Don Bruce continued.

"Now if I understand this right, what you want in return for letting us into this territory is that we lay off Big Julie and Possiltum. Right?"

I count real good up to three.

"And me," I added. "No 'getting even with the guy who thrashed our army plans,' no 'join the Mob or die' pressure. I'm an independent operator and happy to stay that way."

"Sure, sure," Don Bruce waved. "Now that we've seen how you operate, no reason we can't eat out of the same bowl. If anything, we owe you a favor for opening up a new area to our organization."

Somehow, that worried me.

"Um . . . tell you what. I don't want any credit for this . . . inside the Mob or outside. Right now, nobody but us knows I had a hand in this. Let's keep it that way, okay?"

"If that's what you want," Don Bruce shrugged. "I'll just tell the Big Boys you're too rough for us to tangle with, and that's why we're going to leave you alone. Anytime our paths cross, we go ahead with your approval or we back off. Okay?"

"That's what I want."

"Deal?"

"Deal."

We shook hands ceremoniously.

"Very well," I said. "Here's what you need to travel between here and home."

I fished the D-Hopper out of my sleeve.

"This setting is for home. This one is for here. Push this button to travel."

"What about the other settings?" Shai-ster asked.

"Remember the magic wand?" I countered. "Without instructions, you could get lost with this thing. I mean, *really* lost."

"Come on, boys," Don Bruce said, setting the D-Hopper. "We gotta hurry home. There's a world here to conquer, so we gotta get started before somebody else beats us to it. Mister Skeeve, a pleasure doin' business with you."

A second later, they were gone.

I should have been elated, having finally eliminated one set of problems from my horizon. I wasn't.

Don Bruce's last comment about world conquering reminded me of Queen Hemlock's plans. Now that the Mob was neutralized, I had other problems to solve. As soon as I got back to the palace, I would have to . . .

Then it hit me.

The Mob representatives had taken the D-Hopper with them when they left. That thing was my only route back to Klah! I was stranded at the Bazaar with no way back to my own dimension!

Chapter Twelve:

"I'm making this up as I go along!"

—I. JONES

BUT I didn't panic. Why should I?

Sure, I was in a bit of a mess, but if there was one place in all the dimensions I could be confident of finding help, it was here at the Bazaar. Anything could be had here for a price, and thanks to Aahz's training, I had made a point of stocking my pouch with money prior to our departure from Klah.

Aahz!

It suddenly occurred to me that I hadn't thought about my old mentor for days. The crises that had erupted shortly after his departure had occupied my mind to an extent where there was no time or energy left for brooding. Except for the occasional explanation of his absence, Aahz was playing no part in my life currently. I was successfully handling things without him.

Well . . .

Okay. I had successfully handled *some* things without him . . . the Mob, for example. Of course, the training he had gotten me into earlier in our relationship had also provided me with confidence under fire . . . another much-needed commodity these days.

"Face it, kid," I said to myself in my best imitation of Aahz. "You owe a lot to your old mentor."

Right. A lot. Like not making him ashamed of his prize pupil . . . say by leaving a job half done.

With new resolve, I addressed my situation. First, I had to get back to Klah . . . or should I look for a solution right here?

Rather than lose time to indecision, I compromised. With a few specific questions to the nearest vendor, I set a course for my eventual destination, keeping an eye out as I went for something that would help me solve the Queen Hemlock problem.

This trip through the Bazaar was different from my earlier visits. Before, my experience had been of wishing for more time to study the displays at leisure while hurrying to keep up with Aahz. This time, it was me that was pushing the pace, dismissing display after display with a casual "interesting, but no help with today's problem." Things seemed to have a different priority when responsibility for the crisis was riding on *my* shoulders.

Of course, I didn't know what I was looking for. I just knew that trick wands and instant thunderstorms weren't it. Out of desperation, I resorted to logic.

To recognize the solution, I needed to know the problem. The problem was that Queen Hemlock was about to marry me instead of Rodrick. Scratch that. Massha was bringing Rodrick back, and I couldn't help her. I just had to believe she could do it. The problem was Queen Hemlock.

Whether she married me or Rodrick, she was determined to use Possiltum's military strength to wage a war of expansion. If her husband, whoever it was, tried to oppose her, he would find himself conveniently dead.

Killing the Queen would be one solution, but somehow I shrank from cold-blooded murder . . . or hot-blooded murder for that matter. No. What was needed was something to throw a scare into her. A big scare.

The answer walked past me before I recognized it. Fortunately, it was moving slowly, so I turned and caught up with it in just a few steps.

Answers come in many shapes and sizes. This one was in the form of a Deveel with a small tray display hung by a strap around his neck.

"What you just said, was it true?"

The Deveel studied me.

"I said, 'Rings. One size fits all. Once on, never off.' "

"That's right. Is it true?"

"Of course. Each of my rings are pre-spelled. Once you put it on, it self-adjusts so that it won't come off, even if you want it to."

"Great. I'll take two."

". . . Because to lose a ring of such value would be tragedy indeed. Each one worth a king's ransom. . . ."

I rolled my eyes.

"Look," I interrupted. "I know it's a tradition of the Bazaar to bargain, but I'm in a hurry. How much for two? Bottom price."

He thought for a moment and named a figure. My training came to the fore and I made a counteroffer one-tenth of his.

"Hey! You said 'no haggling,' " he protested. "Who do you think you are?"

Well, it was worth a try. According to Massha, I was getting a bit of a reputation at the Bazaar.

"I think I'm the Great Skeeve, since you asked."

". . . And the camel you rode in on," the vendor sneered. "Everyone knows the Great Skeeve isn't a Pervert."

The disguise! I had forgotten about it completely. With a mental wave, I restored my normal appearance.

"No, I'm a Klahd," I smiled. "And for your information, that's Pervect!"

"You mean you're really . . . no, you must be. No one else would voluntarily look like a Klahd . . . or defend Perverts . . . excuse me, Pervects."

"Now that that's established," I yawned, "how much for two of your rings?"

"Here," he said, thrusting the tray forward. "Take your pick, with my compliments. I won a bundle betting on your team at the Great Game. All I ask is permission to say that you use my wares."

It was with a great deal of satisfaction that I made my selection and continued on my way. It was nice to have a reputation, but nicer to earn it. Those two little baubles now riding in my pouch were going to get me out of the Possiltum dilemma . . . if I got back in time . . . and if Massha had found the King.

Those sobering thoughts brought my hat size back to normal in a hurry. The time to gloat was after the battle, not before. Plans aren't victories, as I should be the first to know.

With panic once again nipping at my heels, I quickened my pace until I was nearly running by the time I reached my final destination: the Yellow Crescent Inn.

Bursting through the door of the Bazaar's leading fast food establishment, I saw that it was empty of customers except for a troll munching on a table in the corner.

Terrific.

I was expecting to deal with Gus, the gargoyle proprietor, but I'd settle for the troll.

"Skeeve!" the troll exclaimed. "I say, this is a surprise. What brings you to the Bazaar?"

"Later, Chumly. Right now I need a lift back to Klah. Are you busy with anything?"

The troll set his half-eaten table to one side and raised the eyebrow over one mismatched moon eye.

"Not to be picky about formality," he said, "but what happened to 'Hello, Chumly. How are you?'"

"I'm sorry. I'm in a bit of a hurry. Can we just. . . ."

"Skeeve! How's it going, handsome?"

A particularly curvaceous bundle of green-haired loveliness had just emerged from the ladies' room.

"Oh. Hi, Tananda. How 'bout it, Chumly?"

Tananda's smile of welcome disappeared, to be replaced by a puzzled frown.

" 'Oh. Hi, Tananda?' " she repeated, shooting a look at the troll. "Does anything strike you as strange about that rather low-key greeting, big brother?"

"No stranger than the greeting I just got," Chumly confided. "Just off-hand, I'd say that either our young friend here has forgotten his manners completely, or he's gotten himself into a spot of trouble."

Their eyes locked and they nodded.

"Trouble," they said together.

"Cute," I grimaced. "Okay, so I'm in a mess. I'm not asking you to get involved. In fact, I think I've got it worked out myself. All I want is for you to pop me back to Klah."

Brother and sister stepped to my side.

"Certainly," Chumly smiled. "You don't mind if we tag along, though, do you?"

"But I didn't ask you to . . ."

"When have you had to ask for our help before, handsome?" Tananda scolded, slipping an arm around my waist. "We're your friends, remember?"

"But I think I've got it handled . . ."

". . . In which case, having us along won't hurt," the troll insisted.

"Unless, of course, something goes wrong," Tananda supplied. "In which case, we might be able to lend a hand."

". . . And if the three of us can't handle it, we'll be there to pull you out again," Chumly finished.

I should have known better than to try to argue with the two of them when they were united.

"But . . . if . . . well, thanks," I managed. "I didn't really expect this. I mean, you don't even know what the trouble is."

"You can tell us later," Tananda said firmly, starting her conjuring to move us through the dimensions. "Incidentally, where's Aahz?"

"That's part of the problem," I sighed.

And we were back!

Not just back on Klah, back in my own quarters in the palace. As luck would have it, we weren't alone. Someday I'll have time to figure out if it was good luck or bad.

The King was trussed up hand and foot on my bed, while Massha and J. R. Grimble were each enjoying a goblet of wine, and apparently each other's company. At least, that was the scene when we arrived. Once Massha and Tananda set eyes on each other, the mood changed dramatically.

"Slut," my new apprentice hissed.

"No-talent mechanic," Tananda shot back.

"Is that freak on our payroll?" Grimble interrupted, staring at Chumly.

"Spoken like a true bean-counter," the troll sneered.

I tried to break it up.

"If we can just . . ."

That brought Grimble's attention to me.

"You!" he gasped. "But if you're Skeeve, then who's. . . ."

"King Rodrick of Possiltum," I supplied, nodding to the bound figure on the bed. "And now that everybody knows each other, can you all shut up while I tell you what our next move is?"

Chapter Thirteen:

"Marriage, being a lifelong venture, must be approached with care and caution."

—BLUEBEARD

THE wedding went off without a hitch.

I don't known why I had been worried. There were no interruptions, no missed lines, nobody protested or even coughed at the wrong time. As was previously noted, Queen Hemlock had handled the planning to the last minute detail . . . except for a few surprises we were holding back.

That's why I was worried! My cronies and I knew that as gaudy and overdone as the Royal Wedding was, it was only the warm-up act for the main event. There was also the extra heat on me of knowing that I hadn't shared *all* of my plans with my co-conspirators. It seemed that was another bad habit I had picked up from Aahz.

Grimble and Badaxe were at their usual places as mismatched bookends to the throne, while Chumly, Tananda, Massha, and I, courtesy of my disguise spells and Badaxe's pull as general, were lined up along the foot of the throne as bodyguards. Everything was set to go . . . if we ever got the time!

As dignitary after dignitary stepped forward to offer his or her congratulations and gifts, I found little to occupy my thoughts except how many things could go wrong with my little scheme. I had stuck my neck out a long way with my plan, and if it didn't work, a lot of people would be affected, starting with the king and subjects of Possiltum.

The more I thought, the more I worried until, instead of wishing the dignitaries would hurry, I actually found myself hoping they would take forever and preserve this brief moment of peace.

Of course, no sooner did I start hoping things would last then they were over. The last well-wisher was filing out and the Queen herself rising to leave when Grimble and Badaxe left their customary positions and stepped before the throne.

"Before you go, my dear," Rodrick said, "our retainers wish to extend their compliments."

Queen Hemlock frowned slightly, but resumed her seat.

"The Chancellor of the Exchequer stands ready to support their majesties in any way," Grimble began. "Of course, even with the new influx of wealth into the treasury, we must watch needless expenses. As always, I stand ready to set the example in cost savings, and so have decided that to purchase a present for you equal to my esteem would be a flagrant and unnecessary expense, and therefore . . ."

"Yes, yes, Grimble," the King interrupted. "We understand and appreciate your self-sacrifice. General Badaxe?"

Grimble hesitated, then yielded the floor to his rival.

"I am a fighting man, not a speechmaker," the General said abruptly. "The army stands ready to support the kingdom and the throne of Possiltum. As for myself . . . here is my present.''

He removed the axe from his belt and laid it on the stairs before the throne.

Whether he was offering his pet weapon or his personal allegiance, I found the gesture eloquent beyond words.

"Thank you, General Badaxe, Grimble," Queen Hemlock said loftily. "I'm sure I can . . ."

"My dear," the King interrupted softly. "There *is* another retainer."

And I was on.

Screwing up my courage, I dropped my disguise and stepped before the throne.

"Your majesties, the Great Skeeve gives you his congratulations on this happy event."

The Queen was no fool. For one beat her eyes popped open and on the next she was staring at the King. You could almost hear her thoughts: "If the Magician is there, then the man I just married is . . ."

"That's right, your majesty. As you yourself said in our earlier conversations, 'Royalty has married royalty.' "

While it might have been nice dramatically to savor that moment, I noticed the Queen's eyes were narrowing thoughtfully, so I hurried on.

"Before you decide how to express your joy," I warned, "perhaps I should explain *my* gift to the throne."

Now the thoughtful gaze was on me. I expressed my own joy by sweating profusely.

"My gift is the wedding rings now worn by both king and queen. I hope you like them, because they won't come off."

Queen Hemlock made one brief attempt to remove her ring, then her eyes were on me again. This time, the gaze wasn't thoughtful.

"Just as the fate of the kingdom of Possiltum is linked to the throne, as of the moment you donned those rings, your fates are linked to each other. By the power of a spell so simple it cannot be broken or countered, when one of you dies, so does the other."

The Queen didn't like that at all, and even the King showed a small frown wrinkle on his forehead, as if contemplating something he had not previously considered. That was my signal to clarify things for him . . . that there *was* an implication to the rings that I hadn't mentioned to him.

"This is not intended as a 'one-sided' gift, for just as Queen Hemlock must now protect the health and well-being of her king, so must King Rodrick defend his queen against all dangers . . . *all* dangers."

The King was on his feet now, eyes flashing.

"What is that supposed to mean, Lord Magician?"

As adept as I was at becoming at courtly speech, there were things which I felt were best said in the vernacular.

"It means if you or anybody else kills her, say, on your orders, then, *you're* dead. Now *SIT DOWN AND LISTEN!!*"

All the anger and frustration I had felt since figuring out the King was trying to double-cross me, but had been too busy to express, found its vent in that outburst. It worked. The King sank back into his chair, pale and slightly shaken.

I wasn't done, though. I had been through a lot, and a few words weren't enough to settle my mind.

"Since I accepted this assignment, I've heard nothing but how ruthless and ambitious Queen Hemlock is. Well, that may be true, *BUT SHE ISN'T GETTING*

ANY PRIZE EITHER! Right now, *King* Rodrick, I have more respect for her than I have for you. *She* didn't abandon her kingdom in the middle of a crisis."

I began to pace back and forth before the thrones as I warmed to my topic.

"Everybody talks about 'our duty to the throne.' It's the guiding directive in the walk-a-day life of commoners. What never gets mentioned is 'the throne's duty to the people.' "

I paused and pointed directly at the King.

"I sat in that chair for a while. It's a lot of fun, deciding people's lives for them. Power is heady, and the fringe benefits are great! All that bowing and scraping, not to mention one heck of a wardrobe. Still, it's a job like any other, and with any job you sometimes have to do things you don't like. Badaxe doesn't just parade and review his troops, he has to train them and lead them into battle . . . you know, as in 'I could get killed out here' battle. Grimble spends ungodly hours poring over those numbers of his for the privilege of standing at your side.

"Any job has its pluses and minuses, and if the minuses outweight the pluses, you screw up your courage and quit . . . unless, of course, you're King Rodrick. Then, instead of abdicating and turning the pluses and minuses over to someone else, you stick someone else with doing the job in your name and sneak out a back door. Maybe that's how people do their jobs where you were raised, but I think it's conduct a peasant would be ashamed of."

I faced them, hands defiantly on my hips.

"Well, I've done *my* job. The kingdom has been protected from the immediate threat. With any luck, you two will learn to work together. I trust King Rodrick can dilute the queen's ambition. I only hope that Queen

Hemlock's fiery spirit can put a little more spine and courage into the King.''

This time it was Queen Hemlock who was on her feet.

''Are you going to let him talk to you like that, Roddie? You're the king. Nobody pushes a king around.''

''Guards!'' Rodrick said tightly. ''Seize that man.''

It had worked! King and Queen were united against a common foe . . . me! Now all I had to do was survive it.

One more mind pass, and my comrades stood exposed as the outworlders they were.

Queen Hemlock, unaccustomed to my dealings with demons, dropped into her seat with a small gasp. The King simply scowled as he realized the real reason for the presence of my friends.

''Your Majesties,'' Badaxe said, stepping forward. ''I am sworn to protect the throne and would willingly lay down my life in your defense. I do not see a physical threat here, however. If anything, it occurs to me both throne and kingdom would be strengthened if the Great Skeeve's words were heard and heeded.''

''I am not a fighting man,'' Grimble said, joining Badaxe, ''so my duty here is passive. I must add, though, that I also feel the Lord Magician's words have merit and should be said to every ruler.''

His eyes narrowed and he turned to face me.

''I challenge, though, whether they should be said by a retainer to the court. One of our first duties is to show respect to the throne, in word *and* manner.''

''That much we agree on, Grimble,'' Badaxe nodded, adding his glare to the many focused on me.

''Strange as it may sound,'' I said, ''I agree, too. For that reason, I am hereby tendering my resignation as Court Magician of Possiltum. The kingdom is now secure militarily and financially, and in my opinion there is no point in it bearing the expense of a full-time magician . . . especially one who has been insolent to the throne. There is no need to discuss severance pay. The King's reward for my last assignment, coupled with the monies I have already received from the Exchequer, will serve my needs adequately. I will simply gather my things and depart.''

I saw Grimble blanch slightly when he realized that I would not be returning his bribe. I had faith in his ability to hide anything in his stacks of numbered sheets, though.

With only the slightest of nods to the throne, I gathered my entourage with my eyes and left.

Everything had gone perfectly. I couldn't have asked for the proceedings to have turned out better. As such, I was puzzled as to why I was sweat-drenched and shaking like a leaf by the time I reached my own quarters.

Chapter Fourteen:

"Some farewells are easier than others."
—P. MARLOWE

"SO, where do you go from here?" Tananda asked.

She and Chumly were helping me pack. We had all agreed that having incurred the combined wrath of the King and Queen, it would be wisest to delay my departure as little as possible. Massha was off seeing to Gleep and Buttercup as well as saying her goodbyes to Badaxe.

"I don't really know," I admitted. "I was serious when I said I had accumulated enough wealth for a while. I'll probably hole up someplace and practice my magic for a while . . . maybe at that inn Aahz and I used to use as a home base."

"I say, why don't you tag along with little sister and me?" Chumly suggested. "We usually operate out of the Bazaar at Deva. It wouldn't be a bad place for you to keep your hand in, magik-wise."

It flashed through my mind that the Mob must have started its infiltration of the Bazaar by now. It also occurred to me that, in the pre-wedding rush, I hadn't told Tananda or Chumly about that particular portion of the caper. Having remembered, I found myself reluctant to admit my responsibility for what they'd find on their return.

"I dunno, Chumly," I hedged. "You two travel pretty light. I've got so much stuff, I'd probably be better off settling down somewhere permanent."

It was a pretty weak argument, but the troll seemed to accept it . . . maybe because he could see that mountain of gear we were accumulating, trying to clear my quarters.

"Well, think it over. We'd be glad to have you. You're not a bad sort to have around in a tight spot."

"I'll say," Tananda agreed with a laugh. "Where did you find those rings, anyway?"

"Bought them from a street vendor at the Bazaar."

"On Deva?" Chumly said with a frown. "Two spelled rings like that must have set you back a pretty penny. Are you *sure* you have enough money left?"

Now it was my turn to laugh.

"First of all, they aren't spelled. That was just a bluff I was running on their royal majesties. The rings are plain junk jewelry . . . and I got them for free."

"Free?"

Now Tananda was frowning.

"Nobody gets anything for free at the Bazaar."

"No, really. They were free . . . well, the vendor did get my permission to say that I use his wares, but that's the same as free, isn't it? I mean, I didn't pay him any money."

As I spoke, I found myself suddenly uncertain of my "good deal." One of my earliest lessons about dealing with Deveels was "If you think you've made a good deal with a Deveel, first count your fingers, then your limbs, then your relatives. . . ."

"Permission to use your name?" Tananda echoed. "For two lousy rings? No percentage or anything? Didn't Aahz ever teach you about endorsements?"

There was a soft *BAMPH* in the air.

"Is someone taking my name in vain?"

And Aahz was there, every green scaly inch of him, making his entrance as casually as if he had just stepped out.

Of the three of us, I was the first to recover from my surprise. Well, at least I found my voice.

"Aahz!"

"Hi, kid. Miss me?"

"But, Aahz!"

I didn't know if I should laugh or cry. What I really wanted to do was embrace him and never let go. Of course, now that he was back, I would do no such thing. I mean, our relationship had never been big in the emotional displays department.

"What's the matter with everybody?" my mentor demanded. "You all act like you never expected to see me again."

"We . . . Aahz! I . . ."

"We didn't," Tananda said flatly, saving me from making an even bigger fool of myself.

"What little sister means," Chumly put in, "is that it was our belief that your nephew, Rupert, had no intention of letting you return from Perv."

Aahz gave a derisive snort.

"Rupert? That upstart? Don't tell me anybody takes him seriously."

"Well, maybe not if your powers were in full force," Tananda said, "but as things are . . ."

"Rupert?" Aahz repeated. "You two have known me a long time, right? Then you should get it through your heads that nobody holds me against my will."

Somehow that quote sounded familiar. Still, I was so glad to have Aahz back, I would have agreed to anything just then.

"Yeah!" I chimed in eagerly. "This is Aahz! *Nobody* pushes him around."

"There!" my mentor grinned. "As much as I hate to

agree with a mere apprentice, the kid knows what he's talking about . . . this time."

Chumly and Tananda looked at each other with that special gaze that brother and sister use to communicate non-verbally.

"You know, big brother," Tananda said, "this mutual admiration society is getting a bit much for my stomach. How about you?"

"Ectually," the troll responded. "I wasn't hearing all that much *mutual* admiration. Somehow the phrase 'mere apprentice' sticks in my mind."

"Oh, come on, you two," Aahz waved. "Get real, huh? I mean, we all like the kid, but we also know he's a trouble magnet. I've never met anyone who needs looking after as badly as he does. Speaking of which . . ."

He turned his yellow eyes on me with that speculative look of his.

". . . I notice you're both here . . . *and* I definitely heard my name as I phased in. What I need more than fond 'hellos' is a quick update as to exactly what kind of a mess we have to bail the Great Skeeve out of this time."

I braced myself for a quick but loud lesson about "endorsements," whatever that was, but the troll surprised me.

"No mess," he said, leaning back casually. "Little sister and I just dropped by for a visit. In fact, we were just getting ready to leave."

"Really?" my mentor sounded both surprised and suspicious. "Just a visit? No trouble?"

"Well, there was a *little* trouble," Tananda admitted. "Something to do with the King. . . ."

"I knew it!" Aahz chortled, rubbing his hands together.

". . . But Skeeve here handled it himself," she finished pointedly. "Currently, there are no problems at all."

"Oh."

Strangely, Aahz seemed a bit disappointed.

"Well, I guess I owe you two some thanks, then. I really appreciate your watching over Skeeve here while I was gone. He can . . ."

"I don't think you're listening, Aahz," Chumly said, looking at the ceiling. "Skeeve handled the trouble. We just watched."

"Oh, we would have pitched in if things got tight," Tananda supplied. "You know, the way we do for *you*, Aahz. As it turned out, we weren't needed. Your 'mere apprentice' was more than equal to the task."

"Finished the job rather neatly, you know?" the troll added. "In fact, I'm hard pressed to recall when I've seen a nasty situation dealt with as smoothly or with as little fuss."

"All right, all right," Aahz grimaced. "I get the message. You can fill me in on the details later. Right now, the kid and I have some big things to discuss . . . and I mean *big*."

"Like what?" I frowned.

"Well, I've been giving it a lot of thought, and I figure it's about time we left Possiltum and moved on."

"Um, Aahz?" I said.

"I know, I know," he waved. "You think you need practice. You do, but you've come a long way. This whole thing with the trouble you handled only proves my point. You're ready to . . ."

"Aahz?"

"All right. I know you've got friends and duties here, but eventually you have to leave the nest. You'll just have to trust my judgment and experience to know when the time is right to . . ."

"I've already quit!"

Aahz stopped in midsentence and stared at me.

"You have?" he blinked.

I nodded and pointed at the pile of gear we had been packing. He studied it for a moment as if he didn't believe what he was seeing.

"Oh," he said at last. "Oh well, in that case, I'll just duck over to talk to Grimble and discuss your severance pay. He's a tight-fisted bird, but if I can't shake five hundred out of him, I'll know the reason why."

"I know the reason why," I said carefully.

Aahz rolled his eyes.

"Look, kid. This is *my* field of expertise, remember? If you go into a bargaining session aiming low, they'll walk all over you. You've got to . . ."

"I've already negotiated for a thousand!"

This time, Aahz's "freeze" was longer . . . and he didn't look at me.

"A thousand?" he said finally. "In gold?"

"Plus a hefty bonus from the King himself," Tananda supplied helpfully.

"We've been trying to tell you, Aahz old boy," Chumly smiled. "Skeeve here has been doing just fine without you."

"I see."

Aahz turned away and stared silently out the window.

I'll admit to being a bit disappointed. I mean, maybe I hadn't done a first-rate job, but a *little* bit of congratulations would have been nice. The way my mentor was acting, you'd think he. . . .

Then it hit me. Like a runaway war-chariot it hit me. Aahz was jealous! More than that, he was hurt!

I could see it now with crystal clarity. Up until now I had been blinded by Aahz's arrogant self-confidence, but suddenly the veil was parted.

Aahz's escape from Perv wasn't nearly as easy as he

was letting on. There had been a brawl—physical, verbal, or magikal—some hard feelings, and some heavy promises made or broken. He had forced his way back to Klah with one thing on his mind: his apprentice . . . his *favorite* apprentice, was in trouble. Upon returning, what was his reception? Not only was I not in trouble, for all appearances, I was doing better without him!

Tananda and Chumly were still at it, merrily chattering back and forth about how great I was. While I appreciated their support, I wished desperately I could think of a way of getting it through to them that what they were really doing was twisting a knife in Aahz.

"Umm . . . Aahz?" I interrupted. "When you've got a minute, there *are* a few things I need your advice on."

"Like what?" came the muffled response. "From the sound of things, you don't need anybody, much less a teacher with no powers of his own."

Tananda caught it immediately. Her gadfly manner dropped away like a mask and she signaled desperately to Chumly. The troll was not insensitive, though. His reaction was to catch my eye with a pleading gaze.

It was up to me. Terrific.

"Well, like . . . um."

And Massha exploded into the room.

"Everything's ready downstairs, hot stuff, and . . . oh! Hi there, green and scaly. Thought you were gone for good."

Aahz spun around, his eyes wide.

"Massha?" he stammered. "What are you doing here?"

"Didn't the man of the hour here tell you?" she smiled, batting her expansive eyelashes. "I'm his new apprentice."

"Apprentice?" Aahz echoed, his old fire creeping into his voice.

"Um . . . that's one of the things I wanted to talk to

you about, Aahz," I smiled meekly.

"Apprentice?" he repeated, as if he hadn't heard. "Kid, you and I have got to talk . . . NOW!"

"Okay, Aahz. As soon as I. . . ."

"Now!"

Yep. Aahz was back.

"Um, if you'll excuse us, folks, Aahz and I have to . . ."

For the second time, there was a *BAMPH* in the room.

This one was louder, which was understandable, as there were more beings involved. Specifically, there were now four Deveels standing in the room . . . and they didn't look happy.

"We seek the Great Skeeve," one of them boomed.

My heart sank. Could my involvement with the Mob have been discovered so fast?

"Who's asking?"

Aahz casually placed his bulk between me and the intruders. Tananda and Chumly were also on their feet, and Massha was edging sideways to get a clear field of fire. Terrific. All I needed to complete my day was to have my friends soap up the trouble I had started.

"We are here representing the merchants of the Bazaar on the Deva, seeking an audience with the Great Skeeve."

"About what?" my mentor challenged.

The Deveel fixed him with an icy glare.

"We seek the Great Skeeve, not idle chit-chat with a Pervert."

"Well, this particular Per-*vect* happens to be the Great Skeeve's business manager, and he doesn't waste his time with Deveels unless *I* clear them."

I almost said something, but changed my mind. Concerned or not, this was not the time to take a conversation away from Aahz.

The Deveel hesitated, then shrugged.

"There is a new difficulty at the Bazaar," he said. "A group of organized criminals has gained access to our dimension threatening to disrupt the normal flow of business unless they are paid a percentage of our profits."

Tananda and Chumly exchanged glances, while Massha raised an eyebrow at me. I studied the ceiling with extreme care. Aahz alone was unruffled.

"Tough. So what does that have to do with the Great Skeeve?" he demanded.

Anticipating the answer, I tried to decide whether I should fight or run.

"Isn't it obvious?" the Deveel frowned. "We wish to retain his services to combat this threat. From what we can tell, he's the only magician around up to the job."

That one stopped me. Of all the strange turns events could have taken, this had to be the most unanticipated and . . . well, bizarre!

"I see," Aahz murmured, a nasty gleam in his eye. "You realize, of course, that the Great Skeeve's time is valuable and that such a massive undertaking would require equally massive remuneration?"

Every alarm in my system went off.

"Um . . . Aahz?"

"Shut up, k . . . I mean, be patient, Master Skeeve. This matter should be settled in a moment."

I couldn't watch.

Instead, I went to the window and stared out. Listening over my shoulder, I heard Aahz name an astronomical figure, and realized there might be a way out of this yet. If Aahz was greedy enough, and the Deveels stingy enough . . .

"Done!" said the spokesman.

". . . Of course, that's only an advance," Aahz

pressed. "A full rendering will have to wait until the job is completed."

"Done," came the reply.

". . . And that is the fee only. Expenses will be reimbursed separately."

"Done! The advance will be awaiting your arrival. Anything else?"

In tribute to the Deveel's generosity, Aahz was unable to think of any other considerations to gouge out of them.

There was another *BAMPH*, and the delegation was gone.

"How about that!" Aahz crowed. "I finally put one over on the Deveels!"

"What's that thing you always say about anyone who thinks they've gotten a good deal from a Deveel, Aahz?" Tananda asked sweetly.

"Later," my mentor ordered. "Right now we've got to get our things together and pop over to the Bazaar to scout the opposition."

"We already know what the opposition is."

"How's that, kid?"

I turned to face him.

"The opposition is the Mob. You remember, the organized crime group that was sponsoring Big Julie's army?"

A frown crossed Aahz's face as he regarded me closely.

"And how did you come by that little tidbit of information, if I may ask?"

I regarded him right back.

"That's the other little thing I wanted your advice on."

Chapter Fifteen:

*"In a war against organized crime, survival
is a hit or myth proposition."*

—M. BOLAN

"Now let me see if I've got this right," Aahz scowled,
pacing back and forth in front of our worried gazes.
"What we've got to do is keep the Mob from taking
over the Bazaar, without letting them know we're opposing them or the Deveels know we were the ones who
loosed the Mob on the Bazaar in the first place. Right?"

"You can do it, Aahz," I urged eagerly.

This time, it required no false enthusiasm on my part.
While I had done an adequate job operating on my own,
when it came to premeditated deviousness, I was quick
to acknowledge my master. There might be someone out
there in the multitude of dimensions better than Aahz at
finding under-handed ways out of dilemmas, but I
haven't met them yet.

"Of course I can do it," my mentor responded with a
confident wink. "I just want everyone to admit it isn't
going to be easy. All this talk about the Great Skeeve
has made me a little insecure."

"A little?" Tananda smirked.

"I think it's a bit of all right," Chumly said, nudging

113

his sister with an elbow. "I've always heard how formidable Aahz is when he swings into action. I, for one, am dying to see him handle this rather sticky situation all by himself."

Aahz's shoulders sagged slightly as he heaved a small sigh.

"Whoa! Stop! Perhaps in my enthusiasm I overspoke. What I *meant* to say is that my slimy but agile mind can provide a *plan* to pull off this assignment. Of course, the execution of said plan will rely upon abilities and goodwill of my worthy colleagues. Is that better, Chumly?"

"Quite," the troll nodded.

"Now that that's settled," Gus interrupted impatiently, "can we get on with it? This *is* my place of business, you know, and the longer I keep the place closed, the more money I lose."

For those of you who missed the earlier references, Gus is a gargoyle. He is also the owner/proprietor of the Yellow Crescent Inn, the Bazaar's leading fast-food establishment and our current field headquarters. Like Chumly and Tananda, he's helped me out of a couple scrapes in the past and, as soon as he heard about our current crisis, volunteered again. Like anyone who earns their living at the Bazaar, however, he habitually keeps one eye on the cash register. Even though he had closed his doors to give us a base of operations for the upcoming campaign, there was still a reflexive bristling over missed profits.

An idea struck me.

"Relax, Gus," I ordered. "Come up with a daily figure for your normal trade, bump it for a decent profit, and we'll reimburse you when this thing's over."

"What!" my mentor screeched, losing momentary control. "Are you out of your mind, kid? Who do you think is paying for this, anyway?"

"The merchants of Deva," I answered calmly. "We're on an expense account, remember? I think renting a place while we're on assignment isn't an unreasonable expense, do you?"

"Oh. Right. Sorry, Gus. Old reflexes."

Aahz's confusion was momentary. Then his eyes narrowed thoughtfully.

"In fact, if we put all of you on retainer, your help will fall under the heading of 'consultant fees' and never come near our own profits. I like it."

"Before you get too carried away," Tananda put in quickly, "I think big brother and I would rather work for a piece of the action than on a flat fee."

"But, honey," Massha blinked, "You haven't even heard his plan yet. What makes you think a percentage will net you more than a fee? . . . just between us girls?"

"Just between us girls," Tananda winked, "you've never worked with Aahz before. I have, and while he may not be the pleasantest being to team with, I have unshakeable faith in his profit margins."

"Now that we're on the subject," Aahz said, staring hard at Massha, "we never *have* worked together before, so let's get the rules straight early on. I've got my own style, see, and it usually doesn't allow much time for 'please' and 'thank you' and explanations. As long as you do what you're told, when you're told, we'll get along fine. Right?"

"Wrong!"

My reply popped out before Massha could form her own response. I was vaguely aware that the room had gotten very quiet, but most of my attention was on Aahz as he slowly cranked his head around to lock gazes with me.

"Now look, kid. . . ." he began dangerously.

"No, *you* look, Aahz," I exploded. "I may be your apprentice, but Massha is *mine*. Now if she wants to dump that agreement and sign on with you, fine and dandy. But until she does, she's *my* student and *my* responsibility. If you think she can help, then you suggest it to me and *I* decide whether she's up to it. There's one lesson you've drummed into my head over and over, mentor mine, whether you meant to or not. Nobody leans on your apprentice but you . . . nobody! If you didn't want to teach that lesson, then maybe you'd better be more careful with the example you set the next time you take on an apprentice."

"I see," Aahz murmured softly. "Getting pretty big for your britches, aren't you, kid?"

"Not really. I'm very much aware of how little I know, thank you. But this is my assignment, or at least it was accepted in my name, and I mean to give it my best shot . . . however inadequate that might be. Now for that assignment, I need your help, Aahz . . . heck, I'll always probably need your help. You're my teacher and I've got a lot to learn. But, I'm not going to roll over and die without it. If getting your help means turning my assignment and my apprentice over to you, then forget it. I'll just have to try to handle things without you."

"You'll get your brains beat out."

"Maybe. I didn't say I'd win, just that I'd try my best. *You* bring out my best, Aahz. You push me into things that scare me, but so far I've muddled through somehow. I *need* your help, but I don't *have* to have it. Even if you don't want to admit it to me, I think you should admit it to yourself."

With that, we both lapsed into silence.

Me, I couldn't think of anything else to say. Up until now, I had been carried along by my anger and Aahz's responses. All of a sudden, my mentor wasn't responding. Instead, he stared at me with expressionless yellow eyes, not saying a thing.

It was more than a little unnerving. If there is one characteristic of Aahz's I could always count on, it was that he was expressive. Whether with facial expression, gestures, grunts, or verbal explosions, my mentor usually let everyone in the near vicinity know what he felt or thought about any event or opinion expressed. Right now, though, I didn't know if he was about to explode or just walk away.

I began having regrets over instigating this confrontation. Then I toughened up. What I had said was right and needed to be said. It flashed across my mind that I could lose Aahz over this argument. My resolve wavered. Right or not, I could have said it better . . . gentler. At least I could have picked a time when all our friends weren't watching and listening. Maybe. . . .

Aahz turned away abruptly, shifting his stance to face Tananda and Chumly.

"*Now* I'm ready to believe you two," he announced. "The kid here really *did* handle that mess on Klah all by himself, didn't he?"

"That's what we've been trying to tell you, old boy," the troll winked. "Your apprentice is growing up, and seems to us more than capable of standing on his own two feet lately."

"Yeah, I noticed."

He looked at me again, and this time his eyes were expressive. I didn't recognize the expression, but at least there was one.

"Kid . . . Skeeve," he said. "If I've ever wondered why I bothered taking you under my wing, you just gave me the answer. Thanks."

"Um . . . Thanks. I mean, you're welcome. No. I mean . . ."

As always, I was very glib in the face of the unexpected. I had gotten used to weathering Aahz's tirades, but *this* I didn't know how to handle. Fortunately my pet came to my rescue.

"Gleep?" he queried, shaking his head in through the door.

". . . But if you take anything I've showed you, I mean spell one, and teach it to that dragon," my mentor roared, "you and I are going to go a couple rounds. Do we understand each other, apprentice?"

"Yes, Aahz."

Actually, I didn't. Still, this didn't seem like the time to call for a clarification.

"Butt out, Gleep," I ordered. "Go play with Buttercup or something."

"Gleep!" and my dragon's head was gone as fast as it had appeared.

"Say, hot stuff," Massha drawled. "As much as I appreciate your standing up for me, I'm kinda curious to hear what Big Green has for a plan."

"Right!" I nodded, glad to be off the hot seat. "Sorry, Aahz, I didn't mean to interrupt. What's the plan?"

"Well, first," Aahz said, taking his accustomed place as center of attention once more, "I've got a question for Gus. What's the Mob been doing so far to move in?"

"Judging from what I heard," the gargoyle responded, "a bunch of them move in on a merchant and offer to sell him some 'insurance.' You know, 'pay us so much of your revenue and nothing happens to your business.' If anyone's slow to sign up, they arrange a small demonstration of what could go wrong: some 'accidental' breaking of stock or a couple plug-uglies standing outside hassling customers. So far it's been effective. Deveels don't like to lose business."

"Good," my mentor grinned, showing every last one of his numerous pointed teeth. "Then we can beat them."

"How?"

If nothing else, I've gotten quite good at feeding Aahz straight lines.

"Easy. Just ask yourselves this: If you were a Deveel and paid the Mob to protect your business, and things started going wrong anyway, what would you do?"

"I can answer that one," Massha said. "I'd either demand better protection, scream for my money back, or both."

"I don't get it," I frowned. "What's going to happen to a Mob-protected business?"

"We are," Aahz grinned.

"What our strategist is trying to say," Chumly supplied, "is that the best defense is a good offense. Not terribly original, but effective nonetheless."

"You're darn right it's effective," my mentor exclaimed. "Instead of us defending against the Mob, we're going to start a crime wave right here at the Bazaar. Then let's see how good the Mob is at defending against us!"

Chapter Sixteen:

"It's always easier to destroy than to create."
— ANY GENERAL, ANY ARMY, ANY AGE.

"HEY, Guido! How's it going?"

The big bodyguard spun around, scanning the crowd to see who had hailed him by name. When he saw me, his face brightened.

"Mister Skeeve!"

"Never expected to run into you here!" I lied.

From Gus's description, I had known that both Guido and his cousin Nunzio were part of the Mob's contingent at the Bazaar. This "chance meeting" was the result of nearly half a day's worth of searching and following rumors.

"What are you doing here?" he asked confidentially. "Shopping for a few little items to wow 'em with back at Possiltum?"

"Just taking a bit of a vacation. That new queen and I don't get along so well. I thought things might ease up if I disappeared for a while."

"Too bad. If you was shoppin', I could line you up with some 'special deals,' if you know what I mean."

"You guys are really moving in, then?" I marveled.

"How is it going? Any problems?"

"Naw," the bodyguard bragged, puffing out his chest. "You was right. These Deveels are like shopkeepers anywhere. Lean on 'em a little and they fall in line."

"Don't tell me you're handling this all by yourself! I mean I know you're good, but . . ."

"Are you kiddin'? I'm an executive now . . . well, at least a team leader. Both Nunzio and me have a dozen men to order around, courtesy of our 'extensive knowledge of the Bazaar.' Pretty good, huh?"

"You mean you're running the whole operation?"

"That's Shai-ster's job. Me and Nunzio report to him, but it's us gives the orders to the boys."

I looked around expectantly.

"Is your team around? I'd like to meet them."

"Naw. We worked this area a couple days ago. I'm on my way to meet 'em and give out today's assignments. We're going after the area by the livestock pens today."

"How about Nunzio's team?"

"They're about three hours west of here. You know, this is a really big place!"

I put on my most disappointed face.

"Too bad, I would have liked to have met some of the ones who do the *real* work."

"Tell ya' what," Guido exclaimed, "why don't you drop by Fat's Spaghetti Parlor sometimes? That's where we're all hanging out. If we're not there, they can tell you where we are."

"I'll do that. Well, don't work too hard . . . and be careful. These guys can be meaner than they look."

"Piece of cake," he laughed as he headed off.

I was still waving merrily at his retreating figure as the rest of my "gang" faded out of the crowd around me.

"Did you get all that?" I asked out of the corner of my mouth.

"Two teams, neither one in this area. Shai-ster's running the show and therefore holding the bag," Tananda recited. "This area is both clear and under protection."

"Fat's Spaghetti Parlor is their headquarters, which is where we can find Shai-ster," Chumly completed. "Anything else?"

"Yeah," Aahz grinned. "Skeeve has a standing invite to drop by, and when he does, they're ready to tell him which team is working what area that day. Nice work."

"Lucky," I admitted with no embarrassment. "Well, shall we start?"

"Right," Aahz nodded. "Just like we planned, Tananda and Chumly are a team. Gus, you're with me. Skeeve and Massha, you start here. We all move out in different directions and space our hits so there's no pattern. Okay?"

"One more thing," I added. "Keep an eye on your disguises. I'm not sure of the exact range I can hold that spell at. If your disguise starts to fade, change direction to parallel mine."

"We meet back at the Yellow Crescent Inn," Gus finished. "And all of you watch your backs. I don't stock that much first aid gear."

"Good thought," I said. "Okay. Enough talk. Let's scatter and start giving the Mob a headache."

The other two teams had melted into the crowd of shoppers before I had even turned to Massha.

"Well, anything catch your eye for us to have a go at?"

"You know, you're starting to sound a bit like that troll."

That sounded a bit more abrupt than was Massha's normal style. I studied her curiously.

"Something bothering you?"

"Just a little nervous, I guess," she admitted. "Has it occurred to you all this plan has a major flaw? That to implement it potentially means getting the entire Bazaar after us, as well as the Mob?"

"Yes, it has."

"Doesn't it scare you?"

"Yes, it does."

"Well, how do you handle it?"

"By thinking about it as little possible," I said flatly. "Look, apprentice, aside from doing shtick in court for the amusement of the masses, this profession of ours is pretty dangerous. If we start dwelling on everything that can go wrong in the future, we'll either never move or blunder headlong into the present because our minds aren't on what we're doing right *now*. I try to be aware of the potential danger of a situation, but I don't worry about trouble until it happens. It's a little shaky, but it's worked so far."

"If you say so," she sighed. "Oh, well, gear me up and let's get started."

With a pass of my mind, I altered her features. Instead of being a massive woman, she was now a massive man . . . sort of. I had been experimenting with color lately, so I made her purple with reddish sideburns that ran all the way down her arms to her knuckles. Add some claw-like horns at the points of the ears and rough-textured, leathery skin on the face and hands, and you had a being *I* wouldn't want to mess with.

"Interesting," Massha grimaced, surveying what she could see of herself. "Did you make this up yourself, or is there a nasty dimension I haven't visited yet?"

"My own creation," I admitted. "The reputation you're going to build I wouldn't wish on any dimension I know of. Call it a Hoozit from the dimension Hoo."

"Who?"

"You've got it."

She rolled her eyes in exasperation.

"Hot stuff, do me a favor and only teach me magik, okay? Keep your sense of humor for yourself. I've already got enough enemies."

"We still need a target," I said, slightly hurt.

"How about that one? It looks breakable."

I looked where she was pointing and nodded.

"Good enough. Give me a twenty count head start. If they're not protected, I'll be back out. If you don't see me in twenty, they're fair game. Do your worst."

"You know," she smiled rubbing her hands together, "this could be fun."

"Just remember that *I'm* in there before you decide exactly what today's 'worst' is."

The display she had chosen was a small, three-sided tent with a striped top. It was lined with shelves that were crowded with an array of stoppered bottles of all sizes and colors. As I entered, I noticed there was something in each of the bottles—smoky things that shifted as if they were alive.

"May I help you, sahr?" The Deveel proprietor asked, baring what he doubtless thought was a winning smile.

"Just browsing," I yawned. "Actually, I'm seeking refuge from gossip. All anyone can talk about is this pack of ruffians that's selling insurance."

The Deveel's face darkened and he spat out the door.

"Insurance! Extortion I call it. They ruined two of my treasures before I could stop them long enough to subscribe to their services. It was a dark day when they first appeared at the Bazaar."

"Yes, yes. Believe me, I've heard it before."

Having established that this shop was indeed under

the protection of the Mob, I turned my attention to the displays.

With studied nonchalance, I plucked up a small bottle, no more than a hand's-width high, and peered at the contents. Murky movement and a vague sparkle met my gaze.

"Be careful," the proprietor cautioned. "Once a Djin is released, it can only be controlled if you address it by name."

"A Djin?"

The Deveel swept me with a speculative gaze. Since I wasn't doing the heavy work, I wasn't in disguise and looked like . . . well, me.

"I believe in Klah, they're referred to as Genies."

"Oh. You have quite a collection here."

The Deveel preened at the praise.

"Do not be fooled by the extent of my poor shop's selection, young sahr. They are extremely rare. I personally combed the far reaches of every dimension . . . at great personal expense, I might add . . . to find these few specimens worthy of. . . ."

I had been wondering when Massha was going to make her entrance. Well, she made it. Hoo-boy, did she make it. Right through the side of the tent.

With an almost musical chorus, the stand along the wall went over, dumping the bottles onto the floor. The released Djin rose in a cloud and poured out the open tent side, shrieking with inhuman joy as they went.

The Deveel was understandably upset.

"You idiot!" he shrieked. "What are you doing?"

"Pretty weak shelves," Massha muttered in a gravelly-bass voice.

"Weak shelves?"

"Sure. I mean, all I did was this . . ."

She shoved one of the remaining two shelves, which

toppled obligingly into the last display.

This time the Djin didn't even bother using the door. They streaked skyward, taking the top of the tent with them as they screamed their way to freedom.

"My stock! My tent! Who's going to pay for this?"

"That's Hoozit," Massha retorted, "and I'm certainly not going to pay. I don't have any money."

"No money?" the proprietor gasped.

"No. I just came in here to get out of the rain."

"Rain? Rain? But it isn't raining!"

"It isn't?" my apprentice blinked. "Then, good-bye."

With that she ambled off, making a hole in yet another tent side as she went.

The Deveel sank down in the shattered remains of his display and cradled his face in his hands.

"I'm ruined!" he moaned. "Ruined!"

"Excuse me for asking," I said. "But why didn't you call out their names and get them under control?"

"Call out their names? I can't remember the name of every Djin I collect. I have to look them up each time I sell one."

"Well, at least that problem's behind you."

That started him off again.

"Ruined!" he repeated needlessly. "What am I going to do?"

"I really don't know why you're so upset," I observed. "Weren't you just saying that you were insured?"

"Insured?"

The Deveel's head came up slowly.

"Certainly. You're paying to be sure things like this don't happen, aren't you? Well, it happened. It seems to me whoever's protecting your shop owes you an explanation, not to mention quite a bit of money."

"That's right!" the proprietor was smiling now. "More the latter than the former, but you're right!"

I had him going on now. All that was left to be done was the *coup de grace*.

"Tell you what. Just so your day won't be a total washout, I'll take this one. Now you won't have to stay open with just one Djin in stock."

I flipped him the smallest coin in my pouch. True to his heritage, he was sneering even as he plucked it out of the air.

"You can't be serious," he said. "This? For a Djin? That doesn't even cover the cost of the bottle!"

"Oh come, come, my good man," I argued. "We're both men of the world . . . or dimensions. We both know that's clear profit."

"It is?" he frowned.

"Of course," I said, gesturing at the broken glass on the floor. "No one can tell how many bottles were just broken. I know you'll just include this one on the list of lost stock and collect in full from your insurance in *addition* to what I just gave you. In fact, you could probably add five or six to the total if you were really feeling greedy."

"That's true," the Deveel murmured thoughtfully. "Hey, thanks! This might not turn out so bad after all."

"Don't mention it," I shrugged, studying the small bottle in my hand. "Now that we're in agreement on the price, though, could you look up the name of my Djin?"

"I don't have to. That one's new enough that I can remember. It's name is Kalvin."

"Kalvin?"

"Hey, don't laugh. It's the latest thing in Djins."

Chapter Seventeen:

"The best laid plans often go fowl."
—WILE E. COYOTE

"WELL, except for that, how are things going?"

"Except for that?" Shai-ster echoed incredulously. "Except for that? Except for that things are going rotten. This whole project is a disaster."

"Gee, that's tough," I said, with studied tones of sympathy.

I had gotten to be almost a permanent fixture here at Fat's Spaghetti Palace. Every night I dropped by to check the troops' progress . . . theirs and mine.

It was nice to be able to track the effectiveness of your activities by listening to the enemy gripe about them. It was even nicer to be able to plan your next move by listening to counter-attacks in the discussion stage.

"I still don't get it," Guido protested, gulping down another enormous fork-full of spaghetti. "Everything was goin' terrific at first. No trouble at all. Then BOOM, it hits the fan, know what I mean?"

"Yeah! It was like someone was deliberately workin' to put us out of business."

That last was from cousin Nunzio. For the longest

time I thought he was physically unable to talk. Once he got used to having me around, though, he opened up a little. In actuality, Nunzio was shy, a fact which was magnified by his squeaky little voice which seemed out of place coming from a muscleman.

"I warned you that Deveels can be a nasty lot," I said, eager to get the subject away from the possibility of organized resistance. "And if the shopkeepers are sneaky, it only stands to reason that the local criminal element would have to have a lot on the ball. Right, Guido?"

"That's right," the goon nodded vigorously, strands of spaghetti dangling from his mouth. "We criminal types can beat any honest citizen at anything. Say, did I ever tell you about the time Nunzio and me were . . ."

"Shut up, dummy!" Shai-ster snapped. "In case you haven't noticed, *we're* footing the bill for these local amateurs. We're getting our brains beat out financially, and it's up to you boys to catch up with the opposition and return the favor . . . physically."

"They're scared of us," Guido insisted. "Wherever we are, they aren't. If we can't find 'em, they can't be doin' *that* much damage."

"You know, brains never were your long suit, Guido," Shai-ster snarled. "Let me run this past you once real slow. So far, we've paid out six times as much as we've taken in. Add all our paychecks and expenses to that, and you might have a glimmer as to why the Big Boys are unhappy."

"But we haven't been collecting very long. After we've expanded our clientele . . ."

"Well be paying claims on that many more businesses," Shai-ster finished grimly. "Don't give me that 'we'll make it up on volume' guff. Either an operation is self-supporting *and* turning a profit from the beginning, or it's in trouble. And we're in trouble so deep, even if we could breathe through the tops of our heads we'd *still* be in trouble."

"Maybe if we got some more boys from back home. . . ." Nunzio began.

Shai-ster slapped his hand down on the table, stopping his lieutenant short.

"No more overhead!" he shouted. "I'm having enough trouble explaining our profit/loss statement to the Big Boys without the bottom line getting any worse. Not only are we not going to get any more help, we're going to start trimming our expenses, and I mean *right* now. Tell the boys to . . . what are *you* grinning at?"

This last was directed at me.

"Oh, nothing," I said innocently. "It's just that for a minute there you sounded just like someone I know back on Klah . . . name of Grimble."

"J.R. Grimble?" Shai-ster blinked.

Now it was my turn to be surprised.

"Why, yes. He's the Chancellor of the Exchequer back at Possiltum. Why, do you know him?"

"Sure. We went to school together. Chancellor of the Exchequer, huh? Not bad. If I had known he was working the court of Possiltum, I would have stuck around and said 'hi' when I was there."

Somehow, the thought of Shai-ster and Grimble knowing each other made me uneasy. There wasn't much chance of the two of them getting together and comparing notes, and even if they did, Grimble didn't know all that much about my *modus operandi*. Still, it served as a grim reminder that this was a very risky game I was playing, with some very dangerous people.

"I still think there's another gang out there somewhere," Nunzio growled. "There's too much going down for it to be independent operators."

"You're half right," Shai-ster corrected. "There's too much going down for it to be a gang. Nobody's into that many things . . . not even us!"

"You lost me there, Shai-ster," I said, genuinely curious.

The mobster favored me with a patronizing smile.

"That's right. As a magician, you don't know that much about how organized crime works. Let me try to explain. When the Mob decides to move in, we hit one specialty field at a time . . . you know, like protection or the numbers. Like that. Focusing our efforts yields a better saturation as well as market penetration."

"That makes sense," I nodded, not wanting to admit he had lost me again.

"Now you take a look at what's happening here. We're getting all sorts of claims; vandalism, shoplifting, armed robbery, even a couple cases of arson. It's too much of a mix to be the work of one group. We're dealing with a lot of small-time independents, and if we can make an example of a few of them, the others will decide there are easier pickings elsewhere."

In a way, I was glad to hear this. I owed Aahz one more back-pat. He was the one who had decided that the efforts of our team were too limited. To accelerate our "crime wave," he had introduced the dubious practice of "insurance fraud" to Deva . . . and the Deveels were fast learners.

Is your stock moving too slow? Break it yourself and turn in a claim for vandalism. Trying to sell your shop, but nobody wants to buy, even at a discount? Torch the place and collect in full. Better still, want to fatten up your profit margin a little? Dummy up a few invoices and file a claim for "stolen goods." All profit, no cost.

The Deveels loved it. It let them make money and harass the Mob at the same time. No wonder Shai-ster's table was fast disappearing under a mountain of claims and protests.

It was terrific . . . except for the part about making an example out of everyone they caught. I made a mental note to warn the team about being extra careful.

"If it's not a gang, and they aren't working against us," Nunzio scowled, "why is everything happening in *our* areas? My dad taught me to be suspicious of coincidences. He got killed by one."

"How do you know it's just happening in our area?" Shai-ster countered. "Maybe we picked a bad area of the Bazaar to start our operation. Maybe the whole Bazaar is a bad area. Maybe we should have been suspicious when Skeeve here told us there were no police. You get this much money floating around with no police, of course there'll be crooks around."

"So what are we supposed to do?" Guido snarled, plucking his napkin from under his chin and throwing it on the table. "My boys can't be two places at once. We can't watch over our current clients and sign on new accounts, too."

"That's right," Shai-ster agreed, "so here's what we're going to do. First, we split up the teams. Two-thirds of the boys patrol the areas we've got under protection. The others go after new clients . . .*but* we don't just take anybody. We investigate and ask questions. We find out how much trouble a new area or a new shop has had *before* we take them as a client. Then we know who the bad risks are, and if we protect them at all, they pay double. *Capish?*"

Both Guido and Nunzio were thinking, and it was obvious the process hurt.

"I dunno," Nunzio squeaked at last. "Sumpin'

sounds kinda funny about that plan.''

"Crime wouldn't pay if the government ran it," I murmured helpfully.

"What's that?" Shai-ster snapped.

"Oh, just something my teacher told me once." I shrugged.

"Hey! Skeeve's right," Guido exclaimed.

"What you're sayin' is that we're going to be police-men and insurance investigators."

"Well, I wouldn't use those words. . . ."

" 'Well' nothin'. We ain't gonna do it!"

"Why not?"

"C'mon, Shai-ster. We're the bad guys. You know, crooks. What's it going to do to our reputation if it gets back to the Mob that we've turned into policemen?"

"They'll think we're valuable employees who are working hard to protect their investment."

"Yeah?" Guido frowned, unconvinced.

"Besides, it's only temporary," Shai-ster soothed. "Not only that, it's a smoke screen for what we'll *really* be doing."

"What's that?" I asked blandly.

Shai-ster shot a quick look around the restaurant, then leaned forward, lowering his voice.

"Well, I wasn't going to say anything, but remember that I was telling you about how the Mob focuses on one field at a time? The way I see it, maybe we picked the wrong field here at Deva. Maybe we shouldn't have tried the protection racket."

"So you're going to change fields?" I urged.

"Right," Shai-ster smiled. "We'll put the protection racket on slow-down mode for a while, and in the mean-time start leaning on the bookies."

"Now you're talking," Guido crowed. "There's always good money to be made at gambling."

"Keep your voice down, you idiot. It's supposed to be a secret."

"So who's to hear?" Guido protested.

"How about them?"

Shai-ster jerked his thumb toward a table of four enormous beings, alternately stuffing their faces and laughing uproariously.

"Them? That's the Hutt brothers. They're in here about once a week. They're too busy with their own games to bother us."

"Games? Are they gamblers?"

"Naw . . . well, except maybe Darwin. He's the leader of the pack. But he only gambles on businesses."

"Which one is he?"

"The thinnest one. I hear his fiancée has him on a diet. It's making him mean, but not dangerous to us."

Shai-ster turned back to our table.

"Well, keep your voice down anyway. How about it, Skeeve? The gambling, I mean. You've been here at the Bazaar before. Do you know any bookies we can get hold of?"

"Gee, the only one I know of for sure is the Geek," I said. "He's a pretty high-roller. If you boys are going to try to pull a fast one on him, though, don't tell him I was the one who singled him out."

Shai-ster gave me a broad wink.

"Gotcha. But anything we get from him, you're in for a percentage. You know, a finder's fee. We don't forget our friends."

"Gee, thanks," I managed, feeling more than a little guilty. "Well, I'd better be going. C'mon, Gleep."

"Gleep!" echoed my dragon, pulling his head up out of a tub of spaghetti at the sound of his name.

Fats had taken an instant liking to my pet, founded I suspect on Gleep's newfound capacity for the maggot-like stuff barely hidden by blood-red sauce that was the parlor's mainstay.

I had never been able to screw up my courage enough to try spaghetti, but my dragon loved it. Knowing some of the dubious things, edible and in, living and non, that also met with Gleep's culinary approval, this did little toward encouraging me to expand my dietary horizons to include this particular dish. Still, as long as I had Gleep along, we were welcome at Fats, even though my pet was starting to develop a waddle reminiscent of the parlor's proprietor.

"Say, Skeeve. Where do you keep your dragon during the day?"

I glanced over to find Shai-ster studying my pet through narrowed, thoughtful eyes.

"Usually he's with me, but sometimes I leave him with a dragon-sitter. Why?"

"I just remembered an 'interruption of business' claim we had to pay the other day . . . had to pay! Heck, we're still paying it. Anyway, this guy sells dragons, see, except for over a week now he hasn't sold a one. Usually sells about three a day and says since he paid us to be sure nothing happens to his business, we should make up the difference in his sales drop . . . and, you know, those things are *expensive!*"

"I know," I agreed, "but what does that have to do with Gleep?"

"Probably nothing. It's just that this guy swears that just before everything went to pot, some little dragon came by and talked to his dragons. Now they won't roar or blow fire or nothing. All they do is sleep and frolic . . . and who wants to buy a dragon that frolics, you know?"

"Talked to his dragons?" I asked uneasily.

For some reason, I had a sudden mental image of Gleep confronting Big Julie's dragon, a beast that dwarfed him in size, and winning.

"Well . . . they didn't exactly talk, but they did huddle up and put their heads together and made mumbly puffy noises at each other. Wouldn't let this guy near 'em until it was over. The only thing he's sure of is the little one, the one he says messed up his business, said something like 'Peep!' Said it a couple of times."

"Peep?" I said.

"Gleep!" answered my dragon.

Shai-ster stared at him again.

"C'mon, Shai-ster," Guido said, giving his superior a hearty shove. "Talking dragons? Somebody's pullin' your leg. Sounds to me like he got a bad shipment of dragons and is trying to get us to pay for them. Tell him to take a hike."

"It's not that easy," Shai-ster grumbled, "but I suppose you're right. I mean, all dragons look pretty much alike."

"True enough," I called, heading hastily for the nearest exit. "C'mon, Peep . . . I mean, Gleep!"

Maybe Shai-ster's suspicions had been lulled, but I still had a few of my own as we made our way back to the Yellow Crescent Inn.

"Level with me, Gleep. Did you do anything to louse up somebody's dragon business?"

"Gleep?" answered my pet in a tone exactly like my own when I'm trying too hard to sound innocent.

"Uh-huh. Well, stay out of this one. I think we've got it in hand without you getting in the line of fire."

"Gleep."

The answer was much more subdued this time, and I

realized he was drooping noticeably.

"Now don't sulk. I just don't want anything to happen to you. That's all."

I was suddenly aware that passers-by were staring at us. As strange as the Bazaar was, I guess they weren't used to seeing someone walking down the street arguing with a dragon.

"Let's hurry," I urged, breaking into a trot. "I don't know what we can do about the Mob moving in on the bookies, but I'm sure Aahz will think of something."

Chapter Eighteen:

"Life can be profitable, if you know the odds."

—RIPLEY

THE sports arena we were in was noticeably smaller than the stadium on Jahk where we had played in the Big Game, but no less noisy. Perhaps the fact that it was indoors instead of being open-air did something to the acoustics, but even at half-full the crowd in the arena made such a din I could barely hear myself think.

Then again, there was the smell. The same walls and ceiling that botched up the acoustics did nothing at all for ventilation. Even a few thousand beings from assorted dimensions in these close quarters produced a blend of body odors that had my stomach doing slow rolls . . . or maybe it was just my nerves.

"Could you explain to me again about odds?"

"Not now," the Geek snarled, nervously playing with his program. "I'm too busy worrying."

"I'll give it a try, hot stuff," Massha volunteered from my other side. "Maybe I can say it in less technical jargon than our friend here."

"I'd appreciate it," I admitted.

That got me a black look from the Geek, but Massha was already into it.

"First, you've got to understand that for the most part, bookies aren't betting their own money. They're acting as agents or go-betweens for people who are betting different sides of the same contest. Ideally, the money bet on each side evens out, so the bookie himself doesn't have any of his own money riding on the contest."

"Then how do they make their money?"

"Sometimes off a percentage, sometimes . . . but that's another story. What we're talking about is odds. Okay?"

"I guess so," I shrugged.

"Now, the situation I described is the ideal. It assumes the teams or fighters or whatever are evenly matched. That way, some people bet one side, some the other, but overall it evens out. That's even odds or 1–1."

She shifted her weight a bit, ignoring the glares from our fellow patrons when the entire row of seats wobbled in response.

"But suppose things were different. What if, instead of an even match, one side had an advantage . . . like say if Badaxe were going to fight King Rodrick?"

"That's easy," I smiled. "Nobody would be on the King."

"Precisely," Massha nodded. "Then everybody would bet one side, and the bookies would have to cover all the bets with their own money . . . bets they stood a good chance of losing."

"So they don't take any bets."

"No. They rig things so that people will bet on the king."

I cocked an eyebrow at her.

"They could try, but I sure wouldn't throw my gold away like that. I'd back Badaxe."

"Really?" Massha smiled. "What if, instead of betting one gold piece to win one gold piece, you had to bet ten gold pieces on Badaxe to win one back?"

"Well . . ."

"Let me make it a little harder. How about if you bet one gold piece on the King, and he won, that instead of getting one gold piece back, you got a hundred?"

"I . . . um . . . might take a long shot on the King," I said, hesitantly. "There's always a chance he could get lucky. Besides, if I lose, I'm only out one gold piece."

". . . And *that's* how bookies use odds to cover themselves. Now, how they figure out how many bets they need on the King at 'x' odds to cover the bets they have on Badaxe at 'y' odds is beyond me."

I looked at the Deveel next to me with new respect.

"Gee, Geek. I never really realized how complicated your work is."

The Deveel softened a bit. They're as susceptible to flattery as anyone else.

"Actually, it's even more complicated than that," he admitted modestly. "You've got to keep track of several contests at once, sometimes even use the long bets from one to cover the short bets on another. Then there are side bets, like who will score how often in which period in the Big Game. It isn't easy, but a sharp being can make a living at it."

"So what are the odds tonight?"

The Deveel grimaced.

"Lousy. It's one of those Badaxe and the King matchups, if I was following your example right. In this case, the team you'll see in red trunks are Badaxe.

They're hotter than a ten dollar laser and have won their last fifteen bouts. The weak sisters . . . the King to you . . . will be in white trunks and haven't won a bout in two years. When the Mob put their bet down, the odds were running about two hundred to one against the whites."

I whistled softly.

"Wow. Two hundred in gold return on a one-gold-piece bet. Did you remember to act surprised when they put their money down?"

"I didn't have to act," the Geek said through tight lips. "Not with the size bet they came up with. Being forewarned, I had expected they wouldn't be going small, but still . . ."

He shook his head and lapsed into silence.

I hadn't really paused to consider the implication of the odds, but I did now. If betting one piece could get you two hundred back, then a bet of a thousand would have a potential payback of two hundred thousand! And a ten thousand bet . . .

"How big was their bet?" I asked fearfully.

"Big enough that if I lose, I'll be working for the Mob for the rest of my life to pay it off . . . and Deveels don't have short life-spans."

"Wait a minute. Didn't Aahz tell you that if you lost, we'd cover it out of our expense money?"

"He did," the Deveel said. "And he also pointed out that if you were covering my losses, you'd also take all winnings if things went as planned. I opted to take the risk, and the winnings, myself."

Massha leaned forward to stare.

"Are you that confident, or that greedy?"

"More the latter," the Geek admitted. "Then again, I got burnt rather badly betting against Skeeve here in the Big Game. I figure it's worth at least one pass backing the shooter who's working a streak."

I shook my head in puzzlement.

"Aren't you afraid of losing?"

"Well, it did occur to me that it might be me and not the Mob who's being set up here. That's why I'm sitting next to you. If this turns out to be a double cross . . ."

"You're pretty small to be making threats, Geek," Massha warned.

". . . And you're too big to dodge fast if I decide I'm being had," the Deveel shot back.

"Knock it off, both of you," I ordered. "It's academic anyway. There won't be any problems . . . or if there are, I'll be as surprised as you are, Geek."

"More surprised, I hope," the Deveel sneered. "I'm half expecting this to blow up, remember?"

"But Aahz has assured me that the fix is in."

"Obviously. Otherwise, the Mob wouldn't be betting so heavily. The question is, which fix is going to work, theirs or yours?"

Just then a flurry of activity across the arena caught my eye. The Mob had just arrived . . . in force. Shai-ster was there, flanked by Guido and Nunzio and backed by the remaining members of the two teams currently assigned to the Bazaar. Seen together and moving, as opposed to individually feeding their faces at Fats', they made an impressive group. Apparently others shared my opinion. Even though they were late, no one contested their right to prime seats as they filed into the front row. In fact, there was a noticeable bailing out from the desired seats as they approached.

It was still a new enough experience for me to see other beings I knew in a crowd at the Bazaar that I stood up and waved at them before I realized what I was do-

ing. Then it dawned on me! If they saw me sitting with
the Geek and then lost a big bet, they might put two and
two together and get five!

I stopped waving and tried to ease back into my seat,
but it was too late. Guido had spotted my gyrations and
nudged Shai-ster to point me out. Our eyes met and he
nodded acknowledgement before returning to scanning
the crowd.

Crestfallen, I turned to apologize to the Geek, only to
find myself addressing a character with a pasty complexion and hairy ears who bore no resemblance at all to
the Deveel who had been sitting beside me.

I almost . . . almost! . . . looked around to see where
the Geek had gone. Then I did a little mental arithmetic
and figured it out.

A disguise spell!

I'd gotten so used to fooling people myself with that
spell that when someone did the same to me, I was completely taken in.

"Still kinda new at this intrigue stuff, aren't you?" he
observed dryly from his new face.

Fortunately I was saved the problem of thinking up a
suitable response by the entrance of the contestants.
With the scramble of planning and launching our
counter-offensive, I hadn't really been briefed on what
the Mob was betting on except that it would be a tag-
team wrestling match. No one said what the contestants
would be like, and I had assumed it would be like the
matches I had seen back on Klah. I should have known
better.

The two teams were made up of beings who barely
stood high enough to reach my waist! I mean they were
small! They looked like kids . . . if you're used to having
kids around with four arms each.

"What are those?" I demanded.

"Those are the teams," the Geek said helpfully.

"I mean, *what* are they? Where are they from?"

"Oh. Those are Tues."

"And you bet on them? I mean, I've heard of midget wrestling, but this is ridiculous!"

"Don't knock it," the Deveel shrugged. "They're big on the wrestling circuit. In fact, teams like this are their dimension's most popular export. Everyone knows them as the Terrible Tues. They're a lot more destructive than you'd guess from their size."

"This is a put-on, right?"

"If you really want to see something, you should catch their other export. It's a traveling dance troupe called the Tue Tours."

Massha dropped a heavy hand on my shoulder.

"Hot stuff, remember our deal about my lessons?"

"Later, Massha. The match is about to start."

Actually, it was about to finish. It was that short, if you'll pardon the expression.

The first member of the favored red trunk team simply strolled out and pinned his white-trunked rival. Though the pin looked a bit like someone trying to wrap a package with tangled string, the red-trunker made it seem awfully easy. All efforts of his opponent's partner to dislodge the victor were in vain, and the bout was over.

"Well, that's that," the Geek said, standing up. "A pleasure doing business with you, Skeeve. Look me up again if you tie on to a live one."

"Aren't you going to collect your bet?"

The Deveel shrugged.

"No rush. Besides, I think your playmates are a little preoccupied just now."

I looked where he was pointing and saw Shai-ster storming toward the dressing rooms with Guido and

Nunzio close behind. None of them looked particularly happy, which was understandable, given the circumstances.

"Whoops. That's my cue. See you back at the Yellow Crescent, Massha."

And with that, I launched myself in an interceptor course with the angry mobsters.

Chapter Nineteen:

"These blokes need to be taught to respect their superiors."

—GEN. CORNWALLIS

I ALMOST missed them. Not that I was moving slow, mind you. It's just that they had a real head of steam on.

"Hi guys!" I called, just as Shai-ster was raising a fist to hammer on the dressing room door. "Are you going to congratulate the winners, too?"

Three sets of eyes bored into me as my "friends" spun around.

"Congratulate!" Guido snarled. "I'll give 'em congratulate."

"Wait a minute," Shai-ster interrupted. "What did you mean, 'too'?"

"Well, that's why *I'm* here. I just won a sizable bet on the last match."

"How sizable?"

"Well, sizable for me," I qualified. "I stand to collect fifty gold pieces."

"Fifty," Guido snorted. "You know how much we *lost* on that fiasco?"

147

"Lost?" I frowned. "Didn't you know the Reds were favored?"

"Of course we knew," Shai-ster snarled. "That's why we were set to make a killing when they lost."

"But what made you think they were going to . . . Oh! Was that what you were talking about when you said you were going into gambling?"

"That's right. The red team was supposed to take a graceful dive in the third round. We paid them enough . . . more than enough, actually."

He sounded so much like Grimble I couldn't resist taking a cheap shot.

"Judging from the outcome, it sounds to me that you paid them a little less than enough."

"It's not funny. Now, instead of recouping our losses, we've got *another* big loss to explain to the Big Boys."

"Oh come on, Shai-ster," I smiled. "How much can it cost to fix a fight?"

"Not much," he admitted. "But when you figure in the investment money we just lost, it comes to. . . ."

"Investment money?"

"He means the bet," Guido supplied.

"Oh. Well, I suppose that's the risk you take when you try to make a killing."

An evil smile flitted across Shai-ster's face.

"Oh, we're going to make a killing, all right," he said. "It's time the locals at this Bazaar learned what it means to cross the Mob."

With that, he nodded at Guido who opened the dressing room door.

All four wrestlers were sharing the same room, and they looked up expectantly as we filed in. That's right. I said we. I kind of tagged along at the end of the procession and no one seemed to object.

"Didn't you clowns forget something out there?" Shai-ster said for his greeting. "Like who was supposed to win?"

The various team members exchanged glances. Then the smallest of the red team shrugged.

"Big deal. So we changed our minds."

"Yeah," his teammate chimed in. "We decided it would be bad for our image to lose . . . especially to these stumblebums."

That brought the white team to its feet.

"Stumblebums?" one of them bellowed. "You caught us by surprise, that's all. We was told to take it easy until the third round."

"If you took it any easier, you'd be asleep. We were supposed to be wrestling, not dancing."

Shai-ster stepped between them.

"So you all admit you understood your original instructions?"

"Hey, get off our backs, okay? You'll get your stinking money back, so what's your beef, anyway?"

"Even if you gave us a full refund," Shai-ster said softly, "there's still a matter of the money we lost betting on you. I don't suppose any of you are independently wealthy?"

"Oh, sure," one of the reds laughed. "We're just doin' this for kicks."

"I thought not. Guido. Nunzio. See what you can do about squaring accounts with these gentlemen. And take your time. I want them to feel it, you know?"

"I dunno, Shai-ster," Guido scowled. "They're awfully small. I don't think we can make it last too long."

"Well, do your best. Skeeve? Would you join me outside? I don't think you're going to want to see this."

He was closer to being right than he knew. Even

though I had been through some rough and tumble times during recent years, that didn't mean I enjoyed it—even to watch.

The door was barely shut behind us when a series of thuds and crashes erupted inside. It was painful just to listen to, but it didn't last long.

"I told them to take their time," Shai-ster said, scowling at the silence. "Oh well, I guess . . ."

The door opened, revealing one of the white team.

"If you've got any more lessons out there, I suggest you send them in. These two didn't teach us much at all."

He shut the door again, but not before we caught a glimpse of the two bodyguards unconscious on the floor. Well, Guido was on the floor. Nunzio was kind of standing on his head in the corner.

"Tough little guys," I remarked casually. "It must be the four arms. Think you could find work for them in the Mob?"

Shai-ster was visibly shaken, but he recovered quickly.

"So they want to play rough. Well, that's fine by me."

"You aren't going in there alone, are you?" I asked, genuinely concerned.

He favored me with a withering glance.

"Not a chance."

With that, he put his fingers in his mouth and blew a loud blast. At least, that's what it looked like. I didn't *hear* a thing.

Before I could ask what he was doing, though, a thunder of footsteps announced the arrival of two dozen Mob reinforcements.

Neat trick. I guess the whistle had been too high for me to hear . . . or too low.

"They got Guido and Nunzio," Shai-ster shouted before the heavies had come to a complete halt. "Let's show 'em who's running things around here. Follow me!"

Jerking the door open, he plunged into the dressing room with the pack at his heels.

I'm not sure if Shai-ster had ever actually been in a fight before, much less led a team into a fight. I *am,* however, sure he never tried it again.

The screams of pain and anguish that poured out of that room moved me to take action. I walked a little further down the hall and did my waiting there. It turned out my caution was needless. The wall didn't collapse, nor did the ceiling or the building itself. Several hunks of plaster did come loose, however, and at one point someone poked a hole in the wall . . . with his head.

It occurred to me that if the fight fans in the arena *really* wanted to get their money's worth, they should be down here. Additional thought made me decide it was just as well they didn't. There were already more than enough beings crowded into that dressing room . . . which was as good a reason as any for my staying in the hall.

Eventually the sounds of battle died away, leaving only ominous silence. I reminded myself that I had every confidence in the outcome. As the length of silence grew, I found it necessary to remind myself several times.

Finally the door opened, and the four Tues filed out laughing and chatting together.

"Cute," I called. "Don't hurry or anything. I can worry out here all day."

One of the white team ran up and gave me a hug and a kiss.

"Sorry, handsome. We were having so much fun we forgot about you."

"Um . . . could you do something about the disguises before you kiss me again?"

"Whoops. Sorry about that!"

The taller red team member closed his eyes, and the Tues were gone. In their places stood Aahz, Gus, Tananda, and Chumly. That's why I hadn't been worried . . . much.

"Nice work, Gus," I said, nodding my approval. "But I still think I could have handled the disguises myself."

"Have you ever seen a Tue before?" Aahz challenged.

"Well . . . no."

"Gus has. That's why he handled the disguises. End of discussion."

"Used to have a secretary named Etheyl," the gargoyle explained, ignoring Aahz's order. "She was a big fan of the wrestling circuit."

"A secretary?" I blinked.

"Sure, haven't you ever heard of a Tue Fingered Typist?"

"Enough!" Aahz insisted, holding up his hand. "I vote we head back to the Yellow Crescent Inn for a little celebration. I think we've thwarted the Mob enough for one night."

"Yeah," Tananda grinned. "That'll teach 'em to pick on someone their own size."

"But you are their size," I frowned.

"I know," she winked. "That's the point."

"I say, are you sure, Aahz?" Chumly interjected. "I mean, we gave them a sound thrashing, but will it hold them until morning?"

"If they're lucky," my mentor grinned. "Remember,

once they wake up, they're going to have to report in to their superiors.''

''Do you think they'll try to recoup their losses with another stab at gambling?'' I asked.

''I hope so,'' Aahz said, his grin getting broader. ''The next big betting event on the docket is the unicorn races, and we've got that covered easily.''

''You mean Buttercup? You can't enter him in a race. He's a war-unicorn.''

''I know. Think about it.''

Chapter Twenty:

"Figure the last thing you would expect the enemy to do, then count on him doing precisely that!"

—RICHELIEU

THE Mob did not try another gambit right after their disastrous attempt to move in on Deva's bookies. In fact, for some time afterward, things were quiet . . . too quiet, as Aahz put it.

"I don't like it," he declared, staring out the front window of the Yellow Crescent Inn. "They're up to something. I can feel it."

"Fats says they haven't been around for nearly a week," I supplied. "Maybe they've given up."

"Not a chance. There's got to be at least one more try, if for nothing else than to save face. And instead of getting ready, we're sitting around on our butts."

He was right. For days now, the team's main activity had been hanging around Gus's place waiting for some bit of information to turn up. Our scouting missions had yielded nothing, so we were pretty much reduced to relying on the normal Bazaar gossip network to alert us to any new Mob activity.

"Be reasonable, Aahz," Chumly protested. "We can't plan or prepare without any data to work with.

155

You've said yourself that action in an absence of information is wasted effort, eh what? Makes the troops edgy."

Aahz stalked over to where the troll was sprawled.

"Don't start quoting me at me! You're the one who usually argues with everything I say. If everybody starts agreeing with me, we aren't using all the mental resources we can."

"But you're the one saying that we should be planning," I pointed out.

"Right," my mentor smiled. "So we might as well get started. In absence of hard facts, we'll have to try to second-guess them. Now, where is the Bazaar most vulnerable to Mob takeover? Tananda, have you seen . . . Tananda?"

She abandoned her window-gazing to focus on the discussion.

"What was that, Aahz? Sorry. I was watching that Klahd coming down the street dressed in bright purple."

"Purple?"

Massha and I said it together.

I started to race her for the window, then changed my mind. What if I won? I didn't want to be between the window and her mass when she finally got there. Instead, I waited until she settled into position, then eased in beside her.

"That's him all right," I said out loud, confirming my unvoiced thoughts. "That's Don Bruce. Well, now we know what the Mob's been doing. They've been whistling up the heavy artillery. The question is, what is he doing here at the Bazaar? When we get the answer to that, we'll be able to plan our next move."

"Actually, the question should be what is he doing here at the Yellow Crescent Inn," Gus commented dryly from my elbow. "And I think we're about to get the answer."

Sure enough, Don Bruce was making a beeline for the very building we were watching him from. With his walk, it had taken me a minute to zero in on his direction.

"All right. We know who he is and that he's coming here. Now, let's quit gawking like a bunch of tourists."

Aahz was back in his familiar commander role again. Still, I noticed he was no quicker to leave the window than any of the rest of us.

"Everybody sit down and act natural. Skeeve, when he gets here, let me do the talking, okay?"

"Not a chance, Aahz," I said, sinking into a chair. "He's used to dealing with me direct. If we try to run in a middleman he'll know something's up. Sit at this table with me, though. I'm going to need your advice on this one."

By the time Don Bruce opened the door, we were all sitting. Aahz and I at one table, and two others accommodating Massha and Gus, and the Chumly-Tananda team respectively. I noticed that we had left two-thirds of the place empty to sit at adjoining tables, which might have looked a little suspicious. I also noticed we had reflexively split up into two-person teams again, but it was too late to correct either situation.

"Hi there," Don Bruce called, spotting me at once. "Thank goodness I found you here. This Bazaar is great fun to wander, but simply *beastly* at finding what or who you're looking for."

"You were looking for me?"

This was not the best news I had heard all day. Despite his affected style of speech, I had a healthy respect for Don Bruce. From what I had seen of the Mob, it was a rough group, and I figured no one could hold down as high a position as Don Bruce did, unless there was some real hard rock under that soft exterior. Friendly greeting or not, I began to feel the fingers of cold fear gripping my stomach.

"That's right. I've *got* to have a meet with you, you know? I *was* hoping I could speak with you in private."

The last thing in the world I wanted right now was to be alone with Don Bruce.

"It's all right," I said expansively. "These are my friends. Any business I have with your . . . organization we're in on together . . . I mean, can be discussed in front of them."

"Oh, very well."

The Mob chieftain flounced onto a chair at my table.

"I didn't mean to be rude, and I *do* want to meet you all. It's just that, first thing, there are some pressing matters to deal with."

"Shoot," I said, then immediately wished I had chosen another word.

"Well, you know we're trying to move in on this place, and you know it hasn't been going well . . . no, don't deny it. It's true. Shai-ster has mentioned you often in his reports, so I know how well informed you are."

"I haven't seen Shai-ster lately, but I do know he's been working hard at the project."

"That's right," Aahz chimed in. "From what Skeeve's been telling us, Shai-ster is a good man. If he can't pull it off, you might as well pack up and go home."

"He's an idiot!" Don Bruce roared, and for a moment we could see the steel inside the velvet glove. "The reason you haven't seen him is that I've pulled him from the project completely. He thought we should give up, too."

"You aren't giving up?" I said, fearfully.

"I can't. Oh, if you only knew what I go through on the Council. I made such a thing out of this Deva proj-

ect and how much it could do for the Mob. If we pulled
out now, it would be the same as saying I don't know a
good thing when I see it. No sir. Call it family politics or
stubborn pride, we're going to stay right here."

My heart sank.

"But if the operation is losing money—" I began, but
he cut me off with a gesture.

"So far . . . but not for long. You see, I've figured
out for myself what's going wrong here."

"You have? How? I mean, this is your first visit here
since the project started."

I was starting to sweat a bit. Don Bruce was regarding
me with an oily reptilian smile I didn't like at all.

"I saw it in the reports," he declared. "Clear as the
nose on your face. That's why I know Shai-ster's an
idiot. The problem was right here in front of him and he
couldn't see it. That problem is you."

My sweat turned cold. At the edge of my vision I saw
Tananda run her fingers through her hair, palming one
of her poison darts in the process, and Massha was
starting to play with her rings. Chumly and Gus exchanged glances, then shifted in their chairs slightly. Of
our entire team, only Aahz seemed unconcerned.

"You'll have to be a little clearer for the benefit of us
slow folks," he drawled. "Just how do you figure that
Skeeve here is a problem?"

"Look at the facts," Don Bruce said, holding up his
fingers to tick off the count.

"He's been here the whole time my boys were having
trouble; he knows the Bazaar better than my boys; he
knows magik enough to do things my boys can't handle;
and now I find out he's got a bunch of friends and con-
tacts here."

"So?" my mentor said softly.

"So? Isn't it obvious? The problem with the operation is that he should have been working for us all along."

By now I had recovered enough to have my defense ready.

"But just because I . . . what?"

"Sure. That's why I'm here. Now I know you said before you didn't want to work for the Mob full time. That's why I'm ready to talk a new deal with you. I want you to run the Mob's operation here at the Bazaar . . . and I'm willing to pay top dollar."

"How much is that in gold?"

Aahz was leaning forward now.

"Wait a minute! Whoa! Stop!" I interrupted. "You can't be serious. I don't have the time or the know-how to make this a profitable project."

"It doesn't have to be profitable," Don argued. "Break even would be nice, or even just lose money slower. Anything to get the council to look elsewhere for things to gripe about at our monthly Meetings. You could do it in your extra time."

I started to say something, but Aahz put a casual hand on my shoulder. I knew that warning. If I tried to interrupt or correct him, that grip would tighten until my bones creaked.

"Now let me see if I've got this right," he said, showing *all* his teeth. "You want my man here to run your operation, but you don't care if it doesn't show a profit?"

"That's right."

"Of course, with things as shaky as they are now, you'd have to guarantee his salary."

Don Bruce pursed his lips and looked at me.

"How much does he cost?"

"Lots," Aahz confided. "But less than the total salary of the force you've got here now."

"Okay. He's worth it."

"Aahz . . ." I began, but the grip on my shoulder tightened.

". . . *And* you aren't so much concerned with the Mob's reputation here on Deva as you are with how the Council treats you, right?"

"Well . . . yeah. I guess so."

". . . So he'd have free rein to run the operation the way he saw fit. No staff forced on him or policies to follow?"

"No. I'd have to at least assign him a couple bodyguards. Anybody running a Mob operation has got to have a couple of the Family's boys to be sure nothing happens to him."

Aahz scowled.

"But he's already got . . ."

"How about Guido and Nunzio?" I managed, through gritted teeth.

Abruptly the grip on my shoulder vanished.

"Those losers?" Don Bruce frowned. "I was going to have a severe talk with them after this disaster, but if you want 'em, they're yours."

". . . But since *you're* the one insisting on them, they don't show up on *our* overhead. Right?" Aahz said firmly.

I leaned back, working my shoulder covertly, and tried to ignore the horrified stares my friends were exchanging. I didn't know for sure what Aahz was up to, but knew better than to get in his way when he smelled money.

I could only cross my fingers and hope that he knew what he was doing . . . for a change.

Chapter Twenty-One:

"Stayin' alive! Stayin' alive!"

—V. DRACULA

THE representatives of the Bazaar Merchants didn't look happy, but then Deveels never do when they're parting with money.

"Thank you gentlemen," Aahz beamed, rubbing his hands together gleefully over the substantial pile of gold on the table.

"You're sure the Mob is gone?" the head spokesman asked, looking plaintively at the gold.

"Positive. We've broken their reign of terror and sent them packing."

The Deveel nodded.

"Good. Now that that's settled, we'll be going."

". . . Of course," Aahz yawned, "there's no guarantee they won't be back tomorrow."

That stopped the delegation in their tracks.

"What? But you said . . ."

"Face it, gentlemen. Right now, the only thing between the Mob and the Bazaar is the Great Skeeve here, and once he leaves . . ."

The Deveels exchanged glances.

"I don't suppose you'd consider staying," one said hopefully.

I favored him with a patronizing smile.

"I'd love to, but you know how it is. Expenses are high, and I've got to keep moving to eke out a living."

"But with your reputation, clients will be looking for you. What you really need is a permanent location so you can be found."

"True enough," Aahz smiled. "But to be blunt, why should we give you for free what other dimensions are willing to pay for? I should think that if anybody could understand that, you Deveels would."

"Now we're getting to the heart of the matter," the lead spokesman sighed, pulling up a chair. "Okay. How much?"

"How much?" Aahz echoed.

"Don't give me that," the Deveel snapped. "Innocence looks ridiculous on a Pervert. Just tell us what kind of retainer would be necessary to keep the Great Skeeve around as the Bazaar's magician in residence."

Aahz winked at me.

"I'm sure you'll find his fee reasonable," he said. "Well, reasonable when you stop to think what you're getting for your money. Of course, the figure I'm thinking of is just for making the Bazaar his base of operations. If any specific trouble arises, we'll have to negotiate that separately."

"Of course," the Deveel winced.

I settled back to wait patiently. This was going to take a while, but I was confident of the eventual outcome. I also knew that whatever fee Aahz was thinking of originally just got doubled when the Deveel made that 'Pervert' crack. As a Pervect, Aahz is very sensitive about how he's addressed . . . and this time I wasn't about to argue with him.

"I love it!" Aahz crowed, modestly. "Not only are we getting a steady income from both the Mob and the Deveels, we don't have to do a thing to earn it! This is even better than the setup we had at Possiltum."

"It's a sweet deal, Aahz."

"And how about this layout? It's a far cry from that shack you and Garkin were calling home when we first met."

Aahz and I were examining our new home, provided as an extra clause in our deal with the Bazaar merchants. It was huge, rivaling the size of the Royal Palace at Possiltum. The interesting thing was that from the outside it looked no bigger than an average Bazaar stall.

"Of course, holding out for a lifetime discount on anything at the Bazaar was a stroke of genius, if I do say so myself."

"Yeah, Aahz. Genius."

My mentor broke off his chortling and self-congratulations to regard me quizzically.

"Is something bothering you, Skeeve? You seem a little subdued."

"It's nothing, really."

"Come on. Out with it," he insisted. "You should be on top of the world right now, not moping around like you just heard that your dragon has a terminal illness or something."

"Well, it's a couple of things," I admitted grudgingly. "First, I've got a bad feeling about those deals you just put together."

"Now wait a minute," my mentor scowled. "We talked all this out before we went after the merchants and you said that double-dealing wouldn't bother you."

"It doesn't. If anything, I'm glad to see both the Mob and the Deveels getting a little of their own back for a change."

"Then what's wrong? I got you everything I could think of!"

"That's what's wrong."

My mentor shook his head sharply as if to clear his vision.

"I've got to admit, this time *you* lost *me*. Could you run that one past again, slow?"

"Come on, Aahz. You know what I'm talking about. You've gotten me more money than I could spend in a lifetime, a beautiful house . . . not just anywhere, mind you, but at the Bazaar itself . . . steady work anytime I want it . . . in short, everything I need to not only survive, but prosper. Everything."

"So?"

"So are you setting me up so you can leave? Is that what this is all about?"

I had secretly hoped that Aahz would laugh in my face and tell me I was being silly. Instead, he averted his eyes and lapsed into silence.

"I've been thinking about it," he said finally. "You're doing pretty well lately and, like you say, this latest deal will insure you won't starve. The truth of the matter is that you really don't need me anymore."

"But Aahz!"

"Don't 'but Aahz' me! All I'm doing is repeating what you shoved down my throat at the beginning of this caper. You don't need me. I've been giving it a lot of thought, and you're right. I thought you always wanted to hear me say that."

"Maybe I don't like being right," I said plaintively.

"Maybe I wish I *did* need you more and things could go on forever like they have in the past."

"That's most of growing up, kid," Aahz sighed. "Facing up to reality whether we like it or not. You've been doing it, and I figure it's about time I did the same. That's why I'm going to stick around."

"But you don't have to . . . what?"

My mentor's face split in one of his expansive grins.

"In this case, the reality that I'm facing is that whether you need me or not, I've had more fun since I took you on as an apprentice than I've had in centuries. I'm not sure exactly what's going to happen to you next, but I wouldn't miss it for all the gold on Deva."

"That's great!"

". . . Of course, there's still a lot I can teach you, just like there's a lot I have to learn from you."

"From me?" I blinked.

"Uh huh. I've been learning from you for some time now, kid. I was just never up to admitting it before. You've got a way of dealing with people that gets you respect, even from the ones who don't like you. I haven't always been able to get that. Lots of folks are afraid of me, but not that many respect me. That's why I've been studying your methods, and have every intention of continuing."

"That's . . . umm . . . interesting, Aahz. But how come you're telling me this now?"

"Because if I stay around, it'll be on one condition: that you wake up and accept the fact that you're a full partner in our relationship. No more of this 'apprentice' crud. It's getting too rough on my nerves."

"Gee, Aahz . . . I . . ."

"Deal?"

"Deal."

We shook hands solemnly, and I remembered he had refused this simple act when he first accepted me as an apprentice. A full partner. Wow!

"Now what's the other thing?"

"Hmm, excuse me?"

"If I recall correctly, you said there were a couple of things bothering you. What's the other?"

"Well . . . it's this house."

"What about the house?" Aahz exploded, slipping easily back into his old patterns. "It's got enough room for us *and* our friends *and* your bodyguards when they show up *and* Buttercup and Gleep and anyone else who wanders by."

"That's true."

"What's more, we got it for free. It's a good deal."

"Say that again, Aahz."

"I said, 'it's a good . . . 'Oh."

"From the Deveels, right?"

"Oh come on, Skeeve. It's just a house. What could be wrong?"

"To use your phrase, 'The mind boggles.' I've been trying to spot the catch, and I want you to check me to see if my facts and logic are correct."

"Okay."

"Now. Deveels are experts at dimension travel. If I understand it right, they manage these 'bigger inside than outside' houses by offsetting the dimensions just a bit. That is, if we numbered the dimensions, and Deva was one, then our door is in dimension one and the rest of our house is in dimension one point four or something."

"Now *that's* one I hadn't thought about before," Aahz admitted. "The Deveels have been pretty tight-lipped about it. Makes sense, though. It would be rough to play the poverty-stricken shopowner with a place like this just over your shoulder. If I had thought about it I would have realized a Deveel needs someplace secret to keep his wealth.''

"So we've effectively been given our own dimension," I continued; "An unlisted dimension that's all ours. For free, no less.''

"That's right," Aahz nodded, but there was a note of doubt in his voice now.

"What I wonder about is how many of these offset dimensions do the Deveels have access to, and why is this particular one standing vacant? What's in this dimension?''

"Our house?" my mentor suggested tentatively.

"And what else?" I urged. "I've noticed there are no windows. What's outside our back door that the Deveels were so eager to give away?''

"Back door?"

I pulled away the tapestry to reveal the door I had spotted during our first tour. It was heavy wood with strange symbols painted on it. It also had a massive beam guarding it, and several smaller but no less effective-looking locks around the edge.

"I tried to say something at the time, but you kept telling me to shut up.''

"I did, didn't I."

We both stared at the door in silence for several minutes.

"Tell you what," Aahz said softly. "Let's save investigating this for another day.''

"Right," I agreed, without hesitation.

"... And until we do, let's not mention this to the others.''

"My thoughts precisely."

". . . And, partner?"

"Yes, Aahz?"

"If anyone knocks at this door, don't answer unless I'm with you."

Our eyes met, and I let the tapestry fall back into place.

MYTH-ING PERSONS

Chapter One:

"Reputations are fine up to a point. After
that they become a pain!"

—D.JUAN

THERE is something sinfully satisfying about doing
something you know you aren't supposed to. This was
roughly my frame of mind as I approached a specific
nondescript tent at the Bazaar at Deva with my breakfast under my arm . . . guilty, but smug.

"Excuse me, young sahr!"

I turned to find an elderly Deveel waving desperately
at me as he hurried forward. Normally I would have
avoided the encounter, as Deveels are always selling
something and at the moment I wasn't buying, but since
I wasn't in a hurry I decided to hear what he had to say.

"I'm glad I caught you in time," he said, struggling
to catch his breath. "While I don't usually meddle, you
really don't want to go in there!"

"Why not? I was just. . . ."

"Do you know who lives there?"

"Well, actually I thought. . . ."

"That is the dwelling of the Great Skeeve!"

1

Something about this busybody irritated me. Maybe it was the way he never let me finish a sentence. Anyway, I decided to string him along for a while."

"The Great Skeeve?"

"You never heard of him?" The Deveel seemed genuinely shocked. "He's probably the most powerful magician at the Bazaar."

My opinion of the busybody soared to new heights, but the game was too much fun to abandon.

"I've never had too much faith in magicians," I said with studied casualness. "I've found for the most part their powers are overrated."

The oldster rolled his eyes in exasperation.

"That may be true in most cases, but not when it comes to the Great Skeeve! Did you know he consorts with Demons and has a dragon for a familiar?"

I favored him with a worldly smile.

"So what? Deva is a crossroads of the dimensions. Dimension travelers, or Demons as you call them, are the norm around here. As a Deveel, your main livelihood comes from dealing with Demons. As for the dragon, there's a booth not eight rows from here that sells dragons to anyone with the price."

"No, no! You don't understand! Of course we all deal with Demons when it comes to business. The difference is that this Skeeve is actually *friends* with them . . . invites them into his home and lives with them. One of his permanent house guests is a Pervert, and I don't know of a single Deveel who would stoop that low. What's more, I've heard it said that he has underworld connections."

The game was growing tiresome. Any points the Deveel had made with his tribute to the Great Skeeve had been lost with interest when he started commenting on Demons.

"Well, thank you for your concern," I said, holding out my hand for a handshake. "I promise you I'll remember everything you've said. What was your name again?"

The Deveel grabbed my hand and began pumping it vigorously.

"I am Aliman, and glad to be of assistance," he said with an ingratiating smile. "If you really want to show your gratitude, remember my name. Should you ever be in need of a *reputable* magician, I have a nephew who's just getting started in the business. I'm sure we could arrange some discount prices for you. Tell me, what is *your* name so I can tell him who to watch for?"

I tightened my grip slightly and gave him my widest smile. "Well, my friends call me Skeeve."

"I'll be sure to tell . . . SKEEVE?"

The Deveel's eyes widened, and his complexion faded from red to a delicate pink.

"That's right," I said, retaining my grip on his hand. "Oh, and for your information Demons from Perv are called Pervects, not Perverts . . . and he's not my house guest, he's my partner."

The Deveel was struggling desperately now, trying to free his hand.

"Now then, how many customers have you scared away from my business with your tales about what a fearsome person I am?"

The Deveel tore loose from my grip and vanished into the crowds, sounding an incoherent scream of terror as he went. In short, Aliman left. Right?

I watched him go with a certain amount of mischievous satisfaction. I wasn't really angry, mind you. We literally had more money than we could use right now, so I didn't begrudge him the customers. Still, I had never really paused to consider how formidable our operation must look from the outside. Viewing it now through a stranger's eyes, I found myself more than a little pleased. Considering the dubious nature of my beginning, we had built ourselves quite a reputation over the last few years.

I had been serious when I told Aliman that I didn't have much faith in magicians. My own reputation was overrated to say the least, and if I was being billed as a powerful magician, it made the others of my profession more than a little suspect in my eyes. After several years of seeing the inside of the magic business, I was starting to wonder if *any* magician was really as good as people thought.

I was so wrapped up in these thoughts as I entered our humble tent that I had completely forgotten that I was suppoised to be sneaking in. I was reminded almost immediately.

The reminder came in the form of a huge man who loomed up to block my path. "Boss," he said in a squeaky little voice that was always surprising coming from such a huge body, "you shouldn't ought to go out alone like that. How many times we got to tell you. . . ."

"It's all right, Nunzio," I said, trying to edge around him. "I just ducked out to get some breakfast. Want a bagel?"

Nunzio was botn unconvinced and undaunted in his scolding.

"How are we supposed to be your bodyguards if you keep sneaking off alone every chance you get? Do you know what Don Bruce would do to us if anything happened to you?"

"C'mon, Nunzio. You know how things are here at the Bazaar. If the Deveels see me with a bodyguard, the price of everything goes through the ceiling. Besides, I like being able to wander around on my own once in a while.''

"You can afford the higher prices. What you can't afford is to set yourself up as a target for every bozo who wants the rep of bagging the Great Skeeve.''

I started to argue, but my conversation with Aliman flashed across my mind. Nunzio was right. There were two sides to having a reputation. If anyone believed the rumors at the Bazaar and still meant me harm, they would muster such firepower for the attempt that my odds for survival would be nonexistent.

"Nunzio,'' I said slowly, "you may be right, but in all honesty what could you and Guido do to stop a magical attack on me?''

"Not a thing," he said calmly. "But they'd probably try to knock off your bodyguards first, and that might give you time to get away or hit them yourself before they could muster a second attack."

He said it easily, like you or I might say "The sun rises in the east," but it shook me. It had never really occurred to me how expendable bodyguards are, or how readily they accept the dangers of their profession.

"I'll try to remember that in the future," I said with a certain degree of grave humility. "What's more, I think I owe you and Guido an apology. Where is Guido, anyway?''

"Upstairs arguing with His Nibbs," Nunzio grinned. "As a matter of fact, I was looking for you to break it up when I found you had snuck out again."

"Why didn't you say so in the first place?"

"What for? There's no rush. They'll be arguing until you get there. I figured it was more important to convince you to quit going out alone."

I groaned a little inside, but I had learned long ago the

futility of arguing priorities with Nunzio.

"Well, thanks again for the advice, but I'd better get upstairs before those two kill each other."

With that I headed across the courtyard for the fountain stairs to our offices. . . .

Courtyard? Fountain stairs?

What happened to the humble tent I was walking into a minute ago?

Weelll . . . I said I was a magician, didn't I? Our little stall at the Bazaar is bigger on the inside than it is on the outside. Lots bigger. I've lived in royal palaces that weren't as big as our "humble tent." I can't take any credit for this particular miracle, though, other than the fact that it was my work that helped earn us our current residence. We live here rent-free courtesy of the Devan Merchants Association as partial payment for a little job we did for them a while back. That's also how I got my bodyguards . . . but that's another story.

Devan Merchants Association, you ask? Okay. For the uninitiated, I'll go over this just once. The dimension I'm currently residing in is Deva, home of the shrewdest deal-drivers in all the known dimensions. You may have heard of them. In my own home dimension they were called devils, but I have since learned the proper pronunciation is Deveels. Anyway, my gracious living quarters are the result of my partner and I beating the Deveels at their own game . . . which is to say we got the better of them in a deal. Don't tell anyone, though. It would ruin their reputation and maybe even cost me a cushy spot. You see, they still don't know they've been had.

Anyway, where was I? Oh, yes. Heading for the offices. Normally after sneaking out I would stop by the stables to share breakfast with Gleep, but with a crisis on my hands I decided to forgo the pleasure of my pet's company and get to work. Gleep. He's the dragon Aliman was talking about . . . and I'm *not* going to try to condense *that* story. It's just too complicated.

Long before I reached the offices I could hear their voices raised in their favorite "song." The lyrics changed from time to time, but I knew the melody by heart.

"Incompetent bungler!"

"Who are you calling an incomplete bungler?"

"I stand corrected. You are a *complete* bungler!"

"You better watch your mouth! Even if you are the boss's partner, one more word and I'll. . . ."

"You'll what? If you threw a punch the safest place to be would be where you're aiming."

"Izzat so?"

It sounded like I had arrived in the nick of time. Taking a deep breath, I casually strolled into the teeth of the fracas.

"Hi, guys." I pretended to be totally unaware of what was going on. "Anyone want a bagel?"

"No, I don't want a bagel!" came the sneering response from one combatant. "What I want is some decent help."

". . . and while you're at it see what you can do about getting me a little respect!" the other countered.

The latter comment came from Guido, senior of my two bodyguards. If anything, he's bigger and nastier than his cousin Nunzio.

The former contribution came from Aahz. Aahz is my partner. He's also a demon, a Pervect to be exact, and even though he's slightly shorter than I am, he's easily twice as nasty as my two bodyguards put together.

My strategy had worked in that I now had their annoyance focused on me instead of each other. Now, realizing the potential devastation of their respective temperaments individually, much less collectively, I had cause to doubt the wisdom of my strategy.

"What seems to be the trouble?"

"The trouble," Aahz snarled, "is that your ace bodyguard here just lost us a couple of clients."

My heart sank. I mentioned earlier that Aahz and I have more money than we know what to do with, but old habits die hard. Aahz is the tightest being I've ever met when it comes to money, and, living at the Bazaar at Deva, that's saying something! If Guido had really lost a potential customer, we'd be hearing about it for a long time.

"Ease up a minute, partner," I said more to stall for time than anything else. "I just got here, remember? Could you fill me in on a few of the details?"

Aahz favored Guido with one more dark stare.

"There's not all that much to tell," he said. "I was in the middle of breakfast . . ."

"He was drinking another meal," Guido translated scornfully.

". . . when mush-for-brains here bellows up that there are some customers waiting downstairs in reception. I called back that I'd be down in a few, then finished my meal."

"He kept them waiting at least half an hour. You can't expect customers to. . . ."

"Guido, could you hold the editorial asides for one round? Please?" I interceded before Aahz could go for him. "I'm still trying to get a rough idea of what happened, remember? Okay, Aahz. You were saying?"

Aahz took a deep breath, then resumed his account.

"Anyway, when I got downstairs, the customers were nowhere to be seen. You'd think your man here would be able to stall them or at least have the sense to call for reinforcements if they started getting twitchy."

"C'mon, Aahz. Guido is supposed to be a body-guard, not a receptionist. If some customers got tired of waiting for you to show up and left, I don't see where you can dodge the blame by shifting it to. . . ."

"Wait a minute, Boss. You're missing the point. They didn't leave!"

"Come again?"

"I left 'em there in the reception room, and the next thing I know Mr. Mouth here is hollerin' at me for losing customers. They never came out! Now, like you say, I'm supposed to be a bodyguard. By my figuring we've got some extra people wandering the premises, and all this slob wants to do is yell about whose fault it is."

"I know whose fault it is," Aahz said with a glare. "There are only two ways out of that reception room, and they didn't come past me!"

"Well they didn't come past *me*!" Guido countered.

I started to get a very cold feeling in my stomach.

"Aahz," I said softly.

"If you think I don't know when. . . ."

"AAHZ!"

That brought him up short. He turned to me with an angry retort on his lips, then he saw my expression.

"What is it, Skeeve? You look as if. . . ."

"There are more than two ways out of that room."

We stared at each other in stunned silence for a few moments, then we both sprinted for the reception room, leaving Guido to trail along behind.

The room we had selected for our reception area was one of the largest in the place, and the only large room with easy access from the front door. It was furnished in a style lavish enough to impress even those customers spoiled by the wonders of the Bazaar who were expecting to see the home office of a successful magician. There was only one problem with it, and that was the focus of our attention as we dashed in.

The only decoration that we had kept from the previous owners was an ornate tapestry hanging on the north wall. Usually I'm faster than Aahz, but this time he beat me to the hanging, sweeping it aside with his arm to reveal a heavy door behind it.

Our worst fears were realized.

The door was unlocked and standing ajar.

Chapter Two:

"Success often hinges on choosing a reliable partner."

—REMUS

"WHAT'S that?" Guido demanded, taking advantage of our stunned silence.

"It's a door," I said.

"An open door, to be specific," Aahz supplied.

"I can see that for myself!" the bodyguard roared. "I meant what is it doing here?"

"It would look pretty silly standing alone in the middle of the street now, wouldn't it?" Aahz shot back.

Guido purpled. As I've said, these two have a positive talent for getting under each other's skins.

"Now look, all I'm askin'. . . ."

"Guido, could you just hang on for a few minutes until we decide what to do next? Then we'll explain, I promise."

My mind was racing over the problem, and having Aahz and Guido going at each other did nothing for my concentration.

"I think the first thing we should do, partner," Aahz

11

said thoughtfully, "is to get the door closed so that we won't be . . . interrupted while we work this out."

Rather than answer, I reached out a cautious toe and pushed the door shut. Aahz quickly slipped two of the bolts in place to secure it.

That done, we leaned against the door and looked at each other in silence.

"Well? What do you think?" I asked at last.

"I'm in favor of sealing it up again and forgetting the whole thing."

"Think it's safe to do that?"

"Don't know, really. Not enough information."

We both turned slowly to level thoughtful stares at Guido.

"Say, uh, Guido, could you tell us a little more about those customers who came in this morning?"

"Nothing doin'." Guido crossed his arms. "You're the guys who insist on 'information for information.' Right? Well, I'm not telling you anything more until somebody tells me about that door. I mean, I'm supposed to be your bodyguard and nobody bothers to tell me there's another way into this place?"

Aahz bared his teeth and started forward, but I caught him by the shoulder.

"He's right, partner. If we want his help, we owe him an explanation."

We locked eyes again for a moment, then he shrugged and retreated.

"Actually, Guido, the explanation is very simple. . . ."

"That'll be a first," the bodyguard grumbled.

In a bound, Aahz was across the room and had Guido by the shirt front.

"You wanted an explanation? Then SHUT UP AND LET HIM EXPLAIN!"

Now Guido is no lightweight, and he's never been short in the courage department. Still, there's nothing quite like Aahz when he's really mad.

"O—Okay! Sorry! Go ahead, Boss. I'm listening."

Aahz released his grip and returned to his place by the door, winking at me covertly as he went.

"What happened is this," I said, hiding a smile. "Aahz and I found that door when we first moved in here. We didn't like the looks of it, so we decided to leave it alone. That's all."

"That's all!? A back door that even you admit looks dangerous and all you do is ignore it? And if that wasn't bad enough, you don't even bother to tell your bodyguards about it? Of all the lamebrained, half...."

Aahz cleared his throat noisily, and Guido regained control of himself . . . rapidly.

"Aahh . . . what I mean to say is . . . oh well. That's all behind us now. Could you give *me* a little more information now that the subject's out in the open? What's on the other side of that door, anyway?"

"We don't know," I admitted.

"YOU DON'T KNOW?" Guido shrieked.

"What we *do* know," Aahz interrupted hastily, "is what *isn't* on the other side. What isn't there is any dimension we know about."

Guido blinked, then shook his head. "I don't get it. Could you run that past me again . . . real slow?"

"Let me try," I said. "Look, Guido, you already know about dimensions, right? How we're living in the dimension Deva, which is an entirely different world than our own home dimension of Klah? Well, the people here, the Deveels, are masters of dimension travel to a point where they build their houses across the dimension barriers. That's how come this place is bigger on the inside than it is on the outside. The door is in

Deva, but the rest of the house is in another dimension. That means if we go through that door, the back door that we've just shown you, we'd be in another world . . . one we know nothing about. That's why we were willing to leave it sealed up rather than stick our noses out into a completely unknown situation.''

"I still think you should have checked it out," the bodyguard insisted stubbornly.

"Think again," Aahz supplied. "You've only seen two dimensions. Skeeve here has visited a dozen. I've been to over a hundred myself. The Deveels you see here at the Bazaar, on the other hand, know over a thousand different dimensions.''

"So?"

"So we think they gave us this place because it opens into a dimension that *they* don't want . . . 'don't want' as in 'scared to death of'. Now, you've seen what a Deveel will brave to turn a profit. Do *you* want to go exploring in a world that's too mean for *them* to face?"

"I see what you mean."

"Besides," Aahz finished triumphantly, "take another look at that door. It's got more locks and bolts than three ordinary bank vaults.''

"*Somebody* opened it," Guido said pointedly.

That took some of the wind out of Aahz's sails. Despite himself, he shot a nervous glance at the door.

"Well . . . a good thief with a lockpick working from this side. . . .''

"Some of these locks weren't picked, Aahz.''

I had been taking advantage of their discussion to do a little snooping, and now held up one of my discoveries for their inspection. It was a padlock with the metal shackle snapped off. There were several of them scattered about, as if someone had gotten impatient with the lockpick and simply torn the rest of them apart with his hands.

Guido pursed his lips in a silent whistle. "Man, that's strong. What kind of person could do that?"

"That's what we've been trying to get you to tell us," Aahz said nastily. "Now, if you don't mind, what were those customers like?"

"Three of them . . . two men and a woman . . . fairly young-looking, but nothing special. Klahds by the look of 'em. Come to think of it, they did seem a bit nervous, but I thought it was just because they were coming to see a magician."

"Well, now they're on the other side of the door." Aahz scooped up one of the undamaged locks and snapped it into place. "I don't think they can pick locks, or break them if they can't reach 'em. They're there, which is their problem, self-inflicted I might add, and we're here. End of puzzle. End of problem."

"Do you really think so, Aahz?"

"Trust me."

Somehow that phrase struck a familiar chord in my memory, and the echoes weren't pleasant. I was about to raise this point with Aahz when Nunzio poked his head in the door.

"Hey, Boss. You got visitors."

"See?" my partner exclaimed, beaming. "I told you things could only get better! It's not even noon and we've got more customers."

"Actually," Nunzio clarified, "it's a delegation of Deveels. I think it's the landlord."

"The landlord?" Aahz echoed hollowly.

"See how much better things have gotten?" I said with a disgusted smirk. "And it's not even noon."

"Shall I run 'em off, Boss?" Guido suggested.

"I think you'd better see 'em," Nunzio advised.
"They seem kind'a upset. Something about us harboring fugitives."

Aahz and I locked gazes in silence, which was only
natural as there was nothing more to be said. With a
vague wave that bordered on a nervous tick, I motioned
for Nunzio to show the visitors in.

As expected, it was the same delegation of four from
the Devan Chamber of Commerce who had originally
hired us to work for the Bazaar, headed by our old adversary, Hay-ner. Last time we dealt with him, we had
him over a barrel and used the advantage mercilessly.
While he had agreed to our terms, I always suspected it
had hurt his Devan pride to cut such a generous deal and
that he had been waiting ever since to pay us back. From
the smile on his face as he entered our reception room, it
appeared he felt his chance had finally come.

"Aahh, Master Skeeve," he said. "How good of you
to see us so promptly without an appointment. I know
how busy you are, so I'll come right to the point. I
believe there are certain individuals in residence here
that our organization is *most* anxious to speak with. If
you would be so kind as to summon them, we won't
trouble you further."

"Wait a minute, Hay-ner," Aahz put in before I
could respond. "What makes you think the people
you're looking for are here?"

"Because they were seen entering your tent less than
an hour ago and haven't come out yet," said the largest
of Hay-ner's back-up team.

I noticed that unlike Hay-ner, he wasn't smiling. In
fact, he looked down-right angry.

"He must mean the ones who came in earlier," Nunzio suggested helpfully. "You know, Boss, the two guys
with the broad."

Aahz rolled his eyes in helpless frustration, and for once I was inclined to agree with him.

"Umm, Nunzio," I said, staring at the ceiling, "why don't you and Guido wait outside while we take care of this?"

The two bodyguards trooped outside in silence, though I noticed that Guido glared at his cousin with such disdain that I suspected a stern dressing-down would take place even before I could get to him myself. The Mob is no more tolerant than magicians of staff members who say more than they should in front of the opposition.

"Now that we've established that we all know who we're talking about and that they're here," Hay-ner said, rubbing his hands together, "call them out and we'll finish this once and for all."

"Not so fast," I interrupted. "First of all, neither of us have laid eyes on those folks you're looking for, because, second of all, they aren't here. They took it on the lam out the back door before we could meet them."

"Somehow, I don't expect you to take our word for it," Aahz added. "So feel free to search the place."

The Deveel's smile broadened, and I was conscious of cold sweat breaking out on my brow.

"That won't be necessary. You see, whether I believe you or not is of little consequence. Even if we searched, I'm sure you would be better at hiding things than we would be at finding them. All that really matters is that we've established that they did come in here, and that makes them *your* responsibility."

I wasn't sure exactly what was going on here, but I *was* sure that I was liking it less and less with each passing moment.

"Wait a minute, Hay-ner," I began. "What do you mean 'We're responsible'? Responsible for what?"

"Why, for the fugitives, of course. Don't you remember? When we agreed to let you use this place rent-free, part of the deal was that if anyone of this household broke any of the Bazaar rules, and either disappeared off to another dimension or otherwise refused to face the charges, that you would personally take responsibility for their actions. It's a standard clause in any Bazaar lease."

"Aahz," I said testily, "you cut the deal. Was there a clause like that in it?"

"There was," he admitted. "But I was thinking of Tananda and Chumley at the time . . . and we'll stand behind them anytime. Massha, too. It never occurred to me that they'd try to claim that anyone who walked through our door was a member of our household. I don't see how they can hope to prove. . . ."

"We don't have to prove that they're in your household," Hay-ner smiled. "You have to prove they aren't."

"That's crazy," Aahz exploded. "How can we prove. . . ."

"Can it, Aahz. We can't prove it. That's the point. All right, Hay-ner. You've got us. Now what exactly have these characters done that we're responsible for and what are our options? I thought one of the big sales points of the Bazaar was that there weren't any rules here."

"There aren't many," the Deveel said, "but the few that do exist are strictly enforced. The specific rule your friends broke involves fraud."

He quickly held up a hand to suppress my retort.

"I know what you're going to say. Fraud sounds like a silly charge with all the hard bargaining that goes on here at the Bazaar, but to us it's a serious matter. While we pride ourselves in driving a hard bargain, once the deal is made you get the goods you were promised. Sometimes there are specific details omitted in describing the goods, but anything actually *said* is true. That is our reputation and the continued success of the Bazaar depends on that reputation being scrupulously maintained. If a trader or merchant sells something claiming it to be magical and it turns out to have no powers at all, that's fraud . . . and if the perpetrators are allowed to go unpunished, it could mean the end of the Bazaar as we know it."

"Actually," I said drily, "all I was going to do was protest you billing them as our friends, but I'll let it go. What you haven't mentioned is our options."

Hay-ner shrugged. "There are only three, really. You can pay back the money they took falsely plus a twenty-five percent fine, accept permanent banishment from the Bazaar, or you can try to convince your fr—aahh, I mean the fugitives to return to the Bazaar to settle matters themselves."

"I see . . . Very well. You've had your say. Now please leave so my partner and I can discuss our position on the matter."

Aahz took care of seeing them out while I plunged into thought as to what we should do. When he returned, we both sat in silence for the better part of an hour before either of us spoke.

"Well," I said at last, "what do you think?"

"Banishment from the Bazaar is out!" Aahz snarled. "Not only would it destroy our reputations, I'm not about to get run out of the Bazaar *and* our home over something as idiotic as this!"

"Agreed," I said grimly. "Even though it occurs to me that Hay-ner is bluffing on that option. He wants us to stick around the Bazaar as much as we want to stay. He was the one who hired us in the first place, remem-

ber? I think he's expecting us to ante up and pay the
money. That way he gets back some of the squeeze he so
grudgingly parted with. Somehow the idea of giving in
to that kind of pressure really galls me."

Aahz nodded. "Me too."

There followed several more minutes of silence.

"Okay," Aahz said finally, "who's going to say it?"

"We're going to have to go after them." I sighed.

"Half right," Aahz corrected. "*I'm* going to have to
go after them. Partner or not, we're talking about hitting a totally new dimension here, and it's too dangerous for someone at your level of magical skill."

"*My* level? How about you? You don't have any
powers at all. If it's too dangerous for me, what's supposed to keep you safe?"

"Experience," he said loftily. "I'm used to doing
this, and you aren't. End of argument."

" 'End of argument' nothing! Just how do you propose to leave me behind if I don't agree?"

"That's easy," Aahz grinned. "See who's standing in
the corner?"

I turned to look where he was pointing, and that's the
last thing I remembered for a long time.

Chapter Three:

"Reliable information is a must for successful planning."

—C. COLUMBUS

"HEY! Hot stuff! Wake up!! You okay?"

If I led a different kind of life, those words would have been uttered by a voluptuous vision of female loveliness. As it was, they were exclaimed by Massha.

This was one of the first things that penetrated the fogginess of my mind as I struggled to regain consciousness. I'm never at my best first thing in the morning, even when I wake up leisurely of my own accord. Having wakefulness forced upon me by someone else only *guarantees* that my mood will be less than pleasant.

However groggy I might be feeling, though, there was no mistaking the fact that it was Massha shaking me awake. Even through unfocused eyes, her form was unmistakable. Imagine, if you will, the largest, fattest woman you've ever met. Now expand that image by fifty percent in all directions, top it off with garish orange hair, and false eyelashes and purple lipstick, and adorn it with a wheelbarrow load of gaudy jewelry. See what I mean? I could recognize Massha a mile away on a dark night . . . blindfolded.

"Of course I'm okay, *apprentice*!" I snarled. "Don't you have any lessons you're supposed to be practicing or something?"

"Are you *sure*?" she pressed mercilessly.

"Yes, I'm sure. Why do you ask? Can't a fellow take a little nap without being badgered about it?"

"It's just that you don't usually take naps in the middle of the reception room floor."

That got my attention, and I forced my eyes into focus. She was right! For some reason I was sprawled out on the floor. Now what could have possessed me to. . . .

Then it all came back! Aahz! The expedition into the new dimension!

I sat bolt upright . . . and regretted it immediately. A blinding headache assaulted me with icepick intensity, and my stomach flipped over and landed on its back with all the grace of a lump of overcooked oatmeal.

Massha caught me by the shoulder as I started to list.

"Steady there, High Roller. Looks like your idea of 'okay' and mine are a little out of synch."

Ignoring her, I felt the back of my head cautiously and discovered a large, tender lump behind my ear. If I had had any doubts as to what had happened, they were gone now.

"That bloody Pervert!" I said, flinching at the new wave of pain brought on by the sound of my own voice. "He must have knocked me out and gone in alone!"

"You mean Aahz? Dark, green, and scaly himself? I don't get it. Why would your own partner sucker-punch you?"

"So he could go through the door without me. I made

it very clear that I didn't want to be left behind on this caper."

"Door? What door?" Massha said with a frown. "I know you two have your secrets, Boss, but I think you'd better fill me in on a few more details as to exactly what's going on around here."

As briefly as I could, I brought her up to date on the day's events, including the explanation as to why Aahz and I had never said anything about the house's mysterious back door. Being a seasoned dimension traveler herself, she grasped the concept of an unlisted dimension and its potential dangers much more rapidly than Guido and Nunzio.

"What I don't understand is even if he didn't want you along, why didn't he take *someone* else as a back-up?"

"Like who?" I said with a wry grimace. "We've already established that you're *my* apprentice and he doesn't give you orders without clearing them through me. He's never been impressed with Guido and Nunzio. Tananda and Chumley are off on their own contracts and aren't due back for several days. Even Gus is taking a well-earned vacation with Berfert. Besides, he knows good and well that if he started building a team and excluded me, there'd be some serious problems before the dust settled. I wouldn't take something like that lying down!"

"Don't look now, but you just did," my apprentice pointed out dryly, "though I have to admit he sort of forced it on you."

With that, she slid a hand under each of my armpits and picked me up, setting me gently on my feet.

"Well, now what? I supposed you're going to go charging after him with blood in your eye. Mind if I tag along? Or are you bound and determined to be as stupid as he is?''

As a matter of fact, that was exactly what I had been planning to do. The undisguised sarcasm in her voice combined with the unsettling wobbliness of my legs, however, led me to reconsider.

"No," I said carefully. "One of us blundering around out there is enough . . . or one too many, depending on how you count it. While I still think I should have gone along, Aahz has dealt this hand, so it's up to him to play it out. It's up to me to mind the store until he gets back."

Massha cocked an eyebrow at me.

"That makes sense," she said, "though I'll admit I'm a little surprised to hear you say it."

"I'm a responsible businessman now." I shrugged. "I can't afford to go off half-cocked like a rash kid anymore. Besides, I have every confidence in my partner's ability to handle things."

Those were brave words, and I meant them. Two days later, however, this particular 'responsible businessman' was ready to go off *fully* cocked. Guido and Nunzio ceased to complain about my sneaking off alone . . . mostly because I didn't go out at all! In fact, I spent most of my waking hours and all of my sleeping hours (though I'll admit I didn't sleep much) in the reception room on the off-chance that I could greet Aahz on his triumphant return.

Unfortunately, my vigil went unrewarded.

I did my best to hide my concern, but I needn't have bothered. As the hours marched on, my staff's worries grew until most of my time was spent telling them, "No, he isn't back yet. When he gets here, I'll let you know." Even Guido, who never really got along with Aahz, took to stopping by at least once an hour for a no-progress report.

Finally, as a salve for my own nerves, I called everyone into the reception room for a staff meeting.

"What I want to know is how long are we just going to sit around before we admit that something's gone wrong?" Guido muttered for the fifth time.

"How long do you figure it takes to find a fugitive in a strange dimension?" I shot back. "How long would it take you to find them if they were on Klah, Guido? We've got to give him some time."

"How much time?" he countered. "It's already been two days. . . ."

"Tananda and Chumley will be back any time now," Massha interrupted. "Do you think they'll just sit around on their hands when they find out that Aahz is out there all alone?"

"I thought *you* were the one who thought that going after him was a stupid idea?"

"I still do. Now do you want to know what I think of the idea of doing *nothing*?"

Before I could answer, a soft knock sounded at the door . . . the back door!

"See!" I crowed triumphantly. "I told you he would be back!"

"That doesn't sound like his knock," Guido observed suspiciously.

"And why should he knock?" Massha added. "The door hasn't been locked since he left."

In my own relief and enthusiasm, their remarks went unnoticed. In a flash I was at the door, wrenching it open while voicing the greeting I had been rehearsing for two days.

"It's about time, part . . . ner."

It wasn't Aahz.

In fact, the being outside the door didn't look anything at all like Aahz. What was doubly surprising, though, was that I recognized her!

We had never really met . . . not to exchange names, but shortly after meeting Aahz I had been strung up by an angry mob while impersonating her, and I had seen her in the crowd when I successfully "interviewed" for the job of court magician at Possletum.

What I had never had a chance to observe first-hand was her radiant complexion framed by waves of sungold hair, or the easy grace with which she carried herself, or the . . . .

"It's the Great Skeeve, right? Behind the open mouth?"

Her voice was so musical it took me a few moments to zero in on what she had said and realize that she was expecting an answer.

"Aahh . . . yes. I mean, at your service."

"Glad to finally meet you face-to-face," she said briskly, glancing at Guido and Massha nervously. "I've been looking for an excuse for a while, and I guess this is it. Got some news for you . . . about your apprentice."

I was still having problems focusing on what she was saying. Not only was her voice mesmerizing, she was easily the loveliest woman I had ever met . . . well, girl actually. She couldn't have been much older than me. What's more, she seemed to like me. That is, she kept smiling hesitantly and her deep blue eyes never left mine. Now, I had gotten respect from my colleagues and from beings at the Bazaar who knew my reputation, but never from anyone who looked like . . . .

Then her words sank in.

"My apprentice?"

I stole an involuntary glance at Massha before I realized the misunderstanding.

"Oh, you mean Aahz. He's not my apprentice any more. He's my partner. Please come in. We were just talking about him."

I stood to one side of the door and invited her in with a grand sweeping gesture. I'd never tried it before, but I had seen it used a couple of times while I was working the court at Possletum, and it had impressed me.

"Umm—Boss? Could I talk to you for a minute?"

"Later, Guido."

I repeated the gesture, and the girl responded with a quick smile that lit up the room.

"Thanks for the invite," she said, "but I'll have to take a rain check. I really can't stay. In fact, I shouldn't be here at all. I just thought that someone should let you know that your friend . . . Aahz is it? Anyway, your friend is in jail."

That brought me back to earth in a hurry.

"Aahz? In jail? For what?"

"Murder."

"MURDER!" I shrieked, dropping all attempts to be urbane. "But Aahz wouldn't. . . ."

"Don't shout at me! Oh, I knew I shouldn't have come. Look, I know he didn't do it. That's why I had to let you know what was going on. If you don't do something, they're going to execute him . . . and they know how to execute demons over here."

I spun around to face the others.

"Massha! Go get your jewelry case. Guido, Nunzio! Gear up. We're going to pay a little call on our neighbors."

I tried to keep my voice calm and level, but somehow the words came out a bit more intense than I had intended.

"Not so fast, Boss," Guido said. "There's something you oughta know first."

"Later. I want you to. . . ."

"NOW, Boss. It's important!"

"WHAT IS IT!"

Needless to say, I was not eager to enter into any prolonged conversations just now.

"She's one of 'em."

"I beg your pardon?"

"The three that went out through the back door. The ones your partner is chasing. She's the broad."

Thunderstruck, I turned to the girl for confirmation, only to find the doorway was empty. My mysterious visitor had disappeared as suddenly as she had arrived.

"This could be a trap, you know," Massha said thoughtfully.

"She's right." Guido nodded. "Take it from someone who's been on the lam himself. When you're running from the law and there are only a couple of people who can find you, it gets real tempting to eliminate that link. We've only got her word that your partner's in trouble."

"It wouldn't take a mental giant to figure out that you and Aahz are the most likely hunters for the Deveels to hire. After all, they knew whose house they were cutting through for their getaway," Massha added.

Guido rose to his feet and started pacing.

"Right," he said. "Now suppose *they've* got Aahz. Can you think of a better way to bag the other half of the pair than by feeding you a line about your partner being in trouble so you'll come charging into whatever trap they've laid out? The whole set-up stinks, Boss. I don't know about strange dimensions, but I *do* know about criminals. As soon as you step through that door, you're gonna be a sitting duck."

"Are you *quite* through?"

Even to my ears my voice sounded icy, but for a change I didn't care.

Guido and Massha exchanged glances, then nodded silently.

"Very well. You may be right, and I appreciate your concern for my well-being. HOWEVER . . ."

My voice sank to a deadly hiss.

". . . what if you're wrong? What if our fugitive *is* telling the truth? You've all been on my case about not doing anything to help Aahz. Do you really think I'm just going to sit here while my partner AND friend burns for a crime he didn't commit . . . on the off-chance that getting involved *might* be dangerous to me?"

With great effort I forced my tones back to normal.

"In ten minutes I'm going through that door after Aahz . . . and if I'm walking into a trap, it had better be a good one. Now do any of you want to come with me, or am I going it alone?"

Chapter Four:

> "It's useless to try to plan for the unexpected . . . by definition!"
>
> —A. HITCHCOCK

ACTUALLY, it was more like an hour before we were really ready to go, though for me it seemed like a lot longer. Still, even I had to admit that not taking the proper preparations for this venture would not only be foolish, it would be downright suicidal!

It was decided that Nunzio would stay behind so there would be someone at our base to let Tananda and Chumley know what was going on when they returned. Needless to say, he was less than thrilled by the assignment.

"But I'm supposed to be your bodyguard!" he argued. "How'm I supposed to guard you if I'm sittin' back here while you're on the front lines?"

"By being sure our support troops get the information they need to follow us," I said.

As much as I disliked having to argue with Nunzio, I would rather dig in my heels against half a dozen Mob-type bodyguards than have to explain to Tananda and

Chumley why they weren't included in this rescue mission.

"We could leave a note."

"No."

"We could. . . ."

"NO! I want you *here*. Is that plain enough?"

The bodyguard heaved a heavy sigh. "Okay, Boss. I'll hang in here until they show up. Then the three of us will. . . ."

"No!" I said again. "Then Tananda and Chumley will come in after us. You're going to stay here."

"But Boss. . . ."

"Because if Hay-ner and his crew show up again, someone has to be here to let them know we're on the job and that we haven't just taken off for the tall timber. Assuming for the moment that we're going to make it back, we need our exit route, and you're going to be here making sure it stays open. All we need is for our hosts to move in a new tenant while we're gone . . . say, someone who decides to brick up this door while we're on the other side."

Nunzio thought this through in silence.

"What if you don't come back?" he asked finally.

"We'll burn that bridge when we come to it," I sighed. "But remember, we aren't that easy to kill. At least one of us will probably make it back."

Fortunately, my mind was wrenched away from that unpleasant train of thought by the arrival of Guido.

"Ready to go, Boss."

Despite the desperateness of the situation and the haunting time pressures, I found myself gaping at him.

"What's that?" I managed at last.

Guido was decked out in a long dark coat and wearing a wide-brimmed hat and sunglasses.

"These? These are my work clothes," he said

proudly. "They're functional as well as decorative."

"They're what?"

"What I mean is, not only do people find 'em intimidating, the trench coat has all these little pockets inside, see? That's where I carry my hardware."

"But. . . ."

"Hi, Hot Stuff. Nice outfit, Guido."

"Thanks! I was just telling the Boss here about it."

Massha was dressed . . . or should I say undressed in *her* work clothes. A brief vest struggled to cover even part of her massive torso, while an even briefer bottom was on the verge of surrendering its battle completely.

"Ummm . . . Massha?" I said carefully. "I've always meant to ask. Why don't you . . . ummm . . . wear more?"

"I like to dress cool when we're going into a hot situation," she winked. "You see, when things speed up, I get a little nervous . . . and the only thing worse than havin' a fat broad around is havin' a *sweaty* fat broad around."

"I think it's a sexy outfit," Guido chimed in. "Reminds me of the stuff my old man's moll used to wear."

"Well thanks, Dark and Deadly. I'd say your old man had good taste . . . but I never tasted him."

I studied them thoughtfully as they shared a laugh over Massha's joke. Any hope of a quiet infiltration of this unknown dimension was rapidly disintegrating. Either Guido or Massha alone was eye-catching, but together they were about as inconspicuous as a circus parade and an army maneuver sharing the same road. Then it occurred to me that, not knowing what things were like where we were heading, they might fit in and *I* would stand out. It was a frightening thought. If everybody there looked like this. . . .

I forced the thought from my mind. No use scaring

myself any more than I had to before there was information to back it up. What was important was that
my two assistants were scared. They were trying hard
not to show it, but in doing so, each was dropping into
old patterns, slipping behind old character masks.
Guido was playing his "tough gangster" bit to the hilt,
while Massha was once more assuming her favorite
"vamp" character with a vengeance. The bottom line,
though, was that, scared or not, they were willing to
back my move or die trying. It would have been touching, if it weren't for the fact that it meant they were
counting on me for leadership. That meant I had to stay
calm and confident . . . no matter how scared I felt myself. It only occurred to me as an afterthought that, in
many ways, leadership was the mask *I* was learning to
slip behind when things got tight. It made me wonder
briefly if *anyone* ever really knew what they were doing
or felt truly confident, or if life was simply a mass game
of role-playing.

"Okay. Are we ready?" I asked, shrugging off my
wandering thoughts. "Massha? Got your jewelry?"

"Wearing most of it, and the rest is right here," she
said, patting the pouch on her belt.

While I will occasionally make snide mental comments about my apprentice's jewelry, it serves a dual
purpose. Massha's baubles are in reality a rather extensive collection of magical gimmicks she has accumulated
over the years. How extensive? Well, before she signed
on as my apprentice to learn real magic, she was holding
down a steady job as the magician for the city-state of
Ta-hoe on the dimension of Jahk solely on the strength
of her collected mechanical "powers." While I agreed
with Aahz that real magic was preferable to mechanical
in that it was less likely to malfunction (a lesson learned
from first-hand experience) I sure didn't mind having

her arsenal along for back-up.

"You know that tracking ring? The one you used to find the king? Any chance there's an extra tucked away in your pouch?"

"Only have the one," she said, waggling the appropriate finger.

I cursed mentally, then made the first of what I feared would be many unpleasant decisions on this venture.

"Give it to Nunzio. Tananda and Chumley will need it to find us."

"But if we leave it behind, how are we going to find your partner?"

"We'll have to figure out something, but we can't afford to divide our forces. Otherwise, even if we get Aahz, we could still end up wandering around out there trying to find the other half of the rescue team."

"If you say so, Hot Stuff," she grimaced, handing over the ring, "but I hope you know what you're doing."

"So do I, Massha, so do I. Okay, gang, let's see what our backyard is *really* like!"

From the outside, our place looked a lot more impressive than the side that showed in the Bazaar. It really did look like a castle . . . a rather ominous one at that, squatting alone on a hilltop. I really didn't study it too close, though, beyond being able to recognize it again for our trip out. As might be expected, my main attention was focused on the new dimension itself.

"Kinda dark, ain't it."

Guido's comment was more statement than question, and he was right.

Wherever we were, the lighting left a lot to be desired. At first I thought it was night, which puzzled me, as so far in my travels all dimensions seemed to be on the same sun-up and sun-down schedule. Then my eyes adjusted to the gloom and I realized the sky was simply heavily overcast . . . to a point where next to no light at all penetrated, giving a night-like illusion to the day.

Aside from that, from what I could see, this new land seemed pretty much like any of the others I had visited: Trees, underbrush, and a road leading to or from the castle, depending on which way you were facing. I think it was Tananda who was fond of saying "If you've seen one dimension, you've seen them all." Chumley, her brother, argued that the reason for the geologic similarities was that all the dimensions we traveled were different realities off the same base. This always struck me as being a bit redundant . . . "They're all alike because they're the same? C'mon Chumley!", but his rebuttals always left me feeling like I'd been listening to someone doing readings in another language, so of late I've been tending to avoid the discussions.

"Well, Hot Stuff, what do we do now?"

For a change, I had an answer for this infuriating question.

"This road has to go somewhere. Just the fact that it exists indicates we aren't alone in this dimension."

"I thought we already knew that," Guido said under his breath. "That's why we're here."

I gave him my best dark glare.

"I believe there was *some* debate as to whether or not we were being lied to about Aahz being held prisoner. If there's a road here, it's a cinch that neither my partner nor the ones he was chasing built it. That means we have native types to deal with . . . possibly hostile."

"Right," Massha put in quickly. "Put a sock in it, Guido. I want to hear our plan of action, and I don't like being kept waiting by hecklers."

The bodyguard frowned, but kept his silence.

"Okay. Now, what we've got to do is follow this road
and find out where it goes. Hug the side of the road and
be ready to disappear if you hear anybody coming. We
don't know what the locals look like, and until I have a
model to work from, it's pointless for me to try to disguise us."

With those general marching orders, we made our
way through the dark along the road, moving quietly to
avoid tipping our hand to anyone ahead of us. In a short
time we came up to our first decision point. The road we
were on ended abruptly when it met another, much
larger thoroughfare. My assistants looked at me
expectantly. With a shrug I made the arbitrary decision
and led them off to the right down this new course. As
we went, I reflected with some annoyance that even
though both Massha and Guido knew that I was as new
to this terrain as they were, it somehow fell to me to
choose the path.

My thoughts were interrupted by the sound of voices
ahead, coming our way. The others heard it too, and
without word or signal we melted into the underbrush.
Squatting down, I peered through the gloom toward the
road, anxious to catch my first glimpse of the native life
forms.

I didn't have long to wait. Two figures appeared, a
young couple by the look of them, talking and laughing
merrily as they went. They looked pretty normal to me,
which was a distinct relief, considering the forms I had
had to imitate in some of the other dimensions. They
were humanoid enough to pass for Klahds . . . or Jahks,
actually, as they were a bit pale. Their dress was not dis-
similar from my own, though a bit more colorful. Ab-
sorbing all this in a glance, I decided to make my first
try for information. I mean, after all my fears, they
were so familiar it was almost a letdown, so why not

bull ahead? Compared with some of the beings I've had to deal with in the past, this looked like a piece of cake.

Signaling the others to stay put, I stepped out onto the road behind my target couple.

"Excuse me!" I called "I'm new to this area and in need of a little assistance. Could you direct me to the nearest town?"

Translation pendants were standard equipment for dimension travel, and as I was wearing one now, I had no fear of not being understood.

The couple turned to face me, and I was immediately struck by their eyes. The "whites" of their eyes glowed a dark red, sending chills down my spine. It occurred to me that I might have studied the locals a bit longer before I tried to pass myself off as a native. It also occurred to me that I had already committed myself to this course of action and would have to bluff my way through it regardless. Finally, it occurred to me that I was a suicidal idiot and that I hoped Massha and Guido were readying their back-up weapons to save me from my own impatience.

Strangely enough, the couple didn't seem to notice anything unusual about my appearance.

"The nearest town? That would be Blut. It's not far, we just came from there. It's got a pretty wild night life, if you're into that kind of thing."

There was something about his mouth that nagged at the edges of my mind. Unfortunately, I couldn't look at it directly without breaking eye contact, so, buoyed by my apparent acceptance, I pushed ahead with the conversation.

"Actually, I'm not too big on night life. I'm trying to run down an old friend of mine I've lost touch with. Is there a post office or a police station in Blut I could ask at?"

"Better than that," the man laughed. "The one you want to talk to is the Dispatcher. He keeps tabs on everybody. The third warehouse on your left as you enter town. He's converted the whole second floor into an office. If he can't help you, nobody can."

As vital as the information was, I only paid it partial attention. When the man laughed, I had gotten a better look at his mouth. His teeth were. . . .

"Look at his teeth!" the girl gasped, speaking for the first time.

"My teeth?" I blinked, realizing with a start that she was staring at me with undisguised astonishment.

Her companion, in the meantime, had paled noticeably and was backing away on unsteady legs.

"You . . . you're . . . Where did you come from?"

Trying my best to maintain a normal manner until I had figured out what was going on, I moved forward to keep our earlier conversational distance.

"The castle on the hill back there. I was just. . . ."

"THE CASTLE!?!"

In a flash the couple turned and sprinted away from me down the road.

"Monster!! Help!! MONSTER!!!"

I actually spun and looked down the road behind me, trying to spot the object of their terror. Looking at the empty road, however, it slowly began to sink in. They were afraid of *me*! Monster?

Of all the reactions I had tried to anticipate for our reception in this new land, I had never in my wildest imaginings expected this.

Me? A monster?

"I think we've got problems, High Roller," Massha said as she and Guido emerged from the brush at my side.

"I'll say. Unless I'm reading the signs all wrong, they're afraid of me."

She heaved a great sigh and shook her head.

"That's not what I'm talking about. Did you see their teeth?"

"I saw his," I said. "The canines were long and pointed. Pretty weird, huh?"

"Not all that weird, Hot Stuff. Think about it. My bet is that you were just talking to a couple of vampires!"

Chapter Five:

"To survive, one must be able to adapt to changing situations."

—TYRANNOSAURUS REX

"VAMPIRES," I said carefully.

"Sure. It all fits." Massha nodded. "The pale skin, the sharp fangs, the red eyeliner, the way they turned into bats. . . ."

"Turned into bats?"

"You missed it, Boss," Guido supplied. "You were lookin' behind you when they did it. Wildest thing I ever saw. One second they was runnin' for their lives, and the next they're flutterin' up into the dark. Are all the other dimensions like this?"

"Vampires. . . ."

Actually, my shock wasn't all that great. Realizing the things Aahz and I had run into cruising the so-called "known and safe" dimensions, I had expected something a bit out of the ordinary in this one. If anything, I was a bit relieved. The second shoe had been dropped . . . and it really wasn't all that bad! That is, it could have been worse. (If hanging around with Aahz had

40

taught me anything, it was that things could always be worse!) The repetitive nature of my conversational brilliance was merely a clever ploy to cover my mental efforts to both digest this new bit of information and decide what to do with it.

"Vampires are rare in any dimension," my apprentice replied, stepping into the void to answer Guido's question. "What's more, they're pretty much feared universally. What I can't figure out is why those two were so scared of Skeeve here."

"Then again," I said thoughtfully, "there's the question of whether or not we can safely assume the whole dimension is populated with beings like the two we just met. I know it's a long shot, but we might have run into the only two vampires in the place."

"I dunno, High Roller. They acted pretty much at home here, and they sure didn't think you'd find anything unusual about *their* appearance. My guess is that they're the norm and we're the exceptions around here."

"Whatever," I said, reaching a decision at last, "they're the only two examples we have to work with so far, so that's what we'll base our actions on until proven different."

"So what do we do against a bunch of vampires?"

As a bodyguard, Guido seemed a bit uneasy about our assessment of the situation.

"Relax," I smiled. "The first order of business is to turn on the old reliable disguise spell. Just a few quick touch-ups and they won't be able to tell us apart from the natives. We could walk through a town of vampires and they'd never spot us."

With that, I closed my eyes and went to work. Like I told the staff, this was going to be easy. Maintain everyone's normal appearance except for paler skin, longer canines, and a little artful reddening of the eyes, and the job was done.

"Okay," I said, opening my eyes again. "What's next?"

"I don't like to quote you back at yourself, Hot Stuff," Massha drawled, "but didn't you say something about disguises being the first thing before we went any further?"

"Of course. That's why I just . . . wait a minute. Are you trying to say we still have the same appearance as before I cast the spell?"

One of the problems with casting a disguise spell is that as the caster, I can never see the effects. That is, I see people as they really are whether the spell is on or not. I had gotten so used to relying on the effects of this particular spell that it had never occurred to me that it might not work.

Massha and Guido were looking at each other with no small degree of concern.

"Ummm . . . maybe you forgot."

"Try again."

"That's right! This time remember to. . . ."

"Hold it, you two," I ordered in my most commanding tone. "From your reactions, I perceive that the answer to my questions is 'yes.' That is, that the spell didn't work. Now just ease up a second and let me think. Okay?"

For a change they listened to me and lapsed into a respectful silence. I might have taken a moment to savor the triumph if I wasn't so worried about the problem.

The disguise spell was one of the first spells I had learned, and until now was one of my best and most reliable tools. If it wasn't working, something was seriously wrong. Now I knew that stepping through the door hadn't lessened my knowledge of that particular spell, so that meant that if something was haywire, it would have to be in the. . . .

"Hey, Hot Stuff! Check the force lines!"

Apparently my apprentice and I had reached the conclusion simultaneously. A quick magical scan of the sky overhead and the surrounding terrain confirmed my worst fears. At first I thought there were no force lines at all. Then I realized that they were there, but so faint that it took nearly all of my reserve power just to detect them.

"What's all this about force lines?" Guido demanded.

Massha heaved an impatient sigh.

"If you're going to run with this crowd, Dark and Deadly, you'd best start learning a little about the magic biz . . . or at least the vocabulary. Force lines are invisible streams of energy that flow through the ground and the air. They're the source of power we tap into when we do our bibbity-bobbity-boo schtick. That means that in a land like this one, where the force lines are either non-existent or very weak. . . ."

". . . you can't do squat," the bodyguard finished for her. "Hey, Boss! If what she says is true, how come those two you just met could still do that bat-trick?"

"By being very, *very* good in the magic department. To do so much with so little means they don't miss a trick . . . pardon the pun . . . in tapping and using force lines. In short, they're a lot better than either Massha or me at the magic game."

"That makes sense." Massha nodded. "In any dimension I've been in that had vampires, they were some of the strongest magic-slingers around. If this is what they have to train on, I can see why they run hog-wild when they hit a dimension where the force lines are both plentiful and powerful."

I rubbed my forehead, trying desperately to think and to forestall the headache I felt coming on. Right on schedule, things were getting worse!

"I don't suppose you have anything in your jewelry collection that can handle disguises, do you?"

Despite our predicament, Massha gave a low laugh.

"Think about it, High Roller. If I had anything that could do disguises, would I walk around looking like this?"

"So we get to take on a world of hot-shot magic types with our own cover fire on low ammo," Guido summarized.

"Okay. So it'll be a little tougher than I thought at first. Just remember my partner has been getting along pretty well these last few years without any powers at all."

"Your partner is currently sitting in the hoosegow for murder," Guido said pointedly. "That's why we're here in the first place. Remember?"

"Besides," I continued, ignoring his comment (that's another skill I've learned from Aahz), "it's never been our intention 'to take on the whole world.' All we want to do is perform a quick hit and run. Grab Aahz and get back out with as little contact with the natives as possible. All this means is that we've got to be a little more careful. That's all."

"What about running down the trio we started out to retrieve?"

I thought briefly about the blonde who had warned us of Aahz's predicament.

"That's part of being more careful," I announced solemnly. "If . . . I mean, *when* we get Aahz out of jail, we'll head for home and count ourselves as lucky. So we . . . pay off the Deveels. It's a . . . cheap price to . . . pay for. . . ."

I realized the staff was looking at me a little askance.
I also realized that my words had been gradually slowing to a painful broken delivery as I reached the part
about paying off the Deveels.

I cleared my throat and tried again.

"Ummm, let's just say we'll reappraise the situation
once we've reached Aahz. Okay?"

The troops still looked a little dubious, so I thought it
would be best if I pushed on to the next subject.

"As to the opposition, let's pool our knowledge of
vampires so we have an idea of what we're up against.
Now, we know they can shapechange into bats or
dogs. . . ."

". . . or just into a cloud of mist," Massha supplied.

"They drink blood," Guido said grimly.

"They don't like bright light, or crosses. . . ."

". . . and they can be killed by a stake through their
heart or. . . ."

"They drink blood."

"Enough with the drinking blood! Okay, Guido?"

I was starting to get more than a little annoyed with
my bodyguard's endless pessimism. I mean, none of us
was particularly pleased by the way things were going,
but there was nothing to be gained by dwelling on the
negatives.

"Sorry, Boss. I guess looking on the dark side of
things gets to be a habit in my business."

"Garlic!" Massha exclaimed suddenly.

"What's that?"

"I said 'garlic'," she repeated. "Vampires don't like
garlic!"

"That's right! How about it, Guido? Do you have
any garlic along?"

The bodyguard actually looked embarrassed.

"Can't stand the stuff," he admitted "The other

boys in the Mob used to razz me about it, but it makes me break out in a rash."

Terrific. We probably had the only Mob member in existence who was allergic to garlic. Another brilliant idea shot to hell.

"Well," I said, heaving a sigh, "now we know what we're up against."

"Ummm . . . say, Hot Stuff?" Massha said softly. "All kidding aside. Aren't we a little overmatched on this one? I mean, Dark and Deadly here can hold up his end on the physical protection side, but I'm not sure my jewelry collection is going to be enough to cover us magically."

"I appreciate the vote of confidence," Guido smiled sadly, "but I'm not sure my hardware is going to do us a lick of good against vampires. With the Boss out of action on the magic side. . . ."

"Don't count me out so fast. My magic may not be at full power, but I can still pull off a trick or two if things really get rough."

Massha frowned. "But the force lines. . . ."

"There's one little item I've omitted from your lessons so far, apprentice," I said with a smug little grin. "It hasn't really been necessary what with the energy so plentiful on Deva . . . as a matter of fact, I've kind of gotten out of the habit myself. Anyway, what it boils down to is that you don't always tap into a force line to work magic. You can store the energy internally like a battery so that it's there when you need it. While we've been talking, I've been charging up, so I can provide a bit of magical cover as needed. Now, I won't be able to do anything prolonged like a constant disguise spell, and what I've got I'll want to use carefully because it'll take a while to recharge after each use, but we won't be relying on your jewelry completely."

I had expected a certain amount of excitement from the staff when they found out I wasn't totally helpless. Instead, they looked uncomfortable. They exchanged glances, then looked at the sky, then at the ground.

"Ummm . . . does this mean we're going on?" Guido said at last.

"That's right," I said, lips tight. "In fact, I probably would have gone on even if my powers were completely gone. Somewhere out there my partner's in trouble, and I'm not going to back away from at least *trying* to help him. I'd do the same if it was one of you, but we're talking about Aahz here. He's saved my skin more times than I care to remember. I can't just. . . ."

I caught myself and brought my voice back under control.

"Look," I said, starting again. "I'll admit we never expected this vampire thing when we started out, and the limited magic handicap is enough to give anyone pause. If either or both of you want to head back, you can do it without hard feelings or guilt trips. Really. The only reason I'm pushing on is that I know me. Whatever is up ahead, it can't be any worse than what I would put myself through if I left Aahz alone to die without trying my best to bail him out. But that's me. If you want out, go ahead."

"Don't get your back up, Hot Stuff," Massha chided gently. "I'm still not sure how much help I'm going to be, but I'll tag along. I'd probably have the same problem if anything happened to you and I wasn't there, that you'd have if anything happened to Aahz. I *am* your apprentice, you know."

"Bodyguarding ain't much, but it's all I know," Guido said glumly. "I'm supposed to be guardin' that body of yours, so where it goes, I go. I'm just not wild about the odds, know what I mean?"

"Then it's settled," I said firmly. "All right. As I see it, our next stop is Blut."

"Blut," Massha echoed carefully.

"That's right. I want to look up this Dispatcher character and see what he has to say. I mean, a town is a town, and we've all visited strange towns before. What we really need now is information, and the nearest source seems to be Blut."

"The Dispatcher," Massha said without enthusiasm."

"Blut," Guido repeated with even less joyful anticipation.

It occurred to me that while my assistants were bound and determined to stay with me on this caper, if I wanted wholehearted support, I'd better look for it from the natives . . . a prospect I didn't put much hope in at all.

Chapter Six:

"An agent is a vampire with a tele-
phone!"

— ANY EDITOR

REMEMBER how I said that if you've seen one town,
you've seen 'em all? Well, forget it. Even though I've
visited a lot of dimensions and seen a lot of towns, I had
to admit that Blut looked a little strange.

Everything seemed to be done to death in basic black.
(Perhaps "done to death" is an unfortunate turn of a
phrase. Whatever.) Mind you, when I say everything, I
mean *everything*. Cobblestones, walls, roof tiles, everything had the same uninspired color scheme. Maybe by
itself the black overtones wouldn't have seemed too
ominous, if it weren't for the architectural decorations
that seemed to abound everywhere you looked. Stone
dragons and snakes adorned every roof peak and ledge,
along with the inescapable gargoyles and, of course,
bats. I don't mean "bats" here, I mean "BATS"!!! Big
bats, little bats, bats with their wings half open and
others with their wings spread wide . . . BATS!!! The
only thing they all seemed to have in common (besides

being black) was mouths full of needle-sharp teeth . . .
an image which did nothing to further the confidence of
my already nervous party. I myself felt the tension in-
creasing as we strode down the street under the noses of
those fierce adornments. One almost expected the stone
figures to come to life and swoop down on us for a pint
or two of dinner.

"Cheerful sort of place, isn't it?" Massha asked, eyeing the rooftops.

"I don't like to complain, Boss," Guido put in, lying
blatantly, "but I've been in friendlier-looking grave-
yards."

"Will you both keep your mouths shut!" I snarled,
speaking as best I could through tightly pressed lips.
"Remember our disguises."

I had indeed turned on my disguise spell as we entered
town, but in an effort to conserve magical energy, I had
only turned our eyes red. If any of the others on the
street, and there were lots of them, happened to spot
our non-vampirish teeth, the balloon would go up once
and for all. Then again, maybe not. We still hadn't
figured out why the couple we met on the road had been
so afraid of me, but I wasn't about to bank the success
of our mission on anything as flimsy as a hope that the
whole town would run at the sight of our undisguised
features.

Fortunately, I didn't have to do any magical tinkering
with our wardrobe. If anything, we were a little drab
compared to most of the vampires on the street. Though
most of them appeared rather young, barely older than
me, they came in all shapes and sizes, and were decked
out in some of the most colorful and outrageous garb it
has ever been my misfortune to encounter as they
shouted to each other or wove their way in and out of
taverns along the street.

It was night now, the clouds having cleared enough to show a star-studded night sky, and true to their billing, vampires seemed to love the night life.

"If everybody here is vampires," Guido said, ignoring my warning, "how do they find anybody to bite for blood?"

"As far as I can tell," Massha answered, also choosing to overlook the gag order, "they buy it by the bottle."

She pointed to a small group of vampires sitting on a low wall merrily passing a bottle of red liquid back and forth among themselves. Despite our knowledge of the area, I had subconsciously assumed they were drinking wine. Confronted by the inescapable logic that the stuff they were drinking was typed, not aged, my stomach did a fast roll and dip to the right.

"If you two are through sightseeing," I hissed, "let's try to find this Dispatcher character before someone invites us to join them for a drink."

With that, I led off my slightly subdued assistants, nodding and waving at the merrymaking vampires as we went. Actually, the goings on looked like a lot of fun, and I might have been tempted to join in, if it weren't for the urgency of our quest . . . and, of course, the fact that they *were* vampires.

Following the instructions I had gleaned from the couple on the road before their panicky flight, we found the Dispatcher's place with no problem. Leaving Guido outside as a lookout, Massha and I braved the stairs and entered the Dispatcher's office.

As strange as Blut had appeared, it hadn't prepared me for the room we stepped into.

There were hundreds of glass pictures lining the walls, pictures which depicted moving, living things much like looking into a rack of fishbowls. What was more, the

images being displayed were of incredible violence and
unspeakable acts being performed on seemingly helpless
victims. The overall effect was neither relaxing nor
pleasant . . . definitely not something I'd want on the
wall at home.

I was so entranced by the pictures, I almost missed the
Dispatcher himself until he rose from his desk. Perhaps
"rose" is the wrong description. What he actually did
was hop down to the floor from his chair which was
high to begin with, but made higher by the addition of a
pillow to the seat.

He strode forward, beaming widely, with his hand extended for a handshake.

"Hi there Vilhelm's the name Your problem is my
problem Don't sit down Standing problems I solve for
free Sitting problems I charge for Reasonable rates Just
a minor percentage off the top What can I do for you?"

That was sort of all one sentence in that he didn't
pause for breath. He did, however, seize my hand,
pump it twice, then repeated the same procedure with
Massha, then grabbed my hand again . . . all before he
stopped talking.

All in all, it was a little overpowering. I had a flash
impression of a short, stocky character with plump rosy
cheeks and a bad case of the fidgets. I had deliberately
tried not to speculate on what the Dispatcher would
look like, but a cherub vampire still caught me a little
off-guard.

"I . . . ummm . . . how did you know I have a problem?"

That earned me an extra squeeze of the hand and a
wink.

"Nobody comes in here unless they've got a problem," he said, finally slowing down his speech a bit. "I
mean, I could always use a bit of help, but does anyone

leap forward to lend a hand? Fat chance. Seems like the only time I see another face in the flesh is when it means more work for me. Prove me wrong . . . please! Tell me you came in here to take over for an hour or so to let me duck out for a bite to drink.''

"Well, actually, we've got a problem and we were told. . . .''

"See! What did I tell you? All right. What have you got? A standing or a sitting problem? Standing problems I handle for. . . .''

He was off again. In a desperate effort to keep our visit short, I interrupted his pitch.

"We're looking for a friend who. . . .''

"Say no more! A friend! Just a second!''

With that he vaulted back into his chair, grabbed the top off a strange-looking appliance on his desk, diddled with it briefly, then started talking into it.

"Yea Darwin? Vilhelm. I need . . . sure. . . .''

Leaning back in his chair, he tucked the gadget under one side of his head and grabbed another.

"This is Vilhelm. Is Kay around? . . . Well, put her on when she's done. . . .''

The second gadget slid in under the same ear as the first and he reached for yet another.

"I know I shouldn't ask this,'' I murmured to Massha, "but what's he doing?''

"Those are telephones,'' she whispered back as a fourth instrument came into play. "You talk into one end of it and whoever's at the other end can hear you and talk back. It beats running all over town to find an answer.''

By this time, the little vampire had so many instruments hung from his shoulders and arms he looked like he was being attacked by a nest of snakes. He seemed to be handling it well, though, talking first into one, then another, apparently keeping multiple conversations going at once like a juggler handles a basket full of balls.

"Gee, that's kind of neat!" I exclaimed. "Do you think we could get some of these for our place at the Bazaar?"

"Believe me, they're more trouble than they're worth," Massha said. "In nothing flat you find you're spending all your time on the phone talking to people and not accomplishing anything. Besides, ever since they broke up the corporation. . . ."

"I think I've got it!" Vilhelm announced, jumping down to floor-level again. "I've got one friend for you definite, but to be honest with you he's only so-so. I've got call-backs coming on two others, so let's see what they're like before you commit on the definite. Okay?"

"Ummm . . . I think there's some kind of mistake here," I said desperately, trying to stop the madness before it progressed any further. "I'm not trying to find a *new* friend. I'm trying to locate a friend I already have who may be here in town."

He blinked several times as this news sank in. He started to turn back to his phones in an involuntary motion, then waved a hand at them in disgusted dismissal.

"Heck with it," he said with a sigh. "If they can come up with anything, I can always fob 'em off on someone else for a profit. Now then, let's try this again. You're looking for someone specific. Are they a townie or a transient? It *would* help if you gave me a little something to go on, you know."

He seemed a little annoyed, and I would have liked to do or say something to cheer him up. Before I could think of anything, however, my apprentice decided to join the conversation.

"This is quite a layout you've got, Fast Worker.

Mind if I ask exactly what it is you do?''

As always, Massha's "people sense" proved to be better than mine. The little vampire brightened noticeably at the compliment, and his chest puffed out as he launched into his narration.

"Well, the job was originally billed as Dispatcher . . . you know, as in Dispatcher of Nightmares. But anyway, like any job, it turned out to involve a lot of things that aren't on the job description. Now it's sort of a combination of dispatcher, travel agent, lost and found, and missing persons bureau.''

"Nightmares?'' I questioned, unable to contain myself.

"Sure. Anything that comes out of Limbo, be it dreams or the real thing, comes through here. Where're you from that you didn't know that?''

Obviously, I wasn't wild about continuing on the subject of our place of origin.

"Ahhh, can you really help us find our friend? He's new in town, like us.''

"That's right. You're looking for someone. Sorry. I get a little carried away sometimes when I talk about my work. New in town, hmmm? Shouldn't be that hard to locate. We don't get that many visitors.''

"He might be in jail,'' Massha blurted out before I realized what she was going to say.

"In jail?'' The vampire frowned. "The only outsider in jail right now is. . . . Say! Now I recognize you! The eyes threw me for a minute. You're Skeeve, aren't you?''

"Screen 97B!'' he declared proudly, gesturing vaguely over his shoulder. "There's someone a dozen dimensions over from here, runs a hot dog stand, who features you in his most frequent nightmares. You, a dragon, and a Pervert. Am I correct in assuming that the current resident in our fair jail is none other than your sidekick Aahz?''

"To be correct, that's Pervect, not Pervert . . . but except for that you're right. That's my partner you've got locked up there, and we aim to get him out.''

I was probably talking too much, but being recognized in a dimension I'd never heard of had thrown me off balance. Then again, the Dispatcher didn't seem all that hostile at the discovery. More curious than anything else.

"Well, well. Skeeve himself. I never expected to meet you in person. Sometime you must tell me what you did to that poor fellow to rate the number-one slot on his hit parade of nightmares.''

"What about Aahz?'' I said impatiently.

"You know he's up for murder, don't you?''

"Heard it. Don't believe it. He's a lot of things, but a murderer isn't one of them.''

"There's a fair amount of evidence.'' Vilhelm shrugged. "But tell me. What's with the vampire get-up. You're no more a vampire than I'm a Klahd.''

"It's a long story. Let's just say it seemed to be the local uniform.''

"Let's not,'' the dispatcher grinned. "Pull up a chair . . . free of charge, of course. I've got time and lots of questions about the other dimensions. Maybe we can trade a little information while you're here.''

Chapter Seven:

"I don't see anything thrilling about it!"
—M. JACKSON

"I really don't see how you can drink that stuff," I declared, eyeing Vilhelm's goblet of blood.

"Funny," he smiled in return, "I was about to say the same thing. I mean, you know what W. C. Fields said about water!"

"No. What?"

"Now let me get this straight," Guido interrupted before I could get any answer. "You're sayin' you vampire guys don't really drink blood from people?"

"Oh, a few do," the Dispatcher said with a shrug. "But it's an acquired taste, like steak tartare. Some say it's a gourmet dish, but I could never stand the stuff myself. I'll stick with the inexpensive domestic varieties any night."

We were all sprawled around the Dispatcher's office at this point, sipping our respective drinks and getting into a pretty good rap session. We had pulled Guido in off door watch and I had dropped our disguises so my energy reserve wasn't being drained.

The Dispatcher had played with his phones, calling from one to the other. Then he put them all down and announced that he had them on "hold," a curious expression since it was the first time in half an hour he hadn't been holding one.

Vilhelm himself was turning out to be a priceless source of information, and, as promised, had a seemingly insatiable curiosity about otherworldly things.

"Then how do you account for all the vampire legends around the other dimensions," Massha said skeptically.

The Dispatcher made a face.

"First of all, you've got to realize who you're dealing with. Most of the ones who do extensive touring outside of Limbo are 'old money' types. We're talking about the idle rich . . . and that usually equates to bored thrill-seekers. Working stiffs like me can't afford to take that kind of time away from our jobs. Heck, I can hardly manage to get my two weeks each year. Anyway, there are a lot more of us around the dimensions than you might realize. It's just that the level-headed ones are content to maintain a low profile and blend with the natives. They content themselves with the blood of domestic livestock, much the way we do here at home. It's the others that cause the problems. Like any group of tourists, there's always a few who feel that just because they're in another world or city, the rules don't apply . . . and that includes common manners and good taste. They're the ones who stir up trouble by getting the locals up in arms about 'bloodsucking monsters.' If it makes you feel any better, you human types have a pretty bad rep yourselves here in Limbo."

That caught my attention.

"Could you elaborate on that last point, Vilhelm?

What problem could the locals have with us?''

The Dispatcher laughed.

"The same one you humans have with us vampires. While humans aren't the leading cause of death in vampires any more than vampires are a leading cause of death in humans, it's certainly one of the more publicized and sensational ways to go."

"Is that why the first locals we met took off like bats out of hell . . . if you'll pardon the expression?'' Massha asked.

"You've got it. I think you'll find that the citizens of Blut will react the same way to you that you would if you ran into a vampire in your home dimension."

"I don't notice you bein' particularly scared of us," Guido said suspiciously.

"One of the few advantages of this job. After a few years of monitoring the other dimensions, you get pretty blasé about demons. As far as I can tell, most of 'em are no worse than some of the folks we've got around here."

This was all very interesting, but I was getting a little fidgety about our mission.

"Since you know we aren't all evil or on a permanent vampire hunt, what can you tell us about the mess Aahz is in? Can you give us any help there?"

"I dunno," the Dispatcher said, rubbing his jaw thoughtfully. "Until I found out who he was, I was ready to believe he was guilty as sin. There's an awful lot of evidence against him."

"Such as?" I pressed.

"Well, he was caught with a stake and mallet in his hand, and there are two eyewitnesses who say they saw him kill one of our citizens and scatter his dust to the winds."

"Wait a minute. You mean you ain't got no *corpus*

delecti?" Guido said, straightening in his chair. "Sorry to interrupt, Boss, but you're playin' in my alley now. This is somethin' I know a little about. You can't go on trial for murder without a corpse, know what I mean?"

"Maybe where you come from," Vilhelm corrected, "but things get a little different when you're dealing with vampires. If we *had* a body, or even just the pile of dust, we could revive him in no time flat. As it is, the problem is when there's *no* body . . . when a vampire's been reduced to dust and the dust scattered. That's when it's impossible to pull 'em back into a functional mode."

"But if there isn't a body, how do you know the victim is dead at all?" I asked.

"There's the rub," Vilhelm agreed. "But in this case, there's a matter of two eyewitnesses."

"Two of 'em, eh?" Massha murmured thoughtfully. "Would you happen to have descriptions of these two peepers?"

"Saw 'em myself. They were both off-worlders like yourselves. One was a young girl, the blonde and innocent type. The other was a pretty sleazy-looking guy. It was her who sold us on the story, really. I don't think anyone would have believed him if he said that were-wolves were furry."

My heart sank. I had wanted very badly to believe the girl who had warned us of Aahz's danger was somehow an innocent bystander in the proceedings. Now it looked as if. . . .

"Do the descriptions sound familiar, Hot Stuff? Still think Guido and I were being paranoid when we said this might be a set-up? Sounds like they framed your partner, then came back after you to complete the set."

I avoided her eyes, staring hard at the wall monitors.

"There might be another explanation, you know."

My apprentice gave out a bark of laughter.

"If there is, I'm dying to hear it. Face it, High Roller, any way you look at it the situation stinks. If they cooked up a frame that tight on Green and Scaly on such short notice, I'm dying to see what kind of a trap they've got waiting for you now that they've had time to get ready *before* inviting you to step in."

It occurred to me that I had never been that mouthy when I was an apprentice. It also occurred to me that now I understood why Aahz had gotten so angry on the rare occasions when I had voiced an opinion . . . and the rarer times when I was right.

"I think I missed a lap in this conversation somewhere." Vilhelm frowned. "I take it you know the witnesses?"

Massha proceeded to bring the Dispatcher up to date, with Guido growling counterpoint to the theme. For once I was glad to let them do the talking. It gave me a chance to collect my scattered thoughts and try to formulate a plan. When they finished, I still had a long way to go on both counts.

"I must admit, viewed from the light of this new information, the whole thing does sound a little suspicious," the vampire said thoughtfully.

"A *little* suspicious!" Massha snorted. "It's phonier than a smiling Deveel!"

"Tell ya what," Guido began, "just give us a few minutes alone with these witnesses of yours and we'll shake the truth out of 'em."

"I'm afraid that will be a little difficult," the Dispatcher said, eyeing the ceiling. "You see, they haven't been around for a while. Disappeared right after the trial."

"The trial!?" I snapped, abandoning my efforts to collect my wits. "You mean the trial's already been held?"

The vampire nodded.

"That's right. Needless to say, your friend was found guilty."

"Why do I get the feeling he didn't get a suspended sentence for a first offense?" Guido growled under his breath.

"As a matter of fact, he's been slated for execution at the end of the week," Vilhelm admitted.

That got me out of my seat and pacing.

"We've got to do something," I said needlessly. "How about it, Vilhelm? Can you help us out at all? Any chance of getting the verdict reversed or at least a stay of execution?"

"I'm afraid not. Character witnesses alone wouldn't change anything, and as for new evidence, it would only be your word against the existing witnesses . . . and you've already admitted the defendant is a friend of yours. Mind you, *I* believe you, but there are those who would suspect you'd say anything or fabricate any kind of tale to save your partner."

"But can you *personally* give us a hand?"

"No, I can't," the vampire said, turning away. "You all seem like real nice folks, and your friend is probably the salt of the earth, but I have to live here and deal with these people for a long time. If I sided with outsiders against the town legal system, my whole career would go down the drain whether I was right or not. It's not pretty and I don't like it, but that's the way things are."

"We could fix it so you like it a lot less!" Guido said darkly, reaching into his coat.

"Stop it, Guido," I ordered. "Let's not forget the help Vilhelm's *already* given us. It's a lot more than we expected to get when we first came into this dimension, so don't go making enemies out of the only friend we've got locally. Okay?"

The bodyguard sank back into his chair, muttering something I was just as glad I didn't hear, but his hand came out of his coat empty and stayed in sight.

"So what do we do now, Hot Stuff?" Massha sighed.

"The only thing I can think of is to try to locate those witnesses before the execution date," I said. "What I can't figure is how to go about looking without getting half the town down on our necks."

"What we really need is a bloodhound," Guido grumbled.

"Say, that's not a bad idea!" Vilhelm exclaimed, coming to life. "Maybe I can help you after all!"

"You got a bloodhound?" the bodyguard said, raising his eyebrows.

"Even better," the vampire declared. "I don't know why I didn't think of it before. The ones you need to get in touch with are the Woof Writers."

I studied him carefully to see if this were some kind of joke.

"The Woof Writers?" I repeated at last.

"Well, that's what we in Blut call them behind their backs. Actually, they're a husband-wife team of were-wolves who are on a big crusade to raise sympathy for humans."

"Werewolves," I said carefully.

"Sure. We got all kinds here in Limbo. Anyway, if anyone in this dimension will be willing to stick their necks out for you, they're the ones. They do their own thing and don't really give a hang what any of the other locals think about it. Besides, werewolves are second to none when it comes to sniffing out a trail."

"Werewolves."

Vilhelm cocked his head at me curiously.

"Am I imagining things, Skeeve, or didn't you just say that?"

"What's more," Massha smiled sweetly, "he'll probably say it again. It bears repeating."

"Werewolves," I said again, just to support my apprentice.

"Boss," Guido began, "I don't want to say this, but nobody said anything about werewolves when we. . . ."

"Good," I interrupted brusquely. "You don't want to say it, and I don't want to hear it. Now that we're in agreement, let's just pass on it and. . . ."

"But Boss! We can't team up with werewolves."

"Guido, we just went over this. We're in a tight spot *and* in a strange dimension. We can't afford to be choosy about our allies."

"You don't understand, Boss. I'm allergic to 'em!"

I sank down into a chair and hid my face in my hands.

"I thought you were allergic to garlic," I said through my fingers.

"That, too," the bodyguard said. "But mostly I'm allergic to furry things like kitties or fur coats or. . . ."

". . . or werewolves," Massha finished for him. "Frankly, Dark and Deadly, one starts to wonder how you've been able to function effectively all these years."

"Hey, it doesn't come up all that often, know what I mean?" Guido argued defensively. "How many times have *you* been attacked by somethin' furry?"

"Not as often as I'd like!" Massha leered.

"Enough, you two," I ordered, raising my head. "Guido, have you ever actually been near a werewolf?"

"Well, no. But. . . ."

"Then until we know for sure, we'll assume you're *not* allergic to them. Okay? Vilhelm, exactly where do we find these Woof Writers of yours?"

Chapter Eight:

"First, let's decide who's leading and
who's following."

—F. ASTAIRE

"BOSS, just where the hell *is* Pahkipsee?"

I found myself wondering if all bodyguards spent
most of their time complaining, or if I had just gotten
lucky.

"Look, Guido. You were there and heard the same
instructions I did. If Vilhelm was right, it should be just
up the road here a couple more miles."

"'. . . 'a rather dead bedroom community, fit only for
those not up to the fast-lane life-style of the big city,' "
Massha quoted in a close imitation of the vampire's
voice.

Guido snickered rudely.

"Why do I get the feeling you didn't particularly
warm to Vilhelm, Massha?" I suppressed a grin of my
own.

"Maybe it's because he's the only guy we've met she
hasn't made a pass at?" Guido suggested.

Massha favored him with an extended tongue and

crossed eyes before answering.

"Oh, Vilhelm's okay," she said. "Kinda cute, too
. . . at least the top of his head was. And he did admit
that in general vampires were more partial to cities and
parties while werewolves preferred the back-to-nature
atmosphere of rural living. I just didn't like the crack,
that's all. I grew up on a farm, you know. Country
breakfasts have a lot to do with my current panoramic
physique. Besides, something inside says you shouldn't
trust a smiling vampire. . . . or at least you shouldn't
trust him too far."

I had been about to mention the fact that I had grown
up on a farm, too, but withheld the information. Obviously, farm food hadn't particularly affected my physique, and I didn't want to rob my apprentice of her
excuse.

"If he had wanted to do us harm, all he would have
had to do was blow the whistle on us while we were still
in town," I pointed out. "Let's just take things at face
value and assume he was really being as nice as he
seemed . . . for all our peace of minds."

I wished I was as confident as I sounded. We were a
long way out in the boondocks, and if Vilhelm had
wanted to send us off on a wild goose chase, he couldn't
have picked a better direction to start us off in.

"Yeah, well I'd feel a lot better if we weren't being
followed," Guido grumbled.

I stopped in my tracks. So did Massha . . . in her
tracks, that is. The bodyguard managed to stumble into
us before bringing his own forward progress to a halt.

"What is it, Boss? Something wrong?"

"For a minute there, I thought I heard you say that
we were being followed."

"Yeah. Since we left the Dispatcher's. Why does . . .
you mean you didn't know?"

I resisted an impulse to throttle him.

"No, Guido. I didn't know. You see, my bodyguard didn't tell me. He was too busy complaining about the road conditions to have time to mention anything as trivial as someone following us."

Guido took a few shaky steps backward.

"Hey! C'mon, Boss. Don't be like that. I thought you knew! Honest. Whoever's back there isn't doin' such a hot job of hiding the fact that they're dogging our trail. Any idiot could've spotted . . . I mean. . . ."

"Keep going, Dark and Deadly," Massha urged. "You're digging yourself in further with every word, in case you hadn't noticed."

With great effort I brought myself back under control.

"Whatever," I said. "I don't suppose you have any idea who it is?"

"Naw. There's only one of 'em. Unless. . . ."

His voice trailed off into silence and he looked suddenly worried.

"Out with it, Guido. Unless what?"

"Well, sometimes when you're getting *really* tricky about tailing someone, you put one real clumsy punk out front so's they can be spotted while you keep your real ace-hitter hidden. I hadn't stopped to think of that before. This turkey behind us could be a decoy, know what I mean?"

"I thought you used decoys for ducks, not turkeys," Massha scowled.

"Well, if that's what's happening, then *we're* sitting ducks, if it makes you feel any better."

"Could both of you just be quiet for a few minutes and let me think?" I said, suddenly impatient with their banter.

"Well, maybe it isn't so bad," Guido said in a doubtful voice. "I'm pretty sure I would have spotted the back-up team if there was one."

"Oh sure," Massha sneered. "Coming out of a town full of vampires that can change themselves into mist whenever they want. Of course you'd spot them."

"Hey. The Boss here can chew on me if he wants, but I don't have to take that from you. You didn't even spot the turkey, remember?"

"The only turkey I can see is. . . ."

"Enough!" I ordered, having arrived at a decision despite their lack of cooperation. "We have to find out for sure who's behind us and what they want. This is as good a place as any, so I suggest we all retire into the bushes and wait for our shadow to catch up with us. . . . No, Massha. I'll be over here with Guido. You take the other side of the road."

That portion of my plan had less to do with military strategy than with an effort on my part to preserve what little was left of my nerves. I figured the only way to shut the two of them up was to separate them.

"I'm sorry, Boss," Guido whispered as we crouched side by side in the brush. "I keep forgettin' that you aren't as into crime as the boys I usually run with."

Well, I had been half right. Massha on the other side of the road was being quiet, but as long as he had someone to talk to, Guido was going to keep on expressing his thoughts and opinions. I was starting to understand why Don Bruce insisted on doing all the talking when the bodyguards were around. Encouraging employees to speak up as equals definitely had its drawbacks.

"Will you keep your voice down?" I tried once more. "This is supposed to be an ambush."

"Don't worry about that, Boss. It'll be a while before they catch up, and when they do, I'll hear 'em before. . . ."

"Is that you, Skeeve?"

The voice came from the darkness just up the road.

I gave Guido my darkest glare, and he rewarded it with an apologetic shrug that didn't look particularly sincere to me.

Then it dawned on me where I had heard that voice before.

"Right here," I said, rising from my crouch and stepping onto the road. "We've been waiting for you. I think it's about time we had a little chat."

Aside from covering my embarrassment over having been discovered, that had to be my best understatement in quite a while. The last time I had seen this particular person, she was warning me about Aahz's imprisonment.

"Good." She stepped forward to meet me. "That's why I've been following you. I was hoping we could. . . ."

Her words stopped abruptly as Guido and Massha rose from the bushes and moved to join us.

"Well, look who's here," Massha said, flashing one of her less pleasant smiles.

"If it isn't the little bird who sang to the vampires," Guido leered, matching my apprentice's threatening tone.

The girl favored them with a withering glance, then faced me again.

"I was hoping we could talk alone. I've got a lot to say and not much time to say it. It would go faster if we weren't interrupted."

"Not a chance, Sweetheart," Guido snarled. "I'm not goin' to let the Boss out of my sight with you around."

". . . besides which, I've got a few things to tell you myself," Massha added, "like what I think of folks who think frames look better on people than on paintings.''

The girl's eyes never left mine. For all her bravado, I thought I could detect in their depths an appeal for help.

''Please,'' she said softly.

I fought a brief skirmish in my mind, and, as usual, common sense lost.

''All right.''

''WHAT! C'mon, Boss. You can't let her get you alone! If her pals are around. . . .''

''Hot Stuff, if I have to sit on you, you aren't going to. . . .''

''Look!'' I said, wrenching my eyes away from the girl to confront my mutinous staff. ''We'll only go a few steps down the road there, in plain sight. If anything happens you'll be able to pitch in before it gets serious.''

''But. . . .''

''. . . and you certainly can't think *she's* going to jump me. I mean, it's a cinch she isn't carrying any concealed weapons.''

That was a fact. She had changed outfits since the last time I saw her, probably to fit in more with the exotic garb favored by the party-loving vampires. She was wearing what I've heard referred to as a ''tank top'' which left her midsection and navel delightfully exposed, and the open-sided skirt (if you can call two flaps of cloth that) showed her legs up past her hips. If she had a weapon with her, she had swallowed it. Either that, or. . . .

I dragged my thoughts back to the argument.

''The fact of the matter is that she isn't going to talk in front of a crowd. Now, am I going to get a chance to hear another viewpoint about what's going on, or are we going to keep groping around for information with Aahz's life hanging in the balance?''

My staff fell silent and exchanged glances, each waiting for the other to risk the next blast.

"Well, okay," Massha agreed at last. "But watch yourself, Hot Stuff. Remember, poison can come in pretty bottles."

So, under the ever-watchful glares of my assistants, I retired a few steps down the road for my first words alone with. . . .

"Say, what *is* your name, anyway?"

"Hmmm? Oh. I'm Luanna. Say, thanks for backing me up. That's a pretty mean-looking crew you hang around with. I had heard you had a following, but I hadn't realized how nasty they were."

"Oh, they're okay once you get to know them. If you worked with them on a day-to-day basis, you'd find out that they . . . heck, none of us are really as dangerous or effective as the publicity hype cuts us out to be."

I was suddenly aware of her eyes on me. Her expression was strange . . . sort of a bitter half-smile.

"I've always heard that *really* powerful people tended to understate what they can do, that they don't have to brag. I never really believed it until now."

I really didn't know what to say to that. I mean, my reputation had gotten big enough that I was starting to get used to being recognized and talked about at the Bazaar, but what she was displaying was neither fear nor envy. Among my own set of friends, admiration or praise was always carefully hidden within our own brand of rough humor or teasing. Faced with the undiluted form of the same thing, I was at a loss as to how to respond.

"Ummm, what was it you wanted to talk to me about?"

Her expression fell and she dropped her eyes.

"This is so embarrassing. Please be patient with me,

Skeeve . . . is it all right if I call you Skeeve? I haven't
had much experience with saying 'I'm sorry' . . . heck, I
haven't had much experience with people at all. Just
partners and pigeons. Now that I'm here, I really don't
know what to say.''

"Why don't we start at the beginning?" I wanted to
ease her discomfort. "Did you really swindle the
Deveels back at the Bazaar?"

Luanna nodded slowly without raising her eyes.

"That's what we do. Matt and me. That and running,
even though I think sometimes we're better at running
than working scams. Maybe if we were better at conning
people, we wouldn't get so much practice at running."

Her words thudded at me like a padded hammer. I
had wanted very badly to hear that she was innocent and
that it had all been a mistake. I mean, she was so pretty,
so sweet, I would have bet my life that she was innocent,
yet here she was openly admitting her guilt to me.

"But why?" I managed at last. "I mean, how did you
get involved in swindling people to begin with?"

Her soft shoulders rose and fell in a helpless shrug.

"I don't know. It seemed like a good idea when Matt
first explained it to me. I was dying to get away from the
farm, but I didn't know how to do anything but farm-
work for a living . . . until Matt explained to me how
easy it was to get money away from people by playing
on their greed. 'Promise them something for nothing,'
he said, 'or for so little that they think *they're* swindling
you.' When he put it that way, it didn't seem so bad. It
was more a matter of being smart enough to trick people
who thought they were taking advantage of you."

". . . by selling them magical items that weren't." I
finished for her. "Tell me, why didn't you just go into
the magic trade for real?"

Her head came up, and I caught a quick flash of fire in her sad blue eyes.

"We didn't know any magic, so we had to fake it. You probably can't understand that, since you're the real McCoy. I knew that the first time I saw you at Possletum. We were going to try to fake our way into the Court Magician spot until you showed up and flashed a bit of real magic at the crown. Even Matt had to admit that we were outclassed, and we kind of faded back before anyone asked us to show what we could do. I think it was then that I. . . ."

She broke off, giving me a startled, guilty look as if she had been about to say something she shouldn't.

"Go on," I urged, my curiosity piqued.

"It's nothing, really," she said hastily. "Now it's your turn. Since I've told you my story, maybe you won't mind me asking how you got started as a magician."

That set me back a bit. Like her, I had been raised on a farm. I had run away, though, planning to seek my fortune as a master thief, and it was only my chance meeting with my old teacher Garkin and eventually Aahz that had diverted my career goals toward magic. In hindsight, my motives were not discernibly better than hers, but I didn't want to admit it just now. I kind of liked the way she looked at me while laboring under the illusion that I was someone noble and special.

"That's too long a tale to go into just now," I said brusquely. "There are still a few more answers I'd like from you. How come you used our place as a getaway route from Deva?"

"Oh, that was Vic's idea. We teamed up with him just before we started working our con at the Bazaar. When it looked like the scam was starting to turn sour, he said

he knew a way-off dimension that no one would be
watching. Matt and I didn't even know it was your place
until your doorman asked if we were there to see you.
Matt was so scared about having to tangle with you that
he wanted to forget the whole thing and find another
way out, but Vic showed us the door and it looked so
easy we just went along with him.''

"Of course, it never occurred to you that we'd get
stuck with the job of trying to bring you back."

"You better believe it occurred to us. I mean, we
didn't think you'd *have* to do it. We expected you'd be
mad at us for getting you involved and come after us
yourself. Vic kept saying that we shouldn't worry, that
if you found us here in Limbo he could fix it so you
wouldn't be able to take us back. I didn't know he was
thinking about setting up a frame until he sprang it on
your partner.''

I tried to let this console me, but it didn't work.

"I notice that once you found out that Aahz was
being framed, you still went along with it."

"Well . . . I didn't want to, but Vic kept saying that if
you two were as good as everyone said, that your
partner could get out of jail by himself. We figured that
he'd escape before the execution, but with the whole
dimension hunting him as a fugitive that he'd be too
busy running for home to bother about catching us.''

I was starting to get *real* anxious to meet this guy Vic.
It also occurred to me that of all the potential problems
our growing reputation could bring down on us, this
was one we had never expected.

"And you believed him?"

Luanna made a face, then shrugged.

"Well . . . you're supposed to be able to do some
pretty incredible things, and I don't want you to think I
don't believe in your abilities, but I was worried enough

that I sneaked back to let you know what was going on
. . . just in case.''

It was almost funny that she was apologizing for giving us the warning. Almost, but not quite. My mind
kept running over what might have happened if she *had*
believed in me completely.

"I guess my only other question is who is this citizen
that Aahz is supposed to have killed?"

"Didn't anybody tell you?" she blinked. "It's Vic.
He's from this dimension . . . you know, a vampire.
Anyway, he's hiding out until the whole thing's resolved
one way or another. I don't think even Matt knows
where he is. Vampires are normally suspicious, and
after I sneaked out the first time, he's even gotten cagey
around us. He just drops in from time to time to see
how we're doing."

Now I *knew* I wanted to meet friend Vic. If I was
lucky, I'd meet him before Aahz did.

"Well, I do appreciate you filling me in on the problem. Now, if you'll just come back to Blut with us and
explain things to the authorities, my gratitude will be
complete."

Luanna started as if I had stuck her with a pin.

"Hold on a minute! Who said anything about going
to the authorities? I can't do that! That would be dou-
blecrossing *my* partners. I don't want to see you or your
friends get hurt, but I can't sacrifice my own to save
them."

An honest crook is both incongruous and infuriating.
Aahz had often pointed this out to me when some point
in my ethic kept me from going along with one of his
schemes, and now I was starting to understand what he
was talking about.

"But then why are you here?"

"I wanted to warn you. Vic has been thinking that

you might come into Limbo after your partner, and he's
setting up some kind of trap if you did. If he was right,
I thought you should know that you're walking into
trouble. I figured that if you came, you'd look up the
Dispatcher, so I waited there and followed you when
you showed up. I just wanted to warn you is all. That
and. . . ."

She dropped her eyes again and lowered her voice
until I could hardly hear her.

". . . I wanted to see you again. I know it's silly,
but. . . ."

As flattering as it was, this time I was unimpressed.

"Yeah, sure." I interrupted. "You're so interested in
me you're willing to let my partner sit on a murder rap
just so you can watch me go through my paces."

"I already explained about that," she said fiercely,
stepping forward to lay a hand on my arm.

I stared at it pointedly until she removed it.

"Well," she said in a small voice. "I can see that
there's nothing more I can say. But, Skeeve? Promise
me that you won't follow me when I leave? You or your
friends? I took a big risk finding you. Please don't make
me regret it."

I stared at her for a long moment, then looked away
and nodded.

"I know you're disappointed in me, Skeeve," came
her voice, "but I can't go against my partners. Haven't
you ever had to do something you didn't want to do to
support your partner?"

That hit home . . . painfully.

"Yes, I have," I said, drawing a ragged breath. "I'm
sorry, Luanna. I'm just worried about Aahz, that's all.
Tell you what. Just to show there're no hard feelings,
can I have a token or something? Something to remember you by until I see you again?"

She hesitated, then pulled a gossamer-thin scarf from somewhere inside her outfit. Stepping close, she tucked it into my tunic, then rose on her tiptoes and kissed me softly.

"It's nice of you to ask," she said. "Even if I don't mean anything to you at all, it's nice of you to ask."

With that, she turned and sprinted off down the road into the darkness.

I stared after her.

"You're letting her go!?"

Suddenly Massha was at my side, flanked by Guido.

"C'mon, Boss. We gotta catch her. She's your partner's ticket off death row. Where's she goin'?"

"To meet up with her partners in crime," I said. "Including a surprisingly lively guy named Vic . . . surprising since he's the one that Aahz is supposed to have killed."

"So we can catch 'em all together. Nice work, Hot Stuff. Okay, let's follow her and. . . ."

"No!"

"Why not?"

"Because I promised her."

There was a deathly silence as my assistants digested this information.

"So she walks and Green and Scaly dies, is that it?"

"You're sellin' out your partner for a skirt? That musta been some kiss."

I slowly turned to face them, and, mad as they were, they fell silent.

"Now listen close," I said quietly, "because I'm not going to go over it again. If we tried to follow her back to their hideout, and she spotted us, she'd lead us on a wild goose chase and we'd never catch up with them . . . and we need that so-called corpse. I don't think her testimony alone will swing the verdict."

"But Boss, if we let her get away. . . ."

"We'll find them," I said. "Without us dogging her footsteps, she'll head right back to her partners."

"But how will we. . . ."

In answer, I pulled Luanna's scarf from my tunic.

"Fortunately, she was kind enough to provide us with a means to track her, once we recruit the necessary were-wolf."

Guido gave my back a slap that almost staggered me.

"Way to go, Boss," he crowed. "You really had me goin' for a minute. I thought that chickie had really snowed you."

I looked up to find Massha eyeing me suspiciously.

"That *was* quite a kiss, Hot Stuff," she said. "If I didn't know better, I'd think that young lady is more than a little stuck on you . . . and you just took advantage of it."

I averted my eyes, and found myself staring down the road again.

"As a wise woman once told me," I said, "sometimes you have to do things you don't like to support your partner. . . . Now, let's go find these Woof Writers."

Chapter Nine:

"My colleagues and I feel that independents like ElfQuest are nothing but sheep in wolves' clothing!"

—S. LEE

THE Woof Writers turned out to be much more pleasant than I had dared hope, which was fortunate as my werewolf disguises were some of the shakiest I'd ever done. Guido was indeed allergic to werewolves as feared (he started sneezing a hundred yards from their house) and was waiting outside, but even trying to maintain two disguises was proving to be a strain on my powers in this magic-poor dimension. I attempted to lessen the drain by keeping the changes minimal, but only succeeded in making them incredibly unconvincing even though my assistants assured me they were fine. No matter what anyone tells you, believe, me, pointy ears alone do not wolf make.

You might wonder why I bothered with diguises at all? Well, frankly, we were getting a little nervous. Everyone we had talked to or been referred to in this dimension was so *nice*! We kept waiting for the other shoe to drop. All of our talks and discussions of pos-

79

sible traps had made us so skittish that we were now
convinced that there was going to be a double-cross
somewhere along the way. The only question in our
minds was when and by whom.

With that in mind, we decided it would be best to try
to pass ourselves off as werewolves until we knew for
sure the Woof Writers were as well-disposed toward
humans as Vilhelm said they were. The theory was that
if they weren't, the disguises might give us a chance to
get out again before our true nature was exposed. The
only difficulty with that plan was that I had never seen a
werewolf in my life, so not only was I working with a
shortage of energy, I was unsure as to what the final
result should look like. As it turned out, despite their
knowledgeable advice, my staff didn't know either.

While we're answering questions from the audience,
you might ask, if neither I nor my assistants knew what
a werewolf looked like, how I knew the disguises were
inadequate? Simple. I deduced the fact after one look at
real werewolves. That and the Woof Writers told me so.
Didn't I tell you they were great folks? Of course, they
let us sweat for a while before admitting that they knew
we were poorly disguised humans all along, but I myself
tend to credit that to their dubious sense of humor. It's
Massha who insists it was blatant sadism. Of course, she
was the one who had to eat a bone before they acknowledged the joke.

Anyway, I was talking about the Woof Writers. It
was interesting in that I had never had much opportunity to watch a husband-wife team in action before (my
parents don't count). The closest thing to the phenomenon I had witnessed was the brother-sister team of
Tananda and Chumley, but they spent most of their
conversational time trying to "one-down" each other.

The Woof Writers, in contrast, seemed to take turns playing "crazy partner-sane partner." They never asked my opinion, but I felt that she was much better at playing the crazy than he. He was so good at playing the straight that when he did slip into crazy mode, it always came as a surprise.

"Really, dear," Idnew was saying to Massha, "wouldn't you like to slip out of that ridiculous disguise into something more comfortable? A werewolf with only two breasts looks so silly."

"Idnew," her husband said sternly, "you're making our guests uncomfortable. Not everyone feels as easy about discussing their bodies as you do."

"It's the artist in me," she returned. "And besides, Drahcir, who was it that set her up to eat a bone?—and an old one at that. If you were a little more conscientious when you did the shopping instead of stocking up on junk food. . . ."

"Oh, don't worry about me, Hairy and Handsome," Massha interceded smoothly, dropping into her vamp role. "I've got no problems discussing my body, as long as we get equal time to talk about yours. I've always liked my men with a lot of facial hair, if you get my drift."

I noticed Idnew's ears flatten for a moment before returning to their normal upright position. While it may have been nothing more than a nervous twitch, it occurred to me that if we were going to solicit help from these two, it might not be wise to fan any embers of jealousy that might be lying about.

"Tell me," I said hastily, eager to get the subject away from Massha's obvious admiration of Drahcir, "What got you started campaigning for better relationships between humans and werewolves?"

"Well, there were many factors involved," Drahcir explained, dropping into the lecturer mode I had grown to know so well in such a short time. "I think the most important thing to keep in mind is that the bad reputation humans have is vastly overrated. There is actually very little documented evidence to support the legends of human misconduct. For the most part, werewolves tend to forget that, under the proper conditions, we turn into humans. Most of them are afraid or embarrassed and hide themselves away until it passes, but Idnew and I don't. If anything we generally seize the opportunity to go out and about and get the public used to seeing harmless humans in their midst. Just between us, though, I think Idnew here likes to do it because it scares the hell out of folks to be suddenly confronted by a human when they aren't expecting it. In case you haven't noticed, there's a strong exhibitionist streak in my wife. For myself, it's simply a worthy cause that's been neglected for far too long."

"The other factor, which my husband has neglected to mention," Idnew put in impishly, "is that there's a lot of money in it."

"There is?" I asked.

My work with Aahz had trained me to spot profit opportunities where others saw none, but this time the specific angle had eluded me.

"There . . . umm . . . are certain revenues to be gleaned from our campaign," Drahcir said uneasily, shooting a dark glance at his wife. "T-shirts, bumper stickers, lead miniatures, fan club dues, greeting cards, and calendars, just to name a few. It's a dirty job, but somebody's got to do it. Lest my wife leave you with the wrong impression of me, however, let me point out that I'm supporting this particular cause because I *really* believe in it. There are lots of ways to make money."

". . . and he knows them all, don't you dear?" Idnew said with a smile.

"Really?" I interrupted eagerly. "Would you mind running over a few? Could I take notes?"

"Before you get carried away, High Roller," Massha warned, "remember why we came here originally."

"Oh! Right! Thanks, Massha. For a minute there I . . . Right!"

It took me a few seconds to rechannel my thoughts. While Aahz's training has gotten me out of a lot of tight spots and generally improved my standard of living, there are some unfortunate side effects.

Once I got my mind back on the right track, I quickly filled the werewolves in on our current problem. I kept the details sketchy, both because I was getting tired of going back and forth over the same beginning, and to keep from having to elaborate on Luanna's part in causing our dilemma. Still, the Woof Writers seemed quite enthralled by the tale, and listened attentively until I was done.

"Gee, you're really in a spot," Idnew said when I finally ground to a halt. "If there's anything we can do to help. . . ."

"We can't," Drahcir told us firmly. "You're behind on your deadlines, Idnew, and I've got three more appearances this month . . . not to mention answering the mail that's piled up the last two weekends I've been gone."

"Drahcir. . . ." Idnew said, drawing out his name.

"Don't look at me like that, dear," her husband argued before she had even started her case, "and don't cock your head, either. Someone's liable to shove a gramophone under it. Remember, *you're* the one who keeps pointing out that we have to put more time into our work."

"I was talking about cutting back on your personal appearances," Idnew argued. "Besides, this is important."

"So's meeting our deadlines. I'm as sympathetic to their problem as you are, but we can't let the plight of one small group of humans interfere with our work on the big picture."

"But *you're* the one who insists that deadlines aren't as important as. . . ."

She broke off suddenly and semaphored her ears toward her husband.

"Wait a minute. Any time you start talking about 'big pictures' and 'grand crusades'. . . is our bank account low again?"

Drahcir averted his eyes and shifted his feet uncomfortably.

"Well, I was going to tell you, but I was afraid it might distract you while you were trying to work. . . ."

"All right. Let's have it," his wife growled, her hackles rising slightly. "What is it you've invested our money in this time?"

I was suddenly very uncomfortable. Our little discussion seemed to be dissolving into a family fight I felt I had no business being present for. Apparently Massha felt the same thing.

"Well, if you can't help us, that's that," she said, getting to her feet. "No problem. A favor's not a favor if you have to be argued into it. C'mon, Hot Stuff. We're wasting our time *and* theirs."

Though in part I agreed with her, desperation prompted me to make one last try.

"Not so fast, Massha. Drahcir is right. Time's money. Maybe we could work out some kind of a fee to compensate them for their time in helping us. Then it's not a favor, it's a business deal. Face it, we *really* need their help in this. The odds of us finding this Vic character on our own are pretty slim."

Aahz would have fainted dead away if he had heard me admitting how much we needed help *before* the fee was set, but that reaction was nothing compared to how the Woof Writers took my offer.

"What did you say?" Drahcir demanded, rising to all fours with his ears back.

"I said that maybe you'd help us if we offered to pay you," I repeated, backing away slightly. "I didn't mean to insult you. . . ."

"You can't insult Drahcir with money," his wife snapped. "He meant what did you say about Vic?"

"Didn't I mention him before?" I frowned. "He's the vampire that Aahz is supposed to have. . . ."

There was a sudden loud flapping sound in the rafters above our heads, like someone noisily shaking a newspaper to scare a cat off a table. It worked . . . not on the cat (I don't think the werewolves owned one) but on Massha and me. My apprentice hit the floor, covering her head with her hands, while I, more used to sudden danger and being more svelte and agile, dove beneath the coffee table.

By the time we recovered from our panicky . . . excuse me, our shrewd defensive maneuvers, there was nothing to see except the vague shape of someone with huge wings disappearing out the front door.

"This one's all yours, dear," Drahcir said firmly, his posture erect and unmoved despite the sudden activity.

"Come on, honey," his wife pleaded. "You're so much better at explaining things. You're supposed to help me out when it comes to talking to people."

"It's a skill I polished at those personal appearances you're so critical of," he retorted stiffly.

"Would *somebody* tell me what's going on?" I said

in tones much louder than I usually use when I'm a guest in someone's home.

Before I could get an answer, the door burst open again utterly destroying what little was left of my nervous system.

"Hey, Boss! Did you s—se—Wha—wa. . . ."

"Outside, Guido!" I ordered, glad to have someone I could shout at without feeling guilty. "Blow your nose . . . and I'm *fine*, thanks! Nice of you to ask!"

By the time my bodyguard had staggered back outside, his face half buried in a handkerchief, I had managed to regain most of my composure.

"Sorry for the interruption," I said as nonchalantly as I could, "but my colleague *does* raise an interesting question. What *was* that?"

"Scary?" Massha suggested.

Apparently she had recovered her composure a little better than I had. I closed my eyes and reflected again on the relative value of cheeky apprentices.

"*That*," Drahcir said loftily, barely in time to keep me from my assistant's throat, "was Vic . . . one of my wife's weird artist friends who dropped in unannounced for a prolonged stay *and*, unless I miss my guess, the criminal you're looking for who framed your partner."

"He wasn't really a friend of mine," Idnew put in in a small voice. "Just a friend of a friend, really. Weird artist types tend to stick together and pass around the locations of crash spaces. He was just another charity case down on his luck who. . . ."

". . . who is currently winging his way back to his accomplice with the news that we're on their trail," I finished with a grimace.

"Isn't that 'accomplices' as in plural?" Massha asked softly.

I ignored her.

"Oh, Drahcir," Idnew said, "now we have to help them. It's the only way we can make up for having provided a hideout for the very person they were trying to find."

"If I might point out," her husband replied, "we've barely met these people. We don't really owe them an explanation, much less any help. Besides, you still have a deadline to meet and. . . ."

"Drahcir!" Idnew interrupted. "It could get real lonely sleeping in the old kennel while I work day and night on a deadline, if you catch my meaning."

"Now, dear," Drahcir said, sidling up to his wife, "before you go getting into a snit, hear me out. I've been thinking it over and I think there's a way we can provide assistance without biting into our own schedules. I mean, we *do* have a friend . . . one who lives a little north of here . . . who's temporarily between assignments and could use the work. I'm sure he'd be willing to do a little tracking for them at a fraction of the fee that we'd charge for the same service."

He was obviously talking in the veiled references partners use to communicate or check ideas in front of strangers, as his words went completely over my head, but drew an immediate reaction from Idnew.

"Oh, Drahcir!" she exclaimed excitedly, all trace of her earlier anger gone. "That's perfect! And he'll just *love* Massha."

"There's still the question of whether or not we can get him here in time," her husband cautioned. "And of course I'll want a percentage off the top as a finder's fee. . . ."

"WHAT!" I exclaimed.

"I agree," Idnew said firmly. "A finder's fee is totally. . . ."

"No! Before that," I urged. "What did you say

about there not being enough time? I thought the execution wasn't scheduled until the end of the week!"

"That's right," Drahcir said. "But the end of the week is tomorrow. Your friend is slated to be executed at high midnight."

"C'mon, Massha," I ordered, heading for the door. "We're heading back to Blut."

"What for?" she demanded. "What can we do without a tracker?"

"We've tried being nice about this, and it isn't working," I responded grimly. "Now we do it the other way. You wanted action, apprentice? How do you feel about giving me a hand with a little jailbreak?"

Chapter Ten:

"What's wrong with a little harmless crime
once in a while?"

—M. BLAISE

"BUT I'm telling you, Boss, jailbreak is a bad rap. With
you operating at only half power in the magic department, there's no tellin' what can go wrong, and
then. . . ."

"Before we get all worked up about what can go
wrong, Guido," I said, trying to salvage something con-
structive out of the conversation, "could you give me a
little information on exactly how hard it is to break
someone out of jail? Or haven't you been involved in
any jailbreaks, either?"

"Of course I've been along on some jailbreaks," the
bodyguard declared, drawing himself up proudly. "I've
been an accomplice on *three* jailbreaks. What kind of
Mob member do you take me for, anyway?"

With a heroic effort I resisted the temptation to answer that particular rhetorical question.

"Okay. So how about a few pointers? This is my first
jailbreak, and I want it to go right."

I was all set to settle in for a fairly lengthy lecture, but instead of launching into the subject, Guido looked a bit uncomfortable.

"Umm . . . actually, Boss, I don't think you'd want to use any of the plans I followed. You see, all three of 'em were busts. None of 'em worked, and in two of the capers, the guy we were tryin' to save got killed. That's how I know about what a bad rap a jailbreak is, know what I mean?"

"Oh, swell! Just swell! Tell me, *Mister* bodyguard, with your allergies and zero-for-three record at jail-break, did you ever do *anything* for the Mob that worked?"

A gentle hand fell on my shoulder from behind.

"Hey! Ease up a little, High Roller," Massha said softly. "I know you're worried about your partner, but don't take it out on Guido . . . or me, either, for that matter. We may not be much, but we're here and trying to help as best we can when we'd both just as soon be back at the Bazaar. You're in a bad enough spot with-out starting a two-front war by turning on your allies."

I started to snap at her, but caught myself in time. Instead, I drew a long ragged breath and blew it out slowly. She was right. My nerves were stretched to the breaking point . . . which served me right for not follow-ing my own advice.

We were currently holed up at the Dispatcher's, the only place I could think of for an in-town base of operations, and as soon as we had arrived, I had insisted that both Massha and Guido grab a bit of sleep. We had been going nonstop ever since stepping through the door into Limbo, and I figured that the troops would need all the rest they could get before we tried to spring Aahz. Of course, once I had convinced them of the necessity of racking out, I promptly ignored my own wisdom and stayed up thinking for the duration.

The rationalization I used for this insane action was that I wanted some extra time uninterrupted to recharge my internal batteries, so whatever minimal magic I had at my disposal would be ready for our efforts. In actuality, what I did was worry. While I had indeed taken part in several criminal activities since teaming up with Aahz, they had all been planned by either Aahz or Tananda. This was my first time to get involved in masterminding a caper, and the stakes were high. Not only Aahz's but Massha's and Guido's futures were riding on my successful debut, and my confidence level was at an all-time low. After much pondering, I had decided to swallow my pride and lean heavily on Guido's expertise, which was why it hit me so hard when I discovered that he knew even less about successful jailbreaks than I.

"Sorry, Guido," I said, trying to restructure my thinking. "I guess I'm more tired than I realized. Didn't mean to snap at you."

"Don't worry, Boss," the bodyguard grinned. "I've been expectin' it. All the big operators I've worked with get a little crabby when the heat's on. If anything, your temper gettin' short is the best thing I've seen since we started this caper. That's why I've been so jumpy myself. I wasn't sure if you weren't taking the job seriously, or if you were just too dumb to know the kind of odds we were up against. Now that you're acting normal for the situation, I feel a lot better about how it's goin' to come out in the end."

Terrific! Now that I was at the end of my rope, our eternal pessimist thought things were going great.

"Okay," I said, rubbing my forehead with one finger, "we haven't got much information to go on, and what we do know is bad. According to Vilhelm, Aahz is being held in the most escape-proof cell they have, which is the top floor of the highest tower in town. If we try to take him from the inside, we're going to have to fool or fight every guard on the way up *and* down. To me, that means our best bet is to spring him from the outside."

My assistants nodded vigorously, their faces as enthusiastic as if I had just said something startlingly original and clever.

"Now, with my powers at low ebb, I don't think I can levitate that far *and* spring the cell. Massha, do you have anything in your jewelry collection that would work for rope and climbing hooks?"

"N—no," she said hesitantly, which surprised me. She usually had a complete inventory of her nasty pretties on the tip of her tongue.

"I saw a coil of rope hangin' just inside the door," Guido supplied.

"I noticed it, too," I acknowledged, "but it isn't nearly long enough. We'll just have to use up my power getting up to the cell and figure some other way of opening the window."

"Ummm . . . you don't have to do that, High Roller," Massha said with a sigh. "I've got something we can use."

"What's that?"

"The belt I'm wearing with all my gear hung on it. It's a levitation belt. The controls aren't horribly reliable, but it should do to get us to the top of the tower."

I cocked an eyebrow at my apprentice.

"Wait a minute, Massha. Why didn't you mention this when I asked?"

She looked away quickly.

"You didn't ask about a belt. Only about rope and climbing hooks."

"Since when do I have to ask you specific questions
. . . or any questions, for that matter, to get your input?"

"All right," she sighed. "If you really want to know,
I was hoping we could find a way to do this without
using the belt."

"Why?"

"It embarrasses me."

"It what?"

"It embarrasses me. I look silly floating around in the
air. It's okay for skinny guys like you and Guido, but
when I try it, I look like a blimp. All I'd need is Good-
year tattooed on my side to make the picture complete."

I closed my eyes and tried to remember that I was
tired and that I shouldn't take it out on my friends. The
fact that Massha was worried about appearances while I
was trying to figure out a way to get us all out of this
alive wasn't really infuriating. It was . . . flattering!
That was it! She was so confident of my abilities to get
us through this crisis that she had time to think about
appearances! Of course, the possibility of betraying that
confidence set me off in another round of worrying.
Wonderful.

"You okay, Boss?"

"Hmmm? Yeah. Sure, Guido. Okay. Now Massha
floats up to the window, which leaves you and me free
to. . . ."

"Hold it, Hot Stuff," Massha said, holding up a
hand. "I think I'd better explain a little more about this
belt. I bought it in an 'as-is' rummage sale, and the controls are not all they should be."

"How so?"

"Well, the 'up' control works okay, but the 'altitude'
is shaky so you're never sure how much you can lift or

how high it will go. The real problem, though, is the
'down' control. There's no tapering-off effect, so it's
either on or off.''

I was never particularly good at technical jargon, but
flying was something I knew so I could almost follow
her.

"Let me see if I've got this right," I said. "When you
go up, you aren't sure how much power you'll have, and
when you land. . . ."

". . . it ain't gentle," she finished for me. "Basically,
you fall from whatever height you're at to the ground."

"I don't know much about this magic stuff," Guido
commented dryly, "but that doesn't sound so good.
Why would you use a rig like that, anyway?"

"I don't . . . at least not for flying," Massha said.
"Remember, I told you I think it makes me look silly?
All I use it for is a utility belt . . . you know, like Bat-
man? I mean, it's kind of pretty, and it isn't easy to find
belts in my size."

"Whatever," I said, breaking into their fashion discussion. "We're going to use it tonight to get up to the
cell even if it means rigging some kind of ballast system.
Now all we need to figure out is how to open the cell
window and a getaway plan. Guido, it occurs to me that
we might pick up a few lessons on jailbreaks from your
experiences even if they *were* unsuccessful. I mean,
negative examples can be as instructive as positive examples. So tell me, in your opinion what went wrong in
the plans you followed in the past?"

The bodyguard's brow furrowed as it took on the
unaccustomed exercise of thought.

"I dunno, Boss. It seems that however much planning
was done, something always came up that we hadn't
figured on. If I had to hang our failures on any one
thing, I'd say it was just that . . . overplanning. I mean,

after weeks of lectures and practice sessions, you get a little overconfident, so when something goes wrong you're caught flatfooted, know what I mean?"

Nervous as we were, that got a laugh from both Massha and me.

"Well, that's one problem we won't have to worry about," I said. "Our planning time is *always* minimal, and for this caper we're going to have to put it together in a matter of hours."

"If you take hours, you'll never pull it off," Vilhelm said, entering our planning room just in time to hear my last comment.

"What's that supposed to mean?" Massha growled.

"Say, are you *sure* you guys are on the level?" the vampire said, ignoring my apprentice. "It occurs to me that I've only got your word on all this . . . that Vic is still alive and all. If you're taking advantage of my good nature to get me involved in something crooked. . . ."

"He's alive," I assured him. "I've seen him myself since we were here last . . . but you didn't answer the question. What was that you were saying about what would happen if we took hours to plan the jailbreak?"

The Dispatcher shrugged.

"I suppose you guys know what you're doing and I should keep my mouth shut, but I was getting a little worried. I mean, it's sundown already, and if you're going to make your move before the execution, it had better be soon."

"How do you figure that?" I frowned. "The action isn't slated until high midnight. I had figured on waiting a while until it was dark and things quieted down around town a little."

"Are you kidding?" the vampire said with a start, his eyebrows going up to his hairline. "That's when . . . oh, I get it. You're still thinking in terms of your off-dimension timetables. You've got to . . . umm, you might want to be sitting down for this, Skeeve.''

"Lay it on me," I said, rubbing my forehead again. "What have I overlooked now? Even without the blindfold and the cigarette I'd just as soon take the bad news standing up."

"Well, you've got to remember that you're dealing with a city of vampires here. Sundown is the equivalent of dawn to us. That's when things *start* happening, not when they start winding down! That means. . . ."

". . . that high midnight is a major traffic time and the longer we wait, the more people there will be on the street," I said, trying to suppress a groan.

Once the basic oversight had been pointed out, I could do my own extrapolations . . . with all their horrible consequences. Trying to fight back my own panic, I turned to my assistants.

"Okay, troops. We're on. Guido, grab that rope you saw. We may need it before this is over."

The bodyguard's eyes widened with astonishment.

"You mean we're going to start the caper right now? But Boss! We haven't planned. . . ."

"Hey, Guido," I said, flashing a grin that was almost sane. "You were the one who said that overplanning was a problem. Well, if you're right, this should be the most successful jailbreak ever!"

Chapter Eleven:

"Nice jail. Looks strong."

—H. HOUDINI

VILHELM was right about one thing. The streets were
nowhere nearly as crowded as they had been the times
we navigated their length well after sundown. Only a
few stray beings wandered here and there, mostly making deliveries or sweeping down the sidewalks in front of
their shops prior to opening. Except for the lack of
light, the streets looked just like any town preparing for
a day's business . . . that and the red eyes of the citizens.

We hugged the light as we picked our way across
town. . . .

That's right. I said "hugged the light." I try to only
make the same mistake a dozen times. In other dimensions, we would have "hugged the dark" to avoid being
noticed or recognized. Here, we "hugged the light."
Don't laugh. It worked.

Anyway, as we picked our way through the streets of
Blut, most of my attention was taken up with the task of
trying to map a good getaway route. Getting Aahz out

of jail I would deal with once we got there. Right now I was worried about what we would do once we had him out . . . a major assumption, I know, but I had so little optimism that I clung to what there was with all fours.

The three of us looked enough like vampires in appearance to pass casual inspection. There was no way, however, that we could pass off my scaly green partner as a native without a disguise spell, and I wasn't about to bet on having any magical energy left after springing Aahz. As such, I was constantly craning my neck to peer down sidestreets and alleys, hoping to find a little-traveled route by which we could spirit our fugitive colleague out of town without bringing the entire populace down on our necks. By the time we reached our destination, I was pretty sure I could get us back to the Dispatcher's by the route we were following, and *positively* sure that if I tried to take us there by the back routes, I would get us totally and helplessly lost.

"Well, Boss. This is it. Think we can crack it?"

I don't think Guido really expected an answer. He was just talking to break the silence that had fallen over us as we stood looking at our target.

The Municipal Building was an imposing structure, with thick stone walls and a corner tower that stretched up almost out of sight into the darkness. It didn't look like we could put a dent in it with a cannon . . . if we had a cannon, which we didn't. I was used to the tents of the Bazaar or the rather ramshackle building style of Klah. While I had been gradually getting over being overawed by the construction prevalent here in Blut, this place intimidated me. I'd seen shakier looking mountains!

"Well, one thing's for certain," I began, almost under my breath.

"What's that?"

"Staring at it isn't going to make it any weaker."

Neither of my assistants laughed at my joke, but then again, neither did I.

Shaking off a feeling of foreboding, I turned to my staff.

"All right, Guido. You stay down here and keep watch. Massha? Do you think that belt of yours can lift two? It's time I went topside and took a good look at this impregnable cell."

My apprentice licked her lips nervously and shrugged.

"I don't know, Hot Stuff. I warned you that the controls on this thing don't work right. It could lift us right into orbit for all I know."

I patted her shoulder in what I hoped was a reassuring way.

"Well, give it a try and we'll find out."

She nodded, wrapped one arm around my chest, and used her other hand to play with the jewels on her belt buckle.

There was a sparkle of light, but beyond that nothing.

"Not enough juice," she mumbled to herself.

"So turn it up already," I urged.

Even if the vampires tended to avoid light, we were lit up like a Christmas tree and bound to attract attention if we stayed at ground level much longer.

"Cross your fingers," she said grimly and touched the jewels again.

The light intensified and we started up fast . . . too fast.

"Careful, Boss!" Guido shouted and grabbed my legs as they went past him.

That brought our progress to a halt . . . well, almost. Instead of rocketing up into the night, we were rising slowly, almost imperceptibly.

"That's got it, High Roller!" Massha exclaimed, shifting her grip to hang onto me with both arms. "A little more ballast than I had planned on, though."

I considered briefly telling Guido to let go, but rejected the thought. If the bodyguard released his grip, we'd doubtless resume our previous speed . . . and while a lot of folks at the Bazaar talked about my meteoric rise, I'd just as soon keep the phrase figurative. There was also the minor detail that we were already at a height where it would be dangerous for Guido to try dropping back to the street. There was that, and his death-grip on my legs.

"Don't tell me, let me guess," I called down to him. "You're acrophobic, too?"

The view of Blut that was unfolding beneath us was truly breathtaking. Truly! My life these days was so cluttered with crisis and dangers that a little thing like looking down on buildings didn't bother me much, but even I was finding it hard to breathe when confronted up close with sheer walls adorned with stone creatures. Still, until I felt his fingernails biting into my calves, it had never occurred to me that such things might upset a rough-and-tumble guy like Guido.

"Naw. I got nothin' against spiders," he replied nervously. "It's heights that scare me."

I let that one go. I was busy studying the tower which could be viewed much more clearly from this altitude. If anything, it looked stronger than the portion of the building that was below us. One feature captured my attention, though. The top portion of the tower, the part I assumed was Aahz's cell, was shaped like a large dragon's head. The window I had been expecting was actually the creature's mouth, with its teeth serving as bars.

I should have anticipated something like that, realizing the abundance of stone animals on every other building in town. Still, it came as a bit of a surprise . . .

but a pleasant surprise. I had been trying to figure a way to get through iron bars, but stone teeth might be a bit easier. Maybe with Aahz working from the inside and us working from the outside, we could loosen the mortar and. . . .

I suddenly realized that in a few moments we would be level with the cell . . . and that a few moments after that we'd be past it! Unless something was done, and done fast, to halt our upward progress, we'd only have time for a few quick words with Aahz before parting company permanently. With time running out fast, I cast about for a solution.

The wall was too far away to grab onto, and there was no way to increase our weight, unless. . . .

When Aahz first taught me to fly, he explained the process as "levitation in reverse." That is, instead of using the mind to lift objects, you push against the ground and lift yourself. Focusing my reservoir of magical energy, I used a small portion to try *flying* in reverse. Instead of pushing up, I pushed down!

Okay. So I was desperate. In a crisis, I'll try anything, however stupid. Fortunately, this stupid idea worked!

Our upward progress slowed to a halt with me hanging at eye-level with the cell's dragon mouth.

Trying not to show my relief, I raised my voice.

"Hey, Aahz! When are visiting hours?"

For a moment there was no response, and I had a sudden fear that we were hanging a hundred feet in the air outside an empty cell. Then my partner's unmistakable countenance appeared in the window.

"Skeeve?" he said in a skeptical voice. "Skeeve! What are you doing out there?"

"Oh, we were just in the neighborhood and thought we'd drop in," I replied in my best nonchalant voice. "Heard you were in a bit of trouble and thought we'd better get you out before it got serious."

"Who's we?" my partner demanded, then he focused on my assistants. "Oh no! Those two? Where are Tananda and Chumley? C'mon, Skeeve. I need a rescue team and you bring me a circus act!"

"It's the best I could do on short notice," I shot back, slightly annoyed. "Tananda and Chumley aren't back from their own work yet, but I left a message for them to catch up with us if they could. Of course, I'm not sure how much help they'll be. In case you're wondering why I'm being carried by my apprentice instead of flying free, this particular dimension is exceptionally low on force lines to tap in to. If anything, I think I'm pretty lucky that I brought 'these two' along instead of ending up with a whole team of for-real magicians who are too proud to use gimmicks. It's thanks to 'these two' that I made it this far at all. Now, do you want our help, or do you want to wait for the next team to float past? I mean, you're in no rush, are you?"

"Now don't get your back up, partner," Aahz said soothingly. "You caught me a little off-guard is all. So tell me, just how do you figure to get me out of here?"

That brought me back to earth . . . or as close to it as I could get while suspended in mid-air.

"Umm . . . actually, Aahz, I was kinda hoping *you* might have a few ideas on the subject. You're usually pretty good at coming up with plans to get us out of tight spots."

"What I want to know," Guido snarled, turning slightly in the wind, "is how come your partner hasn't figured a way out of there all by himself, if he's so all-fired smart?"

I started to rebuke my bodyguard, but slowly his words sank in. That was a good question! Aahz was strong . . . I mean STRONG! By rights he should have been able to rip the stone teeth out of the window all by himself. What *was* keeping him here?

"Oh, I'm having so much fun in here I just couldn't bear to leave," Aahz barked back. "I'm in here because I can't get out, that's why. What's more, if any of you have any ideas about how to get me out, I think now's a real good time to share them with the rest of us."

"Wait a minute, Aahz," I said. "*Why* can't you get out . . . and how did they catch you in the first place?"

"I was framed," my partner retorted, but I noticed his voice was a bit more subdued.

"We already know that," I pressed. "What I want to know is why you didn't just bust a few heads and sprint for home? You've never been particularly respectful of local authority before."

To my surprise, Aahz actually looked embarrassed.

"I was drugged," he said in a disgusted tone. "They put something in my drink, and the next thing I knew I had a stake and mallet in my hands and a room full of officials. Whatever it was they used, it kept me groggy all the way through the trial . . . I mean I couldn't walk straight, much less defend myself coherently, and after that I was in *here*!"

"The old Mickey Finn trick!" Massha snorted, rocking our entire formation. "I'm surprised someone as off-worldly as you could get caught by such a corny stunt."

"Yeah. It surprised me, too!" Aahz admitted. "I mean, that gag is so old, who would really expect anyone to try it at all?"

"Only if you figured the mark was louder than he was smart," Guido sneered.

"Is that so!" my partner snapped, ready to renew their old rivalry. "Well, when I get out of here, you and me can. . . ."

"Stop it, you two," I ordered. "Right now the problem is to get us *all* out of here before the balloon goes up . . . no offense, Massha. Now spill, Aahz. What's so special about this cell that's keeping you bottled up?"

My partner heaved a great sigh.

"Take another look at it, Skeeve. A *close* look."

I did. It still looked the same to me: a tower room in the shape of a dragon's head.

"Yeah. Okay. So?"

"So remember where we are. This thing was built to hold *vampire* criminals. You know, beings with super-human strength that can change into mist?"

My gaze flew back to the dragon's head.

"I don't get it," I admitted. "How can any stone cell hold beings like that?"

"That's the point." Aahz winced. "A stone cell *can't*! This thing is made of *living* stone. If whoever's inside tries to bust out, it swallows them. If they try to turn into mist, it inhales them."

"You mean. . . ."

"Now you're getting the picture."

He flashed his toothy grin at me despite his obvious depression.

"The cell is alive!"

Startled by this revelation, I looked at the tower top cell again. As if it had been waiting for the right cue, the dragon's head opened its eyes and looked at me.

Chapter Twelve:

"For the right person, the impossible is easy!"
—DUMBO

To everyone's surprise, particularly my own, I didn't find the revelation about the true nature of Aahz's confinement at all discouraging. If anything, I was doubly pleased. Not only did I have an immediate idea for how to beat the problem, I had arrived at it before my knowledgeable partner . . . well before, as a matter of fact, as he had been pondering his dilemma for days whereas I had only just received the information. Of course, he was probably not in a position to see the easy solution that I could.

"What are you grinning at?" he demanded. "If there's anything funny about this, it eludes me completely."

Unlike my own amiable self, Aahz tends to show his worry by getting mad. Come to think of it, he tends to express almost any emotion by *getting* mad. Well, at least he's consistent.

"Tell me," I said, eyeing the dragon's head, "you say this thing's alive. How alive is it?"

"What do you mean, 'how alive is it'?" Aahz
scowled. "It's alive enough to swallow me if it gets it
into it's head. That's alive enough for me.

"I mean, can it hear and see?"

"Who cares?" my partner said, in a dazzling display
of charm and curiosity that makes him so lovable. "I
hadn't planned on asking it out for a date."

I stared thoughtfully at the beast.

"I was just wondering if it could hear me . . . say, if I
said that I thought it was the ugliest building decoration
I've seen here in town?"

The dragon's head rewarded me by narrowing its eyes
into an evil glare.

"I think it can hear you, Boss," Guido said, shifting
his grip nervously. "It doesn't look like it liked that last
comment."

"Oh, swell!" Aahz grumbled. "Tell you what, partner. Why don't *you* come in here and sit on this thing's
tongue instead of me before you start getting it all riled
up?"

"I was just checking." I smiled. "To tell the truth, I
think it's the most incredible thing I've seen since I
started traveling the dimensions. I just said that other to
test its reactions."

The dragon stopped glaring, but it still looked a little
bit suspicous and wary.

"Well, find some other reaction to test, okay?" my
partner snapped. "For some obscure reason, I'm a little
nervous these days, and every time this thing moves its
tongue I age a few centuries."

I ignored his grumbling and shook one of my legs.

"Hey, Guido! Are you still paying attention down
there?"

His grip tightened fiercely.

"Of course I'm paying attention, you little . . . I

mean, yeah, Boss. There's not much else to do while we're hangin' here, know what I mean? And quit jerking your leg around . . . please?''

I found his verbal slip rather interesting, but now wasn't the time to investigate further.

"Well, listen up," I said. "Here's what I want you to do. I want you to let go with one hand and pass the rope up to me. . . .''

"No way, Boss! Have you seen how far down it is? I'm not lettin' go no matter what you. . . .''

''. . . because if you don't," I continued as if he hadn't interrupted, "I'm going to start squirming around until either you lose your grip with both hands or Massha loses her grip on me. Whichever way it goes, you'll fall. Get my drift? Now for once could you just follow orders without a lot of back-talk? We don't have much time to pull this off.''

There was a stricken silence below as Guido absorbed my ultimatum and weighed the possibilities.

"Pull what off?" Aahz demanded. "Why doesn't anybody tell me anything? If this master plan of yours is riding on that sorry excuse for a bodyguard, you might as well give up right now. I've told you all along that he was too lily-livered to be any good at. . . .''

"Who's lily-livered?!" Guido shouted. "Look, Big Mouth, as soon as we get you out of there, you and me are going to settle this once and. . . .''

"First, we've got to get him out, Guido," I interrupted. "The rope.''

"Right, Boss. One rope coming up. We'll see who's lily-livered. The last person who called me that was my mom, and by the time I got done with her. . . .''

Our whole formation began to rock dangerously as he fumbled through his coat one-handed in search of the rope. For a minute, I was afraid he was mad enough to

108   **Robert Asprin**

let go with both hands to speed his search.

"Easy there, Guido," I cautioned. "We can. . . ."

"Here it is, Boss!" he said, flipping the rope up so violently that it almost whacked me in the face. "I hope you can use it to hang the son of a. . . ."

"Hanging isn't enough!" Aahz taunted. "It takes more than a piece of rope to do me in."

"Yeah. It takes a little girl with blue eyes and a spiked drink," my bodyguard sneered back. "If you think I'm going to let you live *that* one down. . . ."

I forced myself to ignore them. While it was tempting to rally to Luanna's defense, there were other more pressing matters to attend to.

Moving as carefully as I could, I looped one end of the rope up and around Massha's waist. It took a couple of tries and a lot more rope than I would have liked, but finally I managed to catch the dangling end and tie it off securely.

"What's with the rope, Hot Stuff?" Massha said calmly, the only one of our group who had managed to keep her cool through the entire proceedings.

"Well, with any luck, in a little while we're going to be heading down . . . with Aahz," I explained. "Even though I know you're strong, I don't think your hands are strong enough to keep a grip on all three of us while we make the trip. This is to be sure we don't lose anyone *after* we spring the cell."

"Speaking of that," Aahz called, "I'm still waiting to hear how you're going to get me out of this thing. You might even say I'm *dying* to find out."

He wasn't the only one. The dragon's head was watching my every movement through slitted eyes. I'm not sure how much pride it took in its job, but it was obvious the beast wasn't getting ready to overwhelm us with its cooperation.

Everything was as ready as I could make it, so I decided it was time to play my trump card.

"There's nothing to it, really," I told my partner with a smile. "Talk to me."

It isn't often I catch my old mentor totally by surprise . . . I get him upset on a fairly regular basis, but total surprise was a real rarity. This was one of those golden times.

"Say WHAT?" Aahz exclaimed loudly.

"Trust me, Aahz," I insisted. "I know what I'm doing. Just talk to me. Tell me a story. How did you first meet Garkin?"

"Oh, that," he said, rolling his eyes expressively. "Well, we were at the same boring cocktail party, see . . . you know, one of those dreary affairs where the crowd has you pinned against the wall and you get stuck talking to whatever the tide washes up against you? Anyway, he was trying to impress some little bit of fluff with his magic, which really wasn't all that hot in those days . . . let me tell you, partner, anytime you start getting depressed with your lack of progress in the magic business, remind me to tell you what your old teacher Garkin was like when we first met. But, as I was saying, out of respect for the craft, I just had to wander over and show them what the *real* stuff looked like . . . not that I had any interest in her myself, mind you. . . ."

I felt Guido tugging on my pantleg.

"Say, Boss," he complained. "What is this? I thought we were in a hurry."

"This is what we needed the time for," I whispered back.

"For *this*?" he grumbled. "But Boss, if we don't get started. . . ."

"We're started," I answered. "Now pay attention to what he's saying."

I was afraid our side comments might have distracted Aahz, but I needn't have worried. As per normal, once my partner got on a verbal roll, he wasn't that easy to stop.

". . . so there we were, just the three of us, mind you, and remember, our clothes were five floors away at this point. . . ."

"What's going on, Hot Stuff?" Massha hissed from her position above me. "I *know* you've heard this story before. Heck, *I've* heard it four times myself."

"Keep your eye on the dragon," I advised her. "And be ready to act fast."

I was going through the motions of reacting to Aahz's story and fielding the impatient questions of my assistants as best I could, but my real attention was focused on the dragon's head. My strategy was already working. Aahz's droning account of past glories was starting to take effect.

The dragon's eyes were definitely starting to glaze.

". . . of course, after all that, I just *had* to take her home with me. It was the least I could do for the poor thing under the circumstances."

Aahz was winding up his story already! I had to keep him going just a little bit longer.

"Was that the party where you met Tananda?" I said, deliberately feeding him another cue.

"Tananda? No. That's another story completely. I met her when I was sitting in on a cut-throat game of dragon poker over at the Geek's. We had a real pigeon on the line, the kind of idiot who would bet a busted Corp's a' Corp's into a Unicorn Flush showing, you know? Well, I was a little low on funds just then, so. . . ."

Guido was getting restless again.

"Boss, how much longer are we gonna. . . ."

"Not much longer," I interrupted. "Get hold of the rope. We're about to move."

". . . now I was holding Ogres back-to-back . . . or was it Elves? No, it was Ogres. I remember because Tananda had Elves wrapped up. Of course, we didn't know that until the end of the hand. Anyway, as soon as the Geek opened, I bumped him back limit, and Tananda . . ."

That did it. I should have known a hand-by-hand, bet-by-bet description of dragon poker would do the trick.

Without any warning at all, the dragon yawned . . . long and wide.

Aahz broke off his narration, a momentous event in itself, and blinked his surprise.

"Quick, Aahz! Jump for it!"

Bewildered as he was, there was nothing wrong with my partner's reflexes. He was out of the dragon's mouth in a flash, diving through the air to catch the rope below Guido.

As soon as his hands closed on our lifeline, several things happened at the same time.

With the extra weight on Massha's levitation belt, our whole formation started to sink at an alarming rate . . . my apprentice lost her grip on me, giving me minor rope burns as I clutched madly for the rope, almost too late to follow the advice I had been so freely giving to everyone else . . . and the dragon closed his mouth.

I caught one last glimpse of the beast before we sank from sight, and I honestly don't think he even knew we were gone. His eyelids were at half-mast, and the eyes themselves were out of focus from boredom. Aahz's stories tended to have that effect on even vaguely-intelligent beings. I had simply found a practical application for the phenomenon.

"I've gotta change the controls, Hot Stuff!" Massha called, alerting me once more to our current situation.

The ground was rushing up to meet us with frightening speed.

I remembered the faulty controls that held all of us at their mercy.

"No! Wait, Massha! Let me try. . . ."

Exerting my last ounce of reserve power, I worked at levitating our whole crew. Under normal circumstances, I could lift three people easily and four or five in a pinch. Here in Limbo, using everything I had with Massha's belt assisting me, I barely managed to slow our descent to a moderate crawl.

"What happened there, partner?" Aahz called. "How did you know that thing was going to yawn?"

"Call it a lucky guess," I grunted, still concentrating on keeping us from crashing. "I'll explain later."

"Check the landing zone," Guido warned.

I sneaked a peak.

We had been at our task longer than I thought. The sidewalk below was crowded with vampires strolling here and there as Blut's legendary nightlife fired up.

"I don't think we can bluff our way through this one," Aahz said calmly. "Any chance you can steer us around the corner into the alley? There doesn't seem to be as much of a crowd there."

Before I could answer, something flashed past us from above with a flutter of leather wings.

"JAILBREAK!" it screamed, banking around the corner. "Murderer on the loose! JAILBREAK!"

Chapter Thirteen:

"I've never seen so damn many Indians."
—G. A. CUSTER

THE words of alarm had an interesting effect on the crowd below. After a brief glance to see us descending into their midst, to a man they turned and ran. In a twinkling, the street was empty.

"What's going on?" I called to Aahz, unable to believe our good fortune.

"Beats me!" my partner shouted back. "I guess none of the normal citizenry want to tangle with an escaped murderer. Better get us down fast before they figure out how badly outnumbered we are."

I didn't have to be told twice. Our escape had just gotten an unexpected blessing, but I wasn't about to make book on how long it would last. I cut my magical support, and we dropped swiftly toward the pavement.

"What was that that blew the whistle on us?" Massha said, peering up into the darkness where our mysterious saboteur had disappeared.

"I think it was that Vic character," Guido answered from below me. "I got a pretty good look at him when he bolted past me back at the Woof Writers.''

"Really?" I asked, half to myself, twisting around to look after the departed villain. "That's one more we owe him.''

"Later," Aahz commanded, touching down at last. "Right now we've got to get out of here.''

Guido was beside him in a second. I had to drop a ways, as with the extra weight removed from the rope, we had ceased to sink.

"C'mon, Massha!" I called. "Cut the power in that thing. It's not that far to fall.''

"I'm trying!" she snapped back, fiddling with the belt buckle once more. "The flaming thing's malfunctioning again!''

The belt setting had changed. Holding the rope, I could feel that there was no longer an upward pull. Unfortunately, Massha wasn't sinking, either. Instead, she hovered in mid-air about fifteen feet up.

"Hey, Boss! We got company!"

I followed my bodyguard's gaze. There was a mob forming down the street to our left, and it didn't look happy. Of course, it was hard to tell for sure, but I had the definite impression that their eyes were glowing redder than normal, which I was unable to convince myself was a good sign.

"Maasshhhha!" I nagged, my voice rising uncontrollably as I tugged on the rope.

"It's jammed!" she whimpered. "Go on, take off, Hot Stuff. No sense in all of us getting caught.''

"We can't just leave you here," I argued.

"We don't have time for a debate," Aahz snarled. "Guido! Get up there ahead of us and keep the street open. We can't afford to get cut off. Okay, let's go!''

With that, he snatched the rope out of my hand and took off running down the street away from the crowd with Guido out front in point position and Massha floating over his head like a gaudy balloon. For once, I didn't object to him giving orders to my bodyguard. I was too busy sprinting to keep up with the rest of my group.

If the watching mob was having any trouble deciding what to do, the sight of us fleeing settled it. With a howl, they swarmed down the street in pursuit.

When I say "with a howl," I'm not speaking figuratively. As they ran, some of the vampires transformed into large, fierce-looking dogs, others into bats, presumably to gain more speed in the chase. While Aahz and I had been chased by mobs before, this was the first pack of pursuers who literally bayed at our heels. I must say I didn't care much for the experience.

"Where are we going, Aahz?" I panted.

"Away from them!" he called back.

"I mean, eventually," I pressed. "We're heading the wrong way to get back to our hideout."

"We can't hole up until we've shaken our fan club," my partner insisted. "Now shut up and run."

I had certain doubts about our ability to elude our pursuers while towing Massha overhead to mark our position, but I followed Aahz's instructions and pumped the pavement for all I was worth. For one thing, if I pointed out this obvious fact to my partner, he might simply let go of the rope and leave my apprentice to fend for herself. Then again, the option to running was to stand firm and face the mob. All in all, running seemed like a *real* good idea.

Guido was surprisingly good at clearing a path for us. I had never really seen my bodyguard in action, but with his constant carping and allergy problems throughout this venture, I was tending to discount his usefulness. Not so. The vampires we encountered in our flight had not heard the alarm and were unprepared for the whirlwind that burst into their midst. Guido never seemed to break stride as he barreled into victim after victim, but whatever he did to them was effective. None of the fallen bodies which marked his progress attempted to interfere with Aahz or I . . . heck, they didn't even move.

"River ahead, Boss!" he called over his shoulder.

"What's that?" I puffed, realizing for the first time how out of shape I had grown during my prosperous stay at the Bazaar.

"A river!" he repeated. "The street we're on is going to dead-end into a river in a few blocks. I can see it from here. We're going to have to change direction or we'll get pinned against the water."

I wondered whether it wouldn't be a good idea for us to just plunge into the river and put some moving water between us and the vampires, as I seemed to recall a legend that that was one of the things that could stop them. Then it occurred to me that my bodyguard probably couldn't swim.

"Head right!" Aahz shouted. "There! Up that alley."

Guido darted off on the indicated course with my partner and I pounding along about fifteen paces behind him. We had built up a bit of a lead on our pursuers, though we could still hear their cries and yelps a block or so back, and for the first time I started to have the hope that we might actually elude them. Now that we were out of their line of sight. . . .

"Look out. . . ."

There was a sudden cry from above, and Massha came crashing to the ground, gaining the dubious distinction of being the first person I've ever witnessed doing a belly-flop on dry land. I'm sure the ground didn't actually shake, but the impact was enough to leave that impression. I experienced a quick flash of guilt, realizing that my first thought was not for the well-being of my apprentice, but rather unbridled relief that she hadn't landed on one of us.

"I think the controls just came unstuck," Aahz said, rather unnecessarily to my thinking.

"Are you all right, Massha?" I said, crouching over her.

"Wha—ha . . ." came the forced reply.

"Of course, she's not all right," Aahz snapped, assuming translator duties. "At the very least she's got the wind knocked out of her."

Whatever the exact extent of the damages suffered from her fall, my apprentice wasn't even trying to rise. I would have liked to give her a few minutes recovery time, but already the sounds of our pursuers were drawing closer.

"Can you carry her, Aahz?"

"Not on my best day," my partner admitted, eyeing Massha's sizable bulk. "How about you? Have you got enough juice left to levitate her?"

I shook my head violently.

"Used it all supervising our aerial maneuvers back at the jail."

"Hey, Boss!" Guido hissed, emerging from the shadows behind us. "The alley's blocked. This is the only way out!"

And that was that. Even if we got Massha up and moving, all it meant was that we'd have to retrace our steps right back into the teeth of the mob. We had run our race . . . and were about to lose it rather spectacularly.

The others knew it, too.

"Well, it's been nice working with you, Guido," Aahz said with a sigh. "I know I've gotten on your case a couple of times, but you're a good man to have around in a pinch. You did some really nice crowd work getting us this far. Sorry about that last turn call."

"No hard feelings," my bodyguard shrugged. "You gave it your best shot. This alley would have been my choice, too, if I'd been workin' alone. Boss, I warned you I was a jinx when it came to jailbreaks. I gotta admit, though, for a while there I really thought we were goin' to pull this one off."

"It was a long shot at best." I grinned. "At least you can't say that *this* one suffered from over-planning."

Aahz clapped a hand on my shoulder.

"Well, partner?" he said. "Any thoughts on how to play this one? Do we try to surrender peacefully, or go down swinging?"

I wasn't sure the crowd would give us a choice. They were almost at our alley, and they didn't sound like they cared much for talking.

"NOT THIS WAY! THEY'RE DOUBLING BACK TOWARD THE JAIL!"

This unexpected cry came from the street near the mouth of our alley.

I couldn't believe it, but apparently the mob did. There were curses and shouted orders, but from their fast-fading manner it was plain that the crowd had turned and was now heading back the way they had come.

"What was that?" Massha managed, her voice returning at last.

I motioned her to be silent and cocked an eyebrow at Aahz, silently asking the same question.

He answered with an equally silent shake of the head.

Neither of us knew for sure what was going on, but we both sensed that the timely intervention was neither accidental nor a mistake. Someone had deliberately pulled the crowd off our backs. Before we celebrated our good fortune, we wanted to know who and why.

A pair of figures appeared at the mouth of the alley.

"You can come out now," one of them called.

"Sorry to interfere, but it looked like so much fun we just *had* to play, too."

I'd know that voice anywhere, even if I didn't recognize the figure as well as the unmistakable form of her brother.

"Tananda! Chumley!" I shouted, waving to pinpoint our position. "I was wondering when you'd show up."

The sister-brother team of Trollop and Troll hastened to join us. For all their lighthearted banter, I can think of few beings I'd rather have on or at my side when things get tight.

"Are you all right?" Tananda asked, stopping to help Massha to her feet.

"Really never had much dignity," my apprentice responded, "and what little I did have is shot to hell. Except for that I'm fine. I'm starting to see why you Big Leaguers are so down on mechanical magic."

Chumley seized my hand and pumped it vigorously.

"Now don't be too rough on your little gimmicks, ducks," he advised. "That little ring you left us was just the ticket we needed to get here in time for the latest in our unbroken string of last-minute rescues. Except for the typical hash you've made of your end-game, it looks like you've done rather well without us. We've got all present and accounted for, including Aahz, who seems remarkably unscathed after yet one more near-brush with disaster. Seems like all that's left is a hasty retreat and a slow celebration . . . eh, what?"

"That's about the size of it," I agreed. "It's great having the two of you along to ride shotgun on our exit, though. Speaking of which, can you find the castle from here? I've gotten a little turned around. . . ."

"Hold it right there!" Aahz broke in. "Before we get too wrapped up in congratulating each other, aren't there a few minor details being overlooked?"

The group looked at each other.

"Like what?" Tananda said at last.

"Like the fact that I'm still wanted for murder, for one," my partner glared. "Then again, there's the three fugitives we're supposed to be bringing back to Deva with us."

"Oh, come on, Aahz," the Trollop chided, poking him playfully in the ribs. "With the reputation you already have, what's a little thing like a murder warrant?"

"I didn't do it," Aahz insisted. "Not only didn't I kill this Vic character, nobody did. He's still around somewhere laughing down his sleeve at all of us. Now while I'll admit my reputation isn't exactly spotless, it doesn't include standing still for a bum rap . . . or letting someone get away with making a fool of me!"

"Of course, saving the money for paying the swindlers' debts plus the fines involved has nothing to do with it, eh, Aahz?" Chumley said, winking his larger eye.

"Well . . . that, too," my partner admitted. "Isn't it nice that we can take care of both unpleasant tasks at the same time?"

"Maybe we could settle for just catching Vic and let the others go," I murmured.

"How's that again, partner?"

"Nothing, Aahz," I said with a sigh. "It's just that . . . nothing. C'mon everybody. If we're going to go hunting, it's going to require a bit of planning, and I don't think we should do it out here in the open."

Chapter Fourteen:

"Relax, Julie. Everyone will understand."
—ROMEO

FORTUNATELY, Massha's elevated position during our
flight had given her an excellent view of our surroundings, and we were able to find our way back to the
Dispatcher's without being discovered by the aroused
populace. Now that our numbers had increased, however, Vilhelm's greeting was noticeably cooler.

"I'm starting to believe what everybody says," the
little vampire complained. "Let one demon in, and the
next thing you know the neighborhood's crawling with
them. When I decided to talk to you folks instead of
blowing the whistle on you, I didn't figure on turning
my office into a meeting place for off-worlders."

"C'mon, Vilhelm," I said, trying to edge my foot
into the doorway. "We don't have any place else to go
in town. There aren't *that* many of us."

"We could always just wait out on the street until the
authorities come by," Aahz suggested. "I don't imagine
it would take much to convince them that this guy has
been harboring fugitives."

121

"Can it, Green and Scaly," Massha ordered, puffing herself up to twice her normal size. "Vilhelm's been nice to us so far, and I won't listen to anyone threaten him, even you. Just remember that you'd still be cooling your heels in the slammer if it weren't for him. Either he helps of his own free will, or we look elsewhere."

Aahz gave ground before her righteous indignation.

"Are you going to let your apprentice talk to me that way?" he demanded.

"Only when she's right." I shrugged.

"I say, Aahz," Chumley intervened. "Could you possibly curb your normally vile manners for a few moments? We don't really need one more enemy in this dimension, and I, for one, would appreciate the chance to extend my thanks to this gentleman before he throws us out."

When he's working, Chumley goes by the name of Big Crunch and does a Neanderthal that's the envy of half the barbarians at the Bazaar. On his own time, however, his polished charm has solved a lot of problems for us . . . almost as many as Aahz's bluster has gotten us into.

"Oh, come on in," the Dispatcher grumbled. "Enter freely and of your own accord and all that. I never could turn my back on somebody in trouble. Guess that's why I've never traveled the other dimensions myself. They'd eat me alive out there."

"Thanks, Vilhelm," I said, slipping past him into the office before he could change his mind. "You'll have to forgive my partner. He really isn't always like this. Being on death row hasn't done much for his sense of humor."

"I guess I'm a little edgy myself," the vampire admitted. "Strange as it sounds, I've been worried about you folks . . . and your motor-mouthed friend who's been keeping me company hasn't helped things much."

I did a quick nose count of our troop.

"Wait a minute," I frowned. "Who's been waiting for us?"

Now it was Vilhelm's turn to look surprised.

"Didn't one of you send out for a werewolf? He said he was with you."

"Aahh! But I am! My friends, they do not know me yet, but I shall be their salvation, no?"

With that, I was overwhelmed by a shaggy rug. Well, at least that's what I thought until it came off the floor and threw itself into my arms with the enthusiasm of a puppy . . . a very large puppy.

"What's *that*?!" Aahz said, his eyes narrowing dangerously. "Skeeve, can't I leave you alone for a few days without you picking up every stray in any given dimension?"

"That," in this case, was one of the scroffiest-looking werewolves I'd ever seen . . . realizing, of course, that until this moment I'd only seen two. He had dark bushy eyebrows (if you'll believe that on a werewolf) and wore a white stocking cap with a maple leaf on the side. His whiskers were carefully groomed into a handlebar mustache, and what might have been a goatee peered from beneath his chin. Actually, viewed piecemeal, he was very well-groomed. It's just when taken in its entirety that he looked scroffy. Maybe it was the leer. . . .

"Honest, Aahz," I protested, trying to untangle myself. "I've never seen him before in my life!"

"Oh, but forgive me," the beast said, releasing me so suddenly I almost fell. "I am so stupeed, I forget to introduce. So! I am an artist extraordinaire, but also, I am ze finest track-air in ze land. My friends, the Woof Writers, they have told me of your pro-blem and I have flown like ze wind to aid you. No? I am Pepe Le Garou A. and I am at your service."

With that, he swept into a low bow with a flourish that if I hadn't been so flabbergasted I would have applauded. It occurred to me that now I knew why the Woof Writers had snickered when they told us they knew of someone who could help.

"Boss," Guido said, his voice muffled by his hand, which he was holding over his nose and mouth. "Shall I wait outside?"

Tananda cocked an eyebrow at him.

"Allergy problems? Here, try some of this. No dimension traveler should be without it."

She produced a small vial and tossed it to my bodyguard. "Rub some onto your upper lip just below your nose."

"Gee, thanks," Guido said, following her instructions. "What is it?"

"It's a counter-allergenic paste." She shrugged. "I think it has a garlic base."

"WHAT?" my bodyguard exclaimed, dropping the vial.

Tananda favored him with one of her impish grins.

"Just kidding. Nunzio was worried about you and told us about your allergies . . . all of them."

Her brother swatted her lightly on the rump.

"Shame on you, little sister," he said, smiling in spite of himself. "After you get done apologizing to Guido, I suggest you do the same for our host. I think you nearly gave him a heart attack with that last little joke."

This was, of course, just what I needed while stranded in a hostile dimension. A nervous vampire, a melo-dramatic werewolf, and now my teammates decide it's time to play practical jokes on each other.

"Ummm . . . tell me, Mr. A.," I said, ignoring my other problems and turning to the werewolf. "Do you think you can. . . ."

"No, non," he interrupted. "Eet is simply Pepe, eh?"

"Pepe A.," I repeated dutifully.

"Zat's right," he beamed, apparently delighted with my ability to learn a simple phrase. "Now, before we . . . how you say, get down to ze business, would you do me ze hon-air of introducing me to your colleagues?"

"Oh. Sorry. This is my partner, Aahz. He's. . . ."

"But of course! Ze famous Aahz! I have so long wished to meet you."

If there's anything that can coax Aahz out of a bad mood, it's flattery . . . and Pepe seemed to be an expert in that category.

"You've heard of me?" he blinked. "I mean . . . what exactly have you heard? There have been so many adventures over the years."

"Do you not remem-bair Piere? I was raised from a pup on his tales of your fight with Isstvan."

"Piere? You know Piere?"

"Do I know him? He is my uncle!"

"No kidding. Hey, Tananda! Did you hear that? Pepe here's Piere's nephew. Wait'll we tell Gus."

I retired from the conversation, apparently forgotten in the reunion.

"Say, Skeeve," Vilhelm said, appearing at my side. "It looks like this could take a while. Should I break out the wine?"

That got my attention.

"Wine? You've got wine?"

"Stocked up on it after your last visit," the vampire admitted with a grin. "Figured it might come in handy the next time you came through. I may gripe a bit, but talking to you and your friends is a lot more fun than watching the tubes."

"Well bring it out . . . but I get the first glass. Unless you've got lots there won't be much left after my partner there gets his claws on it."

I turned back to the proceedings just in time to see

Pepe kissing my apprentice's hand.

"Do not be afraid, my little flow-air," he was saying. "Here is one who truly appreciates your beauty, as well as . . . how should I say it, its quantity?"

"You're kinda cute," Massha giggled. "But I never did go in much for inter-species dating, if you get my drift."

I caught Aahz's attention and drew him away from the group.

"Could you take over for a while here, partner?" I said. "I've been running nonstop since the start of this thing and could use a little time by myself to recharge my batteries before we fire up again."

"No problem," he nodded, laying a hand on my shoulder. "I figure we won't be moving before sunup . . . and Skeeve? I haven't had a chance to say it, but thanks for the bail-out."

"Don't mention it," I grinned weakly. "Tell me you wouldn't do the same for me."

"Don't know," he retorted. "You've never sucker-punched me at the beginning of a caper."

"Now *that* I still owe you for."

Just then, Vilhelm appeared with the wine, and Aahz hurried away to rejoin the group.

I managed to snag a goblet and retired to a secluded corner while the party went into high gear. Pepe seemed to be fitting in well with the rest of the team, if not functioning as a combination jester and spark plug, but somehow I felt a bit distant. Sipping my wine, I stared off into the distance at nothing in particular, letting my thoughts wander.

"What's the trouble, handsome?"

"Hmmm? Oh. Hi, Tananda. Nothing in particular. Just a little tired, that's all."

"Mind if I join you?" she said, dropping to the floor beside me before I could stop her. "So. Are you going to tell me about it? Who is she?"

I turned my head slowly to look at her directly.

"I beg your pardon?"

She kept her eyes averted, idly running one finger around the rim of her goblet.

"Look," she said, "if you don't want to talk about it, just say so . . . it's really none of my business. Just don't try to kid me or yourself that there's nothing bothering you. I've known you a long time now, and I can usually tell when there's something eating you. My best guess right now, if I'm any judge of the phenomenon, is that it's a girl."

Ever since I'd met Tananda, I'd had a crush on her. With her words, though, I suddenly realized how badly I wanted someone to talk to. I mean, to Guido and Massha I was an authority figure, and I wasn't about to open up to Aahz until I was sure he'd take the problem seriously and not just laugh, and as for Chumley . . . how do you talk about woman problems with a troll?

"Okay. You got me," I said, looking back into my wine. "It's a girl."

"I thought so," Tananda smiled. "Where have you been keeping her? Tell me, is she beautiful and sensitive?"

"All that and more." I nodded, taking another drink from my goblet. "She's also on the wrong side."

"Woops," Tananda said, straightening up. "You'd better run that one past me again."

I filled her in on my encounters with Luanna. I tried to keep it unbiased and informative, but even I could tell that my tones were less controlled than I would have liked.

Tananda sat in silence for a few moments after I'd finished, hugging her legs and with her chin propped up on her knees.

"Well," she said at last, "from what you say, she's

an accomplice at best. Maybe we can let her go after we get them all rounded up.''

"Sure.''

My voice was flat. Both Tananda and I knew that once Aahz got on his high horse there was no telling how merciful or vicious he would be at any given point.

"Well, there's always a chance,'' she insisted. "Aahz has always had a soft spot where you're concerned. If you intercede for her, and if she's willing to abandon her partners. . . .''

". . . and, if a table had wings, we could fly it back to the Bazaar.'' I frowned. "No, Tananda. First of all, she won't give up her partners just because they're in a crunch. That much I know. Besides, if I put that kind of pressure on her, to choose between me and them, I'd never know for sure if she really wanted me or if she was just trying to save her own skin.''

Tananda got to her feet.

"Don't become so wise that you're stupid, Skeeve,'' she said softly before she left. "Remember, Luanna's already chosen you twice over her partners. Both times she's risked her life and their getaway to pass you a warning. Maybe all she needs is what you haven't yet given her—an invitation for a chance at a new life with a new partner. Don't be so proud or insecure that you'd throw a genuine admirer to the wolves rather than run the risk of making a mistake. If you did, I don't think I'd like you much . . . and I don't think you would either.''

I pondered Tananda's advice after she'd gone. There was one additional complication I hadn't had the nerve to mention to her. Whatever Luanna's feelings for me were, how would they change when she found out I'd used her scarf . . . her token of affection, to guide a pack of hunters to their target?

Chapter Fifteen:

"Everybody needs a career manager!"
—LADY MACBETH

"SO where is he?" Aahz grumbled for the hundredth time . . . in the last five minutes.

The sun had been up for hours, or at least as up as it seemed to get in this dimension. Since my arrival in Limbo, I had never seen what I am accustomed to thinking of as full sunlight. Whether the constant heavy overcast condition which seemed to prevail during daylight hours was the result of magic or some strange meteorologic condition I was never sure, but it did nothing to alleviate the air of gloom that clung to the town of Blut like a shroud.

The whole team was impatient to get started, but Aahz was the only one who indulged himself in expressing his feelings as often . . . or as loudly. Of course, it might have been simply that he was making so much of a fuss that the others were willing to let him provide the noise for all of them rather than letting their own efforts get constantly upstaged.

"Just take it easy, partner," I said soothingly, struggling to keep from snapping at him in my own nervous impatience. "There aren't that many all-day stores in this dimension."

"What do you expect, dealing with a bunch of vampires," he snapped. "I still don't like this idea. Nonmagical disguises seem unnatural somehow."

I heaved a quiet sigh inside and leaned back to wait, propping my feet up on a chair. This particular quarrel was old before Vilhelm had left on his shopping trip, and I was tired going over it again and again.

"Be reasonable, Aahz," Tananda said, taking up the slack for me. "You know we can't wander around town like this . . . especially you with half the city looking for you. We need disguises, and without a decent power source, Skeeve here can't handle disguises for all of us. Besides, it's not like we're using mechanical magic. We won't be using magic at all."

"That's what everybody keeps telling me," my partner growled. "We're just going to alter our appearances without using spells. That sounds like mechanical magic to me. Do you know what's going to happen to our reputations if word of this gets back to the Bazaar? Particularly with most of the competition looking for a chance to splash a little mud on the Great Skeeve's name? Remember, we're already getting complaints that our prices are too high, and if this gets out. . . ."

The light dawned. I could finally see what was eating at Aahz. I should have known there was money at the bottom of this.

"But Aahz," I chimed in, "our fees *are* overpriced. I've been saying that for months. I mean, it's not like we need the money. . . ."

". . . and I've been telling you for months that it's the only way to keep the riff-raff from draining away all your practice time," he shot back angrily. "Remember, your name's supposed to be the Great Skeeve, not the

Red Cross. You don't do charity.''

Now we were on familiar ground. Unlike the disguise thing, this was one argument I never tired of.

"I'm not talking about charity," I said. "I'm talking about a fair fee for services rendered."

"Fair fee?" my partner laughed, rolling his eyes. "You mean like that deal you cut with Watzisname? Did he ever tell you about that one, Tananda? We catch a silly bird for this Deveel, see, and my partner charges him a flat fee. Not a percentage, mind you, a flat fee. And how much of a flat fee? A hundred gold pieces? A thousand. No. TEN. Ten lousy gold pieces. And half an hour later the Deveel sells his 'poor little bird' for over a hundred thousand. Nice to know we don't do charity, isn't it?"

"C'mon, Aahz," I argued, writhing inside. "That was only five minutes' work. How was I supposed to know the silly bird was on the endangered species list? Even *you* thought it was a good deal until we heard what the final sale was. Besides, if I had held out for a percentage and the Deveel had been legit and never sold the thing, we wouldn't have even gotten ten gold pieces out of it."

"I never heard the details from your side," Tananda said, "but what I picked up on the streets was that everybody at the Bazaar was really impressed. Most folks think that it's a master-stroke of PR for the hottest magician at the Bazaar to help bring a rarity to the public for a mere fraction of his normal fees. It shows he's something other than a cold-hearted businessman . . . that he really cares about people."

"So what's wrong with being a cold-hearted businessman?" Aahz snorted. "How about the other guy? Everybody thinks he's a villain, and he's crying all the way to the bank. He retired on the profit from that one sale alone."

"Unless Nanny misled me horribly when she taught me my numbers," Chumley interrupted, "I figure your current bankroll could eat that fellow's profit and still have room for lunch. Any reason you're so big on squirreling away so much gold, Aahz? Are you planning on retiring?"

"No, I'm not planning on retiring," my partner snapped. "And you're missing the point completely. Money isn't the object."

"It isn't?"

I think everybody grabbed that line at the same time . . . even Pepe, who hadn't known Aahz all that long.

"Of course not. You can always get more gold. What can't be replaced is time. We all know Skeeve here has a long way to go in the magic department. What the rest of you keep forgetting is how short a life span he has to play with . . . maybe a hundred years if he's lucky. All I'm trying to do is get him the maximum learning time possible . . . and that means keeping him from using up most of his time on nickel-and-dime adventures. Let the smalltime operators do those. My partner shouldn't have to budge away from his studies unless the assignment is something *really* spectacular. Something that will advance his reputation and his career."

There was a long silence while everybody digested that one, especially me. Since Aahz had accepted me as a full partner instead of an apprentice, I tended to forget his role as my teacher and career manager. Thinking back now, I could see he had never really given up the work, just gotten sneakier. I wouldn't have believed that was possible.

"How about this particular nickel-and-dime adventure?" Tananda said, breaking the silence. "You know, pulling your tail out of a scrape? Isn't this a little lowbrow for the kind of legend you're trying to build?"

The sarcasm in her voice was unmistakable, but it

didn't phase Aahz in the least.

"If you'll ask around, you'll find out that I didn't want him along on this jaunt at all. In fact, I knocked him cold trying to keep him out. A top-flight magician shouldn't have to stoop to bill collecting, especially when the risk is disproportionately high."

"Well, it all sounds a little cold-blooded for my taste, Aahz," Chumley put in. "If you extend your logic, our young friend here is only going to work when the danger is astronomically high, and conversely if the advancement to his career is enough, no risk is too great. That sounds to me like a sure-fire way to lose a partner *and* a friend. Like the Geek says, if you keep bucking the odds, sooner or later they're going to catch up with you."

My partner spun to confront the troll nose-to-nose.

"Of course it's going to be dangerous," he snarled. "The magic profession isn't for the faint of heart, and to hit the top he's going to have to be hair-triggered and mean. There's no avoiding that, but I can try to be sure he's ready for it. Why do you think I've been so dead-set against him having bodyguards? If he starts relying on other people to watch out for him, he's going to lose the edge himself. *That's* when he's in danger of walking into a swinging door."

That brought Guido into the fray.

"Now let me see if I've got this right," my bodyguard said. "You don't want me and my cousin Nunzio around so that the Boss here can handle all the trouble himself? That's crazy talk, know what I mean? Now listen to me, 'cause this time I know what I'm sayin'. The higher someone gets on the ladder, the more folks come huntin' for his head. even if they don't do nothin' they got people gunning for them, 'cause they got power and respect and there's always somebody who thinks they can steal it. Now I've seen some of the Big Guys

who try to act just like you're sayin' . . . they're so
scared all the time they don't trust nothin' or nobody.
The only one they can count on is themselves, and
everybody else is suspect. That includes total strangers,
their own bodyguards, their friends, *and* their partners.
Think about *that* for a minute.''

He leaned back and surveyed the room, addressing
his next comments to everyone.

"People like that don't last long. They don't trust
nobody, so they got nobody. Ya can't do everything
alone and sooner or later they're lookin' the wrong way
or asleep when they should be watchin' and it's all over.
Now I've done a lot of jobs as a bodyguard, and they
were just jobs, know what I mean? The Boss here is different, and I'm not just sayin' that. He's the best man
I've met in my whole life because he likes people and
ain't afraid to show it. More important, he ain't afraid
to risk his neck to help somebody even if it *isn't* in his
best interest. I work double hard for him because I
don't want to see anything happen to him . . . and if that
means comin' along on weird trips like this, then that's
the way it is. Anybody that wants to hurt him is gonna
have to come through me . . . and that includes fightin'
any of you if you want to try to turn him into somethin'
he isn't and doesn't want to be.''

Massha broke in with a loud clapping of her hands.

"Bravo, Guido,'' she said. "I think your problem,
Green and Scaly, is that your idea of success is out of
step with everyone else's. We all want to see good things
happen for Skeeve, here, but we also like him just the
way he is. We've got enough faith in his good sense to
back him in whatever move he makes in his development . . . without trying to frog-march or trick him up a
specific path.''

Aahz not only gave ground before this onslaught of
protest, he seemed to shrink in a little on himself.

"I like him too," he mumbled. "I've known him longer than any of you, remember? He's doing fine, but he could be so much more. How can he choose a path if he can't see it? All I'm trying to do is set him up to be bigger than I . . . than *we* could ever think of being ourselves. What's wrong with that?"

Despite my irritation at having my life discussed as if I weren't in the room, I was quite touched, by my friends' loyal defense of me, and most of all by Aahz.

"You know, partner," I said softly, "for a minute there, you sounded just like my father. He wanted me to be the best . . . or more specifically, to be better than he was. My mom always tried to tell me that it was because he loved me, but at that time it just sounded like he was always being critical. Maybe she was right . . . I'm more inclined to believe it today than I was then, but then again, I'm older now. If nothing else, I've had to try to tell people I love them when the words just won't come . . . and gotten upset with myself when they couldn't see it when I tried to show them.

"Aahz, I appreciate your concern and I want your guidance. You're right, there are paths and options I can't even comprehend yet. But I also have to choose my own way. I want to be better eventually than I am today, but not necessarily the best. I think Guido's right, there's a big price tag attached to being at the top, and I'd want to think long and hard if I wanted to pay it . . . even if I was convinced I could, which I'm not. I *do* know that if it means giving up the trust I have in you and everybody else in this room, I'll settle for being a nickel-and-dime operator. *That* price I'll never pay willingly."

Silence started to descend again as each of us retreated into his or her own thoughts, then the werewolf bounded into the middle of the assemblage.

"But what is this, eh?" he demanded. "Surely this

cannot be ze great team of Aahz and Skeeve, ze ones
who can laugh at any dan-gair?''

"You know, Pepe," Aahz said warningly, "you've
got a great future as a stuffed head."

"My head?" The werewolf blinked. "But she is not
. . . oohh. I see now. You make ze joke, eh? Good. Zat
is more like it."

". . . and as far as laughing at danger goes," I joined
in, determined to hold up my end of the legend, "the
only danger I see here is dying of boredom. Where *is*
Vilhelm anyway?"

"I know you and Aahz are fond of each other,
Skeeve," Chumley yawned, "but you've *got* to spend
more time with other people. You're starting to sound
like him. Maybe you can tag along the next time I have
an assignment."

"Over my dead body," my partner said. "Besides,
what could he learn from a troll that I couldn't teach
him myself?"

"I could teach him not to catch birds for Deveels for
ten gold pieces," the troll grinned, winking at his sister.
"That seems to be a part of his education you've neglected."

"Izzat so!" my partner bristled. "You're going to
teach him about price setting? How about the time you
set your own sister up to steal an elephant without
bothering to check. . . ."

And they were off again. As I listened, I found myself
reflecting on the fact that while it was nice to know the
depths of my friends' feelings about me, it was far more
comfortable when they managed to conceal it under a
cloak of banter. For the most part, open sincerity is
harder to take than friendly laughter.

Chapter Sixteen:

"Don't be fooled by appearances."

—MALLOY

THINGS were pretty much back to normal by the time Vilhelm returned with our disguises . . . which was a good thing as the process of masking-up proved to be a test of everybody's sense of humor.

Until I had hooked up with Aahz, I had never had occasion to pretend I was anyone but myself. As such, I had no way of knowing how long it took to don a physical disguise without resorting to magic. By the time we were done, I had a new respect for the skills I had learned, not to mention a real longing for a dimension . . . any dimension with a strong force line to work with.

Tananda was a major help, her experiences with the assassin's guild came into play and she took the lead in trying to coach us into our new roles.

"Guido, straighten up!" she commanded, exasperation creeping into her voice. "You walk like a gangster."

"I am a gangster!" my bodyguard snarled back.

"Besides, what's wrong with the way I walk? It got us to the jail, didn't it?"

"Half the town wasn't looking for you then," Tananda argued. "Besides, then you could pick your own route. We don't know where the opposition's holed up. We're going to have to walk through crowds on this hunt, and that walk just doesn't make it. Ninety percent of costuming is learning to move like the character you're trying to portray. Right now you move like you're looking for a fight."

"Try walking like Don Bruce," I suggested. "He's a gangster, too."

That earned me a black look, but my bodyguard tried to follow my instructions, rising up on the balls of his feet and mincing along.

"Better," Tananda said, leaving Guido prancing up and down the room with a scowl on his face.

"How are we doing?"

"Lousy," she confided in me. "This is taking a lot longer than it should. I wish there were more mirrors in this place . . . heck, any mirrors would be nice."

It hadn't been until we started gearing up that we realized the Dispatcher had no mirrors at all. He claimed they weren't popular or necessary among vampires. This left us with the unenviable job of checking each others' make-up and costumes, a chore which would have been Homeric even if less sensitive egos were involved.

"How're my teeth?" Massha demanded, sticking her head in front of me and opening her mouth.

It was like staring into the depths of an underground cave.

"Umm . . . the left side is okay, but you're still missing a few on the right. Hang on a second and I'll give you a hand."

Teeth were turning out to be a special problem. We had hoped to find some of the rubber fangs so prevalent in the Bazaar novelty stores to aid in our disguises. Unfortunately, none of the shops in Blut had them. The closest thing they had in stock, according to Vilhelm, were rubber sets of human teeth designed to fit over fangs. The vampire assured us that locally they were considered quite frightening. Faced by this unforeseen shortage, we were resorting to using tooth-black to blacken all our teeth except the canines for a close approximation of the vampires we were trying to imitate. When we tried it out, it wasn't a bad effect, but the actual application was causing countless problems. When one tried to apply the stuff on oneself without a mirror, it was difficult to get the right teeth, and if one called on one's friends for assistance, one rapidly found that said friend was soon possessed by an overpowering impulse to paint one's tongue black instead of the teeth.

"I don't like this cloak," Guido announced, grabbing my arm. "I want to wear my trench coat."

"Vampires don't wear trench coats," I said firmly. "Besides, the cloak really looks great on you. Makes you look . . . I don't know, debonair but menacing."

"Yeah?" he retorted skeptically, craning his neck to try to see himself.

"You think you've got problems?" Massha burst in. "Look at what I'm supposed to wear! I'll trade your cloak for this rig any day."

As you might have noticed, the team was having more than a little difficulty adapting to their disguises. Massha in particular was rebelling against her costume.

After having been floated over our escape like a balloon over a parade, we feared that she would be one of the most immediately recognizable of our group. As such, we not only dyed her garish orange hair, we insisted that her new costume cover as much of her as possible. To this end, Vilhelm had found a dress he called a "moo-moo," a name which did nothing toward endearing the garment to my apprentice.

"I mean, *really*, High Roller," she said, backing me toward a corner. "Isn't it bad enough that half the town's seen me as a blimp? Tell me I don't have to be a *cow* now."

"Honest, Massha," Vilhelm put in. "The style is fairly popular here in Blut. A lot of the ladies wear it who are . . . that is, are a bit. . . ."

"Fat!?"

She loomed over the little vampire.

"Is that the word you're groping for, Short and About To Become Extinct?"

"Let's face it, dear," Tananda said, coming to the rescue. "You *are* carrying a little extra weight there. Believe me, if there's one time you can't kid yourself about your body, it's when you're donning costumes. If anything, that outfit makes you look a little slimmer."

"Don't try to kid a kidder, sweetie," Massha sighed. "But you're right about the costuming thing. This thing is so *drab*, though. First I'm a blimp, and now I'm an army tent."

"Now *that* I'll agree with," Tananda nodded. "Trust a man to find a drab mu-mu. Tell you what. There's a scarf I was going to use for a belt, but maybe you could wear it around your neck."

I was afraid that last crack would touch off another explosion, but Massha took it as a helpful suggestion and the two of them went off in search of other possible adornments.

"Got a minute, partner?"

From the tone of Aahz's voice, I knew the moment I had been dreading had arrived.

Chumley didn't have to worry about a disguise at all, as trolls were not uncommon in this dimension. Tananda also insisted that she looked enough like a vampire to pass with only minimal modifications. I hadn't seen any vampires with green hair, but she claimed that she had, so, as always, I yielded to her greater experience in these matters. I was also on the "minimal disguise" list, everyone agreeing that no one in Blut had gotten enough of a look at me to fix the image in their mind. While I wasn't wild about being so unmemorable, I went along with it . . . especially when I saw what Guido and Massha were going through. The problems with those two notables have already been mentioned: troublesome, but not insurmountable. Then there was Aahz. . . .

"Is there something wrong?" I asked innocently.

"You bet your dragon there's something wrong!" my partner snarled. "And don't try to play innocent with me! It didn't work when you were my apprentice, and it sure isn't going to work now."

Aahz's disguise had presented us with some knotty problems. Not only was he the most wanted member of our party, he was also easily the most distinctive. After the trial and his time in jail, it was doubtful that there was a single citizen of Blut who wouldn't recognize him on sight. I mean, there just aren't that many scaly green demons wandering around any dimension . . . except possibly his home dimension of Perv. It was therefore decided . . . almost unanimously . . . that not only would we change my partner's color with make-up, but that it would also be necessary to change his sex.

"Does this, perchance, have something to do with your disguise?" I inquired, trying to keep a straight face.

"Yes, it has something to do with my disguise," he

mimicked, "and, so help me, partner or no, if you let that smile get away, I'll punch your lights out. Understand?"

With a great effort I sucked my cheeks in and bit my lower lip.

"Seriously, though," he said, almost pleading, "a joke's a joke, but you don't really expect me to go out in public looking like *this*, do you?"

In addition to the aforementioned make-up, Aahz's disguise required a dress and a wig. Because of the size of his head (a problem Vilhelm had wisely down-played as much as possible) the selection of wigs available had been understandably small. In fact, the only available in his size was a number called "Lady Go-GoDiva," which involved a high blonde beehive style offset by a long ponytail that hung down to his knees. Actually, the ponytail turned out to be a blessing in disguise, as the dark blue dress Vilhelm had selected for my partner turned out to have an exceptionally low neckline, and the hair draped over his shoulder helped hide the problem we had had finding ample or suitable material to stuff his bosom with.

"As my wise old mentor once told me when I was faced with a similar dilemma," I said sagely, "what does it matter what people think of you? They aren't supposed to know it's you, anyway. That's the whole idea of a disguise."

"But this get-up is humiliating!"

"My words precisely when someone else I could name deemed it necessary for *me* to dress up as a girl, remember?"

"You're enjoying this, aren't you?" Aahz glowered, peering at me suspiciously.

"Well, there are a couple of other options," I admitted.

"That's more like it!" he grinned, reaching for his wig.

"You could stay behind. . . ."

His hand stopped just short of its mission.

". . . or we could forget the whole thing and pay the fine ourselves."

The hand retreated as my partner's shoulders sagged in defeat. I felt no joy at the victory. If anything, I had been half hoping he would be embarrassed enough to take me up on my suggestion of abandoning the project. I should have known better. When there's money involved, it takes more than embarrassment to throw Aahz off the scent . . . whether the embarrassment is his own or someone else's.

"All right, everybody," I called, hiding my disappointment. "Are we ready to go?"

"Remember your sunglasses!" Tananda added.

That was the final touch to our disguises. To hide our non-red eyes, each of us donned a pair of sunglasses. Surveying the final result, I had to admit that aside from Tananda and Chumley, we didn't look like us. Exactly what we *did* look like I wouldn't venture to say, but we sure didn't look like *us*!

"Okay," Aahz chimed in, his discomfort apparently behind him. "Does everyone have their marching orders? Vilhelm? Are you sure you can track us on that thing?"

"No problem," the little vampire nodded. "When things get slow around here I use this rig to do a little window peeking right here in town. Covering the streets is even easier."

"Remember," I told him, "watch for our signal. When we catch up with this Vic character, we're going to want you to get some responsible local witnesses there chop-chop."

"Well now," Aahz grinned evilly, "you don't have to be *too* quick about it. I wouldn't mind having a little time alone with him before we turn him over to the authorities."

My heart sank a little. Aahz sounded determined to exact a bit of vengeance out of this hunt, and I wasn't at all sure he would restrict himself to Vic when it came time to express his ire.

I think Tananda noticed my concern.

"Ease up a little, Aahz," she said casually. "I don't mind helping you out of a tight spot, but count me out when it comes to excessive force for the sake of vengeance. It lacks class."

"Since when did you worry about excessive violence?" Aahz growled, then shrugged his acceptance. "Okay. But maybe we'll get lucky. Maybe he'll resist arrest."

I was still worried, but realized that that was about the most restraint I would get out of my partner.

"Now that that's settled," I said, producing Luanna's scarf, "Pepe, take a whiff of this."

"Enchanting," he smiled, nuzzling the piece of cloth. "A young lady, no? Eef ze body is as good as ze aroma, I will follow her to the end of ze world whether you accompany me or not."

I resisted an impulse to wrap the scarf around his neck and pull.

"All right, everybody," I said, retrieving the scarf and tucking it back into my tunic in what I hoped was a casual manner. "Let's go catch us a renegade vampire."

Chapter Seventeen:

"The trail's got to be 'round here some-where!"

—D. BOONE

IT was only a few hours short of sunset as we set out on our quest, a nagging reminder of exactly how long our efforts at physical disguise had taken. We had agreed to avoid following Pepe as a group so as not to attract attention. Instead, we moved singly or in groups of two, using both sides of the street and deliberately walking at different paces. The faster walkers averaged their progress with the slower by occasionally stopping to look into shop windows, thereby keeping our group together without actually appearing to. Tananda pointed out that not only would this procedure lessen our chances of being noticed, but also that it would maximize our chances for at least some of the group's escape if one of us should be discovered . . . a truly comforting thought.

Even though Luanna had claimed to have been watching for us at the Dispatcher's, it had been so long ago I fully expected her scent would have long since dissipated or at least been masked by the passage of numerous others. As such, I was moderately surprised when the werewolf signaled almost immediately that he had found the trail and headed off with a determined air. Either her scent was stronger than I had thought, or I had grossly underestimated Pepe's tracking ability.

The trail wound up and down the cobblestoned streets, and we followed as quickly as we could without abandoning our pretense of being casual strollers who did not know each other. For a while, our group made up the majority of the beings visible, causing me to doubt the effectiveness of our ruse, but soon the vampires began to emerge to indulge their taste for the nightlife and we became much less obvious.

I was paired up with Chumley, but the troll was strangely quiet as we made our way along. At first I thought he was simply concentrating on keeping the werewolf in sight, but as time wore on, I found the silence somehow unnerving. I had always respected Chumley as being one of the saner, leveler heads among our motley assemblage, and I was starting to have an uneasy impression that he was not wholeheartedly behind this venture.

"Is there something bothering you, Chumley?" I asked at last.

"Hmmm? Oh. Not really, Skeeve. I was just thinking."

"About that?"

The troll let out a small sigh.

"I was just contemplating our adversary, this Vic fellow. You know, from what's been said, he's quite resourceful in a devious sort of way."

That took me a little aback. So far I had considered our vampire foe to be everything from an annoyance to a nemesis. The idea of studying his methods had never entered my mind.

"What leads you to that conclusion?"

The troll pursed his lips as he organized his thoughts.

"Consider what he's accomplished so far. The entire time we've known of him, he's been on the run . . . first from the Deveels, and then from Aahz, who's no slouch at hunting people once he sets his mind to it. Now, assuming for the moment that Vic is actually the brains of the group, he was quick enough to take advantage of being left alone in your waiting room to escape out the back door. He couldn't have planned that in advance, even knowing about the door. He probably had some other plan in mind, and formulated this new course of action on the spot."

We paused for a moment to let a small group of vampires cross the intersection in front of us.

"Now, that would have sufficed for an escape in most instances, but they happened to pick an exit route that left you and Aahz responsible, which set your partner on their trail," Chumley continued. "With nothing to go on but your reputations, Vic not only correctly deduced that he would be followed, but he also managed to spot Aahz's weakness and exploit it to frame him and make it stick . . . again, not the easiest task, particularly realizing it involved convincing and coaching his two accomplices in their roles."

All of this was doing nothing for my peace of mind. I was having enough difficulty forcing myself to believe that we were really hunting a vampire, the sort of creature I normally avoid at all costs, without having to deal with the possibility that he was shrewd and resourceful as well. Still, I had learned that ignoring unpleasant elements of a caper was perhaps the worst way to prepare for them.

"Keep going," I urged.

"Well," the troll sighed, "when you stumbled on his

hiding place at the Woof Writers, he didn't panic. He waited to hear as much of your plans as possible, all the while taking advantage of the opportunity to assess you first-hand, then timed his escape so as to catch you all flat-footed.''

I digested this distasteful addition to the rapidly growing data file. ''Do you really think he was sizing me up?''

''There's no doubt in my mind. Not only was he gauging your skills and determination, he was successful enough at second-guessing you, based on the results of his studies, to be waiting to sound the alarm when you busted Aahz out of jail. . . . a particularly bold move when one realizes that he was running the risk of being recognized, which would have blown his frame-up of your partner.''

''Bold or desperate,'' I said thoughtfully. ''That's probably why he waited until we had actually sprung Aahz and were on the way down before he blew the whistle. If we had gotten away unscathed, then the frame would be useless, so at that point he really wasn't risking anything.''

''Have it your way,'' the troll shrugged. ''The final analysis remains that we have one tough nut to crack. One can only wonder what he will do when we catch up with him this time.''

''If he's performing up to par, it could be rough on us.''

Chumley shot me a sidelong glance.

''Actually, I was thinking it could be rough on your lady fair . . . if he has managed to observe the feelings you have for her.''

I started to protest, then the impact of his theory hit me and my embarrassment gave way to concern.

''Is it really that apparent? Do you think he could

spot it? If so, he might already have done something to Luanna for having contacted us."

"It stands out all over you to anyone who knows you," Chumley said, shaking his head. "As for someone watching you for the first time . . . I just don't know. He'd be more likely to deduce it from the information you had . . . such as his name. That kind of data had to come from somewhere, though there's an outside chance that with your current reputation he'll assume that you gleaned it by some magical source."

I barely heard him. My mind was focused on the possibility that Luanna might be hurt, and that I might indirectly have been the cause. A black well of guilt was rising up to swallow me, when I felt a hand on my shoulder.

"Don't tune out now, Skeeve," Chumley was saying, shaking me slightly. "First of all, we're going to need you shortly. Secondly, even if Vic's figured out that you're in love with her, I don't think he'll have hurt her. If anything, he'll save her for a trump card to use against us."

I drew a deep ragged breath.

". . . and he'll be just the bastard to do it, too," I said. "I don't know what I'll be able to do, for us or for her, but I'll be ready to try. Thanks, Chumley."

The troll was studying me closely.

"Actually, I wasn't thinking that he was such a blighter," he said. "More like a clever, resourceful person who's gotten in over his head and is trying his best to ad-lib his way out. Frankly, Skeeve old boy, in many ways he reminds me of you. You might think about that when attempting to appraise his likely courses of action and how to counter them."

I tried again to weigh what he was saying, but all I could think about was what the consequences of this hunt could mean to Luanna. It was difficult enough for me to accept that we would have to force Luanna and her cohorts to answer to the authorities for their indiscretions, but the thought of placing her in physical danger was unbearable.

I looked around for Aahz, fully intending to put an end to this hunt once and for all. To my surprise, the rest of the group was assembled on the corner ahead, and my partner was beckoning us to join them.

"What's going on?" I asked, almost to myself.

"Just off-hand," Chumley replied, "I'd say we've reached our destination."

A cold wave of fear washed over me, and I hurried to the rendezvous with Chumley close behind.

"We're in luck," Aahz announced as I arrived. "Guido here says he saw Vic entering the building just as we got here. It's my guess they're all inside right now."

"Aahz, I—I want us to quit right now," I blurted, painfully aware of how weak it sounded.

"Oh?" my partner said, cocking an eyebrow at me. "Any particular reason?"

I licked my lips, feeling the eyes of the whole group on me.

"Only one. I'm in love with one of the fugitives . . . the girl."

"Yeah. Now tell me something I didn't know," Aahz smirked, winking at me.

"You knew?"

"All of us knew. In fact, we were just discussing it. Remember, we all know you . . . and me probably best of all. It's already been pretty much decided to let your love-light go. Think of it as a present from us to you. The other two are ours."

Five minutes ago, that would have made me deliriously happy. Now, it only seemed to complicate things.

"But Chumley was just saying that there's a chance they might hurt her if they find out she helped us," I explained desperately. "Can't we just let them all go?"

"Not a chance, partner," Aahz said firmly. "In addition to our original reasons, you've just mentioned the new one. Your girlfriend could be in trouble, and the only way to be sure she's safe is to remove her partners ... Fast."

"Believe him, Skeeve," Tananda urged. "It may not be nice, but it's the best way."

"Really, Boss," Guido said quietly. "Unless we finish this thing here and now, you're never goin' to know if she's safe, know what I mean?"

That almost made sense, but I was still worried. "I don't know, Aahz. . . ."

"Well I do," my partner snapped. "And the longer we stand down here, the more chance there is that they'll either get away or set up a trap. If you're uncertain, stay down here ... in fact, that's not a bad idea. Massha, you stay down here with him in case they try to bolt out this way. While you're waiting, watch for the witnesses that Vilhelm's supposed to be sending along. Tananda, you and Chumley and Guido come along with me. This is a job for experienced hard-cases. Pepe, we appreciate your help, but this isn't really your fight."

"But of course." The werewolf grinned. "Besides, I am a lo-var, not a figh-tar. I will wait here to see the finale, eh?"

"But Aahz. . . ."

"Really, partner, you'll be more help down here. This isn't your kind of fight, and we need someone to deal with the witnesses. You're good at that kind of thing."

"I was going to ask if you had given the signal to Vilhelm."

"Signal?" Aahz blinked. "How's this for a signal?!"

With that, he tore off his wig and threw it on the ground, followed closely by his dress.

"Think he'll get the message? Besides, no way am I going to try to fight in that get-up."

"Now you're talkin'!" Guido crowed.

In a flash he had discarded his cloak and was pulling on his now-familiar trench coat.

"Where did that come from?" I demanded.

"Had it with me all the time," the bodyguard said smugly. "It would have been like leaving an old friend behind."

"Well, if you and your old friend are ready," Tananda murmured, "we'd better get started.

"Itching for action?" Aahz grinned.

"No. More like eager to get off the street," she said. "Since you boys have shown your true colors, we're starting to draw a crowd."

Sure enough, the vampires on the street had ceased whatever they had been doing before and were gathering in knots, whispering together and pointing at our group.

"Umm . . . we'd better finish this fast," Aahz said, shooting a nervous glance around. "All right, gang. Let's go for the gusto!"

"Go for the what?" I asked, but they were already on their way into the building.

I noticed they were all moving faster than normal. I also noticed that Massha, Pepe, and I were the only ones left on the street . . . and now the crowd was pointing at us!

Chapter Eighteen:

> "I didn't come all this way to sit out the fight!"
>
> —R. BALBOA

"WHAT'S going on?"

I looked around to find that one of the vampires had detached himself from his group of friends and was addressing me directly.

"Beats me," Massha interceded. "A bunch of off-worlder types just took off into that building with blood in their eyes. I'm waiting to see what happens next."

"Far out," the vampire breathed, peering toward the structure. "I haven't seen that many off-worlders in one place except in the flickers. Wasn't one of them that escaped murderer, Aahz?"

I really didn't want this character to join our little group. While our disguises seemed to be holding up under casual inspection, I was pretty sure that prolonged close scrutiny would reveal not only the non-local nature of Massha and myself, but also the fact that we were trying to hide it.

"You may be right," I said, playing a hunch. "If so,

it's a good thing you happened along. We're going to need all the help we can get.''

"Help? Help for what?"

"Why to catch the murderer, of course. We can't let him get away again. I figure it's our duty to stop him ourselves or at least slow him up until the authorities arrive."

"We? You mean the three of you? You're going to try to stop a murderer all by yourselves?"

"Four of us now that you're here."

The vampire started backing away.

"Ummm . . . actually I've got to get back to my friends. We're on our way to a party. Sorry I can't help, but I'll spread the word that you're looking for volunteers, okay?"

"Hey, thanks," I called as if I believed him. "We'll be right here."

By the time I had finished speaking, he had disappeared into the crowd. Mission accomplished.

"Nicely done, my friend," Pepe murmured. "He does not, how you say, want to get involved, no?"

"That's right," I said, my eyes on the building again. "And to tell you the truth, I'm not too wild about the idea either. What do you think, Massha? It's awfully quiet in there."

"I'll say," my apprentice agreed. "I'm just trying to figure out if that's a good or a bad sign. Another ten minutes and I'm heading in there to check it out myself."

I nodded my consent, even though I doubted she saw it. We both had our eyes glued to the building, memorizing its every detail.

It was a four-story structure . . . or it would be if it weren't for the curved peak that jutted out from the roof fully half-again as high as the main building. It looked as if the builder had suddenly added the adornment in a last-minute attempt to have his work stand as tall or taller than its neighbors. From the number of windows in the main structure, I guessed it was an apartment building or a hotel or something. In short, it looked like it had a lot of little rooms. I found myself wondering exactly how our strike force was supposed to locate their target without kicking in every door in the place . . . a possibility I wouldn't put past Aahz.

I was about to express this fear to Massha when a loud crash sounded from within.

"What was that?" I demanded of no one in particular.

"Sounded like a loud crash," my apprentice supplied helpfully.

I forced myself to remember that no one out here knew any more about what was going on inside than I did.

After the crash, everything was quiet once more. I tried to tell myself that the noise might have nothing at all to do with the strike force, but I didn't believe it for a minute. The crowd was talking excitedly to each other and straining to see the various windows. They seemed quite confident that something else would happen soon, much more than I, but then again, maybe as city dwellers they were more accustomed to such vigils than I.

Suddenly, Tananda appeared in the doorway.

"Did they come out this way?" she called.

"No one's been in or out since you went in," I responded.

She swore and started to re-enter the building.

"What happened?" I shouted desperately.

"We nailed one of them, but Vic got away. He's loose in the building somewhere, and he's got the girl with him."

With that, she disappeared before I could make any further inquiries.

Terrific.

"Exciting, eh?" Pepe said. "I tell you, I could watch such a chase for hours."

"Well, I can't," I snapped. "I've had it with sitting on the sidelines. Massha? I'm going in there. Want to come?"

"I dunno, Hot Stuff. I'd like to, but somebody should be here to plug this escape route."

"Fine. You wait here, and I'll...."

I turned to enter the building and bumped headlong into Vilhelm.

"What are you doing here?" I demanded, not really caring.

The Dispatcher shook his head slightly to clear it. Being smaller, he had gotten the worse of our collision.

"I'm here with the witnesses, remember? I was supposed to bring them."

"You were supposed to *send* them. Oh well, where are they?"

"Right here," he said, gesturing to a sullen group of vampires standing behind him. "This is Kirby, and Paul, and Richard, and Adele, and Scott . . . some of the most respected citizens in town. Convince them and you're home free."

Looking at the group, I suddenly realized how Aahz had ended up on death row. If the jury had been anything like these specimens, they would have hung their own mothers for jaywalking. While I didn't relish the thought of trying to convince them of anything, I found myself being very glad I didn't have to deal with them on a regular basis.

"Okay. So we're here," the one identified as Kirby growled. "Just what is it we're supposed to be wit-

nessing? If this is one of your cockamamie deals, Vilhelm. . . ."

I interrupted simply by taking my sunglasses off and
opening my eyes wide, displaying their whites. The bad
reputation of humans in this dimension was sufficient to
capture their undivided attention.

"Perhaps you recall a certain murder trial that took
place not too long ago?" I said, trying to work the
toothblack off with my tongue. "Well, the convicted
murderer who escaped is my partner, and right now he's
inside that building. He and a few of our friends are
about to show you one surprisingly lively corpse . . .
specifically the fellow that my partner is supposed to
have killed. I trust that will be sufficient to convince you
of his innocence?"

While the vampires were taken aback by my presence
in their midst, they recovered quickly. Like I said, they
were real hard cases and didn't stay impressed very
long.

"So how much time is this going to take?" Kirby said
impatiently. "I'm giving up my sleep for this, and I
don't get much of it."

That was a good question, so, not having an answer, I
stalled.

"You sleep nights? I thought. . . ."

"I'm a day owl," the vampire waved. "It's easier to
get my work done when the phone isn't ringing every
five minutes . . . which usually means waiting until
everyone else is asleep. But we're getting off the subject.
The bottom line is that my time is valuable, and the
same holds true for my colleagues. If you think we're
going to just stand around here until. . . ."

There was a sudden outcry from the crowd, and we all
looked to find them talking excitedly and pointing up at
the roof.

A figure had emerged, fighting to pick his way across the steeply sloped surface while dragging a struggling girl by one arm.

Vic!

This was the first time I had gotten a clear look at my foe, and I was moderately surprised. He was younger than I had expected, barely older than myself, and instead of a menacing cloak, he was sporting a white turtleneck and sunglasses. It suddenly occurred to me that if sunglasses enabled me to pass for a vampire, that they would also let a vampire pass undetected among humans.

The vampire suddenly stopped as his path was barred by Tananda, who appeared as if by magic over the edge of the roof. He turned to retrace his steps, only to find that the trio of Aahz, Guido, and Chumley had emerged behind him, cutting off his retreat.

"I believe, gentlemen and lady, that up there is the elusive body that started this whole thing," I heard myself saying. "If you can spare a few more moments, I think *my* colleagues will have him in custody so that you might interrogate him at your leisure."

"Don't be too sure of that, High Roller," Massha cautioned. "Look!"

His chosen routes of escape cut off, Vic was now scrabbling up the roof peak itself, Luanna hanging in his grip. While I had to admire his strength, I was at a loss to understand what he was trying to accomplish with the manuever. It was obvious that he had been exposed, so why didn't he just give it up?

The answer became apparent in the next few moments. Reaching the apex of the roof, the vampire underwent a chilling metamorphosis. Before the strike force could reach him, he hunched forward and huge batwings began to grow and spread from his back. His plans gone awry, he was getting ready to escape.

In immediate response to his efforts, Tananda and Guido both produced projectile weapons and shouted something to him. Though the distance was too great to make out the words clearly, it was obvious to me that they were threatening to shoot him down if he tried to take to the air.

"We may have a murder case yet," Kirby murmured, squinting to watch the rooftop drama unfold.

"Murder?" I exclaimed, turning on him. "How can you call it murder if they're only trying to keep from escaping *your* justice?"

"That wasn't what I meant," the vampire said, never taking his eyes from the action. "Check it out."

I looked . . . and my heart stood still.

Aahz had been trying to ease up the roof peak closer to Vic and his hostage. Vic must have seen him, because he was now holding Luanna out over the drop as he pointed an angry finger at my partner. The threat was unmistakable.

"You know, eet is people like zat who give ze vampires a bad name, eh?" Pepe said, nudging me.

I ignored him, lost in my own anxiety and frustration at the stalemated situation. A noticeably harder jab from Massha broke my reverie, however.

"Hey, Hot Stuff. Do you see what I see?"

I tore my gaze away from the confrontation and shot a glance her way. She was standing motionless, her brow furrowed with concentration and her eyes closed.

It took me a few moments to realize what she was doing, then I followed suit, scarcely daring to hope.

There it was! A force line! A big, strong, beautiful, glorious force line.

I had gotten so used to not having any magical energy
at my disposal in this dimension that I hadn't even
bothered to check!

I opened myself to the energy, relished it for a fleet
moment, then rechanneled it.

"Excuse me," I said with a smile, handing my sunglasses to Kirby. "It's about time I took a hand in this
directly."

With that, I reached out with my mind, pushed off
against the ground, and soared upward, setting a course
for the cornered vampire on the roof.

Chapter Nineteen:

"All right, pilgrim. This is between you and me!"

—A. HAMILTON

I had hoped to make my approach unobserved, but as I flew upward, the crowd below let out a roar that drew the attention of the combatants on the roof. Terrific! When I wanted unobtrusive, I got notoriety.

Reaching a height level with that of the vampire, I hovered at a discreet distance.

"Put away the nasties," I called to Tananda and Guido. "He's not getting away by air."

They looked a bit rebellious, but followed the order.

"What's with the Peter Pan bit, partner?" Aahz shouted. "Are you feeling your Cheerioats, or did you finally find a force line?"

"Both." I waved back, then turned my attention to Vic.

Though his eyes were obscured by his sunglasses, I could feel his hateful glare burning into me to the bone.

"Why don't you just call it quits?" I said in what I

hoped was a calm, soothing tone. "It's over. We've got you outflanked."

For a moment he seemed to waiver with indecision. Then, without warning, he threw Luanna at Aahz.

"Why can't you all just leave me alone!" he screamed, and dove off the roof.

Aahz somehow managed to snag the girl's hurtling form, though in the process he lost his balance and tumbled backward down the roof peak, cushioning the impact with his own body.

I hesitated, torn between the impulse to check on Luanna's welfare and the desire to pursue Vic.

"Go get him!" my partner called. "We're fine!"

That was all the encouragement I needed. Wheeling to my right, I plunged after the fleeing vampire.

What followed was one of the more interesting experiences of my limited magical career. As I mentioned before, my form of flying magically isn't really flying . . . it's controlled levitation of oneself. This made enthusiastic pursuit a real challenge to my abilities. To counterbalance the problem, however, Vic couldn't really fly either . . . at least he never seemed to flap his wings. Instead, he appeared content to soar and bank and catch an occasional updraft. This forced him to continually circle and double back through roughly the same area time and time again. This suited me fine, as I didn't want to wander too far away from my energizing force line now that I had found it. The idea of running out of power while suspended fifty feet in the air did not appeal to me at all.

Anyway, our aerial duel rapidly became a curious matching of styles with Vic's swooping and circling in his efforts to escape and my vertical and horizontal maneuverings to try to intercept him. Needless to say, the conflict was not resolved quickly. As soon as I would time a move that came close enough to an interception to justify attempting it again, Vic would realize his danger and alter his pattern, leaving me to try to puzzle out his new course.

The crowd loved it.

They whooped and hollered, their words of encouragement alternately loud and faint as we changed altitude. It was impossible to tell which of us they were cheering for, though for a while I thought it was me, considering the approval they had expressed when I first took off to join the battle. Then I noticed that the crowd was considerably larger than it had been when I entered the fray, and I realized that many of them had not been around to witness the beginning of the conflict. To them, it probably appeared that a monster from another dimension was chasing one of their fellow beings through the sky.

That thought was disquieting enough that I spared some of my attention to scan the surrounding rooftops on the off-chance that a local sniper might be preparing to help his fellow countryman. It turned out to be the wisest decision I had made.

As I was looking over my shoulder, I plowed full force into Vic, who had doubled back on his own path. The feint would have probably worked if I had seen it, but as it was we collided at maximum speed, the impact momentarily stunning us both. I managed to grab a double handful of the vampire's turtleneck as we fell about ten feet before I adjusted my levitation strength to support us both.

"What's the matter with you!" I demanded, trying to shake him, which succeeded only in moving us both back and forth in the air. "Running away won't help."

Then I realized he was crying.

Somehow, this struck me as immensely unfair. I

mean, how are you supposed to stay mad at a villain that cries? Okay. So I'm a soft tough. But the crying really did make a difference.

"I can't fight you all!" he sobbed, tears streaming down his cheeks. "Maybe if I knew some magic I could take one of you with me . . . but at least you're going to have to work for your kill!"

With that he tore loose from my grasp and swooped away.

His words stunned me so much I almost let him escape. Fortunately, I had the presence of mind to call out to him.

"Hey, dummy! Nobody's trying to kill you!"

"Yeah, sure," he shouted back. "You're up here just for the fun of it."

He was starting to bank toward the street, and I knew I'd only have time for one more try.

"Look! Will you stop running if I quit chasing you? I think there's a major misunderstanding here."

He glanced back over his shoulder and saw that I was still where I was when we collided. Altering his course slightly, he flared his wings and landed on a carved gargoyle ornament jutting out from the side of the building.

"Why should you want to talk?" he called, wiping his face with one hand. "I thought nothing I could say would change your mind."

"You'd be surprised," I shouted back. "Say, do you mind if I land on that ledge near you? I feel pretty silly just hanging here."

He glanced at the indicated ledge, and I could see his wings flex nervously.

"C'mon," I urged. "I'll be further away from you there than I was when we started this chase back on the roof. You'll still have a clean shot at getting away if I try anything."

He hesitated, then nodded his consent.

Moving slowly so as not to alarm him, I maneuvered my way to my new perch. Truth to tell, I was glad to get something solid under my feet again. Even using magic, flying can take a lot out of you, and I was relieved to get a chance to rest. Now that I was closer, I could see that Vic was breathing heavily himself. Apparently his form of flying was no picnic either.

"All right," I said in a much more conversational tone. "Let's take this thing from the top. Who says we're trying to kill you?"

"Matt does," the vampire responded. "He's the one who filled me in on you and your pet demon. To be honest with you, I had never even heard of you until Matt explained whose home we had stumbled into."

"Matt?" I frowned.

Then I remembered. Of course. The third member of the fugitive party. Luanna's old con artist partner who nobody had been paying attention to at all. A germ of an idea began to form in my head.

"And he says we're out to kill you?"

"That's right. According to him nobody crosses the Great Skeeve or makes a fool of him and lives . . . and using your house as an escape route definitely qualifies."

The reputation thing again. I was beginning to realize why so many magicians preferred to lead the lives of recluses.

"That's crazy, Vic." I said. "If I tried to kill everybody who's made a fool of me, I'd be armpit-deep in corpses."

"Oh yeah?" he shot back. "Well, if you aren't out to

kill me, why did you send your pet demon after us?''

Despite my resolve to settle this thing amicably, I was starting to get annoyed.

''First of all, he's not my pet demon. He's my partner and his name is Aahz. Secondly, I didn't send him. He knocked me out cold and came himself. Third and final, he was never out to kill you. He was trying to bring you and your cohorts back to Deva so we wouldn't get stuck paying off the people you swindled plus a hefty fine. Are you getting all this, or am I going too fast for you?''

''But I didn't swindle anybody,'' the vampire protested. ''Those two offered me a job helping them sell magic charms. I didn't know they weren't genuine until Matt said the customers were mad and we had to run. I suggested we hide out here because it's the only place I know besides the Bazaar.''

''Uh-huh,'' I said, studying the sky. ''Next you'll be saying you didn't frame my partner *or* sound the alarm on us when we tried to spring him.''

Vic's wings dropped as he hung his head.

''That much I can't deny . . . but I was scared! I framed the demon because it was the only way I could think of to get him off our trail for a while. I really thought he could get loose on his own, and when I saw you at the Woof Writers', I knew he was going to get away. I sounded the alarm hoping you would all get caught and be detained long enough to give us a head start. Looking back on it, they were pretty ratty things to do, but what would *you* do if you had a pack of killer demons on your trail?''

Now *that* I could identify with. Chumley's words about Vic and I being alike echoed in my ears. I had had to improvise in some pretty hairy situations myself.

''Wait a minute!'' I growled. ''Speaking of killer demons, what was that bit with you dangling Luanna over the edge of the building back there?''

"I was bluffing," the vampire shrugged. "Your friends were threatening to shoot me if I tried to fly away, and it was the only thing I could think of to try to get them to back off. I wouldn't deliberately hurt anyone . . . especially Luanna. She's sweet. That's why I was trying to help her escape with me after they caught Matt."

That brought me to the question that had been nagging at my mind since I started this wild chase.

"If you don't mind me asking, why didn't you just change into mist and drift away? We could never have caught you then."

Vic gave a short, bitter laugh.

"Do you know how rough it is to turn into mist? Well, you're a magician. Maybe you do know. Anyway, you might as well know the truth. I'm not much in the magic department . . . in fact, I'm pretty much a bust as a vampire. I can't even change all the way into a bat! These wings are the best I've been able to do. That's why I was looking for a new life in the Bazaar. I'd rather be a first-class anything than a third-rate vampire. I mean, I don't even like blood!"

"You should meet my bodyguard." I grinned despite myself. "He's a gangster who's allergic to garlic."

"Garlic? I love garlic."

I opened my mouth to offer him Guido's job, then shut it rapidly. If this character was half as desperate as he sounded, he'd probably take the offer seriously and accept, and then where would I be? All we needed to complete our menagerie was a magic-poor vampire.

"Well," I said instead, "I guess that answers all my questions except one. Now that you know we aren't trying to kill you, are you ready to quit running and face the music?"

The vampire gnawed his lower lip as he thought.

"You're sure it will be all right?"

"I can't say for sure until I talk to my partner," I admitted, "but I'm pretty sure things will be amenable. The main problem is to get the murder charges against him dropped . . . which I think we've already accomplished. As for you, I think the only thing they could have against you is false arrest, and there's no way Aahz will press charges on that one."

"Why not?"

I gave him my best grin.

"Because if he did, we couldn't take you back to Deva to deal with the swindling charge. Believe me, if given a chance between revenge and saving money, you can trust Aahz to be forgiving every time."

Vic thought about it for a few more moments, then shrugged.

"Embarrassment I'm used to dealing with, and I think I can beat the swindling rap. C'mon, Skeeve. Let's get this thing over with."

Having finally reached a truce, however temporary, we descended together to face the waiting crowd.

Chapter Twenty:

"There's no accounting for taste!"
—COLONEL SANDERS

"BUT Skeeve. . . ."

BANG!

". . . I told you before. . . ."

BANG! BANG!

". . . I could never abandon Matt. . . ."

BANG!

". . . he's my partner!"

BANG! BANG!

"But Lu. . . ."

BANG!

". . . excuse me. HEY, PARTNER! COULD YOU KNOCK OFF THE HAMMERING FOR A MINUTE? I'M TRYING TO HAVE A CONVERSATION HERE!"

"Not a chance," Aahz growled around his mouthful of nails. "I'm shutting this door permanently before anything else happens. But tell you what, I'll try to hammer quietly."

If you deduce from all this that we were back at our place on Deva, you're right. After some long, terse conversations with the citizens of Blut and fond farewells to Vílhelm and Pepe, our whole crew, including our three captives, had trooped back to the castle and through the door without incident.

I had hoped to have a few moments alone with Luanna, but, after several attempts, the best I had been able to manage was this conversation in the reception room under the watchful eyes of Aahz and Matt.

Matt, incidentally, turned out to be a thoroughly unpleasant individual with a twisted needle-nose, acne, a receding hairline, and the beginnings of a beer-belly. For the life of me, I couldn't figure out what Luanna saw in him.

"But that was when you thought he was in a jam," I said, resuming the argument. "Aahz and I have already promised to help defend him *and* Vic when they go before the Merchants Association. There's no need to stand by him yourself."

"I don't understand you, Skeeve," Luanna declared, shaking her head. "If I wouldn't leave Matt when he was in trouble, why should I leave him when things look like they're going to turn out okay? I know you don't like him, but he's done all right by me so far . . . and I still owe him for getting me away from the farm."

"But we're making you a good offer," I tried again desperately. "You can stay here and work for Aahz and me, and if you're interested we could even teach you some real magic so you don't have to. . . ."

She stopped me by simply laying a hand on my arm.

"I know it's a good offer, Skeeve, and it's nice of you to make it. But for the time being I'm content to stay with Matt. Maybe sometime in the future, when I have a little more to offer you in return, I'll take you up on it

. . . if the deal's still open."

"Well," I sighed, "if that's really what you want. . . ."

"Hey! Don't take it so hard, buddy," Matt laughed, clapping his hand on my shoulder. "You win some, you lose some. This time you lost. No hard feelings. Maybe you'll have better luck with the next one. We're both men of the world, and we know one broad's just like any other."

"Matt, *buddy*," I said through clenched teeth, "get that hand off my shoulder before it loses a body."

As I said, even on our short trip back from Limbo I had been so underwhelmed by Matt that I no longer even bothered trying to be polite or mask my dislike for him. He could grate on my nerves faster than anyone I had ever met. If he was a successful con artist, able to inspire trust from total strangers, then I was the Queen of May.

"Matt's just kidding," Luanna soothed, stepping between us.

"Well I'm not," I snarled. "Just remember you're welcome here any time you get fed up with this slug."

"Oh, I imagine we'll be together for quite some time," Matt leered, patting Luanna lightly on her rump. "With you big shots vouching for us we should be able to beat this swindling rap . . . and even if we lose, so what? All it means is I'll have to give them back their crummy twenty gold pieces."

Aahz's hammering stopped abruptly . . . or maybe it was my heart.

I tried vainly to convince myself that I hadn't heard him right.

"Twenty gold pieces?" I said slowly.

"Yeah. They caught on to us a lot quicker here at the Bazaar than I thought they would. It wasn't much of a haul even by my standards. I can't get over the fact that you big shots went through so much trouble to drag us back here over a measly twenty gold pieces. There must be more to this principle thing than I realized."

"Ummm . . . could I have a word with you, partner?" Aahz said, putting down his hammer.

"I was about to ask the same thing," I admitted, stepping to the far side of the room.

Once we were alone, we stared at each other, neither wanting to be the first to speak.

"You never did get around to asking Hay-ner how much was at stake, did you?" Aahz sighed absently.

"That's the money side of negotiations and I thought you covered it," I murmured. "Funny, we both stood right there the whole time and heard every word that was said, and neither of us caught that omission."

"Funny. Right. I'm dying." My partner grimaced.

"Not as much as you will if word of this gets out," I warned. "I vote that we give them the money to pay it off. I don't want to, but it's the only way I can think of to keep this thing from becoming public knowledge."

"Done." Aahz nodded. "But let me handle it. If Matt the Rat there gets wind of the fact that the whole thing was a mistake on our part, he'd probably blackmail us for our eyeteeth."

"Right," I agreed.

With that, we, the two most sought-after, most highly-paid magicians at the Bazaar, turned to deal with our charges, reminded once more why humility lies at the core of greatness.

LITTLE MYTH MARKER

Chapter One:

"The difference between an inside straight and a blamed fool is callin' the last bet!"

—B. MAVERICK

"CALL!"

"Bump."

"Bump again."

"Who're you trying to kid? You got elf-high nothing!"

"Try me!"

"All right! Raise you limit."

"Call."

"Call."

"Elf-high nothing bumps you back limit."

"Fold."

"Call."

For those of you starting this book at the beginning (Bless you! I hate it when readers cheat by reading ahead!), this may be a little confusing. The above is the dialogue during a game of dragon poker. What is dragon poker, you ask? Well, it's reputed to be the most complicated card game ever invented . . . and here at the Bazaar at Deva, they should know.

The Bazaar is the biggest shopping maze and haggling

spot in all the dimensions, and consequently gets a lot of
dimension travelers (demons) passing through. In addition to the shops, stalls, and restaurants (which really
doesn't do justice to the extent or variety of the Bazaar)
there is a thriving gambling community in residence
here. They are always on the lookout for a new game,
particularly one that involves betting, and the more
complicated the better. The basic philosophy is that a
complicated game is more easily won by those who de-
vote full time to its study than by the tourists who have
dabbled in it or are trying to learn it as the game goes
on. Anyway, when a Deveel bookie tells me that dragon
poker is the most complicated card game ever, I tend to
believe him.

"Fold."

"Call."

"Okay, Mr. Skeeve the Grater. Let's see you beat
this! Dragons full!"

He exposed his hole cards with a flourish that bordered on a challenge. Actually, I had been hoping he
would drop out of the hand. This particular individual
(Grunk, I think his name was) was easily two heads
taller than me and had bright red eyes, canines almost as
long as my forearm, and a nasty disposition. He tended
to speak in an angry shout, and the fact that he had been
losing steadily had not mellowed him in the slightest.

"Well? C'mon! What have you got?"

I turned over my four hole cards, spread them next to
the five already face up, then leaned back and smiled.

"That's it?" Grunk said, craning his neck and scowling at my cards. "But that's only . . ."

"Wait a minute," the player on his left chimed in.
"It's Tuesday. That makes his unicorns wild."

"But it's a month with an 'M' in it!" someone else
piped up. "So his ogre is only half of face value!"

"But there's an even number of players. . . ."

I told you it was a complicated game. Those of you
who know me from my earlier adventures (blatant

plug!) may wonder how it is I understand such a complex system. That's easy. I don't! I just bet, then spread the cards and let the other players sort out who won.

You may wonder what I was doing sitting in on a cutthroat game of dragon poker when I didn't even know the rules. Well, for once, I have an answer. I was enjoying myself on my own for a change.

You see, ever since Don Bruce, the Mob's fairy godfather, supposedly hired me to watch over the Mob's interests at the Bazaar and assigned me two bodyguards, Guido and Nunzio, I've rarely had a moment to myself. This weekend, however, my two watchdogs were off making their yearly report to Mob Central, leaving me to fend for myself. Obviously, before they left, they made me give my solemn promise to be careful. Also obviously, as soon as they were gone, I set out to do just the opposite.

Even aside from our percentage of the Mob's take at the Bazaar, our magic business had been booming, so money was no problem. I filched a couple thousand in gold from petty cash and was all set to go on a spree when an invitation arrived to sit in on one of the Geek's dragon poker games at this club, the Even-Odds.

As I said before, I know absolutely nothing about dragon poker other than the fact that at the end of a hand you have five cards face up and four face down. Anything I've tried to get my partner, Aahz, to teach me more about the game, I've been lectured about "only playing games you know" and "don't go looking for trouble." Since I was already looking for mischief, the chance to defy both my bodyguards *and* my partner was too much to resist. I mean, I figured the worst that could happen was that I'd lose a couple thousand in gold. Right?

"You're all overlooking something. This is the forty-third hand and Skeeve there is sitting in a chair facing north!"

I took my cue from the groans and better-censored

expressions of disgust and raked in the pot.

"Say, Geek," Grunk said, his red eyes glittering at me through half-lowered eyelids. "Are you *sure* this Skeeve fellow isn't using magic?"

"Guaranteed," responded the Deveel who was gathering the cards and shuffling for the next hand. "Any game I host here at the Even-Odds is monitored against magic *and* telepathy."

"Weelll, I don't normally play cards with magicians, and I've heard that Skeeve here is supposed to be pretty good in that department. Maybe he's good enough that you just can't catch him at it."

I was starting to get a little nervous. I mean, I wasn't using magic . . . and even if I was going to, I wouldn't know how to use it to rig a card game. The trouble was that Grunk looked perfectly capable of tearing my arms off if he thought I was cheating. I began racking my brain for some way to convince him without admitting to everyone at the table just how little I knew about magic.

"Relax, Grunk. Mr. Skeeve's a good player, that's all. Just because he wins doesn't mean he's cheating."

That was Pidge, the only other human-type in the game. I shot him a grateful smile.

"I don't mind someone winning," Grunk muttered defensively, "But he's been winning all night."

"I've lost more than you have," Pidge said, "and you don't see me griping. I'm tellin' you Mr. Skeeve is *good*. I've sat in on games with the Kid, and I should know."

"The Kid? You've played against him?" Grunk was visibly impressed.

"And lost my socks doing it," Pidge admitted wryly. "I'd say that Mr Skeeve here is good enough to give him a run for his money, though."

"Gentlemen? Are we here to talk or to play cards?" the Geek interrupted, tapping the deck meaningfully.

"I'm out," Pidge said, rising to his feet. "I know

when I'm outclassed—even if I have to go in the hole
before I'll admit it. My marker still good, Geek?"

"It's good with me if nobody else objects."

Grunk noisily slammed his fist down on the table,
causing several of my stacks of chips to fall over.

"What's this about markers?" he demanded. "I
thought this was a cash-only game! Nobody said anything about playing for IOUs."

"Pidge here's an exception," the Geek said. "He's
always made good on his marker before. Besides, you
don't have to worry about it, Grunk. You aren't even
getting all of *your* money back."

"Yeah. But I lost it betting against somebody who's
betting markers instead of cash. It seems to me . . ."

"I'll cover his marker," I said loftily. "That makes it
personal between him and me, so it doesn't involve
anyone else at the table. Right, Geek?"

"That's right. Now shut up and play, Grunk. Or do
you want us to deal you out?"

The monster grumbled a bit under his breath but
leaned back and tossed in another chip to ante for the
next hand.

"Thanks, Mr. Skeeve," Pidge said. "And don't
worry. Like the Geek says, I always reclaim my
marker."

I winked at him and waved vaguely as he left, already
intent on the next hand as I tried vainly to figure out the
rules of the game.

If my grand gesture seemed a little impulsive, remember that I'd been watching him play all night, and I
knew how much he had lost. Even if all of it was on
IOUs, I could cover it out of my winnings and still show
a profit.

You see, Grunk was right. I had been winning steadily
all night . . . a fact made doubly surprising by my ignorance of the game. Early on, however, I had hit on a
system which seemed to be working very well: Bet the
players, not the cards. On the last hand, I hadn't been

betting that I had a winning hand, I was betting that
Grunk had a losing hand. Luck had been against him all
night, and he was betting wild to try to make up for his
losses.

Following my system, I folded the next two hands,
then hit them hard on the third. Most of the other
players folded rather than question my judgment.
Grunk stayed until the bitter end, hoping I was bluffing.
It turned out that I was (my hand wasn't all that strong),
but that his hand was even weaker. Another stack of
chips tumbled into my hoard.

"That does it for me," Grunk said, pushing his remaining chips toward the Geek. "Cash me in."

"Me too."

"I should have left an hour ago. Would have saved
myself a couple hundred."

The Geek was suddenly busy converting chips back to
cash as the game broke up.

Grunk loitered for a few minutes after receiving his
share of the bank. Now that we were no longer facing
each other over cards, he was surprisingly pleasant.

"You know, Skeeve," he said, clapping a massive
hand on my shoulder, "it's been a long time since I've
been whipped that bad at dragon poker. Maybe Pidge
was right. You're slumming here. You should try for a
game with the Kid."

"I was just lucky."

"No, I'm serious. If I knew how to get in touch with
him, I'd set up the game myself."

"You won't have to," one of the other players put in
as he started for the door. "Once word of this game gets
around, the Kid will come looking for you."

"True enough," Grunk laughed over his shoulder.
"Really, Skeeve. If that match-up happens, be sure to
pass the word to me. That's a game I'd like to see."

"Sure, Grunk," I said. "You'll be one of the first to
know. Catch you later."

Actually, my mind was racing as I made my goodbyes. This was getting out of hand. I had figured on one madcap night on my own, then calling it quits without anyone else the wiser. If the other players started shooting their mouths off all over the Bazaar, there would be no hope of keeping my evening's adventure a secret . . . particularly from Aahz! The only thing that would be worse would be if I ended up with some hotshot gambler hunting me down for a challenge match.

"Say, Geek," I said, trying to make it sound casual. "Who is this 'Kid' they keep talking about?"

The Deveel almost lost his grip on the stack of chips he was counting. He gave me a long stare, then shrugged.

"You know, Skeeve, sometimes I don't know when you're kidding me and when you're serious. I keep forgetting that as successful as you are, you're still new to the Bazaar . . . and to gambling specifically."

"Terrific. Who's the 'Kid'?"

"The Kid's the current king of the dragon poker circuit. His trademark is that he always includes a breath mint with his opening bet for each hand . . . says that it brings him luck. That's why they call him the 'Sen-Sen Ante Kid.' I'd advise you to stay away from him, though. You had a good run tonight, but the Kid is the best there is. He'd eat you alive in a head-to-head game."

"I hear that." I laughed. "I was only curious. Really. Just cash me in and I'll be on my way."

The Geek gestured at the stacks of coins on the table.

"What's to cash?" he said. "I pulled mine out the same time I cashed the others' out. The rest is yours."

I looked at the money and swallowed hard. For the first time I could understand why some people found gambling so addictive. There was easily twenty thousand in gold weighing down the table. All mine. From one night of cards!

"Um . . . Geek? Could you hold on to my winnings for me? I'm not wild about the idea of walking around with that much gold on me. I can drop back by later with my bodyguards to pick it up.''

"Suit yourself," the Geek shrugged. "I can't think of anyone at the Bazaar who would have nerve enough to jump you, with your reputation. Still, you might run into a stranger. . . ."

"Fine," I said, heading for the door. "Then I'll be . . ."

"Wait a minute! Aren't you forgetting something?"

"What's that?"

"Pidge's marker. Hang on and I'll get it."

He disappeared before I could protest, so I leaned against the wall to wait. I had forgotten about the marker, but the Geek was a gambler and adhered more religiously to the unwritten laws of gambling than most folks obeyed civil law. I'd just have to humor him and . . .

"Here's the marker, Skeeve," the Deveel announced. "Markie, this is Skeeve."

I just gaped at him, unable to speak. Actually, I gaped at the little blond-headed moppet he was leading by the hand. That's right. A girl. Nine or ten years old at the most.

I experienced an all-too-familiar sinking feeling in my stomach that meant I was in trouble . . . lots of it.

Chapter Two:

"Kids? Who said anything about kids?"
—CONAN

THE little girl looked at me through eyes that glowed with trust and love. She barely stood taller than my waist and had that wholesome, healthy glow that young girls are all supposed to have but so few actually do. With her little beret and matching jumper, she looked so much like an oversized doll that I wondered if she'd say "Mama" if you turned her upside down, then right-side up again.

She was so adorable that it was obvious that anyone with a drop of paternal instinct would fall in love with her on sight. Fortunately, my partner had trained me well; any instincts I had were of a more monetary nature.

"What's that?" I demanded.

"It's a little girl," the Geek responded. "Haven't you ever seen one before?"

For a minute, I thought I was being baited. Then I remembered some of my earliest conversations with Aahz and controlled my temper.

"I realize that it's a little girl, Geek," I said carefully.

9

"What I was really trying to ask is a) who is she? b) what is she doing here? and c) what has this got to do with Pidge's marker? Do I make myself clear?"

The Deveel blinked his eyes in bewilderment.

"But I just told you. Her name is Markie. She's Pidge's marker . . . you know, the one you said you would cover personally?"

My stomach bottomed out.

"Geek, we were talking about a piece of paper. You know, 'IOU, etc.'? A marker! Who leaves a little girl for a marker?"

"Pidge does. Always has. C'mon, Skeeve. You know me. Would I give anyone credit for a piece of paper? I give Pidge credit on Markie here because I know he'll be back to reclaim her."

"Right. *You* give him credit. I don't deal in little girls, Geek."

"You do now," he smiled. "Everyone at the table heard you say so. I'll admit I was a little surprised at the time."

". . . But not surprised enough to warn me about what I was buying into. Thanks a lot, Geek old pal. I'll try to remember to return the favor someday."

In case you didn't notice, that last part was an open threat. As has been noted, I've been getting quite a reputation around the Bazaar as a magician, and I didn't really think the Geek wanted to be on my bad side.

Okay. So it was a rotten trick. I was getting desperate.

"Whoa. Hold it," the Deveel said quickly. "No reason to get upset. If you don't want her, I'll give you cash to cover the marker and keep her myself . . ."

"That's better."

". . . at the usual terms, of course."

I knew I was being suckered. *Knew* it, mind you. But I had to ask anyway.

"What terms?"

"If Pidge doesn't reclaim her in two weeks, I sell her

into slavery for enough money to cover her father's losses."

Check and mate.

I looked at Markie. She was still holding the Geek's hand, listening solemnly while we argued out her fate. As our eyes met, she said her first words since she had entered the room.

"Are you going to be my new daddy?"

I swallowed hard.

"No, I'm not your daddy, Markie. I just . . ."

"Oh, I know. It's just that every time my *real* daddy leaves me with someone, he tells me that they're going to be my pretend daddy for a while. I'm supposed to mind them and do what they tell me just as if they were my real daddy until my real daddy comes to get me. I just wanted to know if you were going to be my new pretend daddy?"

"Ummm . . ."

"I hope so. You're nice. Not like some of the scumbags he's left me with. Will you be my new daddy?"

With that, she reached out and took hold of my hand. A small thrill ran through me like an autumn shiver. She was so vulnerable, so trusting. I had been on my own for a long time, first alone, then apprenticed to Garkin, and finally teamed with Aahz. In all that time, I had never really been responsible for another person. It was a funny feeling, scary and warming at the same time.

I tore my eyes away from her and glared at the Geek again.

"Slavery's outlawed here at the Bazaar."

The Deveel shrugged. "There are other dimensions. As a matter of fact, I've had a standing offer for her for several years. That's why I've been willing to accept her as collateral. I could make enough to cover the bet, the cost of the food she's eaten over the years, and still turn a tidy profit."

"That's about the lowest . . ."

"Hey! The name's 'the Geek,' not 'the Red Cross'! I don't do charity. Folks come to me to bet, not for handouts."

I haven't thrown a punch at anyone since I started practicing magic, but I was sorely tempted to break that record just this one. Instead, I turned to the little girl.

"Get your things, Markie. Daddy's taking you to your new home."

My partner and I were currently basing our operations at the Bazaar at Deva, which is the home dimension of the Deveels. Deevels are reputed to be the sharpest merchants, traders, and hagglers in all the known dimensions. You may have heard of them in various folk tales in your own home dimension. Their fame lingers even in dimensions they have long since stopped trading in.

The Bazaar is the showcase of Deva . . . in fact, I've never seen a part of Deva that wasn't the Bazaar. Here the Deveels meet to trade with each other, buying and selling the choicest magics and miracles from all the dimensions. It's an around-the-clock, over-the-horizon sprawl of tents, shops, and barter blankets where you can acquire anything your imagination can conjure as well as a lot of things you never dreamed existed . . . for a price. Many inventors and religious figures have built their entire career from items purchased in one trip to the bazaar. Needless to say, it is devastating to the average budget . . . even if the holder of the pursestrings has above-average sales resistance.

Normally I enjoy strolling through the booths, but tonight, with Markie beside me, I was too distracted to concentrate on the displays. It occurred to me that, fun as it is for adults, the Bazaar is no place to raise a child.

"Will we be living by ourselves, or do you have a girlfriend?"

Markie was clinging to my hand as we made our way through the Bazaar. The wonders of the stalls and shops dispensing magic reached out to us as they always do, but she was oblivious to them, choosing instead to ply me with questions and hanging on my every word.

" 'No's to both questions. Tananda lives with me, but she isn't my girlfriend. She's a free-lance assassin who helps me out on jobs from time to time. Then there's Chumley, her brother. He's a troll who works under the name of Crunch. You'll like them. They're nice . . . in a lot of ways they're nicer than I am."

Markie bit her lip and frowned. "I hope you're right. I've found that a lot of nice people don't like little kids."

"Don't worry," I said, with more confidence than I felt. "But I'm not done yet. There's also Guido and Nunzio, my bodyguards. They may seem a little gruff, but don't let them scare you. They just act tough because it's part of their job."

"Gee. I've never had a daddy who had bodyguards before."

"That's not all. We also have Buttercup, who's a war unicorn, and Gleep, who's my very own pet dragon."

"Oh, lots of people have dragons. I'm more impressed by the bodyguards."

That took me aback a little. I'd always thought that having a dragon was rather unique. I mean, nobody else I knew had a dragon. Then again, nobody else I knew had bodyguards, either.

"Let's see," Markie was saying. "There's Tananda, Chumley, Guido, Nunzio, Buttercup, and Gleep. Is that all?"

"Well, there's also Massha. She's my apprentice."

"Massha. That's a pretty name."

Now, there are lots of words to describe my apprentice, but unfortunately 'pretty' isn't one of them. Massha is huge, both in height and breadth. There are large people who still manage to look attractive, but my apprentice isn't one of them. She tends toward loud, colorful clothes which invariably clash with her bright orange hair, and wears enough jewelry for three stores. In fact, the last time she got into a fight here at the Bazaar was when a nearsighted shopper mistook her for a display tent.

"Aahh . . . you'll just have to meet her. But you're right. Massha is a pretty name."

"Gee, you've got a lot of people living with you."

"Well . . . umm . . . there *is* one more."

"Who's that?"

"His name is Aahz. He's my partner."

"Is he nice, too?"

I was torn between loyalty and honesty.

"He . . . aah . . . takes getting used to. Remember how I told you not to be scared of the bodyguards even if they were a little gruff?"

"Yes."

"Well, it's all right to be scared of Aahz. He gets a little upset from time to time, and until he cools down it's best to give him a lot of room and not leave anything breakable—like your arm—within his reach."

"What gets him upset?"

"Oh, the weather, losing money, not making money . . . which to him is the same as losing money, any one of a hundred things that I say . . . and you! I'm afraid he's going to be a little upset when he meets you, so stay behind me until I get him calmed down. Okay?"

"Why would he be upset with me?"

"You're going to be a surprise to him, and he doesn't like surprises. You see, he's a very suspicious person and tends to think of a surprise as a part of an unknown plot against him . . . or me."

Markie lapsed into silence. Her blow furrowed as she stared off into nothingness, and it occurred to me that I was scaring her.

"Hey, don't worry," I said, squeezing her hand. "Aahz will be okay once he gets over being surprised. Now tell me about yourself. Do you go to school?"

"Yes. I'm halfway through Elemental School. I'd be

further if we didn't keep moving around."

"Don't you mean Elementary School?" I smiled.

"No. I mean . . ."

"Whoops. Here we are. This is your new home, Markie."

I gestured grandly at the small tent that was our combination home and headquarters.

"Isn't it a little small for all those people?" she frowned, staring at the tent.

"It's bigger inside than it is outside," I explained. "C'mon. I'll show you."

I raised the flap for her and immediately wished I hadn't.

"Wait'll I get my hands on him!" came Aahz's booming voice from within. "After all the times I've told him to stay away from dragon poker!"

It occurred to me that maybe we should wait for a while before introducing Markie to my partner. I started to ease the flap down, but it was too late.

"Is that you, partner? I'd like to have a little chat, if you don't mind!"

"Remember. Stay behind me," I whispered to Markie, then proceeded to walk into the lion's den.

Chapter Three:

"I'm doing this for your own good!"
— ANY ESTABLISHMENT EXECUTIONER . . .
OR ANY PARENT

As I told Markie, our place at the Bazaar was bigger on the inside than on the outside . . . lots bigger! I've been in smaller palaces . . . heck, I've lived and worked in smaller palaces than our current domicile. Back when I was court magician at Possletum, to be exact.

Here at the Bazaar, the Deveels think that any display of wealth will weaken their position when they haggle over prices, so they hide the size of their homes by tucking them into 'unlisted dimensions.' Even though our home looked like just a humble tent from the street, the inside included multiple bedrooms, a stable area, a courtyard and garden, etc., etc. You get the picture.

Unfortunately for me, at the moment it also included my partner, Aahz.

"Well, if it isn't the Bazaar's own answer to War, Famine, Death, and Pestilence! Other dimensions have the Four Horsemen, but the Bazaar at Deva has the Great Skeeve!"

Remember my partner, Aahz? I mentioned him back in Chapter One and again in Chapter Two. Most of my efforts to describe him fail to prepare people for the real thing. What I usually forget to mention to folks is that he's from the dimension Perv. For those of you unfamiliar with dimension travel, that means he is green and scaly with a mouth big enough for any other three beings and teeth enough for a school of sharks . . . if shark's teeth got to be four inches long, that is. I don't deliberately omit things from my descriptions. It's just that after all these years I've gotten used to him.

"Have you got anything at all to say for yourself? Not that there's any acceptable excuse, mind you. It's just that tradition allows you a few last words."

Well . . . I've *almost* gotten used to him.

"Hi, Aahz. Have you heard about the card game?"

"About two hours ago," Massha supplied from a nearby chair where she was entrenched with a book and a huge box of chocolates. "He's been like this ever since."

"I see you've done your usual marvelous job of calming him down."

"I'm just an apprentice around here," she said with a shrug. "Getting between you two in a quarrel is not part of my game plan for a long and prosperous life."

"If you two are *quite* through," Aahz growled, "I'm still waiting to hear what you have to say for yourself."

"What's to say? I sat in on a game of dragon poker. . . ."

"WHO'S BEEN TEACHING YOU TO PLAY DRAGON POKER? That's what there is to say! Was it Tananda? Chumley? How come you're going to other people for lessons all of a sudden? Aren't I good enough for the Great Skeeve any more?"

The truth of the situation suddenly dawned on me. Aahz was my teacher before he insisted that I be elevated to full partner status. Even though we were theoretically equals, old habits die hard and he still considered himself to be my exclusive teacher, mentor, coach, and all-around nudge. What the *real* problem was was that my partner was jealous of someone else horning in on what he felt was his private student! Perhaps this problem would be easier to deal with than I thought.

"No one else has been teaching me, Aahz. Everything I know about dragon poker, I learned from you."

"But I haven't taught you anything."

"Exactly."

That stopped him. At least, it halted his pacing as he turned to peer suspiciously at me with his yellow eyes.

"You mean you don't know anything at all about dragon poker?"

"Well, from listening to you talk, I know about how many cards are dealt out and stuff like that. I still haven't figured out what the various hands are, much less their order . . . you know, what beats what."

"*I* know," my partner said pointedly. "What I don't know is why you decided to sit in on a game you don't know the first thing about."

"The Geek sent me an invitation, and I thought it would be sociable to . . ."

"The Geek? You sat in at one of the Geek's games at the Even-Odds to be sociable?" He was off again. "Don't you know that those are some of the most cutthroat games at the Bazaar? They eat amateurs alive at those tables. And you went there to be sociable?"

"Sure. I figured the worse that could happen would be that I lost a little money. The way things have been going, we can afford it. Besides, who knows, I might get lucky."

"Lucky? Now I know you don't know anything about dragon poker. It's a game of skill, not luck. All you could do was throw your money away . . . money we've both risked our lives for, I might add."

"Yes, Aahz."

"And besides, one of the first things you learn playing any kind of poker is that the surest way to lose is to go in *expecting* to lose."

"Yes, Aahz."

Out of desperation, I was retreating behind my strongest defense. I was agreeing with everything he said. Even Aahz has trouble staying mad at someone who's agreeing with him.

"Well, what's done is done and all the shouting in the world won't change it. I just hope you've learned your lesson. How much did it cost you, anyway?"

"I won."

"Okay. Just to show you there're no hard feelings, we'll split it. In a way it's my fault. I should have taught you . . ."

There was a sudden stillness in the room. Even Massha had stopped with a bonbon halfway to her mouth. Very slowly, Aahz turned to face me.

"You know, Skeeve, for a minute there, I thought you said . . ."

"I won," I repeated, trying desperately not to smile.

"You won. As in 'better than broke even' won?"

"As in 'twenty thousand in gold plus' won," I corrected.

"But if you didn't know how the game was played, how could you . . ."

"I just bet the people, not the cards. It seemed to work out pretty well."

I was in my glory now. It was a rare time indeed that I managed to impress my partner, and I was going to milk it for all it was worth.

"But that's crazy!" Aahz scowled. "I mean, it could work for a while, but in the long run . . ."

"He was great!" Markie announced, emerging from behind me. "You should have seen it. He beat everybody."

My "glory" came tumbling down around my ears. With one hand I shoved Markie back behind me and braced for the explosion. What I really wanted to do was run for cover, but that would have left Markie alone in the open, so I settled for closing my eyes.

Nothing happened.

After a few moments, I couldn't stand the suspense any more and opened one eye to sneak a peek. The view I was treated to was an *extreme* close-up of one of Aahz's yellow eyes. He was standing nose to nose with me, apparently waiting until I was ready before launching into his tirade. It was obvious that *he* was ready. The gold flecks in his eyes were shimmering as if they were about to boil . . . and for all I knew, they were.

"Who . . . is . . . that?"

I decided against trying to play dumb and say "Who is what?" At the range he was standing, Aahz would have bitten my head off . . . literally!

"Umm . . . remember I said that I won twenty thousand plus? Well, she's the plus."

"YOU WON A KID IN A CARD GAME!?!!"

The force of my partner's voice actually knocked me back two steps. I probably would have gone farther if I hadn't bumped against Markie.

"ARE YOU OUT OF YOUR MIND?? DON'T YOU KNOW THE PENALTY FOR SLAVERY IS . . ."

He disappeared in mid-sentence behind a wall of flesh and tasteless color. Despite her earlier claims of valuing self-preservation, Massha had stepped between us.

"Just cool down a minute, Green and Scaly."

Aahz tried to get around her.

"BUT HE JUST . . ."

She took a half step sideways and blocked him by leaning against the wall.

"Give him a chance to explain. He *is* your partner, isn't he?"

From the sound of his voice, Aahz reversed his field and tried for the other side.

"BUT HE . . ."

Massha took two steps and leaned against the other wall, all the while talking as if she wasn't being interrupted.

"Now either he's an idiot . . . which he isn't, or you're a lousy teacher . . . which you aren't, or there's more to this than meets the eye. Hmmm?"

There were several moments of silence, then Aahz spoke again in a voice much more subdued.

"All right, *partner*. Let's hear it."

Massha relinquished her spot and I could see Aahz again . . . though I almost wished I couldn't. He was breathing hard, but whether from anger or from the exertion of trying to get around Massha I couldn't tell. I could hear the scales on his fingers rasp as he clenched and unclenched his fists, and I knew that I'd better tell my story fast before he lost control again.

"I didn't win *her*," I said hastily. "I won her father's marker. She's our guarantee that he'll come back and make his losses good."

Aahz stopped making with the fists, and a puzzled frown creased his features.

"A marker? I don't get it. The Geek's games are always on a cash-and-carry basis."

"Well, he seems to have made an exception in Pidge's case."

"Pidge?"

"That's my daddy," Markie announced, stepping from behind me again. "It's short for Pigeon. He loses a lot . . . that's why everyone is always so happy to let him sit in on a game."

"Cute kid," Aahz said drily. "It also might explain why you did so well in the game tonight. One screwball can change the pace of an entire game. Still, when the Geek *does* take markers, he usually pays the winners in cash and handles the collecting himself."

"He was willing to do that."

"Then why . . ."

". . . and if Markie's father didn't show up in two weeks, he was going to take her off-dimension and sell her into slavery himself to raise the money."

From her chair, Massha gave a low whistle.

"Sweet guy, this Geek."

"He's a Deveel." Aahz waved absently, as if the statement explained everything. "Okay, okay. I can see where you felt you had to accept custody of the kid here instead of leaving her with the Geek. Just answer me one question."

"What's that?"

"What do we do with her if her father doesn't show up?"

Sometimes I like it better when Aahz is ranting than when he's thinking.

"Aahh . . . I'm still working on that one."

"Terrific. Well, when you come up with an answer, let me know. I think I'll stay in my room until this whole thing blows over."

With that he strode out of the room, leaving Massha and me to deal with Markie.

"Cheer up, Hot Stuff," my apprentice said. "Kids aren't all that much of a problem. Hey, Markie. Would you like a piece of chocolate?"

"No, thank you. It might make me fat and ugly like you."

I winced. Up until now, Massha had been my ally on the subject of Markie, but this might change everything. She was very sensitive about her weight, so most of us tended to avoid any mention of it. In fact, I had gotten so used to her appearance that I tended to forget how she looked to anyone who didn't know her.

"Markie!" I said sternly. "That wasn't a very nice thing to say."

"But it's true!" she countered, turning her innocent eyes on me.

"That's why it's not nice," Massha laughed, though I noticed her smile was a little forced. "C'mon, Markie. Let's hit the pantry and try to find you something to eat . . . something low-calorie."

The two of them trooped out, leaving me alone with my thoughts. Aahz had raised a good question. What *were* we going to do if Markie's father didn't come back? I had never been around kids before. I knew that having her around would cause problems, but how many problems? With everything else we had handled as a team, surely Aahz and I could handle a little girl. Of course, Aahz was . . .

"There you are, Boss! Good. I was hopin' you were still up."

I cleared my mind to find one of my bodyguards entering the room.

"Oh. Hi, Guido. How did the report go?"

"Couldn't be better. In fact, Don Bruce was so happy he sent you a little present."

In spite of my worries, I couldn't help smiling. At least *something* was going right.

"That's great," I said. "I could use a little cheering up just now."

"Then I've got just the thing. Hey, Nunzio! Bring her in here!"

My smile froze. I tried desperately not to panic. After all, I reasoned, people refer to a lot of things as "her." Boats, for example, or even . . .

"Boss, this is Bunny. Don Bruce sends her with his compliments on a job well done. She's going to be your moll."

The girl they were escorting into the room bore no resemblance at all to a boat.

Chapter Four:

"A doll is a doll is a doll."

—F. SINATRA

BUNNY was a top-heavy little redhead with her hair in a pixie cut and a vacant stare a zombie would envy. She was vigorously chewing something as she rubbernecked, trying to take in the entire room at once.

"Gee. This is quite a place you guys's got here. It's a lot nicer than the last place I was at, ya know?"

"This is just the waitin' room," Nunzio said with pride. "Wait'll you see the rest of the layout. It's bigger'n any hangout I've ever worked, know what I mean?"

"What'sa matter with you two?" Guido barked. "Ain't ya got no manners? First things first. Bunny, this is the Boss. He's the one you're goin' to be workin' under."

Bunny advanced toward me holding out her hand. From the way her body moved under her tight-fitting clothes, there was little doubt what she was wearing under them . . . or not wearing, as the case may be.

"Pleased ta meetcha, Boss. The pleasure's mutual," she said brightly.

For once, I knew exactly what to say.

25

"No."

She stopped, then turned toward Guido with a frown.

"He means not to call him 'Boss' until you get to know him," my bodyguard assured her. "Around here he's just known as Skeeve."

"Gotcha," she winked. "Okay, *Skeeve* . . . ya know, that's kinda cute."

"No," I repeated.

"Okay. So it's not cute. Whatever you say. You're the Boss."

"NO!"

"But . . ."

I ignored her and turned directly to Guido.

"Have you lost your marbles? What are you doing bringing her in here like this?"

"Like I said, Boss, she's a present from Don Bruce."

"Guido, lots of people give each other presents. Presents like neckties and books . . . not girls!"

My bodyguard shrugged his shoulders helplessly. "So Don Bruce ain't lots of people. He's the one who assigned us to you in the first place, and he says that someone with your standin' in the Mob should have a moll."

"Guido . . . let's talk. Excuse us a minute, Bunny."

I slipped an arm around my bodyguard's shoulders and drew him off into a corner. That may sound easy until you realize I had to reach *up* to get to his shoulders. Both Guido and Nunzio are considerably larger than me.

"Now look, Guido," I said. "Remember when I explained our setup to you?"

"Sure, Boss."

"Well, let's walk through it again. Don Bruce hired Aahz and me on a non-exclusive basis to watch over the Mob's interests here at the Bazaar. Now, he did that because the ordinary methods he employs weren't working . . . Right?"

"Actually, he hired *you* and included your partner. Except for that . . . right."

"Whatever. We also explained to you that the reason

the Mob's usual methods weren't working was that the
Bazaar merchants had hired us to chase the Mob out.
Remember?''

"Yea. That was really a surprise when you told us.
You really had us goin', know what I mean?''

"Now that brings us to the present. The money we're
collecting from the Bazaar merchants and passing on to
Don Bruce, the money he thinks they're paying the Mob
for protection, is actually being paid to us to keep the
Mob away from the Bazaar. Get it?''

"Got it.''

"Good. Then, understanding the situation as you do,
you can see why I don't want a moll or anyone else from
the Mob hanging around. If word gets back to Don
Bruce that we're flim-flamming him, it'll reopen the
whole kettle of worms. That's why you've got to get rid
of her.''

Guido nodded vigorously.

"No,'' he said.

"Then all you have to . . . what do you mean, 'no'?
Do I have to explain it all to you again?''

My bodyguard heaved a great sigh.

"I understand the situation, Boss. But I don't think
you do. Allow me to continue where you left off.''

"But I . . .''

"Now, whatever you are, Don Bruce considers you to
be a minor chieftain in the Mob running a profitable
operation. Right?''

"Well . . .''

"As such, you are entitled to a nice house, which you
have, a couple of bodyguards, which you have, and a
moll, which you don't have. These things are necessary
in Don Bruce's eyes if the Mob is to maintain its public
image of rewarding successful members . . . just as it
finds it necessary to express its displeasure at members
who fail. Follow me?''

"Public image,'' I said weakly.

"So it is in the interests of the Mob that Don Bruce
has provided you with what you have failed to provide

yourself . . . namely: a moll. If you do not like this one, we can take her back and get another, but a moll you must have if we are to continue in our existing carefree manner. Otherwise . . ." He paused dramatically.

"Otherwise . . .?" I prompted.

"If you do not maintain the appearance of a successful Mob member, Don Bruce will be forced to deal with you as if you were unsuccessful . . . know what I mean?"

I suddenly felt the need to massage my forehead. "Terrific."

"My sentiments exactly. Under the circumstances, however, I thought it wisest to accept his gift in your name and hope that you could find an amicable solution to our dilemma at a later date."

"I suppose you're . . . Hey! Wait a minute. We already have Massha and Tananda in residence. Won't they do?"

Guido gave his sigh again. "This possibility did indeed occur to me as well. Then I said to myself: 'Guido, do you really want to be the one to hang the label of moll on either Massha or Tananda, knowing those ladies as you do? Even if it will only be bantered around the Mob?' Viewed in that light, it was my decision to go along with Don Bruce's proposal and leave it to you to make the final decision . . . *Boss*."

I shot a sharp glance at him for that last touch of sarcasm. Despite his affected speech patterns and pseudo-pompous explanations, I occasionally had the impression that Guido was far more intelligent than he let on. At the moment, however, his face was a study in innocence, so I let it ride.

"I see what you mean, Guido. If either Massha or Tananda are going to be known as 'molls,' I'd rather it was their choice, not mine. Until then, I guess we're stuck with . . . what's her name? Bunny? Does she wiggle her nose or something?"

Guido glanced across the room at the other two, then

lowered his voice conspiratorily. "Just between you and me, Boss, I think you would be well advised to accept this particular moll that Don Bruce has personally selected to send. Know what I mean?"

"No, I don't." I grimaced. "Excuse me, Guido, but the mind's working a little slow just now. If you're trying to tell me something, you're going to have to spell it out."

"Well, I did a little checkin' around, and it seems that Bunny here is Don Bruce's niece, and . . ."

"HIS N . . ."

"Ssshh. Keep it down, Boss. I don't think we're supposed to know that."

With a supreme effort, I suppressed my hysteria and lowered my voice again. "What are you trying to do to me? I'm trying to keep this operation under wraps and you bring me Don Bruce's niece?"

"Don't worry."

"DON'T . . ."

"Sshh! Like I said. I've been checking around. It seems the two of them don't get along at all. Wouldn't give each other the time of day. The way I hear it, he doesn't want her to be a moll, and she won't go along with any other kind of work. They fight over it like cats and dogs. Anyway, if you can trust any moll to not feed Don Bruce the straight scoop, it's her. That's why I was sayin' that you should keep this one."

My headache had now spread to my stomach.

"Swell. Just swell. Well, at least . . ."

"The one thing I couldn't find out, though," Guido continued with a frown, "is why he wants her with you. I figure that it's either that he thinks that you'll treat her right, or that he expects you to scare her out of bein' a moll. I'm just not sure which way you should play it."

This was not turning out to be a good night for me. In fact, it had gone steadily downhill since I won that last hand of dragon poker.

"Guido," I said. "Please don't say anything more.

Okay? Please? Every time I think that things might not
be so bad, you drag out something else that makes them
worse."

"Just tryin' to do my job," he shrugged, obviously
hurt, "but if that's what you want . . . well, you're the
Boss."

"And if you say that one more time, I'm liable to
forget you're bigger than me and pop you one in the
nose. Understand? Being the 'Boss' implies a certain
degree of control, and if there's one thing I don't have
right now, it's control."

"Right, B . . . Skeeve," my bodyguard grinned.
"You know, for a minute there you sounded just like
my old B . . . employer. He used to beat up on Nunzio
and me when he got mad. Of course, we had to stand
there and take it. . . ."

"Don't give me any ideas," I snarled. "For now, let's
just concentrate on Bunny."

I turned my attention once more to the problem at
hand, which was to say Bunny. She was still staring va-
cantly around the room, jaws working methodically on
whatever it was she was chewing, and apparently oblivious to whatever it was Nunzio was trying to tell her.

"Well, uh . . . Bunny," I said, "it looks like you're
going to be staying with us for a while."

She reacted to my words as if I had hit her "on"
switch.

"Eeoooh!" she squealed, as if I had just told her that
she had won a beauty pageant. "Oh, I know I'm just
goin' to *love* workin' under you, Skeevie."

My stomach did a slow roll to the left.

"Shall I get her things, Boss?" Nunzio said. "She's
got about a mountain and a half of luggage outside."

"Oh, you can leave all that," Bunny cooed. "I just
know my Skeevie is going to want to buy me a whole
new wardrobe."

"Hold it! Time out!" I ordered. "House rules time.
Bunny, some things are going to disappear from your
vocabulary *right now*. First, forget 'Skeevie.' It's

Skeeve . . . just Skeeve, or if you must, the Great Skeeve
in front of company. Not Skeevie."

"Gotcha," she winked.

"Next, you do not work *under* me. You're . . . you're
my personal secretary. Got it?"

"Why sure, sugar. That's what I'm always called."

Again with the wink.

"Now then, Nunzio. I want you to get her luggage
and move it into . . . I don't know, the pink bedroom."

"You want I should give him a hand, Boss?" Guido
asked.

"*You* stay put." I smiled, baring all my teeth. "I've
got a special job for you."

"Now just a darn minute!" Bunny interrupted, her
cutie-pie accent noticeably lacking. "What's this with
the 'pink bedroom'? Somehow you don't strike me as
the kind that sleeps in a pink bedroom. Aren't I moving
into your bedroom?"

"*I'm* sleeping in my bedroom," I said. "Now isn't it
easier for you to move into one of our spares than for
me to relocate just so you can move into mine?"

As I said, it had been a long night, and I was more
than a little slow. Lucky for me, Bunny was fast enough
for both of us.

"I thought we was goin' to be sharin' a room, Mr.
Skeeve. That's the whole idea of my bein' here, ya
know? What's wrong? Ya think I got bad breath or
sumpin'?"

"Aahh . . . ummm . . ." I said intelligently.

"Hi, Guido . . . Nunzio. Who's . . . oh wow!"

That last witty line didn't come from me. Massha had
just entered the room with Markie in tow and lurched to
a halt at the sight of Bunny.

"Hey, Boss! What's with the kid?"

"Guido, Nunzio, this is Markie . . . our *other* house
guest. Massha, Markie, this is Bunny. She's going to be
staying with us for a while . . . in the *pink* bedroom."

"Now I get it!" Bunny exclaimed. "You want we
should play it cool because of the kid! Well, you can

count on me. Discretion is Bunny's middle name. The pink bedroom it is!"

I could cheerfully have throttled her. If her meaning was lost on Markie, it certainly hadn't gotten past Massha, who was staring out at me from under raised eyebrows.

"Whatever!" I said rather than take more drastic action. "Now, Nunzio, you get Bunny set up in the pink bedroom. Massha, I want you to get Markie settled in the blue bedroom next to mine . . . and knock it off with the eyebrows. I'll explain everything in the morning."

"*That* I want to hear," she snorted. "C'mon, kid."

"I'm not tired!" Markie protested.

"Tough!" I countered. "I am."

"Oh," she said meekly and followed Massha.

Whatever kind of a crumb her father might be, somewhere along the line she had learned when adults could be argued with and when it was best to go with the flow.

"What do you want me to do, Boss?" Guido asked eagerly.

I favored him with my evilest grin.

"Remember that special assignment I said I had for you?"

"Yea, Boss?"

"I'll warn you, it's dangerous."

That appealed to his professional pride, and he puffed out his chest. "The tougher the better. You know me!"

"Fine," I said. "All you have to do is go upstairs and explain Bunny to Aahz. It seems my partner isn't talking to me just now."

Chapter Five:

"Such stuff dreams are made of."
—S. BEAUTY

LUANNA was with me. I couldn't remember when she arrived or how long she had been here, but I didn't care. I hadn't seen her since we got back from the jailbreak on Limbo, and I had missed her terribly. She had left me to stay with her partner, Matt, and a little piece of me went with her. I won't be so cornball as to say it was my heart, but it was in that general vicinity.

There was so much I wanted to tell her . . . wanted to ask her, but it didn't really seem necessary. We just lay side by side on a grassy hill watching the clouds, enjoying each other's company in silence. I could have stayed like that forever, but she raised herself on one elbow and spoke softly to me.

"If you'll just skootch over a little, Skeevie, we can both get comfy."

This was somehow jarring to my serenity. She didn't sound like Luanna at all. Luanna's voice was musical and exciting. She sounded like . . .

"BUNNY!"

I was suddenly sitting bolt upright, not on a grassy knoll, but in my own bed.

33

"Ssshh! You'll wake up the kid!"

She was perched on the edge of my bed wearing something filmy that was even more revealing than the skin-tight outfit she had had on last night.

"What are you doing in my room!?"

I had distinct memories of stacking several pieces of furniture in front of the door before I retired, and a quick glance confirmed that they were still in place.

"Through the secret passageway," she said with one of her winks. "Nunzio showed it to me last night."

"Oh, he did, did he?" I snarled. "Remind me to express my thanks to him for that little service."

"Save your thanks, sugar. You're goin' to need them when I get done with you."

With that she raised the covers and slid in next to me. I slid out the other side of the bed as if a spider had just joined me. Not that I'm afraid of spiders, mind you, but Bunny scares me stiff.

"Now what's wrong?" she whined.

"Um . . . ah . . . look, Bunny. Can we talk for a minute?"

"Sure," she said, sitting up in bed and bending forward to rest her elbows on her knees. "Anything you say."

Unfortunately, her current position also gave me an unrestricted view of her cleavage. I promptly forgot what I was going to say.

"Aaah . . . I . . . um . . ."

There was a knock at the door.

"Come in!" I said, grateful for the interruption.

That is beyond a doubt the dumbest thing I have ever said.

The door opened, sweeping the stacked furniture back with amazing ease, and Chumley walked in.

"I say, Skeeve, Aahz has just been telling me the most remarkable . . . Hal-lo?"

I mentioned before that Chumley is a troll. What I didn't say was that he could blush . . . probably because I didn't know it myself until just now. Of all the sights

I've seen in several dimensions, a blushing troll is in a category all its own.

"You must be Chumley!" Bunny chirped. "The boys told me about you."

"Umm . . . quite right. Pleased to make your acquaintance and all that," the troll said, trying to avert his eyes while still making polite conversation.

"Yeah. Sure, Chum. Don't you have somethin' else to do . . . like leavin'?"

I clutched at his arm in desperation.

"No! I mean . . . Chumley always comes by first thing in the morning."

"Ahh . . . Yes. Just wanted to see if Skeeve was ready for a spot of breakfast."

"Well, I got here first," Bunny bristled. "If Skeevie wants something to nibble on, he can . . ."

"Good morning, Daddy!"

Markie came bounding into the room and gave me a hug before any of us knew she was around.

"Well, well. You must be Skeeve's new ward, Markie," the troll beamed, obviously thankful to have something to focus on other than Bunny.

"And you're Chumley. Hi, Bunny!"

"Hiya, kid," Bunny responded with a noticeable lack of enthusiasm as she pulled the covers up around her neck.

"Are you up, Skeeve?"

The voice wafting in from the corridor was immediately identifiable as Tananda.

Chumley and I had rarely worked together as a team, but this time no planning or coordination was necessary. I scooped Markie up and carried her into the hall while Chumley followed, slamming the door behind him with enough force to crack the wood.

"Pip pip, little sister. Fine day, isn't it?"

"Hi, Tananda! What's new?"

Our cordial greetings, intended to disarm the situation, succeeded only in stopping our colleague in her tracks.

Tananda is quite attractive—if curvaceous, olive-skinned, green-haired women are your type. Of course, she looks a lot better when she isn't pursing her lips and narrowing her eyes suspiciously.

"Well, for openers, I'd say the little girl under your arm is new," she said firmly. "I may not be the most observant person, but I'm sure I would have noticed her if she had been around before."

"Oh. Well, there are a few things I've got to debrief you on," I smiled weakly. "This is one of them. Her name is Markie, and . . ."

"Later, Skeeve. Right now I'm more curious about what my big brother's up to. How 'bout it, Chumley? I've seen you slam doors on the way *into* bedrooms before, but never on the way out."

"Ummm . . . that is . . ." the troll mumbled awkwardly.

"Actually," I assisted, "It's more like . . . you see . . ."

"Exactly what I had in mind," Tananda declared, slipping past us and flinging the bedroom door open.

My room was mercifully empty of occupants. Apparently Bunny had retreated through whatever secret panel she had emerged from. Chumley and I exchanged unnoted glances of relief.

"I don't get it," Tananda frowned. "You two acted like you were trying to hide a body. There's nothing here to be so secretive about."

"I think they didn't want you to see the girl in my daddy's bed," Markie supplied brightly.

I wanted to express my thanks to Markie but decided that I had enough problems without adding murder to the list.

"Well, Skeeve?" Tananda said, her eyebrows almost reaching her hairline.

"Ummm . . . actually, I'm not really her daddy. That's one of the things I wanted to debrief you about."

"I meant about the girl in your room!"

"That's the other thing I wanted to . . ."

"Cut him some slack! Huh, Tananda? It's uncivilized to beat up on someone before breakfast."

That was Aahz, who for once had approached our gathering without being seen . . . or heard. He's usually not big on quiet entrances.

For that matter, I had never known him to be at all reluctant about beating up on someone—say, for example, me—before breakfast. Still, I was grateful for his intervention.

"Hi, Aahz. We were just . . ."

"Do you know what your partner is doing!?" Tananda said in a voice that could freeze wine. "He *seems* to be turning our home into a combination daycare center and . . ."

"I know all about it," Aahz interrupted, "and so will you if you'll just cool down. We'll explain everything over breakfast."

"Well . . ."

"Besides," Markie piped up, "It's not *your* home. It's my daddy's. He just lets you live here. He can do anything he wants in *his* house!"

I released my hold on her, hoping to dump her on her head. Instead she twisted in midair and landed on her feet like a cat, all the while sneering smugly.

Tananda had stiffened as if someone had jabbed her with a pin.

"I suppose you're right, Markie," she said through tight lips. "If the 'Great Skeeve' wants to romp with some bit of fluff, it's none of my business. And if I don't like it, I should just go elsewhere."

She spun on her heel and started off down the hall.

"What about breakfast?" Aahz called after her.

"I'll be eating out . . . permanently!"

We watched her departure in helpless silence.

"I'd better go after her," Chumley said at last. "In the mood she's in, she might hurt someone."

"Could you take Markie with you?" Aahz requested, still staring after Tananda.

"Are you kidding?" the troll gaped.

"Well, at least drop her off in the kitchen. I've got to have a few words with Skeeve in private."

"I want to stay here!" Markie protested.

"Go," I said quietly.

There must have been something in my voice, because both Markie and Chumley headed off without further argument.

"Partner, you've got a problem."

"Don't I know it. If there was any way I could ship her back to Don Bruce, I'd do it in a minute, but . . ."

"I'm not talking about Bunny!"

That stopped me.

"You aren't?"

"No. Markie's the problem, not Bunny."

"Markie? But she's just a little girl."

Aahz heaved a small sign and put one hand on my shoulder . . . gently, for a change.

"Skeeve, I've given you a lot of advice in the past, some of it better than others. For the most part, you've done pretty well at winging it in unfamiliar situations, but this time you're in over your head. Believe me, you don't have the vaguest idea of the kind of havoc a kid can cause in your life . . . especially a little girl."

I didn't know what to say. My partner was obviously sincere in his concern, and for a change expressing it in a very calm, low-key manner. Still, I couldn't go along with what he was saying.

"C'mon, Aahz. How much trouble can she be? This thing with Tananda happened because of Bunny . . ."

". . . after Markie started mouthing off at the wrong time. I already had Tananda cooling off when Markie put her two cents in."

It also occurred to me that Markie was the one who had spilled the beans to Tananda in the first place. I shoved that thought to the back of my mind.

"So she doesn't have enough sense to keep her mouth shut. She's just a kid. We can't expect her to . . ."

"That's my point. Think about our operation for a minute, partner. How many times in one day can things go sour if someone says the wrong thing at the right moment? It's taken us a year to get Guido and Nunzio on board . . . and they're adults. Bringing a kid into the place is like waving a torch around a fireworks factory."

As much as I appreciated his efforts to explain a problem to me, I was starting to weary a bit of Aahz's single-minded pursuit of his point.

"Okay. So I haven't had much experience around kids. I may be underestimating the situation, but aren't you being a bit of an alarmist? What experience are you basing *your* worries on?"

"Are you kidding?" my partner said, laughing for the first time in our conversation. "Anyone who's been around as many centuries as I have has had more than their share of experience with kids. You met my nephew Rupert? You think he was born an adult? And he's only one of more nieces, nephews, and grandchildren than I can count without being reduced to a nervous wreck by the memories."

And I though I couldn't be surprised by Aahz any more.

"Really? Grandchildren? I never even knew you had kids."

"I don't like to talk about it. That in itself should be a clue. When someone who likes to talk as much as I do totally avoids a subject, the memories have got to be less than pleasant!"

I was starting to get a bit worried. Realizing that Aahz usually tends to minimize danger, his warnings were starting to set my overactive imagination in gear.

"I hear what you're saying, Aahz. But we're only talking about one kid here. How much trouble can one little girl be?"

My partner's face suddenly split into one of his infamous evil grins. "Remember that quote," he said. "I'm going to be tossing it back at you from time to time."

"But. . ."

"Hey, Boss! There's someone here to see you!"

Just what I needed! I had already pretty much resolved not to take on any more clients until after Markie's father had reclaimed her. Of course, I didn't want to say that in front of Aahz, expecially considering our current conversation.

"I'm in the middle of a conference, Guido!" I called. "Tell them to come back later."

"Suit yourself, Boss!" came the reply. "I just thought you'd want to know, seein' as how it's Luanna . . ."

I was off like a shot, not even bothering to excuse myself. Aahz would understand. He knew I'd had a thing for Luanna since our expedition into Limbo.

On my way to the waiting room, I had time to speculate as to whether or not this was one of my bodyguard's little pranks. I decided that if it was, I would study hard until I knew enough magic to turn him into a toad.

My suspicions were groundless. She was there. My beautiful blond goddess. What really made my heart leap, though, was that she had her luggage with her.

"Hi, Luanna. What are you doing here? Where's Matt? How have things been? Would you like something to drink? Could I . . ."

I suddenly realized that I was babbling and forced myself to pause.

"Aahh . . . what I'm trying to say is that it's good to see you."

That got me the slow smile that had haunted my dreams. "I'm glad, Skeeve. I was afraid you'd forgotten about me."

"Not a chance," I said, then realized I was leering. "That is, no, I haven't forgotten about you."

Her deep blue eyes locked with mine, and I felt myself sinking helplessly into their depths.

"That's good," she said in that musical voice of hers. "I was worried about taking you up on your offer after all this time."

That got through the fog that was threatening to

envelop my mind. "Offer? What offer?"

"Oh, you don't remember! I thought . . . oh, this is embarrassing."

"Wait a minute!" I cried. "I haven't forgotten! It's just that . . . let me think . . . it's just . . ."

Like a beam of sunlight in a swamp the memory came to me. "You mean when I said that you could come to work for Aahz and me? That's it? Right?"

"That's what I was talking about!" The sun came from behind the clouds as she smiled again. "You see, Matt and I have split, and I thought . . ."

"Do you want any breakfast, Daddy? You said . . . oh! Hello."

"DADDY!!??"

Markie and Luanna stared at each other.

I revised my plans rapidly. I would study hard and turn *myself* into a toad.

"I can explain, Luanna . . ." I began.

"I think you should keep this one, Daddy," Markie said, never taking her eyes off Luanna. "She's a lot prettier than the other one."

"THE OTHER . . . Oh! You mean Tananda."

"No, I mean . . ."

"MARKIE!" I interrupted desperately. "Why don't you wait for me in the kitchen. I'll be along in a minute after I finish talking to . . ."

"Skeevie, are we going to go shopping?" Bunny slithered into the room. "I need . . . who's that!?"

"Me? I'm nobody." Luanna responded grimly. "I never realized until just now how much of a nobody I am!"

"Well, the job's already taken, if that's what you're here for," Bunny smirked.

"Wait a minute! It's a different job! Really! Luanna, I can . . . Luanna??"

Sometime during my hysteria, the love of my life had gathered up her bags and left. I was talking to empty air.

"Gee, Skeevie. What're you talkin' to her for when you got me? Aren't I . . ."

"Daddy. Can I . . ."

"SHUT UP! BOTH OF YOU! Let me think!"

Try as I might, the only thought that kept coming to me was that maybe Aahz was right. Maybe kids were more trouble than I thought.

Chapter Six:

"Bring the whole family . . . but leave the kids at home!"

—R. MCDONALD

"REALLY, Hot Stuff. Do you think this is such a great idea?"

"Massha, please! I'm trying to think things out. I couldn't get my thoughts together back at Chaos Central with Aahz nattering at me, and I won't be able to do it now if you start up. Now, are you going to help or not?"

My apprentice shrugged her massive shoulders. "Okay. What do you want me to do?"

"Just keep an eye on those two and see that they don't get into any trouble while I think."

"Keep them out of trouble? At the Bazaar at Deva? Aren't Guido and Nunzio supposed to . . ."

"Massha!"

"All right. All right. I want it noted, though, that I'm taking this assignment under protest."

I'm *sure* I didn't give Aahz this much back talk when I was apprenticed to him. Every time I say that out loud, however, my partner bursts into such gales of laughter

43

that now I tend to keep the thought to myself, even when he isn't around.

After some resistance, I had agreed to take Bunny and Markie on a stroll through the Bazaar. As I said to Massha, this was more to get a bit of time away from Aahz than it was giving in to Bunny's whining, though that voice was not easy to ignore.

In acknowledgement of Aahz's repeated warnings of trouble, I had recruited my apprentice to accompany us so I'd have a backup if things went awry. Guido and Nunzio were along, of course, but they were more concerned with things coming at me than with anything anyone in our party might do to the immediate environment.

All in all, we made quite a procession. Two Mob bodyguards, a woman-mountain disguised as a jewerly display, a moll, a kid, and me! For a change, I wasn't the "kid" of the party. There was something to be said for having an honest-to-goodness child traveling with you. It automatically made one look older and somehow more responsible.

We had been in residence at the Bazaar for some time now, and the neighborhood merchants were pretty much used to us. That is, they knew that if I was interested, I'd come to them. If I wasn't, no amount of wheedling or cajoling would tempt me into buying. That might seem a little strange to you, after all my glowing accounts of the wonders for sale at the Bazaar, but I had fallen into the pattern quite naturally. You see, if you just visit the Bazaar once in a while, it's all quite impressive, and you feel compelled to buy just to keep from losing out on some really nifty bargains. If you live there, on the other hand, there's no real compulsion to buy anything right now. I mean, if I need a plant that grows ten feet in a minute, I'll buy it . . . when I need it. Until then, the plant can stay in its shop three doors from our tent, and my money can stay in my pocket.

That's how things were, normally. Of course, my

situation today was anything but normal. I had known this all along, of course, but I hadn't really stopped to think through all the ramifications of my current state of affairs.

Okay. So I was dumb. Remember, I was taking this stroll to try to get a chance to think. Remember?

Maybe I hadn't zeroed in on what my party looked like, but the Deveels spotted the difference before we had gone half a block.

Suddenly every Deveel who hadn't been able to foist off some trinket on me for the last two years was out to give it one more try.

"Love potions! Results guaranteed!"

"Snake necklaces! Poisonous and non!"

"Special discounts for the Great Skeeve!"

"Special discounts for any *friend* of the Great Skeeve!"

"Try our . . .

"Buy my . . ."

"Taste these . . ."

Most of this was not aimed at me, but at Bunny and Markie. The Deveels swarmed around them like . . . well, like Deveels smelling an easy profit. This is not to say that Guido and Nunzio weren't doing their jobs. If they hadn't been clearing a path for us, we wouldn't have been able to move at all. As it was, our progress was simply slowed to a crawl.

"Still think this was a good idea, High Roller?"

"Massha! If you . . ."

"Just asking. If you can think in this racket, though, you've got better concentration than I do."

She was right, but I wasn't about to admit it. I just kept staring forward as we walked, tracking the activity around me out of the corners of my eyes without turning my head.

"Skeevie! Can I have . . ."

"No."

"Look at . . .“

"No."

"Couldn't we . . ."

"No!"

Bunny was getting to be a pain. She seemed to want everything in sight. Fortunately, I had developed the perfect defense. All I had to do was say "No!" to everything.

"Why did we go shopping if we aren't going to buy anything?"

"Well . . ."

So much for my perfect defense. Not to be stymied, I switched immediately to Plan B, which was simply to keep our purchases at a minimum. I didn't seem to be too successful at that, either, but I consoled myself by trying to imagine how much junk we would have gotten loaded down with if I hadn't been riding the brake.

Surprisingly enough, despite all of Aahz's dire predictions, Markie wasn't much trouble at all. I found her to be remarkably well mannered and obedient, and she never asked me to buy her anything. Instead, she contented herself with pointing out to Bunny the few booths that individual overlooked.

There weren't many.

My only salvation was that Bunny did not seem interested in the usual collection of whiz-bangs and wowers that most visitors to the Bazaar find irresistible. She was remarkably loyal to her prime passion—apparel. Hats, dresses, shoes, and accessories all had to pass her close scrutiny.

I'll admit that Bunny did not indulge in random purchases. She had a shrewd eye for fabric and construction, and better color sense than anyone I have ever known. Aahz always said that Imps were flashy dressers, and I had secretly tried to pattern my own wardrobe after their example. However, one afternoon of shopping with Bunny was an education in itself. Imps have nothing on molls when it comes to clothes sense.

The more I watched Bunny pursue the fashions avail-

able at the Bazaar, the more self-conscious I became
about my own appearance. Eventually, I found myself
looking over a few items for myself, and from there it
was a short step to buying.

In no time flat, we had a small mountain of packages
to cart along with us. Bunny had stocked up on a couple
of outfits that changed color with her mood, and was
now wearing an intriguing blouse which had a transpar-
ent patch that migrated randomly around her torso. If
the latter sounds distracting, it was. My own indul-
gences were few, but sufficient to add to the overall bulk
of merchandise we had to transport.

Guido and Nunzio were exempt from package-carry-
ing duties, and Massha flatly refused on the basis that
being a large woman trying to maneuver through the
Bazaar was difficult enough without trying to juggle
packages at the same time. Realizing the "you break it,
you bought it" policies of the Bazaar, I could scarcely
argue with her cautious position.

The final resolution to our baggage problem was
really quite simple. I flexed my magic powers a bit and
levitated the whole kit and kaboodle. I don't normally
like to flaunt my powers publicly, but I figured that this
was a necessary exception to the rule. Of course, having
our purchases floating along behind us was like having a
lighthouse in tow; it drew the Deveels out of their stalls
in droves.

To my surprise, I started to enjoy the situation. Humility and anonymity is well and good, but sometimes
its nice to be made a fuss over. Bunny hung on my arm
and shoulder like a boneless falcon, cooing little en-
dearments of appreciation . . . though the fact that I was
willing to finance her purchases seemed to be making as
much as or more of an impression on her than my minor
display of magic.

"Can't say I think much of her taste in clothes,"
Massha murmured to me as we paused once more while
Bunny darted into a nearby booth.

To say the least, I was not eager to get drawn into a discussion comparing the respective tastes in clothes of Bunny and my apprentice.

"Different body types look better in different styles," I said, as tactfully as I coud.

"Yeah? And what style looks best on *my* body type?"

"In all honesty, Massha, I can't picture you dressing any differently than you do."

"Really? Say, thanks, Skeeve. A girl always likes to hear a few appreciative noises about how she looks."

I had narrowly sidestepped that booby-trap and cast about frantically for a new subject before the other interpretation of my statement occurred to her.

"Umm . . . hasn't Markie been well-behaved?"

"I'll say. I'll admit I was a little worried when you first brought her in, but she's been an angel. I don't think I've ever known a kid this patient and obedient."

"Undemanding, too," I said. "I've been thinking of getting her something while we're out, but I'm having trouble coming up with anything appropriate. The Bazaar isn't big on toy shops."

"Are you kidding? It's one big toy shop!"

"Massha . . ."

"Okay, okay. So they're mostly toys for adults. Let me think. How old is she, anyway?"

"I'm not really sure. She said she was in the third grade at Elementary School . . . even though she calls it Elemental School . . . so that would make her . . ."

I realized that Massha was staring at me in wide-eyed horror.

"Elemental School!?"

"That's what she called it. Cute, huh? Why, what does . . ."

My apprentice interrupted me by grabbing my arm so hard that it hurt. "Skeeve. We've got to get her back home . . . QUICK!!"

"But I don't see . . ."

"I'll explain later! Just get her and go! I'll round up Bunny and get her back, but you've got to get moving!"

To say the least, I found her manner puzzling. I had never seen Massha so upset. This was obviously not the time for questions, though, so I looked around for Markie.

She was standing, fists clenched, glaring at a tent with a closed flap.

All of a sudden everyone was getting uptight. First Massha, and now Markie.

"What's with the kid?" I said, tapping Guido on the shoulder.

"Bunny's in trying on some peek-a-boo nighties, and the owner chased Markie out," my bodyguard explained. "She don't like it much, but she'll get over it. It's part of bein' a kid, I guess."

"I see. Well, I was just going to take her back home anyway. Could one of you stay here with . . ."

"SKEEVE! STOP HER!!"

Massha was shouting at me. I was turning toward her to see what she was talking about when it happened, so I didn't see all the details.

There was a sudden WHOOSH followed by the sounds of ripping canvas, wood splintering, and assorted screams and curses.

I whipped my head back around, and my jaw dropped in astonishment.

The booth that Bunny was in was in tatters. The entire stock of the place was sailing off over the Bazaar, as was what was left of the tent. Bunny was trying to cover herself with her hands and screaming her head off. The proprietor, a particularly greasy-looking Deveel, was also screaming his head off, but his emotions were being vented in our general direction instead of at the world in general.

I would say it was a major dilemma except for one thing. The displays on either side of Bunny's tent and

for two rows behind it were in a similar state. *That* is a
major dilemma, making the destruction of a single
booth pale in comparison.

A voice sprang into my head, drowning out the
clamor of the enraged merchants. "If you break it, you
bought it!" the voice said, and it spoke with a Devan accent.

"What happened?" I gasped, though whether to
myself or to the gods, I wasn't sure.

Massha answered.

"What happened was Markie!" she said grimly. "She
blew her cork and summoned up an air elemental . . .
you know, like you learn to do at *Elemental* School? It
appears that when the kid throws a tantrum, she's going
to do it with magic!"

My mind grasped the meaning of her words instantly,
just as fast as it leaped on to the next plateau. Aahz! I
wasn't sure which was going to be worse: breaking the
news to Aahz, or telling him how much it had cost us to
learn about it!

Chapter Seven:

"There's a time to fight, and a time to hide out!"
—B. CASSIDY

I'VE heard that when some people get depressed, they retire to their neighborhood bar and tell their troubles to a sympathetic bartender. The problem with the Bazaar at Deva (a problem I had never noticed before) is that there are no sympathetic bartenders!

Consequently, I had to settle for the next best thing and holed up in the Yellow Crescent Inn.

Now, a fast-food joint may seem to you to be a poor substitute for a bar. It is. This particular fast-food joint, however, is owned and managed by my only friend at the Bazaar who isn't living with me. This last part was especially important at the moment, since I didn't think I was apt to get much sympathy in my own home.

Gus is a gargoyle, but despite his fierce appearance he's one of the friendliest beings I've ever met. He's helped Aahz and me out on some of our more dubious assignments, so he's less inclined to ask "How did you get yourself into this?" than most. Usually, he's more interested in "How did you get out of it?"

"How did you get yourself into this one?" he said, shaking his head.

Well, nobody's perfect . . . especially friends.

"I *told* you, Gus. One lousy card game where I expected to lose. If I had known it was going to backfire like this, so help me I would have folded every hand!"

"You see, there's your problem," the gargoyle said, flashing a grin toothier than normal. "Instead of sitting in and losing, you'd be better off not sitting in at all!"

I rewarded his sound advice by rolling my eyes.

"It's all hypothetical anyway. What's done is done. The question is, 'What do I do now?' "

"Not so fast. Let's stick with the card game for a minute. Why did you sit in if you were expecting to lose?"

"Look. Can we drop the card game? I was wrong. Okay? Is that what you want to hear?"

"No-o-o," Gus said slowly. "I still want to hear why you went in the first place. Humor me."

I stared at him for a moment, but he seemed perfectly serious.

I shrugged. "The Geek sent me an invitation. Frankly, it was quite flattering to get one. I just thought it would be sociable to . . ."

"Stop!" the gargoyle interrupted, raising his hand. "There's your problem."

"What is?"

"Trying to be sociable. What's the matter? Aren't your current round of friends good enough for you?"

That made me a little bit nervous. I was having enough problems without having Gus get his nose out of joint.

"It isn't that, Gus. Really. The whole crew—yourself included—is closer to me than my family ever was. It's just . . . I don't know . . ."

". . . you want to be liked. Right?"

"Yeah. I guess that's it."

"And that's your problem!"

That one threw me.

"I don't get it," I admitted.

The gargoyle sighed, then ducked behind the counter. "Have another milkshake," he said, shoving one toward me. "This might take a while, but I'll try to explain."

I like to think it's a sign of my growing savoir-faire that I now enjoy strawberry milkshakes. When I first visited the Bazaar, I rejected them out of hand because they looked like pink swamp muck. I was now moderately addicted to them, though I still wouldn't eat the food here. Then again, maybe it was a sign of something else completely if I thought a taste for strawberry milkshakes was a sign of savoir-faire!

"Look, Skeeve," Gus began, sipping at a milkshake of his own, "you're a nice guy . . . one of the nicest I've ever known. You go out of your way to 'do the right thing'. . . to be nice to people. The key phrase there is 'go out of your way.' You're in a 'trouble-heavy' profession anyway. Nobody hires a magician because things are going well. Then you add to that your chosen lifestyle. Because you want to be liked, you place yourself in situations you wouldn't go near if it was for your own personal satisfaction. Case in point: the card game. If you had been out for personal gain, i.e., wealth, you wouldn't have gone near it, since you don't know the game. But you wanted to be friendly, so you went expecting to lose. That's not normal, and it resulted in a not-normal outcome, to wit, Markie. That's why you get into trouble."

I chewed my lip slightly as I thought over what he was saying.

"So if I want to stay out of trouble, I've got to stop being a nice guy? I'm not sure I can do that, Gus."

"Neither am I," the gargoyle agreed cheerfully. "What's more, if you could, I don't think I or any of your other friends would like you any more. I don't even think you'd like yourself."

"Then why are you recommending that I change?"

"I'm not! I'm just pointing out that it's the way you are, not any outside circumstances, that keeps getting you into trouble. In short, since you aren't going to change, get used to being in trouble. It's going to be your constant state for a long while."

I found myself massaging my forehead again.

"Thanks, Gus," I said. "I knew I could count on you to cheer me up."

"Don't knock it. Now you can focus on solving your current problem instead of wasting time wondering why it exists."

"Funny. I thought I was doing just that. Someone *else* wanted to talk about what was causing my problems."

My sarcasm didn't faze the gargoyle in the least.

"Right," he nodded. "That brings us to your current problem."

"Now you're talking. What do you think I should do, Gus?"

"Beats me. I'd say you've got a real dilemma on your hands."

I closed my eyes as my headache hammered anew.

"I don't know what I'd do without you, Gus."

"Hey. Don't mention it. What are friends for? Whoops! Here comes Tananda!"

The other disadvantage to holing up at the Yellow Crescent Inn, besides the fact that it isn't a bar, is that it's located right across the street from my home. This is not good for someone who's trying to avoid his housemates.

Fortunately, this was one situation I could handle with relative ease.

"Don't tell her I'm here, Gus," I instructed.

"But . . ."

Not waiting to hear the rest of his protest, I grabbed my milkshake, slipped into a chair at a nearby table, and set to work with a fast disguise spell. By the time

Tananda hit the door, the only one she could see in the place besides Gus was a potbellied Deveel sipping on a strawberry milkshake.

"Hi, Gus!" she sang. "Have you seen Skeeve around?"

"He . . . aahh . . . was in earlier." The gargoyle carefully avoided the lie.

"Oh, well. I guess I'll just have to leave without saying goodbye to him, then. Too bad. We weren't on particularly good terms the last time I saw him."

"You're leaving?"

Gus said it before the words burst out of my own mouth, saving me from blowing my disguise.

"Yea. I figure it's about time I moved on."

"I . . . umm . . . have been hearing some strange things about my neighbors, but I've never been sure how much to believe," the gargoyle said thoughtfully. "This sudden departure wouldn't have anything to do with the new moll that's been foisted off on Skeeve, would it?"

"Bunny? Naw. I'll admit I was a bit out of sorts when I first heard about it, but Chumley explained the whole thing to me."

"Then what's the problem?"

Gus was doing a terrific job of beating me to my lines. As long as he kept it up, I'd be able to get all my questions answered without revealing myself.

It had occurred to me to confront Tananda directly as soon as I heard what she was up to, but then I realized that this was a rare chance to hear her thoughts when she didn't think I was around.

"Well, it's something Markie said . . ."

Markie again. I definitely owed Aahz an apology.

". . . She made some crack about her daddy, that's Skeeve, letting me live there, and it got me to thinking. Things have been nice these last couple years . . . almost too nice. Since we haven't had to worry about overhead, Chumley and I haven't been working much. More important, we haven't been working at working. It's too easy to hang around the place and wait for something to come to us."

"Getting fat and lazy, huh?" Gus grinned.

"Something like that. Now, you know me, Gus. I've always been footloose and fancy free. Ready to follow a job or a whim at the drop of a hat. If anyone had suggested to me that I should settle down, I would have punched their lights out. Now all of a sudden, I've got a permanent address and family . . . family beyond Chumley, I mean. I hadn't realized how domestic I was getting until Skeeve showed up with Markie. A kid, even. When I first saw her, my first thought was that it would be nice to have a kid around the place! Now I ask you, Gus, does that sound like me?"

"No, it doesn't."

The gargoyle's voice was so quiet I scarcely recognized it as his.

"Right then I saw the handwriting on the wall. If I don't start moving again, I'm going to take root . . . permanently. You know, the worst thing is that I don't really want to go. That's the scariest part of all."

"I don't think Aahz or Skeeve want you to go either."

"Now don't you start on me, Gus. This is hard enough for me as it is. Like I said, they're family, but they're stifling me. I've got to get away, even if it's only for a little while, or I'm going to lose a part of me . . . forever."

"Well, if you've made up your mind . . . good luck."

"Thanks, Gus. I'll be in touch from time to time. Keep an eye on the boys in case they buy more trouble than they can sell."

"I don't think you have to worry about Chumley. He's pretty levelheaded."

"Chumley's not the one I'm worried about."

I thought that was going to be her parting shot, but she paused with one hand on the door.

"You know, it's probably just as well that I couldn't find Skeeve. I'm not sure I could have stuck to my guns in a face-to-face . . . but then again, maybe that's why I was looking for him."

I could feel Gus's eyes on me as she slipped out.

"I suppose it's pointless to ask why you didn't say something, *Mister* Skeeve."

Even though I had worried earlier about getting Gus angry with me, somehow it didn't matter anymore.

"At first it was curiousity," I said, letting my disguise slip away. "Then, I didn't want to embarrass her."

"And at the end there? When she flat-out said that you could talk her out of going? Why didn't you speak up then? Do you *want* her to disappear?"

I couldn't even manage a spark of anger. "You know better than that, Gus," I said quietly. "You're hurting and lashing out at whoever's handy, which happens to be me. I didn't try to get her to stay for the same reason you didn't try harder. She feels we're stifling her, and if she wants out, it'd be pretty small of us to try to keep her for our own sakes, wouldn't it?"

There was prolonged silence, which was fine by me. I didn't feel much like talking anymore.

Rising, I started for the door.

"You were looking the other way when she left," the gargoyle said. "You might like to know there were tears in her eyes."

"Mine too," I replied without turning. "That's why I was looking the other way."

Chapter Eight:

"What did I do wrong?"

—LEAR, REX

WITH a heavy heart, I headed back home. I was no longer worried about Aahz yelling at me. If anything, I was rather hoping he would. If he did, I decided that for a change I wouldn't argue back. In short, I felt terrible and was in the mood to do a little penance.

Sliding through the tent flap, I cocked an ear and listened for Aahz. Actually, I was a little surprised that I couldn't hear him from the street, but I was sure I would be able to locate his position in the house with no difficulty. As I've said before, my partner has no problem expressing his moods, particularly anger.

The house was silent.

From the lack of reverberations and/or falling plaster, I assumed that Aahz was out . . . probably looking for me with blood in his eye. I debated going out to look for him, but decided that it would be better to wait right here. He'd be back eventually, so I headed for the garden to make myself comfortable until he showed up.

What I call the garden is actually our courtyard. It has a fountain and an abundance of plants, so I tend to

59

think of it as a piece of the outdoors rather than as an enclosed area. I had been spending more and more time there lately, especially when I wanted time to think. It reminded me of some of the quieter spots I would find from time to time back when I was living on my own in the woods . . . back before I met Garkin, and, through him, Aahz.

That memory led me to ponder a curious point: Were there other successful beings, like myself, who used their new prosperity to recreate the setting or atmosphere of their pre-success days? If so, it made for a curious cycle.

I was so preoccupied with this thought as I entered the garden that I almost missed the fact that I wasn't alone. Someone else was using my retreat . . . specifically, Aahz.

He was sitting on one of the stone benches, chin in his hands and elbows on his knees, staring blankly into the water as it flowed through the fountain.

To say the least, I was surprised. Aahz has never been the meditative type, particularly in times of crisis. He's more the "beat on someone or something until the problem goes away" type. Still, here he was, not agitated, not pacing, just sitting and staring. It was enough out of character for him to unnerve me completely.

"Umm . . . Hi, Aahz," I said hesitantly.

"Hello, Skeeve," he replied without looking around.

I waited for a few moments for him to say something else. He didn't. Finally I sat down on the bench next to him and stared at the water myself a bit.

We sat that way for a while, neither of us saying anything. The trickling water began to have a tranquilizing, hypnotic effect on me, and I found my mind starting to relax and drift.

"It's been quite a day, hasn't it, partner?"

My mind reflexively recoiled into a full defensive

posture before it dawned on me that Aahz was still speaking quietly.

"Y . . . Yes."

I waited, but he seemed off in his own thoughts again. My nerves shot, I decided to take the initiative.

"Look, Aahz. About Markie . . ."

"Yes?"

"I knew about the Elemental School thing. She told me on the way back from the Geek's. I just didn't know enough to realize it was important."

"I know," Aahz sighed, not looking at me. "I hadn't bothered to teach you about elemental magic . . . just like I hadn't taught you about dragon poker."

No explosion! I was starting to get a little worried about my partner.

"Aren't you upset?"

"Of course I'm upset," he said, favoring me with a fleeting glimpse of bared teeth, a barely recognizable smile. "Do you think I'm always this jovial?"

"I mean, aren't you mad?"

"Oh, I'm past 'mad.' I'm all the way to 'thoughtful.' "

I arrived at the startling conclusion that I liked it better when Aahz was shouting and unreasonable. *That* I knew how to deal with. This latest mood of his was a total unknown.

"What are you thinking about?"

"Parenthood."

"Parenthood?"

"Yeah. You know, that state of total responsibility for another being? Well, at least, that's the theory."

I wasn't sure I was following this at all.

"Aahz? Are you trying to say you feel responsible for what happened with Markie because you hadn't taught me more about magic and poker?"

"Yes. No. I don't know."

"But that's silly!"

"I know," he replied, with his first honest grin since I had entered the garden. "That's what got me thinking about parenthood."

I abandoned any hope of following his logic.

"You'll have to explain it to me, Aahz. I'm a little slow today."

He straightened up a bit, draping one arm around my shoulders.

"I'll try, but it isn't easy," he said in a tone that was almost conversational. "You see, regardless of what I said when I was ranting at you about how much of a problem Markie was going to be, it's been a long time since I was a parent. I've been sitting here, trying to remember what it was like. What's so surprising to me is the realization that I've never really stopped. Nobody does."

I started to shift uncomfortably.

"Hear me out. For once I'm trying to share some of my hard-won lessons with you without shouting. Forget the theories of parenthood! What it's really all about is taking pride in things you can never be sure you had a hand in, and accepting the responsibility and guilt for things you either didn't know or had no control over. Actually, it's a lot more complicated than that, but that's the bare bones of the matter."

"You don't make it sound particularly attractive," I observed.

"In a lot of ways, it isn't. Your kid expects you to know everything . . . to be able to answer any question he asks and, more important, to provide a logical explanation of what is essentially an illogical world. Society, on the other hand, expects you to train your kid in everything necessary for them to become a successful, responsible member of the community . . . even if you aren't yourself. The problem is that you aren't the only source of input for the kid. Friends, schools, and other adults are all supplying other opinions, many of which you don't agree with. That means that if your kid succeeds, you don't really know if it was because of or in spite of your influence. On the other hand, if the kid goes bad, you always wonder if there was something else you could have said or done or done differently that could have salvaged things before they hit the wall."

His hand tightened slightly on my shoulder, but I don't think he did it consciously.

"Now, I wasn't a particularly good parent . . . which I like to think places me in the majority. I didn't interact much with my kids. Business was always a good excuse, but the truth was that I was glad to let someone else handle their upbringing as much as possible. I can see now that it was because I was afraid that if I tried to do it myself, that in my ignorance and uncertainty I would make some terrible mistake. The end result was that some of the kids turned out okay, some of them . . . let's say less than okay. What I was left with was a nagging feeling that I could have done better. That I could have—should have—made more of a difference."

He released his hold on my shoulders and stood up.

"Which brings us to you."

I wasn't sure if I should feel uncomfortable because he was focusing on me, or glad because he was pacing again.

"I've never consciously thought of you as a son, but in hindsight I realize that a lot of how I've treated you has been driven by my lingering guilt from parenthood. In you, I had another chance to mold someone . . . to give all the advice I felt I should have given my own kids. If at times I've seemed to overreact when things didn't go well, it's because deep inside I saw it as a personal failure. I mean, this was my second chance. A time to show how much I had learned from my earlier perceived failures, and you know what? Now I'm giving it my full attention and my best shot, and things are *still* going wrong!"

This was doing nothing to brighten my mood. On top
of everything else, now I had the distinct feeling I had
somehow let Aahz down.

"I don't think you can say it's your fault, Aahz. I
mean, you've tried hard and been more patient with me
than anyone I've ever known. Nobody can teach someone else everything, even if they could remember what
should be taught. I've got a certain saturation point.
After that, I'm not going to learn anything new until
I've digested what I've got. Even then, I've got to be
honest and say there are some things I don't believe no
matter how often you tell me. I've just got to find out
for myself. A craftsman can't blame his skill if he has
defective material."

"That's just what I've been thinking," Aahz nodded.
"I can't keep blaming myself for everything. It's very
astute of you to have figured this out at your age . . .
without going through what I have."

"It's no big thing to figure out that I'm a dummy," I
said bitterly. "I've known it all along."

Suddenly, I felt myself being lifted into the air. I
looked past Aahz's hand, which was gripping my shirt
by the collar, down the length of his arm, and into his
yellow eyes.

"Wrong lesson!" he snarled, sounding much like his
old self. "What you're supposed to be learning isn't
that you're dumb. You're not, and if you were listening,
I just complimented you on that fact."

"Then what . . ." I managed, with what little air I
had left.

"The point is that what's happened in the past isn't
my fault, just like what's happening now isn't *your*
fault!"

"Aaggh . . . urk . . ." was my swift rebuttal.

"Oh! Sorry."

My feet hit the floor and air flooded back into my
lungs.

"All a parent, *any* parent, can do is give it their best

shot, right or wrong." Aahz continued as if there had been no interruption. "The actual outcome rests on so many variables, no single person can assume responsibility, blame, or praise for whatever happens. That's important for me to remember in my dealings with you . . . and for you to remember in your dealings with Markie. It's not your fault!"

"It isn't?"

"That's right. We both have strong paternal streaks in us, though I don't know where you got yours from, but all we can do is our best. We've got to remember not to try to shoulder the blame for what other people do . . . like Tananda."

That sobered me up again. "You know about that, huh?"

"Yeah. She told me to tell you goodbye if she didn't see you, but I guess you already know."

I simply nodded, unable to speak.

"I was already worried about how you were going to react to the problems with Markie, and when Tananda left I knew you were going to take it hard. I've been trying to find a way to show you that you aren't alone. Right or wrong, what you're feeling has been around for a long time."

"Thanks, Aahz."

"Has it helped at all?"

I thought for a moment.

"A bit."

My partner heaved another sigh.

"Well," he said, "I tried. That what's important . . . I think."

"Cheerio, chaps. How's every little thing?"

I glanced up to find Chumley striding toward us, beaming merrily. "Oh. Hi, Chumley."

"I thought you'd like to know," the troll announced, "I think I've figured out a way to charge the damage Markie caused this afternoon back to the Mob as a business expense!"

"That's swell, Chumley," Aahz said dully.

"Yeah. Terrific."

"'Allo, 'allo?" he said, cocking his head at us. "Any time the two biggest hustlers at the Bazaar fail to get excited over money, there's got to be something wrong. Out with it now. What's troubling you?"

"Do you want to tell him, Aahz?"

"Well . . ."

"I say, this wouldn't be about little sister leaving the nest, would it? Oh, there's a giggle."

"You know?" I blinked.

"I can see you're all broken up over it," Aahz said in a dangerous tone.

"Tish tosh!" the troll exclaimed. "I don't see where it's anything to get upset about. Tananda's just settling things in her mind, is all. She's found that she likes something that goes against her self-image. It might take a few days, but eventually she'll figure out that it's not the end of the world. Everybody goes through it. It's called 'growing up.' If anything, I think it's bloody marvelous that she's finally having to learn that things don't stay the same forever."

"You do?" I was suddenly starting to feel better.

"Certainly. Why, in just the time we've been chumming around together, Aahz has changed, you've changed, so have I, though I don't tend to show it as dramatically as you two or little sister. You blokes have just got a bad case of the guilts. Poppycock! You can't take the blame for everything, you know."

"That's good advice," I said, standing up and stretching. "Why can't you ever give me good advice like that, partner?"

"Cause any fool can see it without being told," Aahz snarled, but there was a twinkle in his eye. "The problem is that Pervects aren't just any fool."

"Quite right," Chumley grinned. "Now how about joining me in a little Happy Hour spot of wine while I tell you how clever I am at saving you money."

"I'd rather you impressed us with a solution to our baby-sitting problems," my partner said grimly, heading for the lounge.

I followed in their wake, strangely happy. Things were back to normal . . . or as normal as they ever get around here. Between us, I was sure we could find a positive course of action. I mean, after all, how much trouble could one little girl . . .

That thought crumbled in front of an image of elemental-blown tents.

I resolved to do more listening than talking in the upcoming war council.

Chapter Nine:

"They never let you live it down. One little mistake!"

—NERO

RELAXING over drinks with Aahz and Chumley, I felt the tensions and depressions of the day slipping away. It was nice to know that when things really got tough, I had friends to help me solve my problems, however complex or apparently hopeless.

"Well, guys," I said, pouring another round of wine for everyone. "Any ideas as to what we should do?"

"Beats me." Chumley said, toying with his goblet.

"I still think it's *your* problem," Aahz announced, leaning back in his chair and grinning evilly. "I mean, after all, you got into it without our help."

Like I said, it's great to have friends.

"I can't say I go along with that, Aahz old boy," the troll said with a wave. "Although I'll admit it's tempting. The unfortunate reality is that as long as we're living and working as closely as we are, his problems are out problems, don't you know?"

As much as I appreciated the fact that Chumley's logic was moving them closer to lending me assistance, I felt the need to defend myself a little.

"I'd like to think it's a two-way street, Aahz. I've gotten dragged into a few of *your* problems as well."

He started to snap back, then pursed his lips and returned his attention to his wine. "I'll avoid comparing lists of how often which of us has gotten us in how much trouble and simply concede the point. I guess that's part of what a partnership is all about. Sorry if I seem a little snorky from time to time, but I've never had a partner before. It takes getting used to."

"I say! Well said, Aahz!" Chumley applauded. "You know, you're getting more civilized every day."

"Let's not get too carried away just yet. How about you, Chumley? You and your sister have helped us out often enough, but I don't recall either of *you* bringing your problems home with you. Isn't that a little lopsided?"

"I've always figured it's our way of kicking in on the rent," the troll said casually. "If our problems ever start interfering with your work, then I'll figure we've overstayed our welcome."

This came as a total surprise to me. I realized with a start that I was usually so busy with my own life and problems that I never got around to asking much about the work Chumley and Tananda were doing.

"Whoa up a minute here," I said. "Are you two having problems I don't know about?"

"Well, it isn't all beer and skittles," the troll grimaced briefly. "The subject at hand, however, is *your* problems. There's nothing on my plate that has a higher priority just now, so let's get to work on the latest crisis, shall we? I suggest we all put on our thinking caps and brainstorm a little. Let's just stare at the ceiling and each toss out ideas as they occur to us."

I made myself a little promise to return to the subject of Tananda and Chumley's problems at a later date, then joined the others in staring thoughtfully at the ceiling.

Time crawled along, and no one said anything.

"Well, so much for brainstorming," Aahz said, reaching for the wine again. "I'll admit I'm coming up blank."

"Perhaps it would help if we started by defining the problem," Chumley urged. "Now, as I see it, we have two problems: Markie and Bunny. We're going to have trouble figuring out what to do about Bunny until we find out what Don Bruce has up his sleeve, and we've got to come up with a way to keep Markie from totally disrupting our lives until her father comes to pick her up."

"*If* he picks her up," my partner corrected helpfully.

"I'll admit, I still don't know how you did so well in that game to end up with Markie in the first place," the troll said, cocking one outsized eye at me and ignoring Aahz.

"Dumb luck . . . with the emphasis on *dumb*."

"That's not the way I heard it," Chumley smirked. "Whatever your method was, it was successful enough to make you the talk of the Bazaar."

"What!?" Aahz said, sitting up in his chair again.

"You would hear it yourself if you weren't spending all your time sulking in your room," the troll winked. "When I went out after little sister today, it seemed that all I was hearing about was the new dragon poker champion of Deva. Everybody's talking about the game, or what they've heard about the game. I suspect they're embellishing upon the facts, from some of the description of the hands, but there are those who are taking it all as gospel."

I remembered then that when the game broke up, the other players had been very enthusiastic about my playing. At the time, I had been worried about the secret of my night out reaching Aahz (which, you'll recall, it did before I got home). The troubles with Markie and Bunny had occupied my mind and time ever since, so I hadn't stopped to think of other potential repercussions of the game gossip. Now, however . . .

Aahz was out of his seat, pacing back and forth.

"Chumley, if what you're saying is true . . . are you following this, partner?"

"Too bloody well," I growled.

That got my partner to pause momentarily to roll his eyes.

"Watch yourself," he warned. "You're starting to talk like Chumley now."

"You want I should talk like Guido instead, know what I mean?"

"I don't understand," the troll interrupted. "Is something amiss?"

"We don't have two problems," Aahz announced. "We've got *three!* Markie, Bunny, *and* the rumor mill!"

"Gossip? How can that be a problem?"

"Think it through, Chumley," I said. "All I need right now is to have a bunch of hotshot dragon poker players hunting me up to see if I'm as good as everybody says."

"That's only part of it, partner," Aahz added. "This could hurt our business and public images as well."

I closed my eyes and sighed.

"Spell it out for me, Aahz. I'm still learning, remember?"

"Well, we already know your reputation at magic has been growing fast . . . almost too fast. The competition hates you because you're taking all the prime assignments. No big deal! Professional jealousy is the price of success in any field. There comes a time, however, when you can get too big too fast. Then it isn't just your rivals you worry about. Everybody wants you taken down a peg or two if for no other reason than to convince themselves that your success is abnormal . . . that they don't have to feel bad for not measuring up."

He paused to stare at me hard.

"I'm afraid this dragon poker thing just might push you into the second category. A lot of beings excel here at the Bazaar, but they're only noted in one field. The Geek, for example, is a recognized figure among the gamblers, but he doesn't have any reputation to speak of as a magician or merchant. People can accept that . . . work hard and you rise toward the top of your group. You, on the other hand, have just made a strong showing in a second profession. I'm afraid there's going to be some backlash.''

"Backlash?" I echoed weakly.

"It's like I've been trying to tell you: people aren't going to want you to get too much above them. At the very least they might start boycotting our business. At most . . . well, there are ways of sabotaging other people's success.''

"You mean they're going to . . ."

"That's enough!" Chumley declared, slapping his palm down on the table loudly.

It suddenly occurred to me that I had never seen Chumley mad. It also occurred to me that I was glad our furniture was strong enough to withstand even Aahz's tirades. If not, the troll would have destroyed the table just stopping the conversation.

"Now listen up, both of you!" he ordered, leveling a gnarled finger at us. "I think the current crisis has gone to your heads. You two are overreacting . . . snapping at shadows! I'll admit we've got some problems, but we've handled worse. This is no time to get panicky."

"But . . ."

"Hear me out, Aahz. I've listened to you bellow often enough."

I opened my mouth to make a witty comment, then, for once, thought better of it.

"Markie is a potential disaster, but the key word there is *potential*. She's a good kid who will do what we say . . . *if* we learn to watch what we say to her. The same goes for Bunny. She's smart as a whip and . . ."

"Bunny?" I blurted, forgetting myself for a moment.

"Yes, Bunny. It's been a long time since there's been

anyone around here I could discuss literature and
theater with. She's really quite intelligent if you bother
to talk to her.''

"We *are* talking about the same Bunny, aren't we?"
Aahz murmured.

"The one who comes across dumb as a stone,"
Chumley confirmed frimly. "Just remember how *I*
come across when I'm putting on my Big Crunch act . . .
but we're wandering. The subject is problems, and I
maintain with a little coaching Bunny won't be one.''

He paused to glare at us.

"As to the rumor of Skeeve's abilities at dragon
poker, I've never in my life heard anyone get as alarmed
as you, Aahz. Sure, there are negative sides to any
rumor, but you have to get pretty extreme to do the pro-
jections that have been voiced just now.''

"Hey, Boss!" Guido called, sticking his head in the
door. "The Geek's here to see you.''

"I'll handle this," Aahz said, heading for the reception area. "You stay here and listen to what Chumley
has to say. He's probably right. I have been edgy lately
. . . for some unknown reason.''

"If I am right, then you should hear it, too," the troll
called after him.

"Talk to me, Chumley," I said. "That's probably the
closest you'll ever hear to an apology from Aahz, anyway.''

"Quite right. Where was I? Oh, yes. Even if Aahz's
appraisal of the reaction to your success is correct, it
shouldn't have too much impact on your work. The
small fry may go to other magicians, but you've been
trying to cut down on unimportant jobs anyway. When
someone is *really* in trouble, they're going to want the
best available magician working on it . . . and right now,
that means you.''

I thought about what he was saying, weighing it
carefully in my mind.

"Even if Aahz is just a little right," I said, "I'm not

wild about having any ill feeling generated about me at the Bazaar. Admiration I don't mind, but envy makes me uneasy."

"Now that you'll just have to get used to," the troll laughed, clapping a hand lightly on my shoulder. "Whether you know it or not, that's been building for some time . . . long before this dragon poker thing came up. You've got a lot going for you, Skeeve, and as long as you do, there will be blokes who envy it."

"So you really think the dragon poker rumors are harmless?"

"Quite right. Really, what harm can come from idle gossip?"

"You know, Chumley, you aren't wrong very often. But when you miss, you really miss."

We looked up to find Aahz leaning in the doorway.

"What's wrong, Aahz? You look like someone just served you water when you were expecting wine."

My partner didn't even smile at my attempted humor.

"Worse than that," he said. "That was the Geek downstairs."

"We know. What did he want?"

"I was hoping he had come to pick up Markie for her father. . . ."

Aahz's voice trailed off to nothing.

"I take it he didn't?" I prompted.

"No, he didn't. In fact, the subject never came up."

Almost without thinking, my partner's hand groped for his oversized goblet of wine.

"He had an invitation . . . no, make that a challenge. The Sen-Sen Ante Kid has heard about Skeeve here. He wants a showdown match of head-to-head dragon poker. The Geek is making the arrangements."

Chapter Ten:

"A spoonful of sugar helps the medicine go down!"

—L. Borgia

"Just let the energy flow."

"That's easy for you to say!"

"Did I stutter?"

"You know, Hot Stuff, maybe it would be better if I . . ."

"Quit talking and concentrate, Massha."

"You started it."

"And I'm finishing it. Focus on the candle!"

If some of that sounds vaguely familiar, it should. It's the old 'light the candle' game. Theoretically, it builds a student's confidence. In actuality, it's a pain in the butt. Apprentices hate the candle drill. I did when I was an apprentice. It's a lot more fun when you're on the teaching end.

"Come on, Skeeve. I'm getting too old to learn this stuff."

"And you're getting older the longer you stall, *apprentice*. Remember, you came to me to learn magic. Just because we've gotten distracted from time to time doesn't mean I've forgotten completely. Now light the candle.''

She turned her attention to the exercise again with a mutter I chose to ignore.

I had been thinking hard about my conversations with Aahz and Chumley. The whole question of what to do about the challenge from the Kid was touchy enough that for once I decided to seek the counsel of my advisors before making a commitment I might later regret. Wiser heads than mine were addressing the dilemma at this very moment. Unfortunately, aforesaid wiser heads were in total disagreement as to what course of action to follow.

Aahz was in favor of refusing the match, while Chumley insisted that a refusal would only inflame the situation. He maintained that the only sane way out would be to face the Kid and lose (no one seriously thought I would have a chance in such a game), thereby getting me off the hot seat once and for all. The main problem with that solution was that it involved voluntarily giving up a substantial amount of money . . . and Aahz wouldn't hear of it.

As the battle raged on, I thought about the earlier portions of our conversations. I thought about parenthood and responsibilty. Then I went looking for Massha.

When we first met, Massha was holding down a job as court magician for one of the city-states in the dimension of Jahk . . . that's right. Where they hold the Big Game every year. The problem was that she didn't really know any magic. She was what is known in the field as a mechanic, and all her powers were purchased across the counter in the form of rings, pendants, and other magical devices. After she saw us strut our stuff in the Big Game, she decided to try to learn some of the nonmechanical variety of magic . . . and for some unknown reason picked or picked on me to provide her with lessons.

Now, to say the least, I had never thought of Massha
as a daughter, but she was my apprentice and therefore
a responsibility I had accepted. Unfortunately, I had
dodged that responsibility more often than not for the
very reasons Aahz had listed: I was unsure of my own
abilities and therefore afraid of making a mistake. What
I hadn't done was give it my best shot, win or lose. That
realization sparked me into a new resolve that if
anything happened to Massha in the future, it wouldn't
be because I hadn't at least tried to teach her what she
asked.

I was also aware that I wanted to learn more about
any problems Chumley and Tananda were having, as
well as getting a better fix on just who or what Bunny
was. At this moment, however, Tananda was absent
and Chumley was arguing with Aahz, putting that objective on hold. Bunny was around somewhere, but
given a choice between her and Massha, I opted for addressing old obligations before plunging into new ones.
Ergo, I rousted out Massha for a long-overdue magic
lesson.

"It's just not working, Skeeve. I told you I can't do
it."

She sank back in her chair dejected and scowled at the
floor. Curious, I reached over and felt the candle wick.
It wasn't even warm.

"Not bad," I lied. "You're showing some improvement."

"Don't kid a kidder." Massha grimaced. "I'm not
getting anywhere."

"Could you light it with one of your rings?"

She spread her fingers and made a quick inventory.
"Sure. This little trinket right here could do the job, but
that's not the point."

"Bear with me. How does it work? Or, more important, how does it feel when it works?"

She gave a quick shrug.

"There's nothing to it. You see, this circle around the

stone here moves, and I rotate it according to how tight
a beam I want. Pressing the back of the ring activates it,
so all I have to do is aim it and relax. The ring does all
the work."

"That's it!" I exclaimed, snapping my fingers.

"What's it?"

"Never mind. Keep going. How does it feel?"

"Well," she frowned throughtfully, "It sort of tin-
gles. It's like I was a hose and there was water rushing
through me and out the ring."

"Bingo!"

"What's that supposed to mean?"

"Listen, Massha. Listen closely."

I was speaking carefully now, trying hard to contain
my excitement over what I hoped was a major breakthrough.

"Our problem with teaching you non-mechanical
magic is that you don't believe in it! I mean, you know
that it exists and all, but you don't believe that you can
do it. You're working hard at overcoming that every
time you try to cast a spell, and that's the problem: You
try . . . You work hard. You know you've got to believe,
so you work hard at overcoming that disbelief every
time you . . ."

"Yeah. So?"

"It means you tense up instead of relaxing the way
you do when you're working your rings. Tensing blocks
the flow of the energies, so you end up with less power
at your disposal than you have when you're just walking
around. The idea of casting a spell isn't to tense up, it's
to relax . . . if anything, it's an exercise in forced relax-
ation."

My apprentice bit at her lower lip. "I don't know.
That sounds too easy."

"On the one hand it's easy. Viewed a different way,
one of the hardest things to do is relax on cue, especially
if there's a crisis raging around you at the time."

"So all I have to is relax?" she asked skeptically.

"Remember that 'hose' feeling you get when you use the ring? That's the energies being channeled through you and focused on your objective. If you pinch off a hose, how much water gets through?"

"I guess that makes sense."

"Try it . . . now. Reach out your hand and focus on the candle wick as if you were going to use your ring, only don't activate it. Just tell yourself that the ring is working and relax."

She started to say something, then changed her mind. Instead, she drew a deep breath, blew it out, then pointed a finger at the candle.

"Just relax," I urged softly. "Let the energies flow."

"But . . ."

"Don't talk. Keep your mind on the candle and hear me like I'm talking from a long way off."

Obediently, she focused on the candle.

"Feel the flow of energies . . . just like when you're using the ring. Relax some more. Feel how the flow increases? Now, without tensing up, tighten that flow down to a narrow beam and aim it at the wick."

I was concentrating on Massha so much I almost missed it. A small glow of light started to form on the candle wick.

"That's it," I said, fighting to keep my voice calm. "Now . . ."

"Daddy! Guido says . . ."

"Ssshh!!!" I hissed. "Not now, Markie! We're trying to light the candle."

She paused in the doorway and cocked her head quizzically.

"Oh, that's easy!" she beamed suddenly and raised her head.

"MARKIE!! DON'T. . ."

But I was too late.

There was a sudden flash of light in the room, and the candle lit. Well, it didn't exactly light, it melted like a bag of water when you take away the bag. So did the candle holder. The table lit, though . . . briefly. At least one corner of it did. It flared for a moment, then the fire died as abruptly as it had appeared. What was left was a charred quarter-circle of tabletop where the corner used to be. That and a table leg standing alone like a burnt-out torch. The fire had hit so fast and smooth the leg didn't even topple over.

I don't remember reaching for Markie, but somehow I had her by the shoulders shaking her.

"WHAT DID YOU DO THAT FOR??" I·said in my best paternal tones.

"You . . . you said . . . you wanted the . ... candle lit."

"*That's* lighting a candle?!?"

"I still have a little trouble with control . . . but my teacher says I'm doing better."

I realized I was having a little trouble with control, too. I stopped shaking her and tried to calm myself. This effort was aided by the fact that I noticed Markie's lip was quivering and she was blinking her eyes rapidly. It suddenly dawned on me that she was about to cry. I decided that, not knowing what would happen when she cried, I would do my best to stay ignorant by heading her off at the pass.

"Umm . . . that was a Fire Elemental, right? Did you learn that at Elemental School?"

Getting someone to talk often serves to stave off tears . . . at least, it had always worked on me.

"Y . . . Yes," she said meekly. "At Elemental School, we learn Fire for starters."

"It's . . . ummm . . . very impressive. Look, I'm sorry if I barked at you, Markie, but you see, I didn't just want the candle lit. I wanted Massha to light it. It was part of her magic lesson."

"I didn't know that."

"I know. I didn't think to tell you. That's why I'm apologizing. What happened here was my fault. Okay?"

She nodded her head, exaggerating the motion until it looked like she had a broken neck. It was an interesting illusion, one that I vastly preferred to the idea of her crying . . . especially in the mood I was in. The thought of Markie with a broken neck . . .

"Aahh . . . you *did* interrupt Massha's lesson, though," I said, forcing the other concept from my mind. "Don't you think it would be nice if you apologized to her?"

"That's a great idea, Daddy," she beamed. "I'll do that the next time I see her. Okay?"

That's when I realized my apprentice had slipped out of the room.

"What do you think you're doing, Massha?"

Leaning casually in the doorway of Massha's bedroom, I realized my voice lacked the intimidating power of Aahz's, but it's the only voice I've got.

"What does it look like I'm doing?" she snarled, carrying a massive armload of clothes from her closet to dump on the bed.

"I'd say, offhand, that it looks like you're packing. The question is, why?"

"People usually pack because it's the easiest way to carry their things when they travel. Less wear and tear on the wardrobe."

Suddenly, I was weary of the banter. Heaving a sigh, I moved in front of her, blocking her path.

"No more games, Massha. Okay? Tell me straight out, why are you leaving? Don't you owe your teacher that much at least?"

She turned away, busying herself with something on her dresser.

"C'mon, Skeeve," she said in a tone so low I could barely hear it. "You saw what happened downstairs."

"I saw you on the verge of making a major breakthrough in your lessons, if that's what you mean. If Markie hadn't come in, you would have had the candle lit in another few seconds."

"Big deal!"

She spun to face me, and I could see that she was trying not to cry. There seemed to be a lot of that going
around.

"Excuse me, Skeeve, but big fat hairy deal. So I can
light a candle. So what?! After years of study, Massha
can light a candle . . . and a little girl can blow the end
off the table without even trying! What does that make
me? A magician? Ha ha! What a joke."

"Massha, *I* can't do what Markie did downstairs . . .
or what she did in the Bazaar either, for that matter. I
told you when you first approached me to be my apprentice exactly how little magic I knew. I'm still learning, though . . . and in the meantime we're still holding
our own in the magic business . . . and that's here at the
Bazaar. The Magic Capital of the dimensions."

That seemed to settle her a bit, but not much.

"Tell me honestly, Hot Stuff," she said, pursing her
lips. "How good do you think I could ever be with
magic . . . really?"

"I don't know. I'd like to think that with work and
practice you could be better than you are now, though.
That's really all any of us can hope for."

"You may be right, Skeeve, and it's a good thought.
The fact still remains that in the meantime, I'll always
be small potatoes around here . . . magically, of course.
The way things are going, I'm destined to be a hanger-
on. A leech. You and Aahz are nice guys, and you'd
never throw me out, but I can't think of one good
reason why I should stay."

"I can."

My head came around so fast I was in momentary
danger of whiplash. Framed in the doorway was . . .

"TANANDA!"

"In the flesh," she said with a wink. "But that's not
the subject here. Massha, I can't speak for long-term

conditions, but I've got one good reason why you shouldn't leave just now. It's the same reason I'm back.''

"What's that?''

"It involves the Great Skeeve here. C'mon downstairs. I'm going to brief everybody at once at a war council. We've got a full-blown crisis on our hands.''

Chapter Eleven:

"I believe we're under attack."

—COL. TRAVIS

ONE of the rooms in our extra-dimensional palace had a large oval table in it surrounded by chairs. When we moved in, we dubbed it the Conference Room, since there didn't seem to be any other practical use for it. We never used it for conferences, mind you, but it's always nice to have a conference room.

Tonight, however, it was packed to capacity. Apparently Tananda had rounded up the whole household, including Markie and Bunny, before locating Massha and me, and everyone was already seated as we walked in.

"Can we get started now?" Aahz asked caustically. "I *do* have other things to do, you know."

"Really?" Chumley sneered. "Like what?"

"Like talking to the Geek about that invitation," my partner shot back.

"Without talking to your partner first?"

"I didn't say I was going to refuse or accept. I just want to talk to him about . . ."

"Can we table the argument for the moment?" I interrupted. "I want to hear what Tananda has to say."

"Thanks, Skeeve," she said, flashing me a quick
smile before dropping back into her solemn manner. "I
guess you all know I was moving out of here. Well, poking around the Bazaar, I heard a rumor that's changed
my mind. If it's true, we're all going to have our hands
full dealing with it."

She paused, but no one else said anything. For a
change, we were all giving her our undivided attention.

"I guess I should drop the shoe first, then we can all
go on from there. The talk on the street is that someone's hired the Ax to do a number on Skeeve."

There was a few heartbeats of silence; then the room
exploded.

"Why should anyone . . ."

"Who's hired the Ax?"

"Where did you hear . . ."

"Hold it! HOLD IT!" Tananda shouted, holding up
her hands for silence. "I can only answer one question
at a time . . . but I'll warn you in advance, I don't have
that many answers to start with."

"Who's hired him?" Aahz demanded, seizing first
position.

"The way I heard it, a group of magicians here at the
Bazaar is none too happy with Skeeve's success. They
feel he's taking all the choice assignments these days . . .
getting all the glory work. What they've done is pool
their money so they can hire the Ax to do what they're
all afraid to do themselves . . . namely, deal with
Skeeve."

"Do you hear that, Chumley? Still think I'm being
melodramatic?"

"Shut up, Aahz. Where'd you hear this, little sister?"

"Remember Vic? The little vampire that relocated
here from Limbo? Well, he's opened his own magic
practice here at the Bazaar. It seems that he was approached to contribute to the fund. He's new enough
here that he didn't know any of them by name, but they

claim to have the support of nearly a dozen of the smalltime magicians."

"Why didn't he warn us as soon as he heard?"

"He's trying to stay neutral. He didn't contribute, but he also didn't want to be the one to blow the whistle to Skeeve. The only reason he said anything to me was that he was afraid that anyone close to Skeeve might get caught in the crossfire. I must admit, he seems to have a rather exaggerated idea of how much Skeeve here can handle on his own."

"Can I ask a question?" I said grimly. "As the intended victim?"

"Sure, Skeeve. Ask away."

"Who's the Ax?"

At least half the heads at the table swiveled toward me while the faces attached to them dropped their jaws.

"You're kidding!"

"Don't you know who . . ."

"Aahz, didn't you teach him any . . ."

"Whoa! Hold it!" I shouted over the clamor. "I can only take so much of this informative babbling at one time. Aahz! As my friend, partner, and sometimes mentor, could you deign to tell me in simple terms who the Ax is?"

"Nobody knows."

I closed my eyes and gave my head a small shake in an effort to clear my ears. After all this "Gee, why don't you know that?" brouhaha, I could swear he said . . .

"He's right, handsome," Tananda chimed in. "The Ax's real identity is one of the most closely guarded secrets in all the dimensions. That's why he's so effective at what he does."

"That may be true," I nodded. "But from the reaction in this room when you dropped the name, I'd guess that somebody knows *something* about him. Now, let me rephrase the question. If you don't know *who* the Ax is, could someone enlighten me as to *what* he is?"

"The Ax is the greatest Character Assassin in all the

dimensions," Aahz said with a snarl. "He works free-lance and charges fees that make ours look like pocket change. Once the Ax is on your tail, though, you might as well kiss it goodbye. He's ruined more careers than five stock-market crashes. Haven't you ever heard the expression 'take the ax to someone'? Well, that's where it comes from."

I felt that all-too-familiar "down elevator" sensation in my stomach.

"How does he do it?"

"It varies," my partner shrugged. "He tailor-makes his attack depending on the assignment. The only con-stant is that whatever you were when he started, you're not when he's done."

"I wish you'd quit saying 'you' all the time. I'm not dead yet."

"Sorry, partner. Figure of speech."

"Well, that's just swell!" Guido exploded. "How're Nunzio 'n' me supposed to guard the Boss when we don't know what's comin' at him?"

"You don't," Aahz shot back. "This is out of your category, Guido. We're talking about character assas-sination, not a physical attack. It's not in your job description."

"Izzat so!" Nunzio said in his squeaky voice. "Don Bruce says we should guard him. I don't remember him sayin' anything about physical or non-physical attacks. Right, Guido?"

"That's right! If the Boss has got someone after his scalp, guardin' him is our job . . . if that's all right with you, MISTER Aahz!"

"I wouldn't trust you two to guard a fish head, much less my partner!" Aahz roared, surging to his feet.

"Stop it, Aahz!" Tananda ordered, kicking my part-ner's chair so that it cut his legs out from under him and plopped him back into his seat. "If we're up against the Ax, we're going to need all the help we can get. Let's stop bickering about the 'who' and concentrate on the 'how.' Okay? We're all scared, but that doesn't mean we should turn on each other when it's the Ax that's our target.''

That cooled everybody down for the moment. There were a few glares and mutters exchanged, but at least the volume level dropped to where I could be heard.

"I think you're all overlooking something," I said quietly.

"What's that?" Tananda blinked.

"Aahz came close a minute ago. This is my problem . . . and it's not really in any of your job descriptions. We're all friends, and there are business ties between Aahz and me, as well as Guido and Nunzio, but we're talking about reputations here. If I get hit, and everyone seems to be betting against me right now, anyone standing close to me is going to get mud splashed on them, too. It seems to me that the best course of action is for the rest of you to pull back, or, better still, for me to move out and present a solo target. That way, we're only running the risk of having one career ruined . . . mine. I got where I am by standing on your shoulders. If I can't maintain it on my own, well, maybe it wasn't much of a career to start with.''

The whole room was staring at me as I lurched to a halt.

"You know, Skeeve old boy," Chumley said, clearing his throat, "As much as I like you, some times it's difficult to remember just how intelligent you are.''

"I'll say," Tananda snarled. "That's about the dumbest . . . Wait a minute! Does this have anything to do with my leaving?''

"A bit," I admitted. "And Massha leaving and Aahz's talking about responsibility, and . . .''

"Stop right there!" Aahz ordered, holding up his hand. "Let's talk about responsibility, *partner*. It's funny that *I* should have to lecture *you* about this, but there are all sorts of responsibilities. One of the ones that I've learned about from you is the responsibility to one's friends: helping them out when they're in trouble, *and* letting them help you in return. I haven't forgotten how you came into a strange dimension to bust me out of prison after I'd refused your help in the first place; or how you signed us on to play in the Big Game to bail Tananda out after she was caught thieving; or how you insisted that Don Bruce assign Guido and Nunzio here to you when they were in line for disciplinary action after botching their assignment for the Mob. I haven't forgotten it, and I'll bet they haven't either, even if you have. Now, I suggest you shut up about job descriptions and let your friends help you . . . *partner*."

"A-bloody-men." Chumley nodded.

"You could have left me with the Geek for the slavers," Markie said thoughtfully, in a surprisingly adult voice.

"So, now that that's settled," my partner said, rubbing his hands together, "let's get to work. My buddy Guido here has raised a good point. How do we defend Skeeve when we don't know how or when the Ax will strike?"

We hadn't really settled it, and Aahz wasn't about to give me a chance to point it out. I was just as glad, though, since I really didn't know what to say.

"All we can do is be on the lookout for anyone or anything strange showing up." Tananda shrugged.

"Like a showdown match of dragon poker with the Sen-Sen Ante Kid," Chumley said, staring into the distance.

"What's that?"

"You missed it, little sister. It seems our boy Skeeve has drawn the attention of the king of dragon poker. He wants a head-to-head showdown match, and he wants it soon."

"Don't look at me like that, Chumley." Aahz grimaced. "I'm changing my vote. If we want to preserve Skeeve's reputation, there's no way he can refuse the challenge. *Now* I'm willing to admit it'll be money well spent."

"My daddy can beat anybody at dragon poker," Markie declared loyally.

"Your daddy can get his brains beaten out royally," my partner corrected gently. "I just hope we can teach him enough between now and game time that he can lose gracefully."

"I don't like it," Tananda growled. "It's too convenient. Somehow this game has the Ax's fingerprints all over it."

"You're probably right," Aahz sighed. "But there's not much else we can do except accept the challenge and try to make the best of a bad situation."

"Bite the bullet and play the cards we're dealt. Eh, Aahz?" I murmured.

I though I had spoken quietly, but everyone around the table winced, including Markie. They might be loyal enough to risk their lives and careers defending me, but they weren't going to laugh at my jokes.

"Wait a minute!" Nunzio squeaked. "Do you think there's a chance that the Kid is actually the Ax?"

"Low probability," Bunny said, speaking for the first time in the meeting. "Someone like the Ax has to work a low profile. The Sen-Sen Ante Kid is too noticeable. If he were a character assassin, people would notice in no time flat. Besides, when he wins, nobody thinks it's because his opponents are disreputable . . . it's because the Kid is good. No, I figure the Ax has got to be like the purloined letter . . . he can hide in plain sight. Figure the last person you'd suspect, and you'll be getting close to his real identity."

The conversation swirled on around me, but I didn't listen very closely. For some reason, a thought had occurred to me while Bunny was talking. We had all been referring to the Ax as a "he," but if no one knew his real identity, he could just as easily be a "she." If anything, men were much less defensive and more inclined to brag about the details of their careers when they were with a woman.

Bunny was a woman. She had also appeared suddenly on our doorstep right around the time the Ax was supposed to be getting his assignment. We already knew that she was smarter than she let on . . . words like "purloined" didn't go with the vacant stare she so carefully cultivated. What better place for the Ax to strike from than the inside?

I decided that I should have a little chat with my moll as soon as the opportunity presented itself.

Chapter Twelve:

"No one should hide their true self behind a false face."

—L. CHANEY

IT· was with a certain amount of trepidation that I approached Bunny's bedroom. In case you haven't noticed, my experience with women is rather limited . . . like to the fingers of one hand limited.

Tananda, Massha, Luanna, Queen Hemlock, and now Bunny were the only adult females I had ever had to deal with, and thus far my track record was less than glowing. I had had a crush on Tananda for a while, but now she was more of a big sister to me. Massha was . . . well, Massha. I guess if anything I saw her as a kid sister, someone to be protected and sometimes cuddled. I've never really understood her open admiration of me, but it had stood firm through some of my most embarrassing mishaps and made it easy for me to confide in her. Even though I still thought of Luanna as my one true love, I had only spoken to her on four occasions, and after our last exchange I wasn't sure there would ever be a fifth meeting. The only relationship I had had with a woman which was more disastrous than my attempt at love was the one I had had with Queen

Hemlock. She might not shoot me on sight, but there
was no doubt in anyone's mind that she would like to
. . . and she's the one who wanted to marry me!

Of course, none of the women I had dealt with so far
was anything like Bunny, though whether this was good
or bad I wasn't entirely sure. The fact still remained,
however, that I was going to have to learn more about
her, for two reasons: first, if she was going to be a resident of our household, I wanted to get a better fix on
where she was coming from so I could treat her as
something other than a mad aunt in the cellar; and second, if she was the Ax, the sooner I found out, the better. Unfortunately, the only way I could think of to
obtain the necessary information was to talk to her.

I raised my hand, hesitated for a moment, then
rapped on her door. It occurred to me that, even though
I had never been in front of a firing squad, now I knew
how it felt.

"Who is it?"

"It's Skeeve, Bunny. Have you got a minute?"

The door flew open and Bunny was there, grabbing
my arm and pulling me inside. She was dressed in a
slinky jumpsuit with the neck unlaced past her navel,
which was a great relief to me. When I called on Queen
Hemlock in her bedroom, she had received me in the
altogether.

"Geez! It's good to see you. I was startin' to think
you weren't ever comin' by!"

With a double-jointed shift of her hips she bumped
the door shut, while her hands flew to the lacings in her
outfit. So much for being relieved.

"If you just give me a second, hon, I'll be all set to
go. You kinda caught me unprepared, and . . ."

"Bunny, could you just knock it off for a while?
Huh?"

For some reason the events of the last few days suddenly rested heavy on my shoulders, and I just wasn't in
the mood for games.

She stared at me with eyes as big as a Pervect's bar bill, but her hands ceased their activity. "What's the matter, Skeevie? Don't you like me?"

"I really don't know, Bunny," I said heavily. "You've never really given me a chance, have you?"

She drew in a sharp breath and started to retort angrily. Then she hesitated and looked away suddenly, licking her lips nervously.

"I . . . I don't know what you mean. Didn't I come to your room and try to be friendly?"

"I think you *do* know what I mean," I pressed, sensing a weakening in her defenses. "Every time we see each other, you're hitting me in the face with your 'sex-kitten' routine. I never know whether to run or applaud, but neither action is particularly conducive to getting to know you."

"Don't knock it," she said. "It's a great little bit. It's gotten me this far, hasn't it? Besides, isn't that what men want from a girl?"

"I don't."

"Really?"

There was a none-too-gentle mockery in her voice. She took a deep breath and pulled her shoulders back. "So tell me, what *does* cross your mind when I do this?"

Regardless of what impression I may have left on you from my earlier exploits, I do think fast. Fast enough to censor my first three thoughts before answering.

"Mostly discomfort," I said truthfully. "It's impressive, all right, but I get the feeling I should do something about it and I'm not sure I'm up to it."

She smiled triumphantly and let her breath out, easing the tension across her chest and my mind. Of the two, I think my mind needed it more.

"You have just hit on the secret of the sex kittens. It's not that you don't like it. There's just too much of it for you to be sure you can handle it."

"I'm not sure I follow you."

"Men like to brag and strut a lot, but they've got egos as brittle as spun glass. If a girl calls their bluff, comes at them like a seething volcano that can't be put out, men get scared. Instead of fanning a gentle feminine ember, they're faced with a forest fire, so they take their wind elsewhere. Oh, they keep us around to impress people. 'Look at the tigress I've tamed,' and all that. But when we're alone they usually keep their distance. I'll bet a moll sees less actual action than your average coed . . . except our pay scale is a lot better."

That made me think. On the one hand, she had called my reaction pretty close. Her roaring come-on *had* scared me a bit . . . well, a lot. Still, there was the other hand.

"It sounds like you don't think very much of men," I observed.

"Hey! Don't get me wrong. They're a lot better than the alternatives. I just got a little sick of listening to the same old lines over and over and decided to turn the tables on 'em. That's all."

"That wasn't what I meant. A second ago you said 'That's what men want from a girl.' It may be true, and I won't try to argue the point. It's uncomfortably close to 'That's *all* men want from a girl,' though, and that I *will* argue."

She scowled thoughtfully and chewed her lower lip. "I guess that *is* over-generalizing a bit," she admitted.

"Good."

"It's more accurate to say 'That's all men want from a *beautiful* girl.'"

"Bunny. . ."

"No, you listen to me, Skeeve. This is one subject I've had a lot more experience at than you have. It's fine to talk about minds when you look like Massha. But when you grow up looking good like I did—no brag, just a statement of fact—it's one long string of men hitting on you. If they're interested in your mind, I'd say they need a crash course in anatomy!"

In the course of our friendship, I had had many long chats with Massha about what it meant to a woman to be less than attractive. However, this was the first time I had ever been made to realize that beauty might be something less than an asset.

"I don't recall 'hitting on you,' Bunny."

"Okay, okay. Maybe I *have* taken to counterpunching before someone else starts. There's been enough of a pattern that I think I'm justified in jumping to conclusions. As I recall, you were a little preoccupied when we met. How would you have reacted if we ran into each other casually in a bar?"

That wasn't difficult at all to imagine . . . unfortunately.

"Touche!" I acknowledged. "Let me just toss one thought at you, Bunny. Then I'll yield to your experience. The question of sex is going to hang in the air over *any* male-female encounter until it's resolved. I think it lingers from pre-civilization days when survival of the species hinged on propagation. It's strongest when encountering a member of the opposite sex one finds attractive . . . such as a beautiful woman, or, I believe the phrase is, a 'hunk.' Part of civilization, though I don't know how many other people think of it this way, is setting rules and laws to help settle that question quickly: siblings, parents, and people under age or married to someone else are off limits . . . well, usually, but you get my point. Theoretically, this allows people to spend less time sniffing at each other and more time getting on with other endeavors . . . like art or business. I'm not sure it's an improvement, mind you, but it has brought us a long way."

"That's an interesting theory, Skeeve," Bunny said thoughtfully. "Where'd you hear it?"

"I made it up," I admitted.

"I'll have to mull that one over for a while. Even if you're right, though, what does it prove?"

"Well, I guess I'm trying to say that I think you're

focusing too much on the existence of the question.
Each time it comes up, resolve it and move on to other
things. Specifically, I think we can resolve the question
between us right now. As far as I'm concerned, the
answer is no, or at least not for a long time. If we can
agree on that, I'd like to move on to other things . . .
like getting to know you better."

"I'd say that sounds like a pass, if you weren't saying
'no' in the same breath. Maybe I have been a little
hypersensitive on the subject. Okay. Agreed. Let's try it
as friends."

She stuck out her hand, and I shook it solemnly. In
the back of my mind was a twinge of guilt. Now that I
had gotten her to relax her guard, I was going to try to
pump her for information.

"What would you like to know?"

"Well, except for the fact that you're smarter than
you let on and that you're Don Bruce's niece, I really
don't know much about you at all!"

"Whoops," she giggled, "You weren't even supposed to know about the niece part."

It was a much nicer giggle than her usual brain-jarring
squeal.

"Let's start there, then. I understand your uncle
doesn't approve of your career choice."

"You can say that again. He had a profession all
picked out for me, put me through school and everything. The trouble was that he didn't bother to check
with me. Frankly, I'd rather do anything else than what
he had in mind."

"What was that?"

"He wanted me to be an accountant."

My mind flashed back to my old nemesis J. R. Grimble back at Possletum. Trying to picture Bunny in his
place was more than my imagination could manage.

"Umm . . . I suppose accounting is okay work. I can
see why Don Bruce didn't want you to follow his
footsteps into a life of crime."

Bunny cocked a skeptical eyebrow at me. "If you believe that, you don't know much about accounting."

"Whatever. It does occur to me that there are more choices for one's livelihood than being an accountant or being a moll."

"I don't want to set you off again," she smirked, "but my looks were working against me. Most legitimate businessmen were afraid that if they hired me their wives, or partners, or board of directors, or staff would think they were putting a mistress on the payroll. After a while I decided to go with the flow and go into a field where being attractive was a requirement instead of a handicap. If I'm guilty of anything, it's laziness."

"I don't know," I said, shaking my head. "I'll admit I don't think much of your career choice."

"Oh, yeah? Well, before you start sitting in moral judgment, let me tell you . . ."

"Whoa! Time out!" I interrupted. "What I meant was there isn't much of a future in it. Nothing personal, but nobody stays young and good-looking forever. From what I hear, your job doesn't have much of a retirement plan."

"None of the Mob jobs do," she shrugged. "It pays the bills while I'm looking for something better."

Now we were getting somewhere.

"Speaking of the Mob, Bunny, I'll admit this Ax thing has me worried. Do you know offhand if the Mob ever handles character assassination? Maybe I could talk to someone and get some advice."

"I don't think they do. It's a little subtle for them. Still, I've never known Uncle Bruce to turn down any kind of work if the profit was high enough."

It occurred to me that that was a fairly evasive no-answer. I decided to try again.

"Speaking of your uncle, do you have any idea why he picked you for this assignment?"

There was the barest pause before she answered.

"No, I don't."

I had survived the Geek's dragon poker game watching other people, and I'm fairly good at it. To me, that hesitation was a dead giveaway. Bunny knew why she was here, she just wasn't telling.

As if she had read my thoughts, a startled look came over her face.

"Hey! It just dawned on me. Do you think I'm the Ax? Believe me, Skeeve, I'm not. Really!"

She was very sincere and very believable. Of course, if I were the Ax, that's exactly what I would say and how I would say it.

Chapter Thirteen:

"Your Majesty should pay attention to his appearance."

—H. C. ANDERSON

THERE are many words to describe the next day's outing into the Bazaar. Unfortunately, none of them are "calm, "quiet," or "relaxing." Words like "zoo," "circus," and "chaos" spring much more readily to mind.

It started before we even left our base . . . specifically, over whether or not we should go out at all.

Aahz and Massha maintained that we should go to ground until things blew over, on the theory that it would provide the fewest opportunities for the Ax to attack. Guido and Nunzio sided with them, adding their own colorful phrases to the proceedings. "Going to the mattresses" was one of their favorites, an expression which never ceased to conjure intriguing images to my mind. Like I told Bunny, I'm not *totally* pure.

Tananda and Chumley took the other side, arguing that the best defense is a solid offense. Staying inside, they argued, would only make us sitting ducks. The only sane thing to do would be to get out and try to determine just what the Ax was going to try. Markie and

Bunny chimed in supporting the brother-sister team, though I suspect it was more from a desire to see more of the Bazaar.

After staying neutral and listening for over an hour while the two sides went at each other, I finally cast my vote . . . in favor of going out. Strangely enough, my reasons aligned most closely with those of Bunny and Markie: while I was more than a little afraid of going out and being a moving target, I was ever more afraid of being cooped up inside with my own team while they got progressively more nervous and short-tempered with each other.

No sooner was that resolved than a new argument erupted, this time over who was going along. Obviously, everyone wanted to go. Just as obviously, if everybody did, we would look like exactly what we were: a strike force looking for trouble. I somehow didn't think this would assist our efforts to preserve my reputation.

After another hour of name-calling, we came up with a compromise. We would all go. For discretion as well as strategic advantage, however, it was decided that part of the team would go in disguise. That is, in addition to making our party look smaller than it really was, it would also allow our teammates to watch from a short distance and, more important, listen to what was being said around us in the Bazaar. Aahz, Tananda, Chumley, Massha, and Nunzio would serve as our scouts and reserve, while Markie, Bunny, Guido, and I would act as the bait . . . a role I liked less the more I thought about it.

Thus it was that we finally set out on our morning stroll . . . early in the afternoon.

On the surface the Bazaar was unchanged, but it didn't take long before I began to notice some subtle differences. I had gotten so used to maintaining disguise spells that I could keep our five colleagues incognito without it eating into my concentration . . . which was just as well, because there was a lot to concentrate on.

Apparently word of our last shopping venture had spread, and the reaction among the Deveel merchants to our appearance in the stalls was mixed and extreme. Some of the displays closed abruptly as we approached, while others rushed to meet us. There were, of course, those who took a neutral stance, neither closing nor meeting us halfway, but rather watching us carefully as we looked over their wares. Wherever we went, however, I noticed a distinct lack of enthusiasm for the favorite Bazaar pastime of haggling. Prices were either declared firm or counteroffers stacked up with minimum verbiage. It seems that, while they still wanted our money, the Deveels weren't eager to prolong contact with us.

I wasn't sure exactly how to handle the situation. I could take advantage of their nervousness and drive some shameless bargains, or grit my teeth and pay more than I thought the items were worth. The trouble was that neither course would do much to improve my image in the eyes of the merchants or erase the memory of our last outing.

Of course, my life being what it is, there were distractions.

After our talk, Bunny had decided that we were friends and attacked her new role with the same enthusiasm she brought to playing the vamp. She still clung to my arm, mind you, and from a distance probably still looked like a moll. Her attention, however, was now centered on me instead of on herself.

Today she had decided to voice her opinion of my wardrobe.

"Really, Skeeve. We've *got* to get you some decent clothes."

She had somehow managed to get rid of her nasal voice as well as whatever it was she had always been chewing on. Maybe there was a connection there.

"What's wrong with what I'm wearing?"

I had on what I considered to be one of my spiffier

outfits. The stripes on the pants were two inches wide and alternated yellow and light green, while the tunic was a brilliant red and purple paisley number.

"I wouldn't know where to start," she said, wrinkling her nose. "Let's just say it's a bit on the garish side."

"You didn't say anything about my clothes before."

"Right. Before. As in 'before we decided to be friends.' Molls don't stay employed by telling their men how tacky they dress. Sometimes I think one of the qualifications for having a decorative lady on your arm is to have no or negative clothes sense."

"Of course, I don't have much firsthand knowledge, but aren't there a few molls who dress a little flamboyantly themselves?" I said archly.

"True. But I'll bet if you checked into it, they're wearing outfits their men bought for them to dress up in. When we went shopping, you let me do the selecting and just picked up the bill. A lot of men figure if they're paying the fare, they should have the final say as to what their baby-doll wears. Let's face it, molls have to pay attention to how they look because their jobs depend on it. A girl who dresses like a sack of potatoes doesn't find work as a moll."

"So you're saying I dress like a sack of potatoes?"

"If a sack looked like you, it would knock the eyes out of the potatoes."

I groaned my appreciation. Heck, if no one was going to laugh at my jokes, why should I laugh at theirs? Of course, I filed her comment away for future use if the occasion should arise.

"Seriously though, Skeeve, your problem is that you dress like a kid. You've got some nice pieces in your wardrobe, but nobody's bothered to show you how to wear them. Bright outfits are nice, but you've got to balance them. Wearing a pattern with a muted solid accents the pattern. Wearing a pattern with a pattern is trouble, unless you really know what you're doing.

More often than not, the patterns end up fighting each other . . . and if they're in two different colors you've got an all-out war. Your clothes should call attention to you, not to themselves.''

Despite my indignation, I found myself being drawn into what she was saying. If there's one thing I've learned in my various adventures, it's that you take information where you find it.

"Let's see if I'm following you, Bunny. What you're saying is that just buying nice items, especially ones that catch my eye, isn't enough. I've got to watch how they go together . . . try to build a coordinated total. Right?''

"That's part of it," she nodded. "But I think we'd better go back to step one for a moment if we're going to educate you right. First, you've got to decide on the image you want to project. Your clothes make a statement about you, but you've got to know what that statement should be. Now, bankers depend on people trusting them with their money, so they dress conservatively to give the impression of dependability. No one will give their money to a banker who looks like he spends his afternoons playing the ponies. At the other end of the scale, you have the professional entertainers. They make their money getting people to look at them, so their outfits are usually flashy and flamboyant.''

This was fascinating. Bunny wasn't telling me a thing I hadn't seen for myself, but she was defining patterns that hadn't registered on me before. Suddenly the whole clothes thing was starting to make sense.

"So what kind of image do I project?''

"Well, since you ask, right now you look like one of two things: either someone who's so rich and successful that he doesn't have to care what other people think, or like a kid who doesn't know how to dress. Here at the Bazaar, they know you're successful, so the merchants jump to the first conclusion and drag out every gaudy item they haven't been able to unload on anyone else and figure if they price it high enough, you'll go for it.''

"A sucker or a fool," I murmured. "I don't really know what image I want, but it isn't either of those."

"Try this one on for size. You're a magician for hire, right? You want to look well off so your clients know you're good at what you do, but not so rich that they'll think you're overcharging them. You don't want to go too conservative, because in part they're buying into the mystique of magic, but if you go too flashy you'll look like a sideshow charlatan. In short, I think your best bet is to try for 'quiet power.' Someone who is apart from the workaday crowd, but who is so sure of himself that he doesn't have to openly try for attention."

"How do I look like that?"

"That's where Bunny comes in," she said with a wink. "If we're agreed on the end, I'll find the means. Follow me."

With that, she led me off into one of the most incredible shopping sprees I've ever taken part in. She insisted that I change into the first outfit we bought: a light blue open-necked shirt with cream-colored slacks and a matching neck scarf. Markie protested that she had liked the pretty clothes better, but as we made our way from stall to stall, I noticed a change in the manner of the proprietors. They still seemed a little nervous about our presence, but they were bringing out a completely different array of clothes for our examination, and several of them complimented me on what I was wearing . . . something that had never happened before.

I must admit I was a little surprised at how much some of these "simple and quiet" items cost, but Bunny assured me that the fabric and the workmanship justified the price.

"I don't understand it," I quipped at one point. "I thought that accountants were all tightfisted, and here you are: the ultimate consumer."

"You don't see me reaching for *my* bankroll, do you?" she purred back. "Accountants can deal with necessary expenses, as long as it's someone else's money. Our main job is to get you maximum purchase power for your hard-earned cash."

And so it went. When I had time to think, it occurred to me that if Bunny *was* the Ax, she was working awfully hard to make me look good. I was still trying to figure out how this could fit into a diabolical plan when I felt a nudge at my elbow. Glancing around, I found Aahz standing next to me.

Now, when I throw my disguise spell, I still see the person as they normally are. That's why I started nervously before I remembered that to anyone else at the Bazaar he looked like a fellow shopper exchanging a few words.

"Nice outfit, partner," he said. "It looks like your little playmate is doing some serious work on your wardrobe."

"Thanks, Aahz. Do you really like it?"

"Sure. There *is* one little item you might add to your list before we head for home."

"What's that?"

"About five decks of cards. While he might be impressed by your new image, I think it'll make a bigger impact on the Kid if you spend a little time learning how to play dragon poker before you square off with him."

That popped my bubble in a hurry. Aahz was right. Clothes and the Ax aside, there was one thing I was going to have to face up to soon, and that was a showdown with the best dragon poker player in all the dimensions.

Chapter Fourteen:

"Sometimes luck isn't enough."

—L. LUCIANO

"OGRE'S high, Skeeve. Your bet."

"Oh! Umm . . . I'll go ten."

"Bump you ten."

"Out."

"Twenty to me? I'll go twenty on top of that."

"Call."

By now, you should know that sound. That's right. Dragon poker in full gallop. This time, however, it was a friendly game between Aahz, Tananda, Chumley, and me. Of course, I'm using the phrase "friendly" rather loosely here.

Aside from occasional shouting matches, I had never been in a fight with these three before. That is, when there had been trouble, we formed our circle with the horns out, not in. For the first time, I found myself on the opposite side of a conflict from my colleagues, and I wasn't enjoying it at all. Realizing this was just a game, and a practice game at that, I was suddenly very glad I didn't have too face any one of them in a real life-and-death situation.

The banter was still there, but there was an edge on it. There was a cloud of tension over the table as the players focused on each other like circling predators. It had been there at the game at the Even-Odds, but then I was expecting it. One doesn't expect support or sympathy from total strangers in a card game. The trouble was that these three who were my closest friends were turning out to be total strangers when the chips were down . . .if you'll pardon the expression.

"I think you're bluffing, big brother. Up another forty."

I gulped and pushed another stack of my diminishing pile of chips into the pot.

"Call."

"You got me," the troll shrugged. "Out."

"Well, Skeeve. That leaves you and me. I've got an elf-high flush."

She displayed her hand and looked at me expectantly. I turned my hole cards over with what I hoped was a confident flourish.

Silence reigned as everyone bent forward to stare at my hand.

"Skeeve, this is garbage," Tananda said at last. "Aahz folded a better hand than this without his hole cards. I had you beat on the board."

"What she's trying to say, partner," Aahz smirked, "is that you should have either folded or raised. Calling the bet when the cards she has showing beat your hand is just tossing away money."

"Okay, okay! I get the point."

"Do you? You've still got about fifty chips there. Are you sure you don't want to wait until you've lost those, too? Of maybe we should redivide the chips and start over . . . *again*."

"Lighten up, Aahz," Tananda ordered. "Skeeve had a system that had worked for him before. Why shouldn't he want to try it out before being forcefed something new?"

What they were referring to was my original resistance to taking lessons in dragon poker. I had pretty much decided to handle the upcoming game the same way I had played the game at the Even-Odds rather than try to crash-learn the rules. After some discussion (read: argument) it was agreed that we should play a demonstration game so that I could show my coaches how well my system worked.

Well, I showed them.

I could read Aahz pretty well, possibly because I knew him so intimately. Chumley and Tananda, though, threw me for a loop. I was unable to pick up any sort of giveaway clues in their speech or manner, nor could I manage to detect any apparent relationship between their betting and what they were holding. In a depressingly short period of time I had been cleaned out of my starting allotment of chips. Then we divvied the stacks up again and started over . . . with the same results. We were now closing in on the end of the third round, and I was ready to throw in the towel.

As much as I would have liked to tell myself that I was having a bad run of cards or that we had played too few hands to set the patterns, the horrible truth was that I was simply outclassed. I mean, usually I could spot if a player had a good hand. Then the question was "how good," or more specifically, if his was better than mine. Of course, the same went for weak hands. I depended on being able to detect a player who was betting a hand that needed development or if he was simply betting that the other hand in the round would develop worse than his. In this "demonstration game," however, I was caught flatfooted again and again. Too many times a hand that I had figured for guts-nothing turned out to be a powerhouse.

To say the least, it was depressing. These were players who wouldn't dream of challenging the Sen-Sen Ante Kid themselves, and they were cleaning my clock without half trying.

"I know when I'm licked, Aahz," I said. "Even if it does take me a little longer than most. I'm ready to take those lessons you offered . . . if you still think it will do any good."

"Sure it will, partner. At the very least, I don't think it can hurt your game, if tonight's been an accurate sample."

Trust a Pervect to know just what to say to cheer you up.

"Come on, Aahz old boy," Chumley interrupted. "Skeeve here is doing the best he can. He's just trying to hang on in a bad situation . . . like we all do. Let's not make it any rougher for him. Hmmm?"

"I suppose you're right."

"And watch comments like that when Markie's around," Tananda put in. "She's got a bad case of hero-worship for her new daddy, and we need him as an authority figure to keep her in line."

"Speaking of Markie," my partner grimaced, peering around, "where is our portable disaster area?"

The tail end of our shopping expedition had not gone well. Markie's mood seemed to deteriorate as the day wore on. Twice we were saved from total disaster only by timely intervention by our spotters when she started to get particularly upset. Not wishing to push our luck, I called a halt to the excursion, which almost triggered another tantrum from my young ward. I wondered if other parents had ever had shopping trips cut short by a cranky child.

"She's off somewhere with Bunny and the body-guards. I thought this session would be rough enough without the added distraction of Markie cheering for her daddy."

"Good call," Chumley said. "Well, enough chitchat. Shall we have at it?"

"Right!" Aahz declared, rubbing his hands together as he leaned forward. "Now, the first thing we have to do is tighten up your better strategy. If you keep . . ."

"Umm . . . Aren't you getting a little ahead of yourself, Aahz?" Tananda interrupted.

"How so?"

"Don't you think it would be nice if we taught him the sequence of hands first? It's a lot easier to bet when you know whether or not your hand is any good."

"Oh. Yeah. Of course."

"Let me handle this part, Aahz," the troll volunteered. "Now then, Skeeve. The ascending sequence of hands is as follows:

High Card
One Pair
Two Pair
Three Of A Kind
Three Pair
Full House (Three Of A Kind plus a Pair)
Four Of A Kind
Flush
Straight (those last two are ranked higher and reversed because of the sixth card)
Full Belly (two sets of Three Of A Kind)
Full Dragon (Four Of a Kind plus a Pair)
Straight Flush
Have you got that?"

Half an hour later, I could almost get through the list without referring to my crib sheet. By that time, my teachers' enthusiasm was noticeably dimmed. I decided to push on to the next lesson before I lost them completely.

"Close enough," I declared. "I can bone up on these on my own time. Where do we go from here? How much should I bet on the hands?"

"Not so fast," Aahz said. "First, you've got to finish learning about the hands."

"You mean there are more? I thought . . ."

"No. You've got all the hands . . . or will have, with a little practice. Now you've got to learn about *conditional modifiers*."

"Conditional modifiers?" I echoed weakly.

"Sure. Without 'em, dragon poker would be just another straightforward game. Are you starting to see why I didn't want to take the time before to teach you?"

I nodded silently, staring at my list of card hands that I somehow had a feeling was about to become more complex.

"Cheer up, Skeeve," Chumley said gaily, clapping me on the shoulder. "This is going to be easier than if we were trying to teach you the whole game."

"It is?" I blinked, perking up slightly.

"Sure. You see, the conditional modifiers depend on certain variables, like the day of the week, the number of players, chair position, things like that. Now since this match is prearranged, we know what most of those variables will be. For example, there will only be the two of you playing, and as the challenged party you have your choice of chairs . . . pick the one facing south, incidentally."

"What my big brother is trying to say in his own clumsy way," Tananda interrupted by squeezing my arm softly, "is that you don't have to learn *all* the conditional modifiers. Just the ones that will be in effect for your game with the Kid."

"Oh, I get it. Thanks, Chumley. That makes me feel a lot better."

"Right-o. There can't be more than a dozen or two that will be pertinent."

The relief I had been feeling turned cold inside me. "Two dozen conditional modifiers?"

"C'mon, big brother. There aren't that many."

"I was going to say I thought he was underestimating," Aahz grinned.

"Well, let's bloody well count them off and see."

"Red dragons will be wild on even-numbered hands. . . ."

". . . But unicorns will be wild all evening. . . ."

". . . The corps-a-corps hand will be invalid all night,

that's why we didn't bother to list it, partner. . . ."

". . . Once a night, a player can change the suit of one of his up cards. . . ."

". . . Every five hands, the sequence of cards is reversed, so the low cards are high and vice-versa. . . ."

". . . Threes will be dead all night and treated as blank cards. . . ."

". . . And once a four-of-a-kind is played, that card value is also dead. . . ."

". . . Unless it's a wild card, then it simply ceases to be wild and can be played normally. . . ."

". . . If there's a ten showing in the first two face-up cards in each hand, then sevens will be dead. . . ."

". . . Unless there is a second ten showing, then it cancels the first. . . ."

". . . Of course, if the first card turned face up in a round is an Ogre, the round will be played with an extra hole card, four face up and five face down. . . ."

". . . A natural hand beats a hand of equal value built with wild cards. . . ."

"Hey—that's not a conditional modifier. That's a regular rule."

"It will be in effect, won't it? Some of the conditional modifiers nullify standing rules, so I thought we should . . . "

"ARE YOU PUTTING ME ON?!!"

The conversation stopped on a dime as my coaches turned to stare at me.

"I mean, this is a joke. Right?"

"No, partner," Aahz said carefully. "This is what dragon poker is all about. Like Chumley said, just be thankful you're only playing one night and get to learn the abbreviated list."

"But how am I supposed to stand a chance in this game? I'm not even going to be able to remember all the rules."

An awkward silence came over the table.

"I . . . uhh . . . think you've missed the point,

Skeeve,'' Tananda said at last. "You don't stand a chance. The Kid is the best there is. There's no way you can learn enough in a few days or a few years to even give him a run for his money. All we're trying to do is teach you enough so that you won't embarrass yourself—as in ruin the reputation of the Great Skeeve—while he whittles away at your stake. You've got to at least *look* like you know what you're doing. Otherwise you come across as a fool who doesn't know enough to know how little he knows.''

I thought about that for a few.

"Doesn't that description actually fit me to a 'T'?''

"If so, let's keep it in the family. Okay?'' my partner winked, punching me playfully on the shoulder. "Cheer up, Skeeve. In some ways it should be fun. There's nothing like competing in a game without the pressure to win to let you role-play to the hilt.''

"Sure, Aahz.''

"Okay, so let's get back to it. Just listen this time around. We'll go over it again slower later so you can write it all down.''

With that, they launched into it again.

I listened with half an ear, all the while examining my feelings. I had gone into the first game at the Even-Odds expecting to lose, but I had been viewing that as a social evening. It was beyond my abilities to kid myself into believing this match with the Kid was going to be social. As much as I respected the views of my advisors, I was having a lot of trouble accepting the idea that I would help my reputation by losing. They were right, though, that I couldn't gracefully refuse the challenge. If I didn't stand a chance of winning, then the only option left was to lose gracefully. Right?

Try as I might, though, I couldn't still a little voice in the back of my mind that kept telling me that the ideal solution would be to take the Kid to the cleaners. Of course, that was impossible. Right? Right?

Chapter Fifteen:

"I need all the friends I can get."
—QUASIMODO

WHILE my life may seem convoluted and depressing at times, at least there is one being who never turns from me in my hours of need.

"Gleep!"

I've never understood how a dragon's tongue can be slimy and sandpapery at the same time, but it is. Well, at least the one belonging to *my* dragon is.

"Down, fella . . . dow . . . hey! C'mon, Gleep. Stop it!"

"Gleep!" my pet declared as he deftly dodged my hands and left one more slimy trail across my face.

Obedient to a fault. They say you can judge a man's leadership ability by how well he handles animals.

"Darn it, Gleep! This is serious!"

I've often tried to convince Aahz that my dragon actually understands what I say. Whether that was the case here or if he was just sensitive to my tone, Gleep sank back on his haunches and cocked his head attentively.

"That's better," I sighed, daring to breathe through

119

my nose again. Dragons have notoriously bad breath (hence the expression "dragon mouth"), and my pet's displays of affection had the unfortunate side effect of making me feel more than slightly faint. Of course, even breathing through my mouth, I could still taste it.

"You see, I've got a problem . . . well, several problems, and I thought maybe talking them out without being interrupted might . . ."

"Gleep!"

The tongue slicked out again, this time catching me with my mouth open. While I love my pet, there are times I wish he were . . . smaller. Times like this . . . and when I have to clean out his litter box.

"You want I should lean on the dragon for you, Boss?"

I looked around and discovered Nunzio sitting on one of the garden benches.

"Oh. Hi, Nunzio. What are you doing here? I thought you and Guido usually made yourself scarce when I was exercising Gleep."

"That's usually," the bodyguard shrugged. "My cousin and me, we talked it over and decided with this Ax fella on the loose that one of us should stick with you all the time, know what I mean? Right now it's my shift, and I'll be hangin' tight . . . no matter what you're doin'."

"I appreciate that, but I don't think there's any danger of getting hit here. I already decided not to take Gleep outside until the coast is clear. No sense tempting fate."

That was at least partially true. What I had really decided was that I didn't want to give the Ax a chance to strike at me through my pet. Aahz already complained enough about having a dragon in residence without adding fuel to the fire. Of course, if my suspicions were correct and Bunny *was* the Ax . . .

"Better safe than sorry . . . and you didn't answer my question. You want I should lean on the dragon?"

Sometimes the logic of bodyguards eluded me completely.

"No. I mean, why should you lean on Gleep? You look comfortable where you are."

Nunzio rolled his eyes. "I don't mean 'lean on him' like really lean on him. I mean, do you want me to bend him a little? You know, rough him up some. I stay outta things between you and your partner, but you shouldn't have to put up with that kind of guff from a dragon."

"He's just being friendly."

"Friendly, schmendly. From what I've seen, you're in more danger from getting knocked off by your own pet than by anyone else I've seen at the Bazaar. All I've ever asked is that you let me do my job . . . I *am* supposed to be guardin' your body, ya' know. That's how my position got its lofty title."

Not for the first time, I was impressed by Nunzio's total devotion to his work. For a moment I was tempted to let him do what he wanted. At the last minute, though, an image flashed through my mind of my outsized bodyguard and my dragon going at it hammer and tongs in the middle of the garden.

"Umm . . . thanks, but I think I'll pass, Nunzio. Gleep can be a pain sometimes, but I kind of like him jumping all over me once in a while. It makes me feel loved. Besides, I wouldn't want to see him get hurt . . . or you either, for that matter."

"Jumpin' up on you is one thing. Doin' it when you don't want him to is sompin' else. Besides, I wouldn't hurt him. I'd just . . . here, let me show you!"

Before I could stop him, he was on his feet, taking a straddle-legged stance facing my dragon.

"C'mere, Gleep. C'mon, fella."

My pet's head snapped around, then he went bounding toward what he thought was a new playmate.

"Nunzio. I . . ."

Just as the dragon reached him, my bodyguard held out a hand, palm outward.

"Stop, Gleep! Sit! I said SIT!!"

What happened next I had to reconstruct later from replaying my memory, it happened so fast.

Nunzio's hand snaked out and closed over Gleep's snout. With a jerk he pulled the nose down until it was under my pet's head, then pushed up sharply.

In mid-stride the dragon's haunches dropped into a sitting position and he stopped, all the while batting his eyelashes in bewilderment.

"Now stay. Stay!!"

My bodyguard carefully opened his hand and stepped back, holding his palm flat in front of my pet's face.

Gleep quivered slightly but didn't budge from his sitting position.

"See, Boss? He'll mind," Nunzio called over his shoulder. "Ya just gotta be firm with him."

I suddenly realized my jaw was dangling somewhere around my knees. "What . . . that's incredible, Nunzio! How did you . . . what did you . . ."

"I guess you never knew," he grinned, "I used ta be an animal trainer . . . mostly the nasty ones for shows, know what I mean?"

"An animal trainer?"

"Yeah. It seemed like a logical extension of bein' a schoolteacher . . . only without the parents to worry about."

I had to sit down. Between the demonstration with Gleep and the sudden insight to his background, Nunzio had my brain on overload.

"An animal trainer *and* a schoolteacher."

"That's right. Say, you want I should work with your dragon some more now that he's quieted down?"

"No. Let him run for a while. This is supposed to be his exercise time."

"You're the Boss."

He turned toward Gleep and clapped his hands sharply. The dragon bounded backwards, then crouched close to the ground, ready to play.

"Get it, boy!"

Moving with surprising believability, the bodyguard scooped an imaginary ball from the ground and pretended to throw it to the far end of the garden.

Gleep spun around and sprinted off in the direction of the "throw," flattening a bench and two shrubs as he went.

"Simply amazing," I murmured.

"I didn't mean to butt in," Nunzio said, sinking into the seat beside me. "It just looked like you wanted to talk and your dragon wanted to frolic."

"It's all right. I'd rather talk to you, anyway."

I was moderately astounded to discover this was true. I'd always been a bit of a loner, but lately it seemed I not only was able to talk to people, I enjoyed it. I hoped it wouldn't seriously change my friendship with Gleep.

"Me? Sure, Boss. What did you want to talk about?"

"Oh, nothing special. I guess I just realized we've never really talked, just the two of us. Tell me, how do you like our operation here?"

"It's okay, I guess. Never really thought about it much. It's not your run-of-the-mill Mob operation, that much is for sure. You got some strange people hangin' around you . . . but they're nice. I'd give my right arm for any one of them, they're so nice. That's different right there. Most outfits, everybody's tryin' to get ahead . . . so they spend more time watchin' each other than they do scopin' the opposition. Here, everybody covers for each other instead of nudging the other guy out."

"Do you want to get ahead, Nunzio?"

"Yes and no, know what I mean? I don't want to be doin' the same thing the rest of my life, but I'm not pushy to get to the top. Actually, I kinda like workin' for someone else. I let them make the big decisions, then all I gotta do is figure out how to make my part happen."

"You certainly do your part around here," I nodded.

"I never knew before how hard a bodyguard works."

"Really? Gee, it's good to hear you say that, Boss.
Sometimes Guido and me, we feel like dead weight
around here. Maybe that's why we work so hard to do
our jobs. I never thought much about whether I do or
don't like it here. I mean, I go where I'm assigned and
do what I'm told, so it doesn't matter what I think.
Right? What I do know, though, is that I'd be real sorry
if I had to leave. Nobody's ever treated me like you and
your crew do."

Nunzio might not be an intellectual giant or the swift-
est with I've known, but I found his simple honesty
touching . . . not to mention the loyalty it implied.

"Well, you've got a job here as long as I've got
anything to say about it." I assured him.

"Thanks, Boss. I was startin' to get a little tired of
how the Mob operates, know what I mean?" That rang
a bell in my mind.

"Speaking of that, Nunzio, do you think the Mob
would ever get involved with something like this character assassination thing?"

The bodyguard's brow furrowed with the effort of
thinking.

"Naw!" he said at last. "Mostly people pay us *not* to
do things. If we do have to do a number on someone,
it's usually to make an example of them and we do
something flashy like burn down their house or break
their legs. Who would know it if we wrecked their
career? What Tananda was sayin' about the Ax was interesting, but it's just not our style."

"Not even for the right price?" I urged. "How much
do you think it would take to get Don Bruce to send
someone in here after us?"

"I dunno. I'd have to say at least . . . wait a minute!
Are you askin' if Bunny's the Ax?"

"Well, she did . . . "

"Forget it, Boss. Even if she could handle the job,
which I'm not too sure she could, Don Bruce would

never send her after you. Heck, you're one of his
favorite chieftains right now. You should hear him . . ."

Nunzio suddenly pressed his palms against his cheeks
to make exaggerated jowls as he spoke. ". . . Dat
Skeeve, he's really got it on the ball, know what I mean?
Mercy! If I had a hundred like him I could take over dis
whole organization."

His imitation of Don Bruce was so perfect I had to
laugh.

"That's great, Nunzio. Has he ever seen you do
that?"

"I'm still employed and breathin', aren't I?" he
winked. "Seriously, though. You're barkin' up the
wrong tree with Bunny. Believe me, you're the apple of
her uncle's eye right now."

"I suppose you're right," I sighed. "If you are,
though, it leaves me right back where I started. Who is
the Ax and what can . . ."

"Hi guys! Is that a private conversation, or can
anyone join?"

We glanced up to find Bunny and Markie entering the
garden.

"C'mon over, Bunny!" I waved, nudging Nunzio
slightly in the ribs. "We were just going to . . ."

"GLEEP!!!"

Suddenly my dragon was in front of me. Crouching
and tense, he didn't look playful at all. I had only seen
him like this a couple of times before, and then . . .

"STOP IT, GLEEP! GLEEP!!!" I screamed, realizing too late what was about to happen.

Fortunately, Nunzio was quicker than I was. From
his sitting position he threw himself forward in a body
check against my pet's neck, just as the dragon let loose
with a stream of fire. The flames leapt forward to
harmlessly scorch a wall.

Bunny swept Markie behind her with one arm.

"Geez! What was . . ."

"I'll get him!" Markie cried, balling up her fists.

"MARKIE!! STOP!!"

"But Daddy . . ."

"Just hold it. Okay? Nunzio?"

"I've got him, Boss," he called, both hands wrapped securely around Gleep's snout as the dragon struggled to get free.

"Bunny? You and Markie get inside! Now!!!"

The two of them hurried from sight, and I turned my attention to my pet.

Gleep seemed to have calmed down as fast as he had exploded, now that Bunny and Markie were gone. Nunzio was stroking her neck soothingly while staring at me in wide-eyed amazement.

"I dunno what happened there, Boss, but he seems okay now."

"What happened," I said grimly, "was Gleep trying to protect me from something or someone he saw as a threat."

"But Boss . . ."

"Look Nunzio, I know you mean well, but Gleep and I go back a long way. I trust his instincts more than I do my own judgment."

"But . . ."

"I want you to do two things right away. First, put Gleep back in his stable . . . I think he's had enough exercise for one day. Then get word to Don Bruce. I want to have a little talk with him about his 'present'!"

Chapter Sixteen:

"I thought we were friends!"

—BANQUO

"I TELL you, partner, this is crazy!"

"Like heck it is!"

"Bunny can't be the Ax! She's a space cadet."

"That's what she'd like us to think. I found out different!"

"Really? How?"

"By . . . well, by talking to her."

I spotted the flaw in my logic as soon as I said it, and Aahz wasn't far behind.

"Skeeve," he said solemnly, "has it occurred to you that if she's the Ax and you're her target, that you would probably be the last person she would relax around? Do you really think you could trick her into giving away her I.Q. in a simple conversation?"

"Well . . . maybe she was being clever. It could be that it was her way of trying to throw us off the track."

My partner didn't say anything to that. He just cocked his head and raised one eyebrow *very* high.

"It *could* be," I repeated lamely.

"C'mon, Skeeve. Give."

"What?"

"Even you need more evidence than that before you go off half-cocked. What are you holding back?"

He had me. I was just afraid that he was going to find my real reason even less believable than the one I had already stated.

"Okay," I said with a sigh. "If you really want to know, what finally convinced me was that Gleep doesn't like her."

"Gleep? You mean that stupid dragon of yours? That Gleep?"

"Gleep isn't st . . ."

"Partner, your dragon doesn't like *me!* That doesn't make me the Ax!!"

"He's never tried to fry you, either!"

That one stopped him for a moment. "He did that? He really let fly at Bunny?"

"That's right. If Nunzio hadn't been there . . ."

As if summoned by the mention of his name, the bodyguard stuck his head into the room.

"Hey, Boss! Don Bruce is here."

"Show him in."

"I still think you're making a mistake," Aahz warned, leaning against a wall.

"Maybe," I said grimly. "With luck I'll get Don Bruce to confirm my suspicions before I show my cards."

"This I've got to see."

"There you are, Skeeve. The boys said you wanted to see me."

Don Bruce is the Mob's fairy godfather. I've never seen him dressed in anything that wasn't lavender, and today was no exception. His ensemble included shorts, sandals, a floppy brimmed hat, and a sports shirt with large dark purple flowers printed all over it. Maybe my wardrobe sessions with Bunny were making me overly sensitive on the subject of clothes, but his attire hardly seemed appropriate for one of the most powerful men in the Mob.

Even his dark glasses had violet lenses.

"You know, this is quite a place you got here. Never been here before, but I heard a lot about it in the yearly report. It doesn't look this big from the outside."

"We like to keep a low profile," I said.

"Yeah, I know. It's like I keep tellin' 'em back at Mob Central, you run a class operation. I like that. Makes us all look good."

I was starting to feel a little uncomfortable. The last thing I wanted to discuss with Don Bruce was our current operation.

"Like some wine?" Aahz chimed in, coming to my rescue.

"It's a little early, but why not? So! What is it you wanted to see me about?"

"It's about Bunny."

"Bunny? Oh yeah. How's she workin' out?"

Even if I hadn't already been suspicious, Don Bruce's response would have seemed overly casual. Aahz caught it too, raising his eyebrow again as he poured the wine.

"I thought we should have a little chat about why you sent her here."

"What's to chat about? You needed a moll, and I figured . . ."

"I mean the *real* reason."

Our guest paused, glanced back and forth between Aahz and me a couple of times, then shrugged his shoulders. "She told you, huh? Funny, I would have thought that was one secret she would have kept."

"Actually, I figured it out all by myself. In fact, when the subject came up, she denied it."

"Always said you were smart, Skeeve. Now I see you're smart enough to get me to admit to what you couldn't trick out of Bunny. Pretty good."

I shot a triumphant glance at Aahz, who was suddenly very busy with the wine. Despite my feeling of victory over having puzzled out the identity of the Ax, I was still more than a little annoyed.

"What I can't figure out," I said, "is why you tried it in the first place. I've always played it pretty straight with you."

At least Don Bruce had the grace to look embarrassed. "I know, I know. It seemed like a good idea at the time, is all. I was in a bit of a spot, and it seemed like a harmless way out."

"Harmless? Harmless! That's my whole life and career we're talking about."

"Hey! C'mon, Skeeve. Aren't you exaggerating a little bit there! I don't think . . ."

"Exaggerating??"

"Well, I still think you'd make a good husband for her . . ."

"Exaggerating? Aahz, are you listening to . . ."

As I turned to appeal to my partner, I noticed he was laughing so hard he was spilling the wine. Of all the reactions I might have expected from him, laughing wasn't . . .

Then it hit me.

"Husband?!?!?"

"Of course. Isn't that what we've been talkin' about?"

"Skeeve here thinks that your niece is the Ax and that you turned her loose on him to destroy his career," my partner managed between gasps.

"The Ax???"

"HUSBAND????"

"Are you crazy??"

"One of us is!!"

"How about both?" Aahz grinned, stepping between us. "Wine, anyone?"

"But he said . . ."

"What about . . ."

"Gentlemen, gentlemen. It's clear that communications have gotten a little fouled up between the two of you. I suggest you each take some wine and we'll start all over again from the top.''

Almost mechanically, we both reached for the wine, eyeing each other all the while like angry cats.

"Very good," my partner nodded. "Now then, Don Bruce, as the visiting team I believe you have first serve."

"What's this about the Ax!?!" the mobster demanded, leaning forward so suddenly half the wine sloshed out of his glass.

"You know who the Ax is??"

"I know *what* he is! The question is, what does he have to do with you and Bunny?"

"We're heard recently that someone's hired the Ax to do a number on Skeeve," Aahz supplied.

". . . Right about the same time Bunny showed up," I added.

"And that's supposed to make her the Ax?"

"Well, there *has* been some trouble since she arrived."

"Like what?"

"Welll . . . Tananda left because of things that were said when she found out that Bunny was in my bedroom one morning."

"Tananda? The same Tananda that said 'Hi' to me when I walked in here today?"

"She . . . ummm . . . came back."

"I see. What else?"

"She scared off my girlfriend."

"Girlfriend? You got a girlfriend?"

"Well, not exactly . . . but I might have had one if Bunny wasn't here."

"Uh-huh. Aahz, haven't you ever told him the 'bird in the hand' story?"

"I try, but he isn't big on listening."

I can always count on my partner to rally to my defense in times of crisis.

"What else?"

"Ummm . . ."

"Tell him!" Aahz smiled.

"Tell me what?"

"My dragon doesn't like her."

"I'm not surprised. She's never gotten along with animals . . . at least the four-footed kind. I don't see where that makes her the Ax, though."

"It's . . . it's just that on top of the other evidence . . ."

My voice trailed off in front of Don Bruce's stony stare.

"You know, Skeeve," he said at last. "As much as I like you, there are times, like now, I wish you was on the other side of the law. If the D.A.s put together a case like you do, we could cut our bribe budget by ninety percent, and our attorney's fees by a hundred percent!"

"But . . ."

"Now listen close, 'cause I'm only goin' to go over this once. You're the representative for the Mob, and *me*, here at the Bazaar. If you look bad, then we look bad. Got it? What possible sense would it make for us to hire someone to make you, and *us*, look bad?"

On the ropes, I glanced at Aahz for support.

"That was going to be the next question *I* was going to ask, partner."

Terrific.

"Well," Don Bruce announced, standing up. "If that's settled, I guess I can go now."

"Not so fast," my partner smiled, holding up a hand. "There's still the matter of the question that Skeeve asked: if Bunny isn't the Ax, what's she doing here? What was that you were saying about a husband?"

The mobster sank back into his chair and reached for his wine, all the while avoiding my eyes.

"I'm not gettin' any younger," he said. "Some day I'm goin' to retire, and I thought I should maybe start lookin' around for a replacement. It's always nice to have 'em in the family . . . the real family, I mean, and since I got an unmarried niece . . ."

"Whoa! Wait a minute," Aahz interrupted. "Are you saying that you're considering Skeeve as your eventual replacement in the Mob?"

"It's a possibility. Why not? Like I said, he runs a class operation and he's smart . . . at least I used to think so."

"Don Bruce I . . . I don't know what to say," I said honestly.

"Then don't say nothin'!" he responded grimly. "Whatever's goin' to happen is a long way off. That's why I didn't say anything to you direct. I'm not ready to retire yet."

"Oh." I didn't know whether to feel disappointment or relief.

"About Bunny?" my partner prompted.

The mobster shrugged. "What's to say that hasn't already been said? She's my niece, he's one of my favorite chieftains. I thought it would be a good idea to put 'em close to each other and see if anything happened."

"I . . . I don't know," I said thoughtfully. "I mean, Bunny's nice enough . . . especially now that I know she isn't the Ax. I just don't think I'm ready to get married yet."

"Didn't say you were," Don Bruce shrugged. "Don't get me wrong, Skeeve. I'm not tryin' to push you into this. I know it'll take time. Like I said, I just fixed it so you two could meet and see if anything develops . . . that's all. If it works out, fine. If it doesn't, also fine. I'm not about to try to force things or kid myself that you two will make a pair if you won't. If nothing else, you've got a pretty good accountant while you find out . . . and from lookin' over your financial figures you could use one."

"Izzat so?"

He had finally tweaked Aahz close to home . . . or his wallet, which in his case is the same thing.

"What's wrong with our finances? We're doing okay."

"Okay isn't soarin'. You boys got no plan. The way I see it, you've spent so much time livin' hand-to-mouth you've never learned what to do with money except stack it and spend it. Bunny can show you how to make your money work for you."

Aahz rubbed his chin thoughtfully. It was interesting to see my partner caught between pride and greed.

"I dunno," he said at last. "It sounds good, and we'll probably look into it eventually, but we're a little tight right now."

"The way I hear it, you're tight all the time," Don Bruce commented drily.

"No. I mean right now we're *really* tight for finances. We've got a lot of capital tied up in the big game tonight."

"Big game? What big game?"

"Skeeve is going head to head with the Sen-Sen Ante Kid at dragon poker tonight. It's a challenge match."

"That's why I wanted to talk to you about Bunny," I said. "Since I thought she was the Ax, I didn't want her around to cause trouble at the game."

"Why didn't anyone tell me about this game?" Don Bruce demanded. "It wasn't in your report!"

"It's come up since then."

"What are the stakes?"

I looked at Aahz. I had been so busy trying to learn how dragon poker was played that I had never gotten around to asking about the stakes.

For some reason, my partner suddenly looked uncomfortable.

"Table stakes," he said.

"Table stakes?" I frowned. "What's that?"

I half-expected him to tell me he'd explain later, but instead he addressed the subject with surprising enthusiasm.

"In a table stakes game, each of you starts with a cer-

tain amount of money. Then you play until one of you
is out of chips, or . . ."

"I know what table stakes are," Don Bruce interrupted. "What I want to know is how much you're
playing for."

Aahz hesitated, then shrugged. "A quarter of a
million each."

"A QUARTER OF A MILLION???"

I hadn't hit that note since my voice changed.

"Didn't you know?" the mobster scowled.

"We hadn't told him," my partner sighed. "I was
afraid that if he knew what the stakes were, he'd clutch.
We were just going to give him the stack of chips to play
without telling him how much they were worth."

"A quarter of a million?" I repeated, a little hoarser
this time.

"See?" Aahz grinned. "You're clutching."

"But, Aahz, do we *have* a quarter of a million to
spare?"

My partner's grin faded and he started avoiding my
eyes.

"I can answer that one, Skeeve," Don Bruce said.
"*No one* has a quarter of a million to spare. Even if
you've got it, you don't have it to spare, know what I
mean?"

"It's not going to take *all* our money," Aahz said
slowly. "The others have chipped in out of their savings, too: Tananda, Chumley, Massha, even Guido and
Nunzio. We've all got a piece of the action."

"Us too," the mobster declared. "Put the Mob down
for half."

I'm not sure who was more surprised, Aahz or me.
But Aahz recovered first.

"That's nice of you, Don Bruce, but you don't
understand what's really happening here. Skeeve here is
a rank beginner at the game. He had one lucky night,
and by the time the rumor mill got through with it, he
had drawn a challenge from the Kid. He can't refuse

without looking foolish, and with the Ax on the loose we can't afford any bad press we can avoid. That's why we're pooling our money, so Skeeve can go in there and lose gracefully. The actual outcome is preordained. The Kid's going to eat him alive.''

''. . . And maybe you weren't listening earlier,'' the mobster shot back. ''If Skeeve looks bad, we look bad. The Mob backs its people, especially when it comes to public image. Win or lose, we're in for half, okay?''

''If you say so,'' Aahz shrugged.

''. . . And try to save me a couple seats. I'm gonna want to see my boy in action—firsthand.''

''It'll cost!''

''Did I ask? Just . . . ''

I wasn't really listening to the conversation any more. I hadn't realized before just how solidly my friends were behind me.

A quarter of a million . . .

Right then something solidified in my mind that had been hovering there for several days now. Whatever the others thought, I was going to try my best to win this game!

Chapter Seventeen:

"Shut up and deal!"

—F.D.R.

THERE was an aura of expectation over the Bazaar that night as we set out for the Even-Odds. At first I thought I was just seeing things differently because of my anticipation and nervousness. As we walked, however, it became more and more apparent that it was not simply my imagination.

Not a single vendor or shop shill approached us, not a Deveel hailed us with a proposed bargain. On the contrary, as we proceeded along the aisles, conversation and business ground to a halt as everyone turned to watch us pass. A few called out their wishes of "good luck" or friendly gibes about seeing me after the game, but for the most part they simply stared in silent fascination.

If I had ever had any doubts as to the existence or extent of the rumor mill and grapevine at the Bazaar, that night put them to rest forever. Everybody and I mean *everybody* knew who I was, where I was going, and what was waiting for me.

In some ways it was fun. I've noted earlier that I

generally kept a low profile in the immediate neighborhood and have gotten used to walking around unnoticed. My recent shopping trips had gained me a certain notoriety, but it was nothing compared to this. Tonight, I was a full-blown celebrity! Realizing the uncertainty of the game's outcome, I decided to seize the moment and play my part to the hilt.

To a certain degree it was easy. We already made quite a procession. Guido and Nunzio were decked out in their working clothes of trenchcoats and weapons and preceded us, clearing a path through the gawkers. Tananda and Chumley brought up the rear looking positively grim as they eyeballed anyone who seemed to be edging too close. Aahz was walking just ahead of me, carrying our stake money in two large bags. If anyone entertained the thought of intercepting us for the money, all they had to do was look at Aahz's swagger and the gleam in his yellow eyes, and they would suddenly decide there were easier ways to get rich . . . like wrestling dragons or panning for gold in a swamp.

We had left Markie back at our place over her loud and indignant protests. I had stood firm, though. This game was going to be rough enough without having her around as a distraction. Massha had volunteered to stay with her, claiming she was far too nervous about the game to enjoy watching it anyway.

Bunny was decked out in a clinging outfit in brilliant white and hung on my arm like I was the most important thing in her life. More than a few envious eyes darted from her to me and back again.

No one was kidding anyone, though, as to who the center of attention was. You guessed it. Me! After all, I was the one on my way to lock horns with the legendary Sen-Sen Ante Kid on his own terrain . . . a card table. Bunny had chosen my clothes for me, and I was resplendent in a dark maroon open-necked shirt with light charcoal gray slacks and vest. I felt and looked like a million . . . well, make that a quarter of a million. If I was going to have my head handed to me tonight, I was at least going to be able to accept it in style . . . which was the whole point of this exercise anyway.

I didn't even try to match Aahz's strut, knowing I would only suffer by comparison. Instead, I contented myself with maintaining a slow, measured, dignified pace as I nodded and waved at the well-wishers. The idea was to exude unhurried confidence. In actuality, it made me feel like I was on the way to the gallows, but I did my best to hide it and keep smiling.

The crowds got progressively thicker as we neared the Even-Odds, and I realized with some astonishment that this was because of the game. Those without the clout or the money to get space inside were loitering around the area in hopes of being one of the first to hear about the game's outcome. I had known that gambling was big at the Bazaar, but I never thought it was *this* popular.

The assemblage melted away before us, clearing a path to the door. I began to recognize faces in the crowd, people I knew. There was Gus waving enthusiastically at me, and over there . . .

"Vic!"

I veered from our straight line and the whole procession ground to a halt.

"Hi, Skeeve!" the vampire smiled, clapping me on the shoulder. "Good luck tonight!"

"I'm going to need it!" I confided. "Seriously, though, I've been meaning to stop by and thank you for your warning about the Ax."

Vic's face fell. "You might have trouble finding me. I'm about to lose my office."

"Really? Is business that bad?"

"Worse. There's an awful lot of competition here."

"Well, tell you what. Why don't you stop by my place tomorrow and we'll talk. Maybe we can work out a small loan or maybe even subcontract some assignments until you're established."

"Gee. Thanks, Skeeve!"

A sudden inspiration hit me. "Come by around noon. We'll do lunch!"

It seemed like a really good idea to me. I wondered why businessmen hadn't thought of talking out ideas over lunch before! For some reason, Vic winced before returning my smile.

"Lunch it is," he said.

"Umm . . . I hate to interrupt, partner, but you *do* have an appointment you're supposed to be at."

"Right, Aahz. Vic! Tomorrow!"

With that, I allowed myself to be ushered into the Even-Odds.

A ripple of applause broke out as I entered the main bar and gaming room, and I barely caught myself from turning to look behind me. For me or against me, the people were here to watch the game and if nothing else were grateful to me for providing the evening's entertainment.

Terrific. I was about to risk a quarter of a million in gold so that folks wouldn't have to watch summer reruns.

The club had been rearranged since the last time I was there. One card table stood alone in the center of the room, while scores of people lined the walls. While the crowd outside might have been larger, the group inside the club made up with clout what they lacked in numbers. While I didn't begin to recognize everyone, the ones I did spot led me to believe that the 'Who's Who' of Deva was assembled to watch the game. Hayner, my landlord and leader of the Devan Chamber of Commerce was there along with his usual clutch of cronies. He nodded politely when our eyes met, but I suspected he was really hoping to see me lose.

Don Bruce was there as promised, and raised his hands over his head, clenched them together, and gave them a brief shake, smiling all the while. I guessed it was some sign of encouragement. At the very least, I hoped I wasn't being hailed with some secret Mob death sign. Of course, that didn't occur to me until after I had waved back.

"Skeeve. SKEEVE! Have you got a moment?"

I glanced around to find the Geek standing at my elbow.

"Sure, Geek," I shrugged. "What can I do for you?"

The Deveel seemed extremely nervous, his complexion several shades off its normal hue. "I . . . you can promise not to hold a grudge. I promise you that tonight was none of my doing. All I did was make the arrangements after the Kid issued the challenge. I didn't give him your name . . . honest."

To say the least, I found his attitude surprising.

"Sure, Geek. I never thought you . . ."

"If I had known it would lead to this, I never would have invited you to my game in the first place, much less . . ."

I was suddenly very alert.

"Wait a minute, Geek! What are you talking about?"

"You're outclassed!" the Deveel explained, glancing around fearfully. "You don't stand a chance against the Kid. I just want you to understand, if you lose all your money tonight, that I didn't mean to set you up. I don't want you or your crew looking for me with blood in your respective eyes."

Now, as you know, I knew that I was outclassed. What intrigued me was that the Geek knew it, too.

"Geek, I think we'd better . . ."

A loud burst of applause and cheers interrupted me. By the time I got through craning my neck to see what was going on, the Geek had disappeared into the crowd. With that discussion closed, I turned my attention again to the subject at hand.

"Who's that?" I said, nodding toward the figure that had just entered the club.

Aahz slid a comforting arm around my shoulders.

"That's him. That's the Sen-Sen Ante Kid."

"THAT'S the Kid???!!"

The man in the door was enormous, he was huge . . . that is to say, he was Massha's size. For some reason, I had been expecting someone closer to my own age. This character, though, was something else.

He was totally hairless, no beard, no eyebrows, and completely bald. His skin was light blue in color, and that combined with his fat and wrinkles gave the overall impression of a half-deflated blue bowling ball. His eyes were extremely dark, however, and glittered slightly as they fixed on me.

"That's the Kid?" I repeated.

Aahz shrugged. "He's had the title for a long time."

The man-mountain had two bags with him which looked very similar to the ones Aahz had carried for us. He handed them casually to one of the onlookers.

"Cash me in!" he ordered in a booming voice. "I hear there's a game here tonight."

For some reason, this brought a loud round of laughter and applause from the audience. I didn't think it was all that funny, but I smiled politely. The Kid's eyes noted my lack of enthusiasm and glittered with increased ferocity.

"You must be the Great Skeeve."

His voice was a dangerous purr, but it still reverberated off the walls. He moved toward me with a surprisingly light tread, holding out his hand in welcome.

The crowd seemed to hold its breath.

". . . And you must be the one they call the Sen-Sen Ante Kid." I responded, abandoning my hand into his grip.

Again I was surprised . . . this time by the gentleness of his handshake.

"I just hope your magic isn't as good as your reputation."

"That's funny, I was just hoping your luck is as bad as your jokes."

I didn't mean to be offensive. The words just kind of slipped out before I could stop them.

Chapter Eighteen:

"Cast your fate to the winds."

—L. BERNSTEIN

THE table was waiting for us. There were only two chairs with chips stacked neatly in front of them.

I had a sudden moment of panic when I realized I didn't know which chair was facing south, but Aahz came to my rescue. Darting out of the crowd, he pulled out one chair and held it for me to sit in. To the crowd it looked like a polite gesture, but my friends knew I had come dangerously close to changing the rules I had labored so hard to memorize.

"Cards!" the Kid ordered, holding out one hand as he eased into the chair facing me.

A new deck materialized in his hand. He examined it like a glass of fine wine, holding it up to the light to be sure the wrapping was intact and even sniffing the seal to be sure the factory glue was the same.

Satisfied, he offered the deck to me. I smiled and spread my hands to show I was satisfied. I mean, heck! If he hadn't found anything wrong, it was a cinch that I wouldn't be able to detect any foul play.

The gesture seemed to impress him though, and he

gave me a small bow before opening the deck. Once the cards were out of the box, his pudgy fingers seemed to take on a life of their own. Moving swiftly, they removed the jokers and cast them aside, then began peeling cards off the deck two at a time, one from the top and one from the bottom.

Watching the process, I began to realize why his handshake had been so gentle. Large as they were, this fingers were graceful, delicate, and sensitive as they went about their task. These were not the hands of a rough laborer, or even a fighter. They existed to do one thing: to handle a deck of cards.

By now the deck had been rough mixed. The Kid scooped up the pile, squared it, then gave it several quick shuffles. His moves were so precise he didn't even have to re-square the deck when he was done . . . just set it on the center of the table.

"Cut for deal?" he asked.

I repeated my earlier gesture. "Be my guest."

Even this seemed to impress the Kid . . . and the crowd. A low murmur rippled around the room as the pluses and minuses of my move were discussed. The truth of the matter was that after watching the Kid handle the deck, I was embarrassed to show my own lack of skill.

He reached for the deck, and the cards sprang to life again. With a hypnotic rhythm he began cutting the deck and riffing the cards together, all the while staring at me with unblinking eyes. I knew I was being psyched out, but was powerless to fight the effect.

"For the ante, shall we say one thousand?"

"Let's say five thousand." I returned.

The rhythm faltered. The Kid realized he had slipped and moved swiftly to cover it. Setting the cards aside for a moment, he reached for his chips.

"Five thousand it is," he said, tossing a handful into the center of the table. "And . . . my trademark."

A small white breath mint followed the chips into the pot.

I was counting out my own chips when something occurred to me.

"How much is that worth?" I said, pointing at the mint.

That surprised my opponent.

"What? The mint? One copper a roll. But you don't have to . . ."

Before he had finished speaking I added a small coin to my chips, pushed them into the center of the table, grabbed his mint, and popped it into my mouth.

This time the audience actually gasped before lapsing into silence. For several heartbeats there was no sound in the room except the mint crunching between my teeth. I almost regretted my bold move. The mint was incredibly strong.

Finally the Kid grinned.

"I see. You eat my luck, eh? Good. Very good. You'll find, though, that it takes more than that to disturb my game."

His tone was jovial, but his eyes darkened even more than they had been and his shuffling took on a sharper, more vengeful tone. I knew I had scored a hit.

I stole a glance at Aahz, who winked at me broadly.

"Cut!"

The deck was in front of me. Moving with forced nonchalance, I cut the deck roughly in half, then leaned back in my chair. While I tried to appear casual, inside I was crossing my fingers and toes and everything else crossable. I had devised my strategy on my own and hadn't discussed it with anyone . . . not even Aahz. Now we got to see how it worked.

One card . . . two cards . . . three cards came gliding across the table to me, face down. They slid to a stop neatly aligned, another tribute to the Kid's skill, and lay there like land mines.

I ignored them, waiting for the next card.

It came, coasting to a stop face up next to its brethren. It was the seven of diamonds and the Kid dealt himself . . .

The ten of diamonds. A ten!

The rules came back to me like a song I didn't want to remember. A ten face up meant my seven was dead . . . valueless.

"So much for eating my luck, eh?" the Kid chuckled, taking a quick glance at his hole cards. "My ten will go . . . five thousand."

". . . And up five."

The gasp from the crowd was louder this time . . . possibly because my coaches had joined in. I heard Aahz clear his throat noisily, but wouldn't look in his direction. The Kid was staring at me in undisguised surprise. Apparently he had either expected me to fold or call . . . possibly because that would have been the sane thing to do.

"You're awfully proud of that dead card," he said thoughtfully. "All right. I'll call. Pot's right."

Two more cards floated onto the table face up. I got a ten! The ten of clubs, to be specific. That canceled his ten and made my seven live again.

The Kid got the unicorn of hearts. Wild card! Now I had ten-seven high against his pair of tens showing.

Terrific.

"I won't try to kid you." My opponent smiled. "A pair of tens is worth . . . twenty thousand."

". . . And up twenty."

The Kid's smile faded. His eyes flicked quickly to my cards, then he nodded. "Call."

No comment. No witty banter. I had him thinking.

The next cards were en route. The three of hearts slid into my lineup. A dead card. Opposing it, the Kid got . . .

The ten of hearts!

I was now looking at three tens against my ten-seven

high! For a moment my resolve wavered, but I shored it up again. I was in too far to change now.

The Kid was eyeing me thoughtfully. "I don't suppose you'd go thirty on that?" he said.

"I'll not only go it, I'll raise you thirty."

There were muffled exclamations of disbelief in the room . . . and some not so muffled. I recognized the voices of some of the latter.

The Kid just shook his head and pushed the appropriate number of chips into the pot without a word. The crowd lapsed into silence and craned their necks to see the next cards.

The dragon of spades to me, and the ogre of hearts to the Kid.

No apparent help for either hand . . . except that now the Kid had three hearts face up.

We both studied each other's cards for a few moments.

"I'll admit I can't figure out what you're betting, Skeeve," my opponent sighed. "But this hand's worth fifty."

". . . And up fifty."

Instead of responding, the Kid leaned back in his chair and stared at me.

"Check me on this," he said. "Either I've missed it completely, or you haven't looked at your hole cards yet."

"That's right."

The crowd started muttering again. At least some of them had missed that point.

"So you're betting blind?"

"Right."

". . . And raising into me to boot."

I nodded.

"I don't get it. How do you expect to win?"

I regarded him for a moment before I answered. To say the least, I had the room's undivided attention.

"Kid, you're the best there is at dragon poker.

You've spent years honing your skills to be the best, and nothing that happens here tonight is going to change that. Me, I'm lucky . . . if you can call it that. I got lucky one night, and that somehow earned me the chance to play this game with you tonight. That's why I'm betting the way I am.''

The Kid shook his head. "Maybe I'm slow, but I still don't get it.''

"In the long run, your skill would beat my luck. It always does. I figure the only chance I've got is to juice the betting on this one hand . . . go for broke. All the skill in the dimensions can't change the outcome of one hand. That's luck . . . which puts us on an equal footing.''

My opponent digested this for a few moments, then threw back his head and gave a bark of laughter.

"I love it!" he crowed. "A half million pot riding on one hand. Skeeve, I like your style. Win or lose, it's been a pleasure matching wits with you.''

"Thank you, Kid. I feel the same way.''

"In the meantime, there's this hand to play. I hate to keep all these people hanging in suspense when we already know how the betting's going to go.''

He swept the rest of his chips into the pot. "I'll call your raise and raise you back . . . thirty-five. That's the whole stake,''

"Agreed," I said, pushing my chips out.

"Now let's see what we got," he winked, reaching for the deck.

The two of diamonds to me . . . the eight of clubs to the Kid . . . then one more card each face down.

The crowd pressed forward as my opponent peered at his last card.

"Skeeve," he said almost regretfully. "You had an interesting strategy there, but my hand's good . . . real good.''

He flipped two of his down cards over.

"Full Dragon . . . four Ogres and a pair of tens."

"Nice hand," I acknowledged.

"Yeah. Right. Now let's see what you've got."

With as much poise as I could muster, I turned over my hole cards.

Chapter Nineteen:

"Can't you take a joke?"

—T. EULENSPIEGEL

MASSHA looked up from her book and bon-bons as we trooped through the door.

"That was quick," she said. "How did it go?"

"Hi, Massha. Where's Markie?"

"Upstairs in her room. After the second time she tried to sneak out, I sent her to bed and took up sentry duty here by the door. What happened at the game?"

"Well, I still say you were wrong," Aahz growled. "Of all the dumb stunts you've pulled . . ."

"C'mon, partner. What's done is done. Okay? You're just mad because I didn't check with you first."

"That's the least of . . ."

"WILL SOMEBODY TELL ME WHAT HAP-PENED?"

"What? Oh. Sorry, Massha. I won. Aahz here is upset because . . ."

I was suddenly swept up in a gargantuan hug and kiss as my apprentice expressed her delight at the news.

"I'll say he won. In one hand he won," Tananda grinned. "Never seen anything like it."

153

"Three unicorns and the six of clubs in the hole," Aahz raged. "Three wild cards, which, when used with the once-a-night suit shift rule on the seven of diamonds, yields . . ."

"A straight-bloody-flush!" Chumley sang. "Which took the Kid's Full Dragon and the largest pot that's ever been seen at the Bazaar."

"I knew you could do it, Daddy!" Markie shrieked, emerging from her hiding spot on the stairs.

So much for sending her to bed early.

"I wish you could have seen the Kid's face, Massha," the troll continued merrily. "I'll bet he wishes now that he carries antacids instead of breath mints."

"You should have seen the crowd. They're going to be talking about this one for years!"

Massha finally let me down and held up a hand.

"Hold it! Wait a minute! I get the feeling I've missed a lap here somewhere. Hot Stuff here won. Right? As in walked away with all the marbles?"

The brother and sister team nodded vigorously. I just tried to get my breath back.

"So how come Green and Scaly is breathing smoke? I should think he'd be leading the cheering."

"BECAUSE HE GAVE THE MONEY AWAY! THAT'S WHY!!!"

"Yes. That would explain it." Massha nodded thoughtfully.

"C'mon, Aahz! I didn't *give* it away."

As I've discovered before, it's a lot easier to find your breath when you're under attack.

"Whoa! Wait!" my apprentice said, stepping between us. "Before you two get started again, talk to Massha. Remember, I'm the one who wasn't there."

"Well, the Kid and I got to talking after the game. He's really a nice guy, and I found out that he had pretty much been betting everything he had . . ."

"That's what he *claimed*," Aahz snorted. "I think he was making a play for our sympathies."

". . . and I got to thinking. I had worked hard to be sure that both the Kid's and my reputations would be intact, no matter how the game came out. What I really wanted to do was to retire from the dragon poker circuit and let *him* take on all the hotshot challengers . . ."

"That much I'll agree with."

"Aahz! Just let him tell it. Okay?"

". . . But he couldn't keep playing if he was broke, which would leave me as the logical target for the up-and-comings, so I let him keep the quarter of a million he had lost . . ."

"See! SEE!!! What did I tell you?"

". . . as a LOAN so he could use it as a stake in future games. . . ."

"That's when I knew he had . . . a loan??"

I grinned at my partner.

"Uh-huh. As in 'put your money to work for you instead of stacking it,' a concept I believe you found very interesting when it was first broached. Of course, you had already gone off half-cocked and stomped away before we got to that part."

Any sarcasm I had managed to load into my voice was lost on Aahz, which is not surprising when you realize we were talking about money.

"A loan, eh?" he said thoughtfully. "What were the terms?"

"Tell him, Bunny."

"BUNNY??"

"Hey! You weren't there, remember? I decided to see what our accountant could do. Bunny?"

"Well, I've never dealt with stake money before, no pun intended, so I had to kind of feel my way along. I think I got us a pretty good arrangement, though."

"Which was . . ."

"Until the Kid pays us back . . . and it's got to be paid back in full, no partial payments, we get half his winnings."

"Hmmm," my partner murmured. "Not bad."

"If you can think of anything else I should have asked for, I'm open to . . ."

"If he could think of anything else," I said, winking at her, "you can believe he would have roared it out by now. You did great, Bunny."

"Gee. Thanks, Skeeve."

"Now then, if someone would be so kind as to break out the wine, I feel like celebrating."

"Of course, Boss, you realize that now a lot of people know that you've got a lot of cash on hand," Guido pointed out, edging close to me. "As soon as Nunzio gets back, I think we'd better take a look at beefin' up security on the place, know what I mean?"

"Where is Nunzio, anyway?" Massha said, peering around.

"He'll be along in a bit," I smiled. "I had a little errand for him after the game."

"Well, here's to you, Skeeve!" Chumley called, lifting his goblet aloft. "After all our worrying about whether your reputation could survive a match with the Kid, I dare say you came out of it well ahead of where you were before."

"That's right," his sister giggled. "I wonder what the Ax thinks about what happened."

That was the cue I had been waiting for. I took a deep breath and a deeper drink of wine, then assumed my most casual manner.

"Why bother speculating, Tananda? Why not ask direct?"

"What's that, Skeeve?"

"I said, why not ask the Ax directly? After all, she's in the room right now."

The gaiety of the mood vanished in an eyeblink as everybody stared at me.

"Partner," Aahz murmured, "I thought we settled this when we talked to Don Bruce."

I cut him off with the wave of a hand.

"As a matter of fact, I'm a little curious about what the Ax is thinking myself. Why don't you tell us . . . Markie?"

My young ward squirmed under the room's combined gaze.

"But, Daddy . . . I don't . . . you . . . oh, heck! You figured it out, huh?"

"Uh-huh." I nodded, not feeling at all triumphant.

She heaved a great sigh. "Oh, well. I was about to throw in the towel anyway. I had just hoped I could beat a retreat before my cover was blown. If you don't mind, I'd like to join you in some of that wine now."

"Help yourself."

"MARKIE?!?"

Aahz had finally recovered enough to make noise. Of course, it comes reflexively to him. The others were still working on it.

"Don't let the little-girl looks fool you, Aahz," she winked. "Folks are small and soft on my dimension. In the right clothes, it's easy to pass yourself off as being younger than you really are . . . lots younger."

"But . . . but . . ."

"Think about it for a minute, Aahz," I said. "You had all the pieces the first day. Kids, particularly little girls, are embarrassing at best, trouble at worst. The trick is that you *expect* them to be trouble, so you don't even consider the possibility that what they're doing could be premeditated and planned."

I paused to take a sip of wine, and for once no one interrupted me with questions.

"If you look back on it, most of the problems we've been having have originated directly or indirectly from Markie. She mouthed off about Bunny being in my bed to get Tananda upset, and when that didn't work she made a few digs about her living here free that got her thinking about leaving . . . just like she deliberately made Massha look bad in the middle of her magic lesson for the same reason, to get her to leave."

"Almost worked, too," my apprentice observed thoughtfully.

"The business in the Bazaar was no accident, either," I continued. "All she had to do was wait for the right opportunity to pretend to get mad so we wouldn't suspect she was blasting things deliberately. If you recall, she even tried to convince me that I didn't need to take dragon poker lessons."

"Of course," Markie put in, "that's not easy to do when people think you're a kid."

"The biggest clue was Gleep. I thought he was trying to protect me from Bunny, but it was Markie he was really after. I keep telling you that he's smarter than you think."

"Remind me to apologize to your dragon," Aahz said, still staring at Markie.

"It was a good plan," she sighed. "Ninety-nine percent of the time it would have worked. The problem was that everyone underestimated you, Skeeve . . . you and your friends. I didn't think you'd have enough money to pay off the irate merchants after I did a number on their displays, and your friends . . ."

She shook her head slowly.

"Usually if word gets out that I'm on assignment, it makes my work easier. The target's associates bail out to keep from getting hit in the crossfire, and trying to get them to stay or come back only makes things worse. Part of sinking someone's career is cutting them off from their support network."

She raised her wine in a mock toast to me.

"Your friends wouldn't run . . . or if they did, they wouldn't stay gone once they heard you were in trouble. That's when I started to have second thoughts about this assignment. I mean, there are some careers that shouldn't be scuttled, and I think yours is one of them. You can take that as a compliment . . . it's meant as one. That's why I was about to call it quits anyway. I realized my heart just wasn't in my work this time around."

She set down her wine and stood up.

"Well, I guess that's that. I'll go upstairs and pack now. Make you a deal. If you all promise not to tell anyone who the famous Ax is, I'll spread the word that you're so invincible that even the Ax couldn't trip you up. Okay?"

Watching her leave the room, I realized with some surprise that I would miss her. Despite what Aahz had said, it had been kind of nice having a kid around the place.

"That's it?" my partner frowned. "You're just going to let her walk?"

"I was the target. I figure it was my call. Besides, she didn't do any real damage. As Chumley pointed out a second ago, we're further ahead than we were when she arrived."

"Of course, there's the matter of the damages we had to pay for her little magic display at the Bazaar."

For once, I was ahead of my partner when it came to money.

"I haven't forgotten that, Aahz. I just figure to recoup the loss from another source. You see, what finally tipped me off was . . . wait. Here they are now."

Nunzio was just coming into the room, dragging the Geek with him.

"Hello, Skeeve," the Deveel said, squirming in my bodyguard's grasp. "Your . . . ah, associate here says you wanted to see me?"

"He tried to sneak out after I told him, Boss," Nunzio squeaked. "That's what took me so long."

"Hello, Geek," I purred. "Have a seat. I want to have a little chat with you about a card game."

"C'mon, Skeeve. I already told you . . ."

"Sit!"

The Geek dropped into the indicated chair like gravity had suddenly trebled. I had borrowed the tone of voice from Nunzio's dragon-training demonstration. It worked.

"What the Geek was starting to say," I explained, turning to Aahz, "is that before the game tonight he warned me that I was overmatched and asked me not to have any hard feelings . . . that the game with the Kid wasn't his idea."

"That's right," the Deveel interjected. "Word just got out and . . ."

"What I'm curious about, however, is how he knew I was outclassed."

I smiled at the Geek, trying to show my teeth the way Aahz does. "You see, I don't want to talk about tonight's game. I was hoping you could give us a little more information about the *other* game . . . you know, the one where I won Markie?"

The Deveel glanced nervously around the group of assembled scowls.

"I . . . I don't know what you mean."

"Let me make it easy for you. At this point I figure the game had to be rigged. That's the only way you would know in advance what a weak dragon poker player I am. Somehow you were throwing hands my way to be sure I won big, big enough to include Markie. I'm just curious how you did it without triggering the magic or telepathy monitors."

The Geek seemed to shrink a little in his chair. When he spoke, his voice was so low we could barely hear him.

"Marked cards," he said.

The room exploded.

"MARKED CARDS??"

"But how . . ."

"Wouldn't that . . ."

I waved them back to silence.

"It makes sense. Think about it," I instructed. "Specifically, think back to our trip to Limbo. Remember how hard it was to disguise ourselves without using

magic? Everybody at the Bazaar gets so used to things
being done magically, they forget there are non-magical
ways to do the same things . . . like false beards, or
marked cards.''

The Geek was on his feet now.

"You can't hold that against me! So someone else
paid me to throw the game your way. Heck, I should
think you'd be happy. You came out ahead, didn't you?
What's to be mad about?''

"I'll bet if I try real hard I could think of something.''

"Look, if it's revenge you want, you already got it. I
lost a bundle tonight betting against you. You want
blood, I'm bleeding!''

The Deveel was sweating visibly now. Then again,
he's always been a little nervous around me for some
reason.

"Relax, Geek. I'm not going to hurt you. If anything,
I'm going to help you . . . just like you helped me.''

"Yeah?'' he said suspiciously.

"You say you're short of cash, we'll fix it.''

"What!!??'' Aahz roared, but Tananda poked him in
the ribs and he subsided into sullen silence.

"Bunny?''

"Yeah, Skeeve?''

"First thing tomorrow I want you to run over to the
Even-Odds. Go over the books, take inventory, and
come up with a fair price for the place.''

The Geek blinked.

"My club? But I . . .''

". . . Then draw up an agreement for us to take it off
the Geek's hands . . . at half the price you arrive at.''

"WHAT!!??'' the Deveel screeched, forgetting his
fear. "Why should I sell my club for . . .''

". . . More than it will be worth if the word gets out
that you're running rigged games?'' I finished for him.
"Because you're a shrewd businessman, Geek. Besides,

you need the money. Right?"

The Geek swallowed hard, then licked his lips before he spoke. "Right."

"How was that, Geek?" Aahz frowned. "I didn't quite hear you."

"I did," I said firmly. "Well, we won't keep you any longer, Geek. I know you'll want to get back to your club and clean up a bit. Otherwise we'll have to reduce the amount of our appraisal."

The Deveel started to snarl something, then thought better of it and slunk out into the night.

"Do you think that will make up for what we had to pay in damages, partner?" I said innocently.

"Skeeve, sometimes you amaze me," Aahz said, lifting his wine in a salute. "Now if there are no more surprises, I'm ready to party."

It was tempting, but I was on a roll and didn't want to let the moment slip away.

"There is one more thing," I announced. "Now that we've taken care of the Ax and the Kid, I think we should address the major problem that's come up . . . while everyone is here."

"Major problem?" my partner scowled. "What's that?"

Taking a deep breath, I went for it.

Chapter Twenty:

"So what else is new?"

—W. CRONKITE

THE whole crew was staring at me as I rolled my goblet of wine back and forth in my hand, trying to decide where to start.

"If I've seemed a little distracted during this latest crisis," I said at last, "it's because I've been wrestling with another problem that's come to my attention . . . a big one. So big that, in my mind, the other stuff took a lower priority."

"Whatever you're talking about, partner," Aahz frowned, "I've missed it."

"You just said it, Aahz. The magic word is 'partner.' Things have been going real well for you and me, but we aren't the only ones in this household. When we were talking to Chumley and he said that his life wasn't all beer and skittles, it took me a while to puzzle out what he was talking about, but it finally came clear."

I looked at the troll.

"Business is off for you, isn't it, Chumley?"

"Well, I don't like to complain . . ."

"I know, but maybe you should once in a while. I had

never stopped to think about it before, but you've been getting fewer and fewer assignments since you moved in with us, haven't you?"

"Is that true, Chumley?" Aahz said. "I never noticed . . ."

"No one's noticed because the attention has always been on us, Aahz. The Aahz and Skeeve team has been taking priority over everything and everyone else. We've been so busy living up to our big-name image that we've missed what it's doing to our colleagues, the ones who have to a large extent been responsible for our success."

"Oh, come now, Skeeve old boy," Chumley laughed uneasily. "I think you're exaggerating a bit there."

"Am I? Your business is off, and so is Tananda's. I hate to say it, but she was right when she left, we are stifling her with our current setup. Guido and Nunzio knock themselves out trying to be super-bodyguards because they're afraid we'll decide we don't really need them and send them packing. Even Massha thinks of herself as a non-contributing team member. Bunny's our newest arrival, and she tried to tell me that the only way she could help us is as an ornament!"

"I feel better about that after tonight, Skeeve," Bunny corrected. "Between negotiating with the Kid and getting the assignment to price out the Even-Odds, I think I can do something for you besides breathe heavy."

"Exactly!" I nodded. "That's what's giving me the courage to propose the plan I've cooked up."

"Plan? What plan?"

"That's what I wanted to talk to you about, Aahz. Actually, what I wanted to talk to all of you about. What we're dealing with in this household isn't really a partnership . . . it's a company. Everybody in this room contributes to the success of our group as a whole, and I think it's about time we restructured our setup to reflect that. What we really need is a system where all of us have a say as to what's going on. Then clients will be able to approach us as a group, and we quote prices, hand out assignments or subcontract, and share the profits as a group. That's my proposal, for what it's worth. What do the rest of you think?"

The silence stretched on until I started to wonder if they were trying to think of a tactful way to tell me I belonged in a rubber room.

"I don't know, Skeeve," Aahz said at last.

"What aren't you sure of?" I urged.

"I don't know if we should call ourselves Magic, Inc., or Chaos, Ltd."

"Magic, Inc., has already been used," Tananda argued. "Besides, I think the name should be a little more dignified and formal."

"You do that, then the clients are goin' to be surprised when they actually see us, know what I mean?" Guido put in. "We ain't exactly dignified and formal ourselves."

I leaned back in my chair and took a deep breath. If that was their only concern, my idea was at least deemed worthy of consideration.

Massha caught my eye and winked.

I toasted her back, feeling justifiably smug.

"Does this company accept new applicants?"

We all turned to find Markie in the door, suitcase in her hand.

"I don't think I have to tell you all about my qualifications," she continued, "but I admire this group and would be proud to be a part of it."

The crew exchanged glances.

"Well, Markie . . ."

"It's still nebulous . . ."

"You've got the Elemental stuff down cold . . ."

"What do you think, Skeeve?" Aahz said. "You're the one who's usually big on recruiting old enemies."

"No," I said firmly.

They were all looking at me again.

"Sorry to sound so overbearing right after claiming I

wanted everybody to have a say in things," I continued,
"but if Markie's in, I'm out."

"What's the problem, Skeeve?" Markie frowned. "I
thought we were still on pretty good terms."

"We are," I nodded. "I'm not mad at you. I won't
work against your career or hit you or hold a grudge.
You were just doing your job."

I raised my head and our eyes met.

"I just can't go along with how you work, is all. You
say you admire our group—well, the glue that holds us
together is trust. The way you operate is to get people to
trust you, then betray it. Even if you stayed loyal to our
group, I don't think I want to be associated in business
with someone who thinks that's the way to turn a
profit."

I stopped there, and no one else raised a voice to con-
tradict me.

Markie picked up her suitcase and started for the
door. At the last moment, though, she turned back to
me and I could see tears in her eyes.

"I can't argue with what you're saying, Skeeve," she
said, "but I can't help wishing you had settled for hitting me and let me join."

There was total silence as she made her departure.

"The young lady has raised a valid point," Chumley
said at last. "What is our position on new members?"

"If we're open, I'd like to put Vic's name up for consideration," Massha chimed in.

"First we've got to decide if we need anyone else,"
Tananda corrected.

"That raises the whole question of free-lance vs. exclusive contracts," Nunzio said. "I don't think that it's
realistic to have all our shares equal."

"I've been doodling up a plan on just that point,
Nunzio," Bunny called, waving the napkin she had been
scribbling on. "If you can hold on for a few minutes,
I'll have something to propose officially."

As interested as I was in the proceedings, I had trouble concentrating on what was being said. For some reason, Markie's face kept crowding into my mind.

Sure, what I said was rough, but it was necessary. If you're going to run a business or a team, you've got to set a standard and adhere to it. There's no room for sentimentality. I had done the right thing, hadn't I? Hadn't I?

Also available in Arrow by Robert Asprin

THE MYTH-ING OMNIBUS

The first three books in a *seriously* funny series!

MEET SKEEVE . . . An apprentice masquerading as a magician.
MEET AAHZ . . . A clapped out demon.
MEET GLEEP . . . A dragon of very little brain.

Together with a varied cast (and we *do* mean 'varied'), they stagger from crisis to disaster and from dimension to dimension. Here, collected together for the first time, are the three adventures which introduced them to a gobsmacked public and set them on the road to staggering success (via the M1).

MYTH-ING IN ACTION

The stuff that myths are made of . . .

Queen Hemlock is conquering planets at a most alarming rate. Not really in Skeeve's best interests. So why has he chosen now, of all times, to go looking for Aahz on Perve? And who's going to mastermind the troops while he's away?

As Guido says, 'We is far more comfortable taking orders than givin' 'em'. So when he and Nunzio are promoted to rank sergeant in Hemlock's army, it looks like another crazy myth-adventure is about to start . . .

ANOTHER FINE MYTH

This is the first book in a series (which is very big news in the US of A) that only very clever and witty people will really appreciate (they are very sophisticated over there) which we know thousands of you here will really tune into.

You might not appreciate the fact that a magician's apprentice, only half-way through his indentures, a purple-tongued demon, a universe populated by deveels, imps, dragons and unicorns is the basis of a hilariously funny, non-stop switchback of magic, mayhem and mythadventure. (That's where the clever, witty, discerning readers come in.)

But we assure you, it is . . .

MYTH CONCEPTIONS

THE SCENARIO . . .
Skeeve, the apprentice masquerading as court magician in Possiltum.
Aahz, the clapped-out demon.
Gleep, a dragon of very little brain.

THE PROBLEM . . .
One invading army marching steadily on Possiltum.

THE PROBABLE OUTCOME . . .
Either Skeeve, whose magic isn't up to much, won't be able to spot it. Result, instant death. Or Aahz will pull a rabbit out of the hat and repel the hairy invader. Result – instant execution.

For all those discriminating readers who have been sucked under the spell of the Myth books (a million-selling series which has transfixed our cousins in the States) here is another hilarious story of mayhem and magic.

MYTH DIRECTIONS

When a girl (lushly curved, with a mane of light green hair) asks for a favour, a chap would have to possess a heart of stone (or a testosterone deficiency) to refuse.

Court magician to the kingdom of Possiltum, Skeeve is a chap all right – and heads off with Tanda into the dimensions. The quest: to steal The Trophy on which Tanda has set her feminine little heart.

Naturally, he bogs it.

Discriminating readers who have been with us all the way in this BRILLIANTLY SUCCESSFUL, INTERNATIONALLY TALKED ABOUT series will know that MYTH DIRECTIONS is sure to be an uproarious switch-back of magic, mayhem and mirth.

They are right.

MYTH-NOMERS AND IM-PERVECTIONS

A myth-begotten Myth-tery tour to the Perv-ect Planet
. . . Nobody's perv-ect and we all make myth-stakes
sometimes! So when the cold-blooded demon Aahz does
a hot-headed bunk on Skeeve, the great magician sets off
in hot pursuit.

The Planet Perv is his destination – the nastiest of the
known dimensions, where low-life villains cruise hi-rise
streets and a mad axeman wanders free.

No myth-ion is too difficult for the scheming Skeeve, but
will he find Aahz before his credit expires, his welcome
expires, and possibly even his life expires, following some
shady dealing in dodgy contraband?

M.Y.T.H. INC. LINK

All rise for the Great Skeeve! Our hero has finally made it all the way – from lowly magician's apprentice to President of the all-conquering M.Y.T.H. Inc.

But when you're in charge of a myth-chievous team made up of magicians, trollops and trolls (not forgetting the gangsters and molls) trouble has a habit of finding you out.

Especially if you're wearing a suit.

Call it luck (of the bad variety). Call it myth-guided loyalty. Or just call it the latest chapter in the BRILLI-ANT new series of INTERNATIONALLY SUCCESS-FUL magical myth-adventures in some very out-of-the-way (and dangerous) dimensions.

At least, that's what the Boss reckons.

PHULE'S PARADISE

'One of the funniest, best-written, fast paced novels I've read. The only feeling you're likely to be left with is hunger for more' *Fear* for *Little Myth Maker*

'Broad comedy . . . when it comes to ridicule, everyone gets it in the neck' *The Dark Side* for *Phule's Company*

OMEGA MOB, *THE* – Once the most dubious *phorce* in the whole Space Legion. Captain Willard Phule, the galaxy's youngest trillionaire, has turned a gang of oddballs, nerds and *touph*nuts into a lean, mean *phighting* machine. Well, nearly.

NEW ASSIGNMENT, *PHAAAB* – security guards for Lorelei's biggest, most gaudy casino. Too *phabulous* to be true!

Whoops, don't *phorget*:

PRUET, *MAXINE* – head of all organised crime on Lorelei. The deadliest granny of them all. Someone you should never, ever teach to suck eggs . . .!

MORE TITLES AVAILABLE IN ARROW
BY ROBERT ASPRIN

☐ ANOTHER FINE MYTH	£3.99
☐ MYTH CONCEPTIONS	£3.99
☐ MYTH DIRECTIONS	£3.99
☐ HIT OR MYTH	£3.50
☐ MYTH-ING PERSONS	£3.99
☐ LITTLE MYTH MARKER	£3.50
☐ M.Y.T.H. INC. LINK	£3.99
☐ MYTH-NOMERS AND IM-PERVECTIONS	£3.99
☐ MYTH-ING IN ACTION	£3.99
☐ THE MYTH-ING OMNIBUS	£8.99
☐ PHULE'S COMPANY	£3.99
☐ PHULE'S PARADISE	£3.99

ARROW BOOKS, BOOKSERVICE BY POST, PO BOX 29,
DOUGLAS, ISLE OF MAN, BRITISH ISLES

NAME _____

ADDRESS _____

_____

_____

Please enclose a cheque or postal order made out to Arrow
Books Ltd. for the amount due and allow the following for
postage and packing.

U.K. CUSTOMERS: Please allow 75p per book to a maximum
of £7.50

B.F.P.O. & EIRE: Please allow 75p per book to a maximum
of £7.50

OVERSEAS CUSTOMERS: Please allow £1.00 per book.

Whilst every effort is made to keep prices low it is sometimes
necessary to increase cover prices at short notice. Arrow Books
reserve the right to show new retail prices on covers which may
differ from those previously advertised in the text or elsewhere.